To Po
With m...
Patrick ...
12/12/03

The Far-Away Hearts Club

American Book Classics™
An Imprint of American Book Publishing
P.O. Box 65624
Salt Lake City, UT 84165
www.american-book.com

Printed in the United States of America on acid-free paper.

The Far-Away Hearts Club

Designed by Mynderd Vosloo, design@american-book.com

Library of Congress Cataloging-in-Publication Data is available upon request.

ISBN 1-58982-081-9

Spadaccino, Patrick R., The Far-Away Hearts Club

Special Sales

These books are available at special discounts for bulk purchases. Special editions, including personalized covers, excerpts of existing books, and corporate imprints, can be created in large quantities for special needs. For more information e-mail orders@american-book.com or call 801-486-8639.

The Far-Away Hearts Club

Patrick R. Spadaccino

Dedication

To my Savior, Jesus Christ, and to my wife, Natalie.

Foreword

The Far-Away Hearts Club is not a story one can encounter passively. Reading this book is, in fact, a total body experience—heart-wrenching, head-scratching, knee-slapping, and soul-stirring. In these pages you will find action, adventure, comedy, romance, suspense, intrigue, coming-of-age pathos, family drama, and truth. Somehow Patrick Spadaccino has managed to make his debut novel as redemptive as it is entertaining. This is no small feat.

But don't read this book because it's good for you (even though it is). Read this book because it's a good read. A great read. *The Far-Away Hearts Club* is a tale as old and universal as prodigal sons (and their jealous brothers), yet somehow as new and particular as Spadaccino's vividly drawn cast of characters. Spend a little time with Jake and Nick and the rest of the engaging crew who inhabit these pages. You'll fast become a member of *The Far-Away Hearts Club* fan club, and before you know it, your own heart will emerge more than a little changed.

Enjoy.

Carolyn Arends
Recording artist, author

Chapter One

This story is fresh in my mind, despite the passage of almost fifty years. When I close my eyes, I can still feel the wind as it swept over our wheat fields. I can taste Mom's cherry pie. I can even catch a glimpse of the special gift Dad built for me in our backyard. I have a good memory for a man my age.

Of course, thinking about the past isn't always enjoyable. Like most people, I've had my share of bad times. As I think back, though, it's the good times that my mind returns to over and over again. The pain is there, but it can't spoil the memories of friends and laughter and summer afternoons.

We all have a story to tell. This one is about being home, leaving home, and returning home.

I suppose the best place to start is my last day at school.

I'd wished it hadn't rained that day. I'd wanted my homecoming to be perfect in every way, from the polished buttons on my uniform to the fresh, clean smell of spring in the air. Buzz had checked his sources, and he'd informed me that the coming cold front would extend south to my home state. I tried to remain optimistic despite the weather, but I had to admit that the thought of going home made me feel a little sick. I'd been gone a long time.

I'd learned in history class that commanders of ancient armies sometimes toured the length and breadth of territories they'd conquered. I suppose I was doing something along those lines as I walked around the campus one last time, surveying a place that had tried its best to break me.

My boots crunched along the gravel-covered concourse that was so different from the main street of my hometown. Instead of friendly townspeople who called out a greeting as you passed, there were uniformed guards who watched your every movement with cold, suspicious eyes. Instead of brightly painted stores, there were drab, clapboard structures devoid of variation or creativity. In fact, all the buildings at Ashur-Kesed Preparatory School wore the same industrial gray, as if they desired to remain anonymous.

The campus was quiet as I walked its perimeter. They never cancelled outdoor exercises at AKPS due to rain. I could hear shouts in the distance and the wet *plop-swish-plop* of young men doing calisthenics in the sodden athletic field. *No rest, no weakness, no regrets.* It shocked me how easily the school mantra invaded my mind. I checked my watch and quickened my pace. Despite my mixed emotions about returning home, I needed to get away from AKPS.

I reached the central courtyard and looked up at the one building that deviated from the uninspired architecture around me. Its official name was Merodach Hall, but we simply called it the Hub. The combination office/classroom facility stood on a hill and watched over the campus like a brooding gargoyle, dominating every moment of our lives, disapproving of our every action. It was the bequest of some rich and long-forgotten benefactor whose portrait hung in the stuffy lobby, glaring disdainfully at all who entered. Despite its elegant pillars, high windows, and white paint—a rare commodity at AKPS—you would never admire Merodach Hall for its architectural or aesthetic beauty if you knew what went on there.

I continued my tour and paused briefly in front of Barracks 894, where I'd first seen Buzz put his latest inventions to use. I gazed fondly at the library where old Eli had fascinated me with stories of undersea adventures. I walked past the drafty classrooms where the professors alternated between droning and bellowing. Finally, I reached the main gate and gazed upward at that forbidding barrier. It was made of iron, but I'd learned that no bars are stronger than the ones we erect in our own minds, and that no freedom is sweeter than liberation from past mistakes.

Standing in front of the gate, finally able to leave, I grasped those implacable bars that had so often denied me passage. I smiled in triumph.

My smile faded quickly. Pondering my escape from school inevitably reminded me of the years I'd been separated from my family. I was only hours away from a reunion with them, but somehow I missed them more than ever. I missed Mom and her gentle encouragement. I missed my brother and his innocent way of questioning the things I took for granted. Most of all, I missed my...

"Dad!"

My shout echoed through the barn as I found my father grooming Chestnut, one of our horses.

"Yes, Jake?"

"When can I have a dog? I've been waiting forever."

My father looked down at me and stopped mid-stroke. Chestnut neighed in mild protest. "Soon," Dad said. "And you haven't waited nearly forever," he added as his strong hands resumed their rhythmic movements over Chestnut's coat. My father's voice was deep and could be as soothing as the purring of a cat, but when he used that tone, he was serious. I'd been harassing him all day, and he'd had enough.

I mumbled a reluctant "yes, sir" and left the barn. When I knew Dad couldn't see or hear me, I kicked the dust in frustration. Was a dog so much to ask? I would take good care of it. After all, I wasn't a kid anymore; I had just turned ten. Another voice—one I wished I had listened to more often—told me to stop being such a baby. Dad had said "soon," and he always meant what he said. I chose the middle ground and decided to return to the house to see if Mom had baked any cookies.

My family lived on a farm in Lancaster, a medium-sized town in southeastern Pennsylvania. I loved everything about that farm, from the cow stalls to the fruit orchards. Our vast fields, stretched out over 153 acres of fertile soil, were the envy of every other farmer in the county.

If you drove into the farm, you'd see a barn and silo off to the left, the garage and maintenance sheds on the right, and a sprawling, white colonial house at the end of the driveway.

Mom and Dad loved for people to drop by, and my father had built the house with guests in mind. There was one room in particular that caught the attention of everyone who came for a visit. In the rear of the house next to the kitchen, family and friends gathered in the spacious room where we did most of our talking, laughing, and even crying. A skylight provided a good breeze in the summer, and two bay windows in the west wall allowed us to enjoy the sunsets and a panoramic view of the farm. A massive fireplace made from slabs of flagstone dominated the room. It had a Dutch oven built into it where Mom baked bread and cookies. The aroma of her baking permeated the room even on the rare days when she didn't bake.

Memories covered the walls: photos of Mom and Dad on their wedding day (they never seemed to age), me in diapers, and friends we'd made over the years. Dad and I hand-waxed the hardwood floors, and the furniture was simple and comfortable—a rocking chair, three couches, and Dad's big leather armchair. It was a family room in the true sense of the term.

The most striking feature of our home and farm was the attention to detail evident in every paving stone, flower bed, and blade of grass. No one ever passed by and said, "Hmm. Looks like the old place needs a coat of paint," or, "Uh-oh, it seems the old man's slipping a bit on the lawn work."

Dad worked constantly, but he always found time to help others. In the days when my father was determining how best to use his farmland, he decided to plant two separate cornfields. He planted the main field behind the house, but he planted a second, smaller field (in addition to a vineyard) in the front yard within easy reach of anyone passing by. My father's philosophy was simple: "Let 'em pick what they need. There's plenty to go around."

Mom was his perfect counterpart. In addition to being a great cook, she excelled at keeping the business end of the farm running smoothly. She was serious about Mom-type things like keeping mud off the carpet and washing up thoroughly before dinner, but her sense of humor and optimism provided never-ending encouragement to Dad and me.

She and my father possessed a special bond: each seemed to always know what the other was thinking (a source of occasional frustration for me, particularly when I was trying to get away with something). They helped each other, treated each other with kindness and respect, and shared a dignified—yet often playful—affection for each other that never faded with the years. They were my best friends—the ones I ran to when I was sad, excited, angry, happy, and every emotion in between.

I was born several years after Dad purchased the farm. I grew up in a self-contained world of pigs, horses, tractors, and of course, a virtually limitless yard in which to play. I had quite an imagination, and since I had no brothers or sisters, I made the most of my surroundings.

When the corn was on the stalk, I used to climb up on the stone wall, look out over those rows and rows of plants and imagine they were soldiers awaiting my orders. "Ten-hut!" I would bellow. They swayed in the breeze as they obeyed my every command. "Attack! Repel the invaders!" I would cry, referring to the vineyard just across the long, winding driveway. The grapevines, resorting to guerilla tactics, hunched down low and responded to the invasion with plump, purple salvos. The corn would counter-strike with heavy, yellow corncob missiles. Neither side ever won, but I oversaw their battles from my vantage point with great delight.

I grabbed a handful of cookies from the kitchen and took up my familiar post on the wall, but I was suddenly tired of the game. I needed a second-in-command, and a dog would fit the bill perfectly. I wanted one so much that I had offered to give up my whole allowance to feed him. Imaginary puppies ran back and forth in my mind all day long, and I begged Dad every opportunity I got. He had listened silently to my pleas, evaluated my sincerity, motives, and priorities, and told me that I would get a dog "in due time."

As I ate my last cookie, Perry came tearing down the road.

"Jake, you gotta help me," he cried.

"What did you do now?"

"Nothing! I didn't do nothing."

"Then why do you look so scared?"

"Okay, okay. I borrowed Mal's glove."

"Again? You know what he said would happen if you took it without asking."

"I *know* that. That's why he's…"

"Peeerrrryyy!"

Perry looked over his shoulder in panic.

I could hear Mal pounding up the street. "Quick. Hide in the corn," I said. "I'll distract him."

Perry jumped over the wall, fell to his belly and wriggled along the ground. Once he was hidden, I turned to face Mal.

"Jake, have you seen the weasel?"

"Why? What's wrong?" I asked.

"He took my glove again. This time he broke one of the laces. I told him his hand is too big for it, but he swiped it anyway."

I took the glove from Mal and examined the broken lace.

"Aw, this doesn't look too bad. I can fix you up. C'mon."

Mal momentarily forgot his anger and followed me to the barn. I frequently had to act as the neighborhood peacemaker. Some of my attempts worked out better than others, but that day I succeeded. Perry slunk home and lived to see another day. As I re-laced Mal's glove, he and I talked about my dog dilemma.

"I mean, how long should I have to wait?" I said. "If I can take care of every other farm animal, why can't I have a dog?"

Mal listened sympathetically. He also wanted a dog.

"Well, you could try pouting," he suggested.

"How would that help?"

"Whenever I really want something, I just pout about it. Eventually, my mom or dad say, 'I'm sick of seeing that puss on your face,' and give me whatever I want."

"Whatever you want, huh? Then where's *your* dog?"

"Well, I didn't say it was foolproof. When did your dad say he'd get you a dog?"

"He said, 'In due time,'" I replied, uttering the term with great contempt.

"Oh, I hate that. 'Due time' means forever, in my book."

"Tell me about it."

I finished the lace job, and Mal gratefully ran down to the ball field to try it out. I grabbed my glove and joined him. Mal's advice wasn't great, but he had given me a possible fallback plan. I'd have to see how things turned out.

Chapter One

I didn't know it then, but Dad had noticed my growing impatience. He'd decided that a lesson was in order.

The next day Dad and I were out by the peach orchard. The trees were full and green, but peaches were still a long way off. Suddenly, Dad looked sharply out into the orchard. He ran down a row of peach trees, his large boots making deep imprints in the soft earth. He looked up into the boughs and thundered, "Grow. Didn't you hear me? I said *grow!*" Dad kept this up for about a minute.

At first, I have to admit, I was confused. My dad had a great sense of humor, but this was bizarre even for him. As he continued to leap and shout among the peach trees, however, I started to snicker, then to laugh until my stomach hurt. Dad looked so silly. I didn't know a man who was nearly six and a half feet tall could move like that.

When Dad saw me laughing, he zeroed in for the kill. He abruptly stopped and walked over to me. He knelt down, clapped me on the shoulder and chuckled a bit.

"I looked pretty silly, didn't I, son?"

Still laughing, I said, "Dad, you've lost it. What'd Mom put in your coffee?"

"I sounded pretty silly, too, hmm?"

"You sure did."

Dad leaned a little closer. The smell of his after shave mingled with the earthy scent of the farm as he said, "Son, while I was shouting at those peach trees, you didn't happen to see any peaches grow, did you?" His eyes, green like the color of the sea, bored into mine with great intensity.

"Aw, Dad. You know I didn't. Even *you* can't make peaches grow by shouting at trees."

"Then what was the point of my getting all riled up?"

I shrugged my shoulders. I was dense sometimes, but I could easily see Dad's point. Just in case I missed it, he leaned in close and said one word firmly but gently.

"Patience."

Patience: that hated word, the curse of young boys everywhere. I mumbled something lame about how hard he was on me, but soon we were laughing again. We laughed all the way back to the house.

I laughed because I loved my dad. I laughed because I couldn't get the image of his leaping and hollering out of my mind. I laughed because I'd discovered the solution to my problem. All I had to do was demonstrate patience for a couple of days, and the dog was as good as mine.

Or so I thought.

The first day was easy. I made no mention of the dog and went about my chores with unusual vigor. I even stayed with the pigs after I slopped them, just to make sure they all got an equal portion of the feast (Little Sue, despite her name, always ate more than her share). I found the next day a bit harder, but I hung in there. The goal was in sight; tomorrow I would get my dog.

When I came in from the barn on the third day, the house was full of the usual dinnertime bustle, but I heard no pitter-patter of tiny paws. I'd made a serious error in judgment. I had only laid aside a three-day reserve of patience. My anger grew. This wasn't right. I had learned my lesson and followed through. Where was my reward? I grew noticeably colder towards my father, and I made my second serious mistake of the week: I sulked at the dinner table.

Dinners at our house were crowded, boisterous affairs. Hired men, neighbors, and friends—all were welcome and all made themselves at home on a regular basis. They came not only for Mom's cooking but also for the camaraderie. We told jokes and stories and often swapped ideas about farming.

Mr. and Mrs. Kaleb were visiting that night, along with Mr. Modau, our gruff but good-hearted neighbor. I'd been giving Dad the cold shoulder since I sat down, but no one seemed to notice at first. Mr. Modau was in the middle of relating a recent "outrage" at the hardware store.

"So the little twerp looked me square in the face and told me I needed a receipt if I wanted a refund." Mr. Modau said. "Me, a faithful customer for over twenty years. For a box of wing nuts, no less!" He usually punctuated his remarks with whatever utensil he was holding. In this case, it was a fork. A piece of roast flew off the end and splattered Mr. Kaleb, who made a fuss. Everyone laughed except me.

"Aw, the boy's new, Jack. Cut him some slack," my dad said as he handed Mr. Kaleb a fresh napkin. "He doesn't know how much trouble it would be for you to sift through that filing cabinet of yours."

"Filing cabinet?" Mr. Kaleb said. "You mean the one in that disaster area he calls an office? Jack couldn't find his own head in there if he hung a bell around his neck." Everyone laughed again.

"Jake, help me out here. They're killing me," Mr. Modau said.

I gave a sad sort of half-smile and continued eating.

"Jake, you're quiet tonight," Mrs. Kaleb observed.

"Yeah. Just tired, I guess." I hung my head and tried to appear piti-ful. I couldn't see Dad's reaction, but I hoped that my display had dem-onstrated how important it was to get a dog for me at first light the next day.

After dinner, our guests remained in the kitchen while Mom put on coffee and prepared dessert. Dad called me into the family room. An excited chill ran down my spine. I was sure that he was going to ask me what kind of dog I wanted. I entered the room cheerfully, pleased that my performance at dinner had been so effective. I sat down across from Dad as he settled into the huge chair he inhabited every evening.

"Son, are you feeling all right? Dad asked. "It's not like you to be so quiet at dinner, especially when Mr. Modau is off on one of his ti-rades."

"I'm fine," I said, with what I hoped was the right mixture of sad-ness and anger. *This better work, Mal.*

"Hmmm. I think I understand," Dad said, leaning forward. "Jake, I know you want a dog. Do you know what else I know?"

Uh-oh, I thought as I shook my head.

"I know that the way you treated me three days ago and the way you treated me tonight are very different. Do you know what that tells me?"

Again, I shook my head. I grew even more miserable. I suspected where this was leading.

Quietly, Dad said, "It tells me that you care more about a dog than about your relationship with me."

I was silent. Protest was futile, and the tears would be coming any-time now. To make a feeble attempt at self-defense would only hasten my shame.

Dad paused, and then spoke again. "I noticed some ears were miss-ing along the east wall. Quite a few of them, actually. I guess some-body's hungry."

That threw me. I thought we were talking about dogs and relationships. I looked up into Dad's face. I knew that he didn't mind when people helped themselves to an ear now and then, but what relevance did that have now?

He locked eyes with me for a moment then stood up. "I know you want a dog, son. We'll talk about this again."

With that, I knew two things. One, the conversation was over for the time being. Two, Dad had given me a clue. There was something I needed to do, something that would show him that I was ready for the responsibility of caring for a dog.

You may be wondering how I knew this, but please don't give me too much credit. That was Dad's way. I assumed that everyone's father taught in riddles. I learned that wasn't true. When I told my friends about our family discussions, they shook their heads in awe.

"My dad doesn't even look my way unless I forget to take out the trash," one of them said.

"My dad sorta grunts," said another, a bit sadly. "I guess you could call that a riddle."

This particular riddle had me stumped. What in the world did corn have to do with my dog? I repeated his words over and over to myself. "I noticed some ears were missing along the east wall. Quite a few of them, actually. I guess somebody's hungry." What did he mean?

The answer came to me three days later. Dad had just given me my allowance, and he'd made no further reference to our discussion. After I laid aside a portion of it in a special container as he'd taught me to do, I put the rest in my pocket. It jingled there, full of promise. I'd told Dad that I was willing to sacrifice my allowance in order to feed my dog, but since I didn't have one yet, I intended to walk into town to buy some licorice.

Manny Corander was a master candy maker. He made the licorice himself, and instead of selling it in strings or twists, he cut it into thick, three-inch-wide strips. I could hardly wait to roll one of them into a tube and slowly relish its sharp, sweet flavor on the way home.

I stopped briefly by the east wall and noticed that not one ear of corn remained on a row of about twenty stalks. *"I guess somebody's hungry,"* I thought, echoing Dad's words. Then, in a flash of realization, it hit me. I immediately tried to suppress it, deny it, squash it. It was unthinkable. Dad *can't* have meant that. Yet, as I looked at the empty husks, I knew what Dad wanted me to do. I went into town and resolutely passed by the candy store and walked instead into the general store. Miss Molly smiled and said, "Hi, Jake."

I called out a quick "hello" but was too intent on my business to socialize. I bought what I needed and hurried out. I passed by the candy store again. This time it was a bit easier. I ran the last quarter mile or so back to the house, eager to execute my plan. When I got to the east wall, I opened my package and laid it out. It contained a small loaf of freshly baked bread, some Vermont cheddar, a stick of pepperoni, and a shiny red apple.

I ripped a square of paper off the grocery sack and realized I didn't have a pen. I ran up the driveway and into the house, grabbed the pen off the foyer phone table and ran back out before Mom could ask me what I was up to. I leaned breathlessly against the stone wall and wrote this note:

Dear Poor Person,

I'm sorry you're so hungry. I got you something better to eat. You must be sick of all that corn. I hope things get better for you soon.

Bone appateet, Jake

I double-checked the note and decided my use of French might seem pretentious (I'd heard the term *bon appétit* on a cooking show my mother watched), so I crossed it out and replaced it with "Sincerely." As I looked upon the miniature feast, I realized that as I'd prepared it, I hadn't thought about my dog. Not once.

That was Dad. He asked a question here, made an observation there, pointed you in this or that direction, and before you knew what was happening, you'd learned something about yourself that had never occurred to you before. That day I learned that I had a selfish streak a country mile wide, and that patience means waiting for something for as long as it takes without becoming angry or bitter.

After dinner I told Dad what I had done.

Dad listened intently, then smiled a glorious smile. "That's wonderful, son. I'm proud of you. I knew you'd figure it out." He called to Mom, who was in the next room. "Dear, listen to what Jake did…" Dad repeated the story, giving me far more credit than I deserved. My parents' happiness washed over me like sunlight in late August.

Dad bought me a puppy two days later. He was a beautiful, fluffy golden retriever. I named him Skipper, and I loved him from his moist nose to his eagerly wagging tail. We spent every waking moment together. I brushed him three times a day, chased him back and forth among the crops, and showed him off to all my friends. Even Mal was happy for me, despite the fact that his pouting idea had backfired.

About a week later, I received a different kind of reward. I was on my way out to the mailbox with Skipper at my heels. I was so intent on making sure that he stayed out of the road that I almost walked right past a small piece of paper wedged into the stone wall.

I grabbed the mail and ran over to investigate. Someone had put the piece of paper on the exact spot I'd left the food. I plucked it out and discovered it was a note for me. The handwriting was unusually neat (I thought, in my youthful ignorance, that all poor people wrote with poor penmanship), but it was the words that captured my attention:

Dear Jake,

Thank you for the meal you left for me. Your kind gesture gave me new strength. I hope that someday I can repay you.

A grateful friend

I picked up Skipper, hugged him, and ran back to the house with the note clenched in my fist. I showed the note to Mom and Dad, who were as delighted about it as I was.

I've wished a thousand times since then that I had paid more attention to that lesson. I've also wished that I had continued to cultivate and enjoy my relationship with Mom and Dad. It's hard to believe that things turned out the way they did.

Chapter Two

I showed my discharge pass to the gatekeeper. He wordlessly stamped it before pressing a button on his control panel. The gate swung open, screaming in protest as if it realized I was leaving and would never return. I took the few cherished steps that led to freedom, splashing through puddles that were now the only barriers between me and the world beyond AKPS.

A battered suitcase and a canvas attaché protected my few belongings from the rain. I'd owned the old piece of luggage since I was eight; a decade later, it still served me well. The attaché was a gift from the best friend I'd made during my stay at AKPS. It was one of the few tangible mementos I had of her. There were memories, of course, but memories weren't enough on a day like this. I needed her next to me, not somewhere distant and unreachable. We'd said our good-byes, my friend and I, and it hadn't been easy.

No rest, no weakness, no regrets.

My lips twisted into an imitation of a smile.

Tucked into the case were a few cherished possessions: letters from home, a cleverly designed device made to resemble an electric shaver, two journals, and my travel documents. As I stood just outside the gate, I considered my two pieces of luggage and thought about my time at Ashur-Kesed. A battered, worn case on my left and a pristine, leather-trimmed case on my right; the old leaving with the new. I reflected on the many ways I had remained the same over the last few years, and marveled at the many ways I had changed. My life had been filled with scores of new lessons and experiences, and my old way of thinking had to make room for them. When it was time to go home, I still needed the suitcase, but that old piece of luggage was insufficient to carry the precious things I had acquired during my stay. New things needed—and even deserved—a new carrying case. I wondered what would happen when I got home and unpacked.

I waited for the airport shuttle, alone except for the gatekeeper, the rain, and the memories.

I loved the tree in our backyard. It was a massive chestnut oak that stood like a guardian behind our house, watching over the farm and all that went on there. I'd been told that it was about four hundred years old, but it seemed ageless. Many birds visited that tree in the course of a day, and squirrels leaped playfully from branch to branch. I deeply envied them all. I wondered what it would be like to dwell among those sturdy branches and deep green leaves. I often ate my lunch at the base of the tree, sheltered from the sun by its outspread branches. One day, as I reclined against the ancient trunk and polished off several of my mother's homemade biscuits, Dad ambled toward me. He seemed particularly thoughtful as he looked up into the branches of the tree. I called out a greeting and rose to meet him. Skipper, who was now a year old and still growing, leaped up and followed me.

"Hi, Jake," Dad said.

"Hi, Dad. What's up?"

"I've been thinking. Do you see those two branches? The ones nearest the ground there?"

"Yup."

"Do you suppose that would be a good place to build a tree house?" he asked.

At first, I was speechless. Then, I let out a delighted yell. Skipper shared my excitement and ran playfully around Dad and me.

"A tree house for me? How come?" I asked.

"Just because," Dad replied. "You're old enough, summer's almost here, and well, it would be a lot of fun."

I hugged Dad, almost knocking him down, and then ran to tell

Mom the good news.

I hadn't asked for a tree house—not once. How did Dad know? How did he always know?

Mom thought the tree house was a great idea and offered to pitch in.

"I'll help you decorate it, Jake. Let's see…a nice, pastel yellow for the walls and…"

"Don't even think about it, Mom."

"Oh, and I just had another idea. After I play tennis on Saturday, I'll invite my whole league up to the tree house for iced tea."

"Dad, say something, will you? It's gonna be one hundred percent guy territory up there, right?"

"Well…" Dad said, eyeing Mom, whose hands were planted squarely on her hips and whose eyes encouraged him to choose his words carefully. "C'mon, Jake. Let's go draw up some rough plans, okay?"

Construction began a week later. Those days of fresh lumber, shiny nails, and bright paint were some of the best days of my life.

Dad put the same meticulous care into that tree house that he put into everything he did. He worked on it during lunch and after dinner and let me help when my farm chores were done. I watched him build a twenty-five foot high scaffold on the north side of the oak, where the two branches formed a V. I marveled at the skill with which he laid down the thick floor planks, erected the walls, and angled the roof. As the small, sturdy house grew before my eyes, I reveled in my father's generosity and dreamed about all the wonderful afternoons I would spend in my little fortress. I planned to watch every sunset from my vantage point high above the ground. I envisioned the envy of Mo, Perry, and especially Gib. I put together a loose set of guidelines as to who could enter and what we would do.

The day before Dad finished the tree house, I wasn't allowed near it. He said he had some "finishing touches" to add, and he wanted me to be surprised. Dad alternated between making mysterious, mechanical noises in his basement workshop and lugging plastic-wrapped bundles out to the work site. The night before the unveiling I was desperate to discover what Dad was up to, but security was airtight. No sooner would I drift over to the window to sneak a glimpse of the tree house than my mother would thwart my effort. I thought she was enjoying her role as security guard a little too much.

I tossed and turned that night and woke up early the next day. By then, my anticipation had reached fever pitch. I went about my usual chores with unbearable restlessness. Dad had forbidden me from venturing anywhere near the backyard. I waited in the house after dinner as per my father's instructions. After vainly attempting to read, I gave up and took to pacing. I heard the distant sound of a shovel. What would Dad be doing with a shovel?

My mother was sewing upstairs, an outrageously casual activity on such a momentous occasion as this. I was left alone with my excitement as I walked up and down, up and down, up and…

"Jake?"

"Yes, Mom?"

"Make sure you pace the whole floor. I don't want you wearing out that carpet."

I knew that, from where she was sitting in her sewing room, she could see everything Dad was doing. I decided to beat her at her own game. I ran up the stairs.

"Jake, don't you dare come up here," she said with a laugh. I heard her get up and run to the door of the sewing room. I reached the top of the stairs, turned the corner and reached for the door just as I heard the *click* of the lock.

"Mom, that's not fair!" I bellowed, rattling the door. "Tell me what you see—what's Dad doing? It's all painted, the roof's on. What else needs to be done?"

From inside the sewing room, I heard my mother whistling. I fumed quietly as I paced the hallway. She sure knew the game—she loved to tease Dad and me, and had become an expert in that department. Suddenly, I heard a distant shout from the yard and then heard Mom get up and gasp. "It's amazing," she said, just loudly enough for me to hear. That did it; I pounded on the door.

"Mom! Tell me what you see. Open this…"

The door flew open, and Mom, her eyes bright with excitement, leaned down and whispered, "Go down and see—your father says it's finished."

I flew down the steps two at a time, exploded out the backdoor and ran across the yard. In the dusk, with the sky painted a light shade of purple, I could just make out the top of the oak over the small hill behind our house. The tree house was not yet in view. When I reached the top of the rise, I saw it.

I stopped short and drank in the sight: the red paint of the walls, the white trim, the slate-shingled roof, the working door, and—what incredible detail—real glass windows. I'd seen the tree house during its construction, of course, but the finished product filled me with admiration. Dad had outdone himself. I walked the rest of the way, not wanting to rush the moment.

As I got closer, I saw that my name was engraved on a brass plate that was affixed to the door. There was also a miniature mailbox and a small porch that extended out past the front of the house. Attached to the porch between a break in the railing was the only way into the house: a sturdy rope ladder that hung down to the ground, inviting me to ascend. The tree house blended naturally with the tree. It nestled there, as if it belonged among those branches.

When I reached the foot of the tree, I noticed a furrow of fresh earth about six inches wide stretching back to our house. A black plastic tube extended from the freshly disturbed earth all the way up to the tree house.

I began to climb the rope ladder, savoring every moment. Mom had hand-woven the ladder (it was her special contribution to the project), and I loved the feel of the thick, coarse rope in my hands. When I had almost reached the top, I heard a click. Light poured out of the tree house, surprising me into immobility.

Electric lights? I had a tree house with electric lights?

As I paused on the ladder, lost in the wonder of every boy's dream-come-true, Dad stuck his head over the side of the tree house porch. His smile stretched from ear to ear and illuminated his face even more brightly than the lights. He whispered only two words: "Welcome home."

Where is that stupid shuttle? I thought irritably. Waiting by the gate of the school gave me far too much time to think. Eight years had passed since Dad had built that tree house, and two years had passed since I'd left home. The pain was still fresh, and the memories remained clear.

My accommodations at school differed drastically from those I knew on the farm—in fact, they weren't even as luxurious as the tree house. The transition from the freedom of the farm to the confinement of boarding school was difficult. When I arrived at school, I found myself missing the strangest things—things I'd taken for granted.

Instead of the polished hardwood of our dining room floor, which spoke of elegance and solidity, institutional linoleum, scuffed by the passage of many students, covered the mess hall. Instead of the curtains and flowerpots that adorned the windows of our farmhouse, welcoming the fresh air and sunlight, gray, nondescript blinds lay grimly against the security glass of the barracks, obscuring any trace of the outside world. Instead of the comforting nighttime backdrop of clucking chickens, mooing cows, and the low murmur of my parents' conversation, I could hear only the distant shouts of drill officers and the nearer sounds of twenty-plus boys snoring, and sometimes (in the darkest part of the night) weeping. Instead of the welcoming scent of Mom's kitchen spices, potpourri jars, and scented candles, the sharp smell of industrial cleanser coated everything in the barracks with its unwelcome embrace.

Sometimes, as I lay in bed with my classmate's foot dangling over the edge of the top bunk, I would try to recapture the sounds of the farm or remember things like the feel of my horse's thick mane against my cheek. I would close my eyes and imagine that Mom had just removed a raspberry rhubarb pie from the oven, or that she had lit a candle that smelled of apples or vanilla. These sights, sounds, and smells—and the joy of experiencing them every day—had seemed a lifetime away.

As much as I've missed my mom, the absence of my father felt like a hole—a vacuum—in my heart. Even when our relationship deteriorated almost to the point of mutual silence, I still loved him and couldn't stand to be far from him. My feelings for my father sprung not only from the fact that he *was* my father, but also from the fact that he was an extraordinary man.

My dad did three things, and he did them exceptionally well: he built things, he grew things, and he loved people. Despite these talents, many people—myself included—misunderstood him.

He was sometimes accused of being aloof: a hard man who was cold and distant. Others claimed he was uncaring or that he showed favoritism. None of those accusations were true, and none of the people who made them knew my dad at all. They didn't know what it was like to sit next to him on the couch as he told one of his innumerable stories. They had no idea what security there was in his huge, farm-hardened arms when they threw you into the air and unerringly caught you every time. They didn't know that when the least popular man in town suffered, Dad suffered with him; when that same man laughed, Dad's guffaw, which rumbled out of his throat like an avalanche, could be heard clear down to the barbershop. I missed my dad these past two years. I missed him a lot.

Once I finally left AKPS, I would never again be subjected to, *"Okay, buttercups, listen up. I'm your mommy, your daddy, and your little pet parakeet. Without my blessing you don't eat, sleep, walk, or live. You do what I say, when I say it. If you have a problem, solve it. If you have an issue, get over it. If you have a question, forget it. Now, fall in, and I mean* now!*"*

I especially missed the times Dad and I spent together first thing in the morning and last thing before bedtime. We had our own little ritual. Dad would get up before dawn, followed about an hour later by the rest of the family. After writing in his journal and making his morning rounds of the farm, he would grab a mug of coffee from the kitchen—Mom had a strong, steaming pot brewing by this time—and walk out to the west fields.

Dad grew oats, wheat, and soybeans there. He would stand and look toward the east and wait for me. I also had a mug, but mine usually contained fresh orange juice or milk from our cows; in the fall I sometimes had tart, hot cider, mulled with nutmeg and cloves. We would turn back toward the farm and watch the day begin as the rising sun painted our house with rich colors.

We would meet together that way, father and son, every day. When it rained and we couldn't enjoy the sunrise, we'd go into the dairy barn and sit on bales of hay. It was during those mornings that Dad taught me lessons like the one in the peach orchard. I could fill a book, maybe two, with all the things I learned during those daily meetings.

Mornings at AKPS tended to be somewhat less relaxing. I usually awoke to, *"Get up, you lazy morons! Do you think you were sent here to sleep? If I don't hear twenty-four sets of feet smack that floor by the time I light this cigar, you'll all wish you were dead!"* Never again.

The time my family spent at night was just as enjoyable as the morning. After dinner in the kitchen, we would gather in the family room. Any conversation about the activities of the farm had taken place during the meal; now we simply sat together and pursued our various hobbies.

Mom loved needlework. During the fall and winter, she would busily knit mittens, sweaters, and comforters. In the spring, she would mend socks and replace buttons. During the summer, she would cross-stitch just for the fun of it. Sometimes I would forgo my own hobbies for a while just to watch her.

I never tired of admiring how her fingers darted about, seemingly independent of any conscious thought on her part. She could carry on a conversation with me and still unerringly tuck that needle under the pattern, plunge it upward, push it back down, and start all over again. The way she called forth order and beauty from an endless supply of disorganized, multicolored yarn was a source of encouragement to me in later years.

"Do you realize how useless you are? Get off the ground, all of you! Now, try it again—march, march, march. Mid-classman, if you fall in that mud one more time you'll launder the dirty socks of your entire class with your ration of water—move! Precision, order, discipline..." Never again.

As the days dragged on at school, I thought of the way Mom had worked on those cross-stitch patterns. She preferred tranquil scenes from nature, such as my childhood favorite: two cardinals resting on a snow-covered branch. Although she usually used brightly colored thread, she would sometimes have to use darker colors—gray, brown, black. They were necessary evils, those dark colors. When used in conjunction with colors like red and green and white, they made those cheerful hues seem somehow brighter and more refreshing by contrast.

I shifted from one foot to the other as I waited for the shuttle, and mused that the darkness of Ashur-Kesed had become, in my mind, like those dark threads: a necessary evil brought about by my own choices.

My experiences at school served to highlight everything else about my life that was good and bright and happy. I hoped that when I finally arrived home I could lay aside those dark threads and begin to use lighter shades once again.

Dad's hobbies, like Mom's, also tended toward the creative. His workshop in the basement housed all of his heavy tools; but after dinner he preferred to work at his neatly organized worktable in the corner of the family room so he could be near us. He often puttered at that table, making the most beautiful objects from a variety of leftover pieces of wood or scraps of metal. Although he rarely used blueprints, he always seemed to know exactly what he was doing.

Sometimes Dad made birdhouses or squirrel feeders. Other times, he built a top, or a doll, or a toy soldier. He kept these items scattered around the house, perched on the mantel or occupying a shelf. When guests with children came for a visit, the children would often go home with an unexpected gift.

When I wasn't watching my parents pursue their hobbies, I enjoyed my own: reading. How I loved to lie by the fire on cold nights with a treasured book open in front of me. What adventures I had in those pages—I was a pirate (a good and kind pirate, of course), a soldier, an adventurer, an explorer, and countless other things. I traveled the world and even to the farthest reaches of space. I had many friends, a great many enemies (all of whom I unerringly defeated), and amassed quite a storehouse of stories and experiences.

"My precious flowers, welcome to your worst nightmare. Please do me the favor of abandoning all hope of having a pleasant stay with us here at Ashur-Kesed Preparatory School. Perhaps you're wondering what you're being prepared for. I'll tell you—you are being groomed into people who will no longer think, move, or act without an express command from my lips. You're here to become model citizens. Keep in mind that when you're making a model, sometimes the molds get broken..." Never again.

When bedtime came around, Mom would kiss me good night and Dad would often walk me upstairs. Some of my friends might have said that having your Dad put you to bed was somewhat babyish, but they would have received a belt in the nose for offering such an opinion. It wasn't babyish at all. Those were the times when I got to teach Dad.

After I was settled under the thick covers, my dad would ask me what I had learned that day. "What did the fields tell you, son?" he would inquire, or, "Did the animals have anything to say today, Jake?" He would then listen carefully as I told him what I had gathered from the vast school of creation. Dad asked questions along the way, but offered few comments. He was content to let me be the teacher during those bedtime chats. It never mattered to me that Dad already knew everything that I had taken so long to learn. What mattered was that he cared enough to hear it in my own words, from my perspective. Sometimes we'd chat about nothing in particular, and I enjoyed those conversations just as much. The night the tree house was unveiled, there was only one thing on my mind.

"Dad, thanks again," I said. "The tree house is perfect."

"I'm glad you like it. I'm still going to whip you in chess, though, so don't think the high altitude will be an advantage."

"Yeah, yeah, we'll see."

"So how's the view from up there? Is it everything you hoped?"

"Better. The leaves block my view a little, but I can see almost to the end of the south cornfield. I'll be able to see farther in the fall."

"That's great."

We talked some more and the conversation shifted to farming. I wanted to enter our sow in an upcoming fair, and we discussed the steps I needed to take to get her ready.

When my eyes grew heavy, Dad kissed my forehead (another practice which would have scandalized my male friends, had they known of it) and I went to sleep in the secure knowledge that no matter what the next day would bring, I was important in the eyes of my father.

"You are nothing, do you hear me? Nothing. And my mission in life is to make sure you never forget that. Learn and accept your own inherent uselessness, and I will have done my job, gentlemen." Never again.

Over the years, Dad's lessons settled on me like a garment you can never take off and wouldn't want to even if you could. When I came to school, those lessons served me well.

The teachers at AKPS could have learned a thing or two from my father.

As I stood at the school gate waiting to go home, I was particularly saddened by the fact that I had managed to hurt the people I loved the most despite my dad's attempts to lead me in another direction.

Despite a deep sense of shame and remorse, I was willing to stand up, brush myself off, and try again. I set my jaw against the rain that was attempting to discourage me, the gate that was trying to snatch back my freedom, and the shuttle that refused to pick me up.

I was going home.

Chapter Three

The summer after I turned eleven was one of the best I can remember. I continued to spend more time in my tree house than I did in our farmhouse. I'd covered the walls with photos and posters and carefully arranged my baseball cards on the shelves Dad had built. Basic necessities were stored in a wooden milk crate. My supplies included several decks of cards, a well-worn copy of the Boston Red Sox yearbook, an emergency reserve of bubble gum, a Frisbee that Skipper had all but chewed into pieces, and my baseball equipment. Mom gave me an old beanbag chair that she was happy to get rid of, and Yasha and Remmy, our two year-round hired men, built me a small table and chair. A plaid horse blanket served as a carpet.

Dad visited often, and he sometimes brought a few of Mom's sweet rolls and a thermos of coffee. As we enjoyed a game of cards or chess, he and I would talk about the farm and the upcoming harvest, trade predictions about which streams would offer the best fishing that year, or discuss the things I'd learned in school that day. Sometimes we just leaned out the window and admired the view.

One day after our work was done, we sat up in the tree house until dinnertime. We were playing chess, and the match was unusually close.

"Your king is toast, Dad," I said gleefully.

"Is he, now? He looks alive and well to me."

Dad still had his queen, but I had just gobbled up his last rook, narrowing his options.

"By the way, did you hear that squeak in the tiller?" he said.

"Hey! No distracting me."

"Oh, sorry. I know what a sensitive ear you have. I was just looking for a little help, is all…"

"It's funny…you don't say a word when you're planning a move."

"You're right, son. I'll be quiet."

I pored over the board. Dad had just made a seemingly inconsequential move with one of his last pawns. I had to be careful. When he made a move like that, he usually had a broader plan to snatch victory right out of my hand. I could feel him watching me. I looked up and just barely caught him making a face.

"Dad!" I tried hard not to laugh and succeeded for about two seconds. "Cut it out. You win enough."

"Sorry, sorry," he said, also laughing. "I'll be as quiet as a mouse."

"Yeah, right." I looked back down at the board. Aha! There it was: a neatly coordinated attack by the queen, a bishop, and a knight. The pawn had been a decoy. I casually leaned forward and nudged my king out of harm's way, while simultaneously placing Dad's king in check.

"Check, big man," I cried triumphantly.

Dad glared at the board in dismay. He suddenly cocked his head to one side.

"Yes, dear? Are you calling us?"

I laughed again. "Come on, Dad, admit it. Tip over your king and then I'll let you beat me arm wrestling to make you feel better."

Dad grunted, then smiled. I looked at the board again and suddenly saw Dad's real trap—the one I'd missed. He slid his queen all the way across the board, eliminating my threat and presenting his own. I gaped and searched for a way out. All my options were temporary, and all my potential attacks were neutralized. Stalemate. I screamed.

Now, Mom did call us. "Are you two all right up there?"

"Perfectly, dear," Dad called back.

"I can never beat him, Ma."

"Neither can I," she called back. "There's no time for a rematch, either. Come on down and knock the mud off your feet before you come in."

"Good game, son," Dad said as we climbed down the ladder. "You get better every time."

"I can still beat you back to the house."

"You're welcome to try."

We ran side by side. Dad gave it a good try, but I outpaced him. We burst into the house and invaded Mom's kitchen.

"Food, Mom. We need food."

"What did I tell you about mud? Out, both of you, or no dessert."

We fled and cleaned off our shoes as we watched the sunset. It was just another great day in a long string of great days.

My friends were frequent visitors to the tree house, too. I loved the look of envy on their faces when they stepped into the tree house for the first time. Whenever possible, I invited them up at night so I could show off my electric lights.

Gib was the first. He was something of a liar and his clothes were always dirty, but he could spit really far, so I welcomed him despite his faults. He was impressed but informed me that his Dad had built him a tree house just like mine. Sadly, termites had consumed *his* tree house. "Yeah, we had to tear down what they didn't wreck. No sense lettin' the little buggers migrate over to our house," he said.

It was a typically transparent lie. I felt bad for Gib and pretended not to know that he'd never had a tree house.

"Cannon" was the second visitor. His real name was Hammond—a distant relative's name, I think—but he'd pound you if you ever called him that. He had the best arm in the neighborhood. If you weren't on his team in baseball, you learned to hit to the field opposite where he was playing. Cannon was duly impressed with the tree house and asked me how I'd managed to swing a place like that. I shrugged; I honestly didn't know. I was still in awe of Dad's generosity.

Word quickly spread about "the coolest tree house in the neighborhood." All my other close friends made the pilgrimage as soon as they heard. Perry, Jeb, Mo, Philip, and Mal were jealous, too. Other visitors followed, neighborhood kids who I barely knew but who now greeted me as their "best friend."

Diane was the first girl to visit the tree house. I was leery about letting her come up; after all, what would the guys say? However, she wore an old pair of overalls and tied her hair up in a bun under a Red Sox cap; I couldn't justifiably refuse her admittance. I soon regretted my decision. She climbed up the rope ladder and before both of her sneakered feet were flat on the floor, she looked around with an eye toward redecorating.

"Nice place you got here, Jake," she said in her best fit-in-with-the-guys voice. "A couple little touches and it would be perfect."

"What 'touches'?" I growled. The tree house had no flaws that I could see.

"Oh, I don't know. Curtains for the windows, maybe a different color paint for the walls...and that milk crate? Totally gross. Now, the first thing we need to..."

"Diane?"

"Yes, Jake?" She was deceptively sweet, but I was blind to her charms at that point.

"I don't dare put up curtains in here," I said.

"Why not?"

"Because of the earwigs."

I was rewarded with an instant look of alarm. Diane stopped examining the rug and stood up abruptly. "Earwigs?" she said, trying hard to sound casual.

"Yeah," I replied. "There's a whole bunch of 'em in here already. They hide between the floorboards, but they really love curtains. The whole place would be crawling with earwigs if I put up curtains." My conscience elbowed me a bit; there wasn't a single insect in the tree house. Didn't fibbing like that make me as bad as Gib? I justified the lie as being my only practical option. I couldn't have some girl telling me what paint to put on my walls or how to decorate my windows.

Diane believed me. She smiled thinly, complimented me once again on the accommodations and then suddenly remembered she had a piano lesson. I watched her descend the rope ladder with great satisfaction. She would return under different circumstances, but not for a few years.

As August made way for September, my family prepared for the harvest. I wasn't able to spend as much time in the tree house. The days grew cooler and shorter, and as the trees put on their glorious displays of color, everyone on our farm shared a sense of nervous anticipation.

The harvest is both exciting and frightening. There is nothing like harvesting grain that you planted. It was you who had driven the plow, scattered the seeds, and cultivated the crops. You had watched with growing wonder as the first green sprouts emerged from the soil, and it was your face that had felt the sun as it bathed the fields with nourishing warmth. Now, as you raked cornstalks, ran the harvester, or helped square-bale the hay, you saw the results of all your hard work and felt both powerful and humbled. That was the exciting part. The frightening part arose from that peculiar mixture of self-sufficiency and dependence that every farmer experiences. Farming requires a delicate balance of many variables. You could work hard all season, but if the rain doesn't fall, the crops don't grow. Too much rain, on the other hand, can saturate the air spaces in the soil and suffocate the crops.

Nevertheless, excitement always won out over fear, and the hard work kept us too busy to worry. From the first seeding in spring until the end of October, everyone on our farm worked even harder than usual. Dad employed about twenty-five men for the season and two year-round. They were a good crew, and I loved to hear them out in the fields as they laughed and sang and swapped stories.

I helped wherever I was needed during the harvest, but my year-round job was to tend to the lawn and take care of the livestock. Ours was a produce farm, but we enjoyed the animals, which included twenty Jersey cows, a small flock of sheep, a brood of chickens, six pigs, three horses, and a donkey. Even though they were expensive to care for and barely provided us with enough milk, wool, and eggs to justify keeping them, it wouldn't have seemed like a farm without them.

I reported to the cow barn every morning after I met with Dad. I ate a quick breakfast on the way—usually an egg sandwich—and set up the automatic pumps under the first four cows. The pumps were efficient, but I often milked a few cows by hand so I wouldn't get out of practice.

After finishing the milking, I fed the pigs. Little Sue was the matriarch of the sty, and she and her clan always enjoyed the mixture of leftovers and milk that I poured into their trough. As they ate their breakfast, I crossed the yard to the horse stalls and bid good morning to Swish, Polo, Chestnut, and Issachar. Swish was my horse, Polo belonged to Dad, and Chestnut was Mom's. Issachar was our donkey, and he protected the sheep during the day. I brushed, fed, and watered each of them, then grabbed some egg cartons and headed for the chicken coop. I checked for eggs as the hens sat contentedly on their nests, then I spread a thick layer of feed corn into their little courtyard and let them out for the day. After all this was done, I grabbed my staff and club from the corner of the barn and took the sheep out to pasture.

These morning tasks gave me a good appetite, so I usually had a snack and chatted with Mom before attending to the grounds. I weeded wherever necessary, did some light repairs, and (twice a week) mowed the several acres of grass that surrounded our house. School took up the rest of the afternoon. Mom and Dad were flexible about my home schooling. They avoided morning classes because of the demands of the farm, and I worked hard at my studies to keep it that way. Just before dinner, I brought the sheep in and bedded down all the animals for the night.

I enjoyed my daily routine, but autumns were hectic. The faster pace around the farm may have contributed to my losing a sheep one afternoon.

It had been a good day and I was on my way out to the pasture to bring the sheep in for the evening. I'd wanted to take Skipper along, but he harassed the sheep too much. He loved to dart among them, yipping playfully as they scolded him with loud bleats and did their best to stay out of his way. He whimpered when he realized I was leaving him behind. I patted his head and promised I'd make it up to him later with a game of fetch-the-tennis-ball. For now, I had work to do. I strolled through the ankle-deep grass, twirling my staff and whistling.

I caught sight of the flock peacefully grazing on the gentle slope of a hill. From a distance, they looked like fluffy cotton balls spread over a lush green carpet. They stood with their heads down, quietly munching the special mixture of grasses we'd planted for them.

Sheep are gentle and quiet. They don't ask for much except that you protect them, feed them, and keep the bugs out of their noses. However, some sheep possess the irritating habit of wandering away from the flock. In retrospect, I should have been more careful. Our farm was too large to completely fence in and I knew that the dry weather was making the sheep restless, but my thoughts were on the harvest, the weather, my dog—anywhere but in that pasture.

When the sheep caught sight of me, they trotted towards me and bleated their customary welcome. Issachar had been faithfully standing guard. He followed the sheep as they headed for the barn, where they would drink deeply from the watering troughs before settling down for the night.

"Issy! Everything okay?" I called out. "No visitors today, I hope." Issachar didn't reply, but his nuzzle gave me all the information I needed. He was as vigilant as a sheepdog, and his powerful kick was an excellent deterrent to any predators that might attack the flock. I threw my arm around the donkey's neck and walked him in as the sheep surrounded us. I rubbed the closest sheep behind the ears and enjoyed the sight of my flock: it was like walking in the midst of a slow-moving cloud. I got halfway back to the farm before I realized I'd forgotten to count them.

I counted aloud, pointing to each sheep with my index finger and humming a little tune as I did so. When I finished, I counted again, more carefully this time, and still came up with thirty-nine. We had forty sheep.

I scanned the horizon wildly, straining to see one tiny, errant blot of white in all that green. There was no sign of the sheep. The sun would go down in about a half hour, and then what? Losing a sheep was a serious matter to any true shepherd. It wasn't that they were expensive, or that they were especially rare. My sheep depended on me, and I took that responsibility seriously. Sheep lack the directional skills and natural defenses of other animals, so a lost sheep often ends up a dead sheep. I couldn't bear that thought.

I left Issachar in charge of the flock and tore across the field to find my dad. When I got to the house, Dad was just coming in. He heard me yelling and stopped at the backdoor to wait for me. When I reached him, he placed his hands on my shoulders and calmly asked what was wrong.

"Sheep…thirty-nine…can't find…"

That was all I needed to say.

"Son, get the rifle, the lantern, and a rope. I'll meet you in the pasture." Then Dad was off and running. I scrambled to follow his directions. I burst through the barn door, startling Yasha and Remmy. I didn't stop to explain. I slid across the dirt floor to the storehouse where we keep the tools. I draped the rope around my neck, took the lantern off its hook and placed it at my feet, then grasped the rifle. It was a .30-30, and my hands trembled as I slid seven shells into the chamber and crammed a handful more into my pocket. Fully equipped, I headed back out to the pasture after breathlessly instructing the men to bring the rest of the sheep home.

When I caught up with Dad, he was studying the tracks, trying to determine where number forty had gone. I knew better than to say anything. This was a time to watch and learn. I scanned the nearby forest for any nocturnal visitors. Dusk had settled on us.

I wasn't usually afraid of the dark, but the memory of a recent visit from the game warden kept replaying in my mind. He'd warned us that red wolves had been seen in the area, and he told us to pay special attention to our livestock. Whether wolves were starting to move back into Pennsylvania from the north, or a rogue pack had simply wandered far out of their usual range, he didn't know. Either way, I'd spotted wolf tracks near the western border of our farm just a few days after the warden's visit. One wolf didn't scare me much, but a pack of wolves....

That night, as we searched for our sheep, I took comfort in Dad's presence and gripped the worn stock of the rifle a little more firmly.

"This way. I think she headed for the river." Dad strode off and I followed, wondering how he knew it was one of the ewes. Perhaps the size and depth of the print? I fell in beside him as we walked across the field.

I heard the ewe before I saw her. We followed the tracks around a thick stand of sycamore trees and caught sight of her. She was the one we called Princess, and she regularly got into trouble. She'd earned her nickname because of the way she dominated the flock, demanding the best patches of turf and often leading other sheep astray. I was thankful that more sheep hadn't followed her bad example this time. Princess had somehow found her way up the side of the riverbank, following a few sparse tufts of clover. Sheep are like that. They are attracted to food that is inferior to that which they enjoy in their own pasture.

Princess was trapped on a small outcropping of rock, bleating piteously. She was lying on her back, unable to roll over and regain her feet. I'd seen this many times before. Princess was what shepherds called a "cast" sheep. Our ewe had probably lain down on her side to rest. In trying to get up, her center of gravity had shifted, causing her to panic, flail her legs, and roll over onto her back. It would have been a funny sight if it weren't so dangerous. When a sheep rolls over like that, gases build up in its digestive system. If we hadn't found her, Princess would surely have died a horrible death by morning.

Dad assessed the situation and then we waded across the river, which narrowed at that point to little more than the width of a creek. The sheep was about twelve feet up, and it would be a hard climb. Even if Dad could find sufficient hand- and toeholds, I couldn't see how he was going to get her down. I thought the matter through from several angles. As much as I hated the thought, the safest thing for us to do was leave her; the most humane thing to do was shoot her. It would be a terrible loss, but it was getting dark, the climb was dangerous, and she'd gotten herself into this mess, hadn't she?

I looked up at Dad and was startled to discover that he was now assessing me, too. His deep voice reverberated against the cliff face as he said, "Never underestimate the value of one." How did he always seem to know what I was thinking?

I heard a distant howl. It sounded more like a coyote than a wolf, but I thought about the tracks I'd seen by the west wall, and I cast a wary eye into the woods. I'd faced wolves before, and even a bear once, but on both occasions I'd been in an open field with a clear shot. That night, Dad and I had a rock wall on one side and an overgrown riverbank on the other. It was a good place to get cornered.

I saw that Dad was determined to save the sheep, so I asked him to hurry. He took the rope from around my shoulders.

"Hold the lantern high and the gun steady. I'm going to fetch Princess, and we need to watch for trouble. Can I count on you?"

I would just as soon have drowned myself in the river as disappoint my father. "Yes," I said. I hardened my expression and scanned the darkening woods around us. Dad started to climb. His rough, strong hands found a root here, a stone there. His boots were planted firmly against the side of the rock face as he slowly ascended.

Behind me, a twig snapped and I wheeled around, the blood hammering in my ears, my senses razor-sharp. I tried to keep my voice calm as I said, "Dad? Almost there?"

He grunted in reply. I leaned against the cliff wall, the better to accost a potential attacker. I couldn't see what my dad was up to, and I still had no idea how he was going to get that sheep down. The ewe probably weighed 125 pounds, so lowering her with the rope was impossible. Dad could probably handle the weight, but the built-up gas in the sheep's abdomen could rupture her stomach, killing her as surely as leaving her behind would do.

I heard more rustling in the underbrush. My finger tightened on the trigger as I saw a pair of eyes glowing in the bushes. I raised the rifle, too frightened to call for Dad. The undergrowth parted, and I sighed with relief as I spotted a familiar black mask and ambling gait; it was just a coon.

I felt safe enough to turn my back on the forest for a moment, and just as I did, I heard a loud *thud* off to my left, followed by a *whoop* from above. I looked up just in time to see my dad glide down from the overhang as if he were an eagle. His strong arms cradled the lost sheep, and his triumphant grin erased all my fears. I burst out laughing when I realized what my father, the consummate king of resourcefulness, had done.

Upon arriving at the top of the cliff, Dad had wrapped the rope around a boulder and then tied the other end around his waist. He'd hefted the boulder up and over a nearby tree limb (that was the *thud*), picked up the sheep, and slid down the bank while hollering at the top of his lungs (that was the *whoop*). The boulder had counterbalanced the weight of man and sheep, slowing their descent and delivering them safely at my feet. Dad landed on his backside and his great barks of laughter probably made every animal within a half mile stop and cock its ears. I looked down at him as we laughed together. Although he had mud smeared all over his face and clothes, his eyes sparkled.

Still holding the ewe, he said breathlessly, "The value of one."

We massaged the sheep's legs to restore circulation. Once she could walk on her own, we trudged back home. After we washed and watered her, Dad and I went inside to celebrate.

* * *

I waited in relentless rain for about an hour. I hoped to spot the shuttle through the line of pine trees that ran along the driveway of the school.

I knew an easy alternative to waiting. I could ask the gatekeeper to let me back inside, so I could use the battered pay phone in the common room to call the airport. I delayed as long as possible.

I could just hear the gatekeeper saying, *"No one ever really escapes from here, Jake. You know that. Come back in where it's warm and dry. They don't really want you to come home anyway."*

I also entertained the irrational notion that once I stepped back onto school property, the vice-chancellor would pop out of his hiding place and tell me that, regretfully, my release papers were not in order after all. A technicality. Such a pity, but another year wouldn't kill me, would it?

As the minutes crawled by, I had to bow to practicality. I was soaked, despite my black rain slicker and waterproof cap, and I was concerned about the contents of my luggage. I felt as though the rain had washed away my confident determination. After examining my limited options, I clenched my jaw, turned around, and asked if I could reenter school grounds to use the telephone. Wordlessly, the gatekeeper pressed the button again.

The memory of Dad's phrase, "the value of one," stung me a little as I dialed the phone. I'd been at AKPS for almost two years, figuratively lost, but Dad hadn't come to get me. I had wandered off, but there had been no grand rescue. It was true that I had brought my troubles upon myself, but now I couldn't even *pay* someone to pick me up and take me home.

On the brink of freedom, I had never felt more alone.

Chapter Four

Ashur-Kesed was described in its promotional literature as a "preparatory school." Its mission: *"To prepare young men for the challenges they will face in life by administering a strict regimen of high academics, challenging physical discipline, and the most demanding code of honor and respect for authority."*

To my knowledge no such instruction occurred at AKPS except by accident, and no admiration was due to the majority of teachers who were tenured there. I would describe the daily classes as senseless exercises in futility. The teachers cared nothing for us—they didn't even care about the subjects they taught. We, in turn, cared little for their teaching. If a wall were erected between the faculty and students of Ashur-Kesed, the level of communication would not have diminished one bit.

I tried to make the best of my experience at AKPS. When the shock of my new environment wore off, I started to pay attention during the long, dull classes. I studied, read, wrote, and found that I could learn despite my circumstances. My thoughts often returned, however, to the education I'd received at home.

It was early November. We'd finished the harvest, cleared the fields, and packed away the silage. The sight of our farm in late autumn always made me a little sad. Rows and rows of green crops had given way to bare, brown fields. The large crew that helped with the harvest was gone for the season, and I missed that exciting sense of urgency as everyone pitched in and worked together.

We'd had a good harvest. The silo was brimming with fresh grain, the loft above the cow stalls was full of sweet-smelling bales of hay, and Dad was pleased with our yield for the season. The pace of every-day life relaxed, and autumn brought the World Series and the country fairs I loved so much. I'd entered Little Sue in the swine competition that year. She didn't win the blue ribbon, but I enjoyed the fair anyway.

It was also time for my official school year to begin. Mom and Dad didn't follow the public school schedule because doing so would have made it difficult for me to both work on the farm and study. My home schooling followed a regular pattern, just as my share of the sowing and harvest duties did. I woke at the usual time of 5:00 A.M. and completed my morning chores; Yasha and Remmy handled the rest of my duties. I ate breakfast, spent about a half hour with Dad, then reported upstairs to the library where Mom waited for me.

She, like Dad, was an excellent teacher. My mother handled literature, grammar, music, art, and practical things not often taught to young boys, such as sewing, cooking, and the proper way to turn out a rug. It was important to her and Dad that I become "well-rounded." In addition to his daily (and often spontaneous) father-son lessons, Dad taught me geography, science, math, and history.

Mom used textbooks and loosely followed a curriculum, but some of her favorite lessons were more abstract. She was fond of helping me explore my emotions.

One morning, I walked into the library and saw that there were no schoolbooks laid out. That usually meant that something unconventional was afoot.

It was a beautiful day. The sun slanted in through the open window, casting slivers of light upon the floor. The wonderful smell of autumn wafted in, rustling the curtains and mingling with the rich odor of paper and leather bookbindings.

My mother smiled when I entered. In front of her on a study table were seven small bottles. They looked like the vials of food coloring that she kept on the top shelf in the kitchen, but each contained a clear liquid with a label on the back that I couldn't read. I put my books down and studied the bottles.

"What gives?" I asked.

"A lesson in aromatics," she said.

"What's that?"

"Uh-uh. Questions later. Close your eyes."

"Aromatics? That's a fake word, isn't it?"

"Why don't you look it up?" my mother suggested with a confident glance at the bookshelf.

I wondered if she were bluffing as I crossed over to the row of large books next to the window. I chose the thick, hardcover dictionary to give my mom the best possible chance and ran a finger slowly down the row of *A* words.

"Let's see. Aroma, aromatherapy, aromatic...nope. It's not here. 'Aromatic' was close, but you're busted, Mom."

My mother scratched her head in a comical fashion. "Really? There's no such thing as aromatics? Oh, well. Sorry, Jake, I guess there'll be no lesson today. I certainly can't teach you about something that doesn't exist." With that, she began to pack up her materials.

"Wait a minute," I objected. "What's all that stuff for?"

She looked up slyly and asked, "Would you really like to know?"

"Yes!"

"Then that brings us back to my original instruction: close your eyes."

I sighed loudly and smiled as I scrunched my eyes shut. I waited a moment then opened my eyes to slits so I could see what was going on.

"All right, if that's the way you want it," Mom said, suddenly behind me. I heard a rustling then felt a strip of soft fabric across my eyes.

"Aw, Ma. Why can't I see?"

"Questions later. Focus." She waited a minute, then I heard her voice in front of me again. "You saw the bottles, Jake. Each contains a scent with which you're familiar. I want you to identify the scent."

"Oh! That sounds cool."

I could hear the smile in my mother's voice as she said, "We'll see."

She took her time bringing the first bottle over to me, allowing me to become acclimated to the lack of visual input. I heard a scratchy metallic sound as she unscrewed the cap from the first bottle, the swish of her house shoes as she walked over to my chair, and the background noises of the farm through the open window.

"Ready?"

"Ready."

I felt a slight breeze as she waved the vial under my nose. I cautiously inhaled the first scent. "Gasoline," I said confidently, and then added, "Unleaded."

"Very good, very technical," she said. "Care to tell me the octane, too?"

"Smells like 89, but since that's the only kind we use for the mowers and the cars, you could've slipped some 90 in there. That was an easy one, Mom. I hope they get more challenging."

"That's only the first part of the test. Here's the second: how does that smell make you feel?"

"What?"

"You heard me."

Now I knew why Mom had sounded so smug. She knew I despised exercises like this.

"You want me to tell you how gasoline makes me *feel*?"

"Yup."

"No hints?"

"How can I give you hints? They're your feelings."

"But I don't have any feelings about gasoline."

"Okay, let's look at this from a different direction. What do you *think* of when you smell gasoline? Paint a picture in your mind then describe it to me."

"I think of the riding mower."

"What about it?"

"How you have to be careful not to pour the gas in too fast because otherwise it spills, and I can't stand wiping it up, but you have to because otherwise it'll spoil the paint."

"What else? What does this smell remind you of?"

"Um, I think of walking into the barn and how I love cutting the grass because it looks great when I'm done. I always grab the rag off the work bench first and make sure that the spout on the gas can is on tight, 'cause one day it wasn't, and...I think I get it."

"I think you do, too. Paint a picture in your mind. Become more aware of your feelings and any memories that spring up as a result of these olfactory cues."

"Huh? Did you make up that word, too?"

Mom giggled. "Olfactory, dear son, means 'having to do with the sense of smell.'"

Still blindfolded, I did my best impression of an English accent. "You might have said so in the first place."

She responded by tickling me, and I screamed all the louder because I hadn't seen it coming.

"Next scent," Mom said, after I had been properly "punished" for my impertinence.

Another wave of the vial, another whiff.

"Um, grease?"

"More specific."

"Bacon grease."

"Right. Feelings? Paint a picture."

"Um, lying in bed and waking up to that smell. Brushing my teeth and coming downstairs on a Saturday morning, seeing you by the stove, snitching a piece before I go and milk the cows. The saltiness, the flavor of it lasting a long time and making me want more."

"Smells are powerful, aren't they?"

"Yeah—I'm hungry, Ma."

"Here's another…"

Breeze, sniff…

"Gross! I don't trust that guy one bit, and I don't think Dad does either."

"Who's that?"

"That salesman who sells seed from door-to-door. He doesn't look like he ever touched a clod of soil in his life. He wears that cologne."

"You're a fast learner, Jake."

"Give me another one."

The lesson went on for another half hour and I loved every minute of it. Such was my early education at home. It was little wonder that I found it difficult to adjust to the often-brutal instruction at Ashur-Kesed.

"Well, Mid-classman Louis? Do you or do you not understand?"

I was jarred awake by the bellowed question, and my head jerked on my hand where it had been resting. Dr. Crednast stood at the front of the classroom, rearing up behind his lectern like an angry bear. I thought a bear would look more cheerful.

Agar Crednast was our mathematics teacher. He was subject to an unusual amount of stress, due largely to our total incomprehension of the numerical principles he loved so dearly. The blank stares and mumbled, incorrect answers we offered frustrated him.

Louis was his current victim, and he squirmed under the teacher's gaze like a beetle speared by a specimen pin. Dr. Crednast had the terrifying habit of fixating on the student who least understood his daily lesson. He would grill that student until he reduced him to a gibbering, red-faced mass of shattered confidence. In Louis's case, that was rather short work.

We'd had a comprehensive test the day before. Many of us, including me, had just barely passed. A few, like Louis, had not. Since everyone suffered from the failure of even one student, we were reviewing word problems when Dr. Crednast noticed that Louis failed to grasp the concepts (probably because the latter had been doodling on his assignment pad). The livid instructor had drilled Louis ceaselessly for the past ten minutes. It had become exceedingly tiresome and as I glanced around, I saw that I was not the only one who had dozed off. Unfortunately for Louis, in trying to cram more information through the slim window of his intelligence, Dr. Crednast was unwittingly closing that window forever.

"I asked you a question, mid-classman. Don't make me repeat myself." When Dr. Crednast spaced out his words like that, he was not to be trifled with.

"Uh, no, sir. I do not fully understand, sir," Louis reluctantly admitted.

"You do not fully understand? Does that mean, sir, that you partially understand? If so, *which* part do you understand?"

"Uh, I guess I don't understand at all, sir."

"Fine. A little confession is good for the soul. Don't you agree, class?"

We murmured the expected agreement, and wondered if it was possible to die of boredom. Such dramas frequently played out during the course of the school day. The only thing we could do was wait them out and hope that we weren't the next targets.

"Now, you addled little twit, this is x. It always represents a numerical value. When we 'solve for x,' we are attempting to discover what that value is. Hello? Are any brain cells available for a response?" The doctor's voice had hardened. He was finished with the pleasantries.

A few of us saw it coming but hoped we were wrong. We certainly would have tried to stop it if we'd been sure. Louis had simply had enough. His broad back tensed and the pencil snapped in half in his hand and dropped to the floor. He stood.

Dr. Crednast told him to sit down, but Louis moved between the rows of desks and chairs like a lion stalking a zebra. The unfortunate mathematics teacher had time to scream once before Louis's beefy hands grasped him around the throat. We all jumped to our feet but didn't dare intervene.

Dr. Crednast had cried out, and that meant a guard was only seconds away from bursting into the room. If he should find any of us in a suspicious position, we would suffer the same fate as Louis.

Sure enough, the door banged open and two guards rushed in. Dr. Crednast had turned an alarming shade of purple by the time they pried Louis's fingers from around his neck. Dr. Crednast staggered back, gasping. That's when the beating began.

I'm sure they did it in front of us to send a message. None of us wanted to look, but we looked anyway. The two guards deftly stripped off Louis's shirt and pants and then wielded the thin fiberglass rods they carried. The rods were hollow and about as thick as a man's finger. They rarely caused permanent damage, but they could raise welts, draw blood, and in this case, disfigure a student with brutal efficiency. We didn't dare move or try to interfere, though I saw Jerry flinch when the first drops of blood hit him (he sat in the front). Louis's screams sent chills down my spine. They eventually ended in husky whispers when his vocal cords became too swollen to produce sound.

I didn't see Louis for about two weeks after that. When I did, I marveled once again at the degree of his injuries. I'd heard that several students had rallied and begun to tutor him in algebra in the hopes of helping him avoid more beatings. It was a pity none of us had thought of it sooner, and I wondered if it would even help. Louis's frustrated attack on Dr. Crednast had precipitated his beating; he needed lessons in self-control as much as he did in algebra. Still, I wondered for the hundredth time how Ashur-Kesed got away with such vicious cruelty, and I vowed for the hundredth time to bring about an end to this school if I ever escaped its oppressive grasp.

I stopped and offered Louis some encouragement, but I didn't stop long. I had a test that I didn't dare fail. In the real world, failure meant that you dusted yourself off and tried again. At AKPS, as Louis had graphically illustrated, failure could result in significantly greater damage than a bruised ego.

I hoped his limp wasn't permanent.

Chapter Five

Autumn turned into winter, and everyone on the farm began to settle in for our least active season of the year.

Skipper was a stout, energetic two-year-old by then. He followed me around as usual, and he loved the snow. One of my favorite games was tying his leash to the back fence while I made a large, crude snowman. I inserted sticks for his arms, stones for his eyes, and the usual carrot for his nose. When I finished, I would incite Skipper into an absolute frenzy by leaping around the snowman, pretending that he was attacking me. When Skipper could stand it no more, I would release him and laugh until it hurt. He promptly attacked the snowman, reducing it to a lumpy, muddy pile. I, in turn, would "attack" Skipper, and we'd tumble in the snow until we were both exhausted. I loved that dog. I suppose he took the place of a brother or sister.

Mom and Dad didn't talk much about why they never had any more kids after me, but I didn't mind not having any siblings. I had many friends, I had Mom and Dad, and I had a dog. What more did I need? I would have been happy if things around the farm had never changed. Unfortunately, change was coming, and it appeared that very night in the form of an unexpected visitor named Paul.

We had eaten dinner and were settling down for the evening when there was a knock on the front door. We weren't expecting anyone;

Dad got up with raised eyebrows and walked down the hall. I heard the door open, then an exclamation: "Paul!" Sounds of backslapping and laughter reached me, and then my father appeared with a rugged, middle-aged man. Paul had a longish beard, rough hands, and dark eyes framed by deep crow's feet. Despite his coarse appearance, he seemed full of joy, as if he'd just heard some good news.

When I saw who our guest was, I was horrified. I recognized him. I'd often seen his gloating picture atop the gossip column in our local newspaper. He was infamous for "exposing the truth" (or spreading rumors, depending on your point of view). How was it that my father not only welcomed him into our home but was actually glad to see him?

I glanced at my mother, waiting for her to say something, but she merely got up, cordially greeted Paul, and went to put on the coffee. Dad introduced me, and I shook Paul's hand as quickly as possible before taking a step back. Our guest noticed.

"Ah, I see you've heard of me, young Jake. Your father's also told me a lot about you."

The man was too loud, too forceful. I wanted him to leave. My father observed my obvious struggle with an amused expression and offered Paul a chair. Paul was determined to win me over.

"You don't mean to say that your father hasn't told you my story?"

There was something different about him, an air of goodwill that was inconsistent with his reputation. I was curious despite myself. "What story?" I ventured.

"The story of how your grand old dad here laid me out one afternoon, right in broad daylight on a public street." Paul seemed to notice my wide eyes and, delighted as a fisherman who had just hooked a bass, he continued.

"That's right, every word of it's true. And, I'm sorry to say, everything you've heard about me is true—or was. I made a living out of destroying people's lives. Oh, not with guns or bombs, but with words. If there were some dirt on you, Jake, I'd find it and broadcast it to the world. That was my job: Paul Tarsean, investigative reporter. Anyway, I recently did a story—what we call in my business an 'exposé'—on the allegedly corrupt practices of certain farmers in this state. I happened to mention your father's name in the article."

That perked up my ears even more. There wasn't a corrupt cell in my father's body. He never cheated on his taxes, he never lied, and he even threw back fish when we were over the limit, even when no one was looking. Why would Paul have mentioned my dad's name in an article about corrupt farmers? Paul could see that I was trying to figure that out by myself and exchanged a conspiratorial glance with my father before continuing.

"One day, I was walking downtown, soaking up the local atmosphere, feeling pretty good about myself. I was on my way to research another story up north, when suddenly I heard this voice boom out of nowhere: 'What do you think you're doing?' Then I felt a thud right against my head and found myself lying flat out on the sidewalk. I looked up and saw that giant of a man"—he indicated my father—"looming over me like an executioner, holding a newspaper as if it were an axe. It seems I picked the wrong name to mention in my article."

Paul paused as Mom reentered the room with a tray of steaming mugs and a plate of chocolate chip cookies she'd baked the day before. Paul took one of the mugs with obvious delight and inhaled deeply.

"Your mom makes the best coffee in the state—maybe even the country," he proclaimed.

By this time, I was ready to leap out of my seat. Dad had literally "laid someone out"?

After three cookies and a few cautious sips from his coffee mug, Paul continued. "Well, your dad helped me up, and we had a long talk. He asked me why I had printed those lies, and why I was persecuting him. I marveled at that, young Jake. I had only mentioned your father in a passing way, but he told me that if I attacked one farmer, I attacked every one of them, and him most of all. Then your dad introduced me to a man. He was a poor man, and he wore dirty clothes and didn't smell so good." Paul soured his face and held his nose for effect.

I smiled. The man was quite a storyteller. I could see why he and Dad got along.

"'This is one of the men your story put out of work,' your dad told me. 'Some people believed the lies you wrote. They don't trust this good farmer anymore, and they get their produce elsewhere. He and his family have suffered because of your actions. That's wrong.'"

Paul paused, and I could see that he was no longer merely telling a story. His eyes grew moist and he leaned forward in his chair. "Your father was right," he continued. "I never knew until that day how much my words impacted the lives of real people. I took a leave of absence from the paper and took a good look at my life. Your father's influence changed me, made me a new man. I wrote a retraction and helped that farmer get back on his feet. Your dad and I have been friends ever since." Paul leaned back and winked. "Now, what do you think about *that*?"

I looked at Paul, and then back at my father, trying to decide which part of the story was the most fantastic. I asked timidly, "Do you still write for the newspaper?"

Paul's eyes grew even more earnest as he said, "Yes, but now I spread good news. I only write the truth. And nothing, young Jake, is more important than the truth."

I couldn't resist one more question, and I wasn't sure whether to ask Paul or Dad. I finally decided to get the story straight from the source.

"Dad, did you really...lay him out?"

Paul and my parents exchanged another glance before bursting into laughter. My father laughed the loudest, roaring and wiping his eyes, and I joined in without understanding. After our laughter subsided, Paul answered my question.

"Well, young Jake, you'll have to excuse the journalist in me. I admit I embellished that part of the story a bit." He grew serious again, just for a moment. "Being confronted with the truth by a man like your father is just like being laid out, Jake. The truth often hits you like a firm right cross."

I listened to them talk for hours. Paul told amazing stories. I found myself admiring him. He'd been all over Europe and was in the process of compiling a travelogue that he hoped to publish someday.

Despite my interest, it was getting late. I stifled a yawn and was about to say good night when the conversation took a turn I didn't like at all.

"By the way, I know you're fond of taking in guests," Paul said to my parents. "I wonder if you might be interested in a long-term arrangement."

"Go on," my father replied.

"I'm sure you've heard of that horrible tragedy in Chicago. Skyscraper fire. A boy was left without his parents and his home was destroyed."

My father nodded thoughtfully. Of course he'd heard about it; everyone had. A fire as catastrophic as that one was big news.

"He's been bounced around from orphanage to foster home, from town to city, and then back again. I can't help but wonder what a good, stable home would do for him." Paul suddenly addressed me. "How would you like a brother, Jake?"

I was shocked. I wouldn't like a brother—not now, not ever. I liked things the way they were. I liked having Mom, Dad, the farm, my dog, and the whole world all to myself. Who did Paul think he was? Coming into our home, spinning his stories about European travels and horrible fires and orphaned boys?

The worst part was that Mom and Dad looked as though they were actually considering the idea. I didn't know what to do. I wanted to argue, but I was reluctant to express my true feelings in front of this meddling journalist. I decided to retreat. I stood up abruptly, yawned, and asked to be excused. I mumbled something about having to get up early, and politely thanked Paul for stopping by. I kissed my parents, shook hands with Paul, and ran upstairs.

I didn't really want to go upstairs; I wanted to escape. I wanted to go to my tree house. I would find refuge there and peace from Paul's suggestion. The problem was that my room was located on the east side of the house, so I couldn't even see my tree house from the window. I crept across the hall to the sewing room, and I could just make out the red planks and white trim as I pressed my nose against the cold glass. I could hear the adults talking downstairs, and I wished I could fly across the yard. Things were safe there; things didn't change there.

After a half hour of painful contemplation, I crawled into bed and felt a terrible rush of adrenaline. Fear was not an emotion I was used to experiencing. Not here. Not in my safe, structured world.

I stared at the ceiling while the low sounds of conversation and clinking coffee mugs continued downstairs. It took a while for sleep to come. The grandfather clock at the end of the hall tick-tocked its disapproval of my thoughts, and seemed to repeat Dad's words at the river the night we rescued Princess: *the value of one the value of one the value of one.* The phrase echoed in my mind, but it no longer sounded wise to me. I was *one*, too. Didn't my needs and desires count? I finally fell asleep and dreamed of fire and brothers and change.

I adjusted my uniform cap to better shield my face from the rain. It was driving in sheets now, as if it would push me back through the gates and away from these painful memories. I had called the airport, been connected to the shuttle dispatcher, and told that someone would "check on it." I was once again alone with my thoughts. *Fire and brothers and change.*

I came to enjoy a certain kind of brotherhood at AKPS. You needed brothers in a place like that. Change, on the other hand, was in short supply. It was not part of the curriculum; you couldn't find it in the daily routine, nor was it stocked in the stainless steel pantries of the mess hall. Everything that happened at that school did so against a backdrop of endless, mind-numbing sameness.

Despite my feelings about it, Ashur-Kesed wasn't a prison or a military school. It tried to be both, but in various ways failed to be either.

The academy had been co-founded by two men who shared a common vision: to provide parents who suffered the grief of having "problem children" with a place where those wayward offspring would learn the true meaning of obedience.

Shem Ashur was a slick, wealthy entrepreneur who owned a large tract of land in Whitlock, Vermont. He was a harsh man who specialized in shady business deals and hostile takeovers, and others who shared his lust for money and power admired him. Ashur established the school in response to his own problems at home: for some unfathomable reason, his sons caused no end of trouble for the servants whose job it was to raise them. Ashur's wife had left him, and his stream of lady friends had no interest in helping to raise his children.

Rodney Kesed had much in common with his partner. He broke into the business world at a young age, became extraordinarily rich (and insufferably proud), and generally took what he wanted by whatever means were most expedient. A clever leader who rarely resorted to intimidation, he was able to turn unwilling business associates to his purpose by making them believe it was in their best interests to cooperate. Kesed co-founded the school purely as a business venture; he had his eye on some of Ashur's European holdings and hoped that the partnership might spawn a lucrative friendship.

The philosophy of the school mirrored the ideology of its two founders. The underlying principle was simple: keep students mindlessly, endlessly busy; root out weakness; and stamp out any hint of compassion or conscience. If they had been trying to raise sharks at AKPS, that philosophy would have served them well. As it ended up, only three types of graduates emerged from the school: those who embraced the AKPS philosophy and thus went forth emotionally and morally dead; those who couldn't bear the brutal, monotonous learning process and were therefore broken by it; and those who somehow held on to who they were and survived. Naturally, I hoped to fall into the third category.

The school followed a basic military pattern because both Shem and Rodney had been in the service. Unfortunately for their students, they had learned only partial lessons from the military, as though they had only been listening half the time. They adopted strict discipline and efficient chains of command, but ignored the higher purposes that discipline and structure were meant to achieve. They constructed a campus that was meant to resemble a military base, but which more closely resembled a stalag. They custom-designed a school uniform, but forgot to instill pride, honor, and loyalty into the institution that those uniforms represented.

I'd outgrown the clothes I'd worn on the day of my arrival. I would have preferred not to wear my uniform on the trip home, but I had nothing else. The uniforms were, not surprisingly, gray in color, with purple and deep red accents on the sides of the legs and on the shoulders. On our right breast, we wore the standard of Ashur-Kesed: a golden crest that depicted a knight brandishing a lance as he sat bravely on his mighty steed. The school motto, written in Greek, was *anesis, meketi asthenes, ametanoeo*, which is translated "no rest, no weakness, no regrets." On our left breast, there was an embroidered patch where the instructors affixed our seldom-awarded medals of achievement.

The uncomfortable garments represented everything I hated about the school. They had remained the same throughout my term, but I had changed. I had overcome the beatings, the long hours of study, the cruelty of both faculty and students, and the separation from everything that was comfortable and familiar to me. Most of all, though, I had come to understand why I had been sent here, and I was actually grateful for the experience. When viewed in that light, the uniform became a symbol of my victory.

Of course, I didn't win the victory alone. Under the harsh yoke of the discipline we were forced to endure, my fellow students and I quickly learned to band together. We shared the kind of brotherhood that doesn't come from birth or adoption, but results from a common experience.

I had arrived at school alone, afraid, and angry. My parents had packed my bags and sent me away, and I'd spent the long trip in detached, shocked silence. I rode in from the airport on a shuttle. As the aged vehicle finally wheezed up to the front gate of AKPS, the air brakes caught the tires and spat like an irate mammoth, forcing every passenger to lurch forward slightly. Once I saw the school, I froze in my seat. A rebuke from the harried driver, however, motivated me to gather my belongings and reluctantly disembark.

I stood in front of the gate as the shuttle abandoned me with a deep, diesel roar and a sharp cloud of exhaust. I didn't know that as I walked through the gate, a pair of eyes had followed me, appraised me, and approved of me. I probably wouldn't have cared if I had known. I didn't want to make friends, I didn't want to stay; I just wanted to go home.

I absorbed every detail of my surroundings with the intensity of a cornered animal. The dull color of the place caught my attention first. The sterile rows of low buildings were so different from the farm, so depressingly plain. A forest of conifers surrounded the school, peeking over the black, metal fence, but inside the fence there was no shrubbery of any kind. It seemed that every living thing had instinctively fled from the academy, and then turned back to look from a safe distance. As I walked onto the grounds, carrying my small suitcase, I noted the low, grinding creak of the gate as it swung shut. I heard the heavy *thunk* as the hasp of the lock sank home. It sounded like a judge's gavel, condemning me to isolation in this horrible gray place for the rest of my life.

With every detail I took in, my sense of desperation grew, and my hopes for deliverance diminished. My parents would not arrive at the end of the day to pick me up. I was here—and I would be staying for a while.

The owner of the blue eyes that examined me that first day knew all of this, but chose to remain in the shadows until later in the week.

The officer who met me at the gate ordered me to report immediately for a haircut and a uniform fitting. The barber looked right through me. He cut off most of my hair with rough, quick movements. After the electric razor devoured the last remnants of my hair, the barber dismissed me with a wave of his hand.

The quartermaster, who fitted me for the uniform, discharged his duties with the same stony, joyless air. When he was through, he directed me to the registrar's office for my barracks assignment. As I waited at the high, marble counter, I was handed a thick booklet of rules and protocol. The registrar, who didn't break the pattern of perpetual frowning that I'd observed so far, handed me a slip of paper with my barracks assignment written on it and pointed me to the mess hall.

My first meal at AKPS cemented my impression of the school: it was the worst place on earth. We were fed a piece of dried, dark-brown matter that pretended to be meat, a lump of gray potatoes, some mushy carrots, and our choice of coffee, tea, or water. I dined with a table full of "newbies," as we were unofficially called. I didn't say much, nor did I eat much.

The other students around me seemed to share my apprehension and discomfort, yet none of us reached out to each other. It was as if we had decided, by mutual consent, to suffer our first day here in silence and isolation. That would change; we soon learned to depend upon one another. We soon became friends.

After dinner, we were lined up and escorted to our barracks. I tried to do the only thing that would grant me relief from this torment—sleep. I wasn't interested in my surroundings, nor was I curious about my fellow students, or even my bunkmate; I simply wanted to sleep. I had no idea what the next day would bring, but I suspected it wouldn't be pleasant.

As I lay there, I suddenly felt that I was being watched. I opened my eyes and saw that the student in the bunk above mine was looking at me. He seemed curious, and his face lacked the fear I'd observed in most of the other new students. I closed my eyes quickly and hoped he would leave me alone. After a moment I heard him lay back down. Some time later, sleep finally, mercifully came.

Chapter Six

"Pick 'em for all you're worth, Jakey-boy! And no nibblin' on the job."

Laughing, I threw a squirrel-eaten corncob at Yasha in reply. He would not beat me again, not this year. The hired man and I were feverishly picking corn in the smaller field in front of our house. Yasha always picked more than I did, and every year he reminded me of that fact. When I was younger, I used to admire him. Now, just a few months before my twelfth birthday, it was my mission to defeat him.

Life on the farm was the same as always, but the possibility of a stranger living with us loomed over me like a thunderhead. Several months had passed since Paul's visit, and I wished that he'd never come at all. Mom and Dad regularly discussed the orphaned boy, whose name was Niko. A foolish name. A name that promised trouble.

One of the things my parents discussed was the possibility of inviting him out to the farm, just for a visit. Niko sounded like the most unlikely of houseguests. He had lived in the city all his life. What in the world would he do on a farm? I asked that question over dessert one night.

"Well, Jake, I think Nick might enjoy the quieter pace of farm life," Dad replied. "From what Paul tells me, he's never even been to the country."

"I guess, but the farm isn't a safe place for someone like Nick. You remember what happened to Jeb's cousin? How he fell off the tiller?"

"That's where you come in, son. You're a natural when it comes to farming. Wouldn't it be fun to show Nick around, give him a taste of how we live?"

"I s'pose."

"I think you two will have a lot to talk about, Jake," Mom added. "Nick has seen and done a lot of things you've never had the opportunity to do. That seems to be the...Skipper, so help me! Jake!" Skipper was gnawing on the chair leg again. He often resorted to that when I ignored his pleas for table scraps.

"Come here, boy! You wanna get us both in trouble?" Skipper skulked over, but quickly got over his shame as I scratched behind his ears. Secretly, I was grateful. Skipper's bad habit had stalled the conversation until I could regroup.

I tried to sow seeds of doubt in my parents' minds. Mom and Dad listened to me, but I failed to convince them. It became clear that in the fall, when the harvest was over and things quieted down a bit, Niko would come for a visit. Worse, if things went well, Niko might even become a permanent member of our household.

Paul stopped by a few more times to update my parents on Niko's situation. I always disappeared during those visits, so everything I knew about Niko was pieced together from conversations I overheard. I never asked questions about him directly. I didn't want my parents to assume I supported their decision to invite him for a visit.

Nick, as we came to call him, was a savage by my standards. He was a year younger than me, and Paul cautioned my parents that even when Nick's parents were alive, he lived very much by his own rules. I chuckled to myself at that one. We would see how this boy would do the first time he opposed one of Dad's fair but nonnegotiable "family guidelines."

Nick had been to school, but not the school of experience and hard work. He had spent a large chunk of his childhood at an exclusive academy that sounded more like a country club than a school. His education came entirely from books. I loved books, but sooner or later you had to *live* life, not just read about it. Nick had never done important things like take the carburetor out of an engine, plow a field, or chop wood. That was how you learned something—by doing it.

Chapter Six

I felt certain that Nick would strut around like a peacock, trying hard to gloss over his obvious deficiencies, attempting to impress me and win over my family. My parents loved people and had taught me to be the same way, but I intended to be the voice of caution on behalf of all of us. I didn't plan to lavish one ounce of affection on this intruder until and unless he proved himself in my eyes. Then—and only then— would I welcome him.

I had his visit all planned out. The first day I would graciously give him a tour of the farm and tell him what was expected of him. (Guest or no guest, he would obey the rules and do his share of the chores.) The second day and every day thereafter, I would proceed to run him ragged—for his own good, of course. He would learn to milk the cows by hand, he would sling manure in the barn, and he would pull weeds and cut grass. As long as Nick followed my instructions, all would be well. I looked forward to teaching him a lesson he would never forget.

As it turned out, I ended up being the one to learn a lesson: my plans concerning Nick never turned out the way I expected.

About two months later, Dad and I were on our way back to the house. It was dusk and the harvest had just ended. Everyone on the farm was in high spirits. As we walked along the south path, I talked enthusiastically while Dad listened. He never seemed to mind that I often dominated our discussions, perhaps because he always managed to make his few words count.

It was a nice night, the kind when you look forward to an evening by the fire, maybe drinking some cocoa and watching the play-offs. We walked past the small grove of sycamores that line the south side of our property. I was busy jabbering about one of Skipper's antics when Dad lifted his hand for silence. I stopped and cocked my ear; I heard it, too. A bird chirped from a rough collection of twigs, grass, and leaves that was balanced precariously amidst the low branches of a nearby tree. Dad and I tiptoed over to the nest.

When I looked down, I was disappointed. Just one tiny baby bird sat in the nest. His beak gaped open as he cried out for food. The cracked remains of his shell and the shells of his siblings lay scattered around him, but there was no trace of his parents or nest mates. Judging by the color of the shells—off-white with brown spots—I narrowed down the species of bird, but it was hard to tell with no adults around. I looked up at Dad.

"Warbler?"

"Looks like."

"What do you think happened?" I whispered, even though there was no risk of frightening the bird out of the nest. He was weeks away from being able to fly.

Dad was just as disappointed as I was. He glanced up at the sky. "Well, it's certain the nest fell from a higher branch. Warblers don't nest this close to the ground. Maybe it was the wind," he said doubtfully, "or maybe some crows got a little too rowdy. Hard to tell for sure. It's a real shame, isn't it?"

Suddenly, inspiration struck me. "Dad, lets take him home and keep him in the barn. I'll dig up some worms and feed him, and in the morning, after I milk the cows, I'll take him into town. Mr. Tishbite can raise him, and then let him go after he's grown a little."

Unfortunately, Dad didn't share my enthusiasm. "A pet store is no place for a warbler, son. Mr. Tishbite knows all about parrots and mynah birds and macaws, but this kind of bird is something else. On top of that," Dad continued, still gazing into the nest, "no human being can teach this bird how to survive in the wild. Only his parents can do that."

"Then I'll take care of him—I'll keep him in the barn. I'm doing a good job with Skipper, aren't I?" I knew I had Dad on that point. Many of my friends promised to care for a dog or cat but quickly reneged. I, on the other hand, cared for Skipper as well as I cared for myself.

Dad mulled it over. "You sure you have the time?"

"Yup."

"Important to you, is it?"

"Yes."

"Why?"

I tore my eyes away from the pitiful, abandoned bird and looked up at my father. His question surprised me. Why? All you had to do was look at this bird and you *knew* why. There it sat, alone in the nest. It's pinkish skin, gaping mouth, and half-opened eyes cried for help. How could I—how could anyone—ignore that cry?

"Dad, I don't get you," I said. "You're always telling me how important life is. How can we just leave it?"

"It's just one bird," he said calmly. "It may already be too late. He may not survive."

Now it was my turn to gape. I must have looked just like the little creature I wanted to save. My mind raced. It's just one bird? That was just about as strange a thing as I'd ever heard Dad say. I wondered what he was...

I had it. This was a test, and I knew the answer. "But, Dad," I declared triumphantly, "we must never underestimate the value of one." Gavel down, case closed. I waited for Dad to concede. He looked into my eyes for a moment longer. The corners of his mouth rose slightly, and then he turned and scooped up the bird in his huge hand. He gently placed it into my cupped palms and we carried it safely to the barn.

With each step we took, my pride grew. I wondered why Dad had not praised me. He always encouraged and often rewarded me when I did something that pleased him, especially when it had to do with a lesson of his. Now, as we strode on through the dusk, he was strangely silent. When we reached the barn, Dad made it clear that he had a broader interpretation of "the value of one" in mind. "By the way, Jake, I have some good news."

"What's that, Dad?"

"Nick is coming for a visit two weeks from Tuesday."

I nearly dropped the bird.

It wasn't that the news shocked me. I had already accepted the inevitability of Nick's visit. What distressed me was the fact that I had stumbled square into the middle of another lesson. Some of Dad's lessons could trip you if you weren't careful; other lessons could fall on your head and crush you. My response to this lesson caused a darkness to begin to grow within me. This was the beginning of my rebellion against my father.

I wondered if he had known that the baby bird was there. Had he guided me to that spot simply to reveal my selfishness? I bitterly asked myself why Dad had to go and make a big production out of everything. He could as easily have said, "Son, we're going to help Nick because it's the right thing to do," without all the theatrics.

I wasn't used to thinking that my father was wrong. I couldn't understand his apparent insensitivity, and I began to wonder if he really listened when I spoke. On the other hand, I knew that I was wrong, too, and that made me even angrier. I hated Nick, but I didn't want to hate him. And since I didn't know how *not* to hate him, I just wanted him to go away.

These thoughts raced through my mind in the twinkling of an eye. All of my arguments, all of my outrage, all of my growing bitterness and fear were distilled into one potent cry: "Dad, that's not fair!"

Dad turned around and looked down at me. "No. It isn't fair for Nick to lose his entire family, his home, his friends, and his life. Nevertheless, this family is going to do it's best to help make a difference. Nick has fallen out of the tree and his nest is breaking apart, but someone came by, noticed him and rescued him. I know I can count on you to help him. You understand the value of one." With that he was gone, melting like a shadow into the inner recesses of the barn. He checked on the horses while I tended to the bird, then we went inside and ate dinner.

Dinner that night was not pleasant, but I felt worse for Mom than for myself. She knew the hearts of both her men, and she knew when things weren't right between us. Mom wasn't one to gloss over things, though. She didn't try to paste a happy face onto the grim mood that now pervaded our home. She just sat there and watched for an opening that she could use to help foster peace. It never came.

That night, dinner served only one purpose: to eat dinner. The lively conversation that usually filled the room dried up like a creek bed in July. Strangely, now that food was our sole focus, we were singularly uninterested in it. Skipper was the only one who seemed unaffected by the uncomfortable atmosphere in the kitchen; he gobbled down his meal and nuzzled his golden snout against my leg, hoping for something a little more appetizing than dry dog food.

When I had rearranged the food on my plate for the eleventh time, I asked to be excused. As I walked toward my room, I heard a chair push out from the table. Dad followed me.

"Jake, can I have a word with you?"

I turned around, dreading the conversation. We sat down in the living room.

"Jake, I'm surprised by your reaction to all this. I'd thought you'd enjoy having a brother. Do you feel like talking about it?"

I wanted very much to talk about it, but I was reluctant to say what I really thought. *Dad, I don't want a brother because I want you and Mom all to myself. Plus, I don't want to share my dog, my baseball cards, or my tree house with anyone else. End of explanation.* Even I knew that such thoughts were selfish. I doubted that expressing them would help my cause.

"Not really," I finally replied.

"Well, this is an important decision, and we want you to be a part of it," Dad said. "We'll talk when you're ready, all right, son?"

"Okay," I mumbled.

Dad was good about letting me say whatever was on my mind. He had firm beliefs, but he wasn't judgmental. Like my earlier doubts about Dad's fairness, my reluctance to share my feelings with him was also a new experience. I didn't like it.

I walked slowly up to my room. As I flopped down on my bed, I could hear Mom and Dad in the kitchen. I decided to take a chance and eavesdrop. I had to know how they really felt about all this. I needed some hope that they understood me.

A heating register was set into the floor at the end of the hall. I lay down with my ear against the metal and could barely make out my parents' voices.

"I know it, dear," my father said. "It doesn't make any sense to me."

"Do you think we should reconsider?"

"I'd hate to do that. I think there's more at stake here than just Nick's welfare. This whole mess has brought out something in Jake that I've never seen before."

"He's almost a teenager. I guess it's normal."

"Yes, but I just don't seem to be getting through to him anymore. It hurts. I remember how his eyes used to shine whenever I'd tell a story or take him aside about this or that. Now…I don't know."

"We'll have to keep an eye on this. I don't want to destroy our family by trying to add to it."

Dad was silent, but I'd heard enough. I hated the tears that had sprung to my eyes at Dad's mention of the way things used to be. Still, I hadn't heard what I'd wanted to hear. They hadn't reconsidered, and a pessimistic voice in my head whispered that they wouldn't.

I complained to myself as I took up my now familiar position at the sewing room window. Even the night sky withheld its sympathy. The moon glared down at me, and the stars twinkled their unanimous disapproval. As I knelt there, my face, reflected in the glass, revealed my conflicting emotions. Outside, a mass of clouds moved in as though the sky was hiding its face, unwilling to look any longer at a bitter, angry young man like me. I was alone in the dark, in more ways than one.

The two weeks before Nick's visit passed quickly. I spent a great deal of time in my tree house, and I played a lot of baseball at our neighborhood field down the road. Nothing I did, however pleasant, was much of a diversion. I didn't know what lay ahead, but I knew I wouldn't like it. I arrived at a kind of peace with Dad, but my opinion of him had changed. Nick hadn't even arrived and already he had come between my father and me.

Dad showed no signs of loving me any less than he always had. However, the knowledge that there soon would be two boys by my father's side changed every lesson he tried to teach me, every meal or story we shared together, every walk we took. He was only one man. It didn't matter that I was his first (and natural-born) son. Dad's attention would soon be divided by a factor of two, and I didn't like that equation one bit.

The day arrived. The sun, obnoxious turncoat that it was, shone brightly as if to more clearly illuminate Nick's entry into our world. I stood between my mother and father at the front door as Paul (another traitor) arrived with Nick. When I saw the boy's face, I received my first disappointment of the day.

I'd expected a dark, brooding boy whose lip curled in an arrogant sneer. I'd anticipated a spoiled child whose every move reeked of over-privileged coddling. I'd hoped that Nick would immediately alienate my parents with his city-boy attitude and that this unfortunate little exercise would come to a swift and decisive end.

What I saw instead was a stooped, pale boy whose eyes were devoid of light and joy. He was well-dressed and seemed to be properly nourished, but he walked as if in a daze and appeared to tremble slightly. I felt the first of many pangs of guilt. Nick had lost everything he'd ever loved—it was only natural that he should look and act that way.

Paul, in contrast to his young charge, was full of energy. The large smile behind his beard testified to his high hopes for this visit. He took Nick's bag in one hand, threw his other arm around his shoulder and led him up the walk. Halfway up, Nick stumbled a bit on the cobblestones. I shook my head slightly, but my disgust was increasingly difficult to maintain.

"Kind sir, generous lady, and young master of the homestead," Paul began with a grandiose bow, "may I present Niko Hellane, your grateful guest." He thrust Nick forward, and the boy extended his hand to my father, then to my mother.

"Thank...thank you for having me," he stuttered in a wispy voice that was utterly devoid of arrogance or pretension. His eyes were downcast and humble, and his smile bespoke only gratitude. I was crushed but had little time to dwell on it. It was my turn to shake his hand.

I'd wondered for two weeks what I would say to Nick when I finally met him. Now that the time was at hand, all I could manage was: "I'm Jake. Glad to have you." It was not what I'd wanted to say, but I was actually grateful that my good upbringing had overridden my childish impulse to harden my voice and broadcast the fact that I was anything but glad to have him.

We went into the house, where my mother had prepared a delicious buffet lunch to welcome Nick. He was shy, but I could see that the warmth of our home and the kindness of my parents were already working to dispel some of his apprehension. I had to interact with him, of course. My father was watching me carefully, and I wanted to avoid unnecessary trouble. As I spoke with Nick—just small talk, really—a horrible thing began to happen. I didn't expect it, I certainly didn't welcome it, but something unthinkable was burgeoning in my heart. I was beginning to like Nick.

"Good morning, maggots. You have officially entered the pit of utter despair. You have no friends here, you have no hope here, and you're not welcome anywhere else. What friends you do succeed in making will be like rats—a large clump of rats, all clinging to the same scrap of debris as you collectively get flushed down the toilet."

This dubious welcome was delivered by Dr. Charles Senna, Vice-Chancellor of Ashur-Kesed Preparatory School for Young Men. At first, I was shocked by his colorful speeches, but I soon became used to them.

At the start of my second day at school, I assembled with the 364 other new students in the large field house at the far end of the campus. The building was state-of-the-art, and boasted bright halogen lamps, a sound system, and bleachers that could be pushed back into the walls when not in use. We were seated on the floor (presumably to emphasize our inferiority) and were obliged to stare up at Dr. Senna as he lurked behind his towering podium. Among his many other disturbing habits, the administrator traveled in the company of a sleek, menacing Doberman. The dog was chained to the platform next to him, and as her master spoke, she bared her teeth and growled almost as if on cue. I later discovered that Sabrina (an absurd name for such a dangerous animal) never left Senna's side, either on campus or off.

This was our indoctrination assembly, and we listened to two solid hours of rules, regulations, ordinances, and most of all, penalties for breaking any of the above. I had to admit that the vice-chancellor was a clear communicator. We had no doubt as to what was expected of us as the list of excessive—even ridiculous—expectations grew. I shared quick, disbelieving glances with my fellow students while trying not to draw undue attention to myself; disruptive behavior during an assembly was cause for a half-day of isolation without meals. Dr. Senna didn't seem to think the school regulations were unreasonable. He spoke of honor and discipline, justice and order. His bird-like eyes swept over us as he blared his conclusion in that thunderous, gravelly voice of his.

"Remember: I'm not here to pamper you, befriend you, or mentor you. I'm not even here to teach you. Teaching is something I do to pass the time in between the fulfillment of my true calling. What is that, you ask? I'm glad you inquired."

He leaned over the top of the podium and melted us with an acidic glare before hosing us down with his closing remarks. "I'm here to break you of whatever bad habit, bad decision, or bad character trait got you here in the first place." There was silence in that cavernous room as he hissed: "And the best way to break a bad habit is suffering. *Dismissed!*"

There was a squeal of feedback, as if the microphone itself objected to this man, and then the guards corralled us and marched us out to our first official school day.

So that was it, I thought, as we were herded out of the main doors and onto the joyless, treeless campus. That's why I was sent here. I wasn't enrolled at AKPS to learn or to grow; I was here to suffer. I was here to be—what was the word Senna had used earlier in his speech?— broken. I recoiled at the cruelty of it all. This school was the complete opposite of my dad's way of thinking (and teaching). How could Dad have sent me here? Didn't he know what kind of place this was?

Dr. Senna had mentioned bad habits. I had accumulated quite a number of them. I remembered, too late, my father's teaching on that subject: "Jake, the best way to break a bad habit is to replace it with a good habit. If someone's bad habit is to lie, he should cultivate the habit of always telling the truth. If someone wrongly criticizes others, that person should work on encouraging others. If someone is greedy, he should learn to give. Remember this principle, son."

As I thought more about Dr. Senna's speech, I realized that my worst habit of all had been ignoring Dad's lessons.

I marched back to the barracks with my classmates. I concluded that Dad must have known about this place. Whenever he was about to buy a new tractor, invest in new silo elevators, or even repair the family car, he pored over catalogs and researched the equipment for weeks before arriving at a decision. He would never leave the choice of his son's school to chance. That conclusion left me with a nagging question: why *did* Dad send me here, of all places? Home seemed farther away than ever on that second, dark day of school, but I soon had little time to think about much of anything except survival. Although I was deeply hurt at having been sent away, I wasn't ready to give up. I needed to find a way to make it in this foreign environment.

After the morning address, we engaged in physical activity for four solid hours. We did every kind of callisthenic known to man, followed by a brisk run around the athletic field. We ate lunch and then reported to our afternoon classes. Our professors dressed in hooded black robes that made them look like executioners. They, like Dr. Senna, showed far more interest in frightening us than they did in teaching us.

When classes were over, we ate dinner before reporting back to our barracks. I undressed but didn't dare try to brush my teeth. A raucous group of well-built students was harassing anyone who tried to use the bathroom. I decided to wait until they tired of their game. I hoped that would be soon.

In the meantime, I lay on the thin mattress, thoroughly exhausted. *Well, that was a nice day*, I thought sarcastically. As I tried to relax, the student on the bunk above mine stuck his head over the side as he'd done the night before.

"Hey, newbie. I'm Buzz, your landlord. You seem to be in a better mood than you were last night, so I thought it was high time for your orientation. That's your footlocker there, and those are your toiletries on the second shelf below the mirror. We'll get along fine as long as you don't snore or make obscene noises in the night. Warm air rises, you know."

With that eloquent welcome, he thrust out his hand, which I cautiously shook.

"You're not mute, are you?" he asked. "I've always wanted to meet a mute."

"No, I can speak."

"Oh," he said, with obvious disappointment. "I invented a tongue-stretching device that I want to test out some day. I think it might really work."

I thought he was joking, but I soon experienced some of his inventions firsthand. Like the tongue-stretching device, they weren't always practical.

"A word of advice for you," he continued. "Don't walk around here looking so scared. It'll get you a real serious beating. Actually, you'll probably get one anyway, but why hasten the experience, right?" He laughed at my look of horror. I glanced around to make sure we weren't being watched and decided to trust him enough to ask a question.

"Um, Buzz, you said your name was? What *is* this place? I thought it was supposed to be a school. It seems more like a concentration camp."

"How true, how true," he said, stroking his chin. "It is a school of sorts, but they never tell your parents—or whoever dumped you here—what really goes on when the bell rings in the morning."

"What goes on?" I prodded him.

"Weren't you listening in assembly? We're here to be corrected, not taught. This is obedience school for humans. It's a place where you're programmed to behave. You'll probably fit better into society, but the price tag is high: you'll lose your personality in the process."

"Look, are you trying to frighten me? That's not good manners where I come from."

Buzz put on a wounded look. "Listen, newbie—wait, what did you say your name was?"

"I didn't. You were too busy telling me my life is over to ask. It's Jake."

"Listen, Jake," he continued, ignoring my jab, "I'm doing you the best favor anyone could do for you: I'm telling you how it is. You'll do okay—but don't have any illusions. You'll probably be here for a while, and you'll most likely hate every second of it. However, if you adapt, if you find out who your friends are and treat them right, you'll make it."

"And who are my friends?"

"Well, I'm probably going to be one of them, as long as you obey the rules I laid out."

"What rules?"

"You know…" He pressed his bare arm against his mouth and blew with all his strength. The resulting noise caused several students to look up and made my lips curl upward a bit. It wasn't my usual smile, but it was a start. I was terrified, confused, and lonely, but it looked as though I had a friend.

Buzz said good night and left me to my thoughts. I heard something crinkle as I lay down, and I slipped my hand under the pillow to see what it was.

It was a slip of paper, folded in half. I glanced around. There were several other students sitting or lying on their bunks, but none seemed the least bit interested in my paper or me. I opened it up and read this typewritten note:

Dear Jake,

Welcome to AKPS. I know you'd rather be home, but I'm sure you'll do well here—especially since you have friends you don't know about. I'll be in touch, and maybe we can meet soon.

Best regards, E. (light brown)

What in the world? It had to be a prank. I'd met only a few class-mates. The boy who slept in the bunk above mine seemed friendly enough, but his name didn't begin with *E*. And what did "light brown" mean?

Though I was curious about this unexpected note, I was too tired. I just wanted to sleep. I tucked the note under my mattress, closed my eyes, and hoped that I would dream of home.

Chapter Seven

"So, why does your father always tell those stories and stuff?" Nick asked the question as we lay contentedly on bales of hay after lunch. Below us, the cows also rested on fresh hay as they munched their cud. It was a typical late autumn day on the farm—typical, that is, except for Nick's presence.

I was fond of him, and I was even getting used to the idea of having another kid around the farm, but I still thought he didn't really belong there.

"He tells stories to teach me things. I don't know why he does it that way. It's sure better than the way Phil's father teaches him."

"How's that?"

"With a strap."

"Oh. Well, at least it's direct."

"Spoken by someone who's never been strapped. I was over at Phil's house one day when his pa came in. He was drunk as a skunk, and…"

"Just how drunk do skunks get?"

"Don't interrupt. Do I mock your little city expressions?"

"All the time."

"Well, anyway. His pa came in drunk, ripping mad, and asked Phil why he hadn't slopped the pigs. Well, Phil had slopped 'em. I was there. He started to tell his dad that he'd done it, but his dad started yelling, 'Don't give your pa no backtalk.' He yanked his belt out of his pants and laid into Phil—with me right there in the room."

"What'd you do?"

"I took off. It was awful. Phil was screaming and trying to get away. I guess it happens a lot."

We sat quietly for a few moments.

"Do you always get it?" Nick asked.

"Get what?"

"What your dad's trying to say."

"Mostly, but sometimes I don't get it until later, and sometimes he has to explain it to me. He's a pretty cool dad. Oh. Sorry," I said.

I realized that in praising my own father, I had unintentionally belittled Nick's deceased father. It had happened more than once during Nick's visit, and I felt bad about it.

"Forget it," he said. "I'm trying to. My dad didn't care about me anyway."

"Why do you say that?"

"He was never around. When he did spend time with me, it was like he was only doing it to get it over with. You have it pretty good. My dad never tried to teach me anything." Nick paused and looked off into the distance. "I still miss him, though."

I didn't know what to say. Nick's family life was so foreign to me that I had no idea how to help him. I was grateful for my mother and father, even as I struggled to understand their reasons for wanting to adopt another son, and I pitied Nick as he lay there thinking about parents he would never see again.

"You know, if you ever want to know what Dad means, just ask me," I said, attempting to cheer him up. Nick didn't reply, but I could see a glimmer of gratitude in his dark eyes. Our growing friendship, coupled with the mention of his father, led me to ask a question I'd wanted to ask for almost two weeks.

"Nick, what happened the night your parents died?"

"What do you mean?"

"I mean—just tell me if you don't want to talk about this—what started that fire? The story was in all the papers, but the reporters said that it was still 'under investigation.'"

Nick continued to rest his chin on his hands as he looked out the small loft window. A tear rolled down the side of his face. I felt terrible for having brought up the subject. "Hey, Nick, I didn't mean to…"

"That's all right." His voice was calm and quiet, almost resigned. "I think I have a pretty good idea what started the fire—a couple idiots were playing with matches in the basement."

"Really? Did you tell the firemen or the police or somebody?"

"No," he replied.

"Why not? Maybe it was arson. Whoever did it should…"

"It was me."

I didn't know what to say.

"Me and my friend," Nick continued, "were lighting old rags in the janitor's room. We knew he sometimes forgot to lock the door. The rags had cleaning stuff on them so they burned blue when we lit them on fire. We thought it was cool." He swallowed and closed his eyes for a moment before continuing. "We also thought the fire was out, but the rags must have smoldered for a while and caught fire during the night. I guess I passed out from the smoke and a neighbor got me out of the building, but my parents were—there was nothing anyone could do." The volume of Nick's voice decreased and the emotion drained out of it. "We were just trying to have a little fun, but I ended up killing my parents, and a lot of other people, too. Sometimes I see them when I sleep. They're trapped in a burning room, pointing at me and asking me why I did it. I tell them I didn't mean to, that I'll never play with matches again, but it's always too late."

We sat in silence for what seemed an eternity while I tried to think of something to say that would make him feel better. Finally, I seized on something he'd said.

"Nick, you said the fire started at night?"

"Yeah. Sometime after midnight."

"When were you burning the rags?"

"In the morning. It was a Saturday."

"Then you can't be sure it was the rags that did it. Maybe it was something that somebody else did. Maybe it wasn't your fault."

"That would be a pretty big coincidence," Nick said quietly.

"Maybe, but you can't rule it out. Listen, you don't know that those rags caused the fire. Why torture yourself?" He was silent. I saw that I wasn't getting through, but then I had an idea.

"Hey, why don't you call the city fire chief? They probably finished the investigation by now, right? They'll know where the fire started, and then…"

"Yeah, that's fine if something else caused the fire. But what if I find out it *was* my fault? Then I'll be even worse off. Then I'll be sure."

Nick was right and I admitted to myself that I was grasping at straws. He started crying again, and I decided that we'd talked about this enough. Secretly, I promised myself that I would help him somehow. For now, I needed to distract him.

"Hey, you wanna swing?"

"Okay."

We trotted to the far end of the loft where a thick, knotted rope hung from a ceiling beam. We took turns swinging out over the cows, hollering as we flew through the air, let go of the rope, and landed safely on a pile of soft hay below. Nick's tears disappeared and the physical exertion helped to cleanse away any residual discomfort from our conversation.

We had a long way to go, Nick and I, but I thought we were doing fine. We'd crossed a boundary, moving beyond the superficial and closer to brotherhood. I wasn't sure why, but in my heart I knew he hadn't caused that fire. I looked forward to seeing his face when I proved it to him. Unfortunately, neither of us knew that we were only days away from learning just how different we were. It would turn out to be a hard lesson: friendships have to be built on stronger foundations than rope and secrets and hay.

"Hey, newbie. Get your carcass up."

This charming wake-up call came from Buzz. He had interrupted a good dream. For that, he earned my wrath. Dreams were precious commodities at AKPS and not to be disrupted, even by one's closest friend.

I had been at Ashur-Kesed for about six months and had settled into the rigid routine. The shock of being torn from home started to fade. I don't believe that time heals all wounds, but I did come to understand that time can act as a bandage, protecting the wound so that healing can occur. Buzz was a friend who promoted healing. He certainly didn't replace my family, nor did he try. He was simply someone who cared enough to draw me out of my self-imposed isolation.

Buzz was tall, blond, and good-looking in a rugged, casual way. His nickname came from his childhood pronunciation of his family name: Bussford. He possessed limitless energy and enthusiasm, and he was a brilliant thinker. When I asked him why he'd been sent here, he snorted one word: "Paperwork."

He explained that he, like Nick, was an orphan. His parents had died while he was a baby, and he'd had no close relatives willing to take him in. He'd grown up in an orphanage and soon learned to overcome his constant boredom by inventing things. Little Buzz drove his guardians crazy by "borrowing" a wide variety of items and putting them to a new (and often messy) use. Sometimes, he actually improved the quality of life in the orphanage by tweaking the air conditioning unit, adjusting the ovens or fixing a leak in the kitchen faucet. At any rate, life was never dull whenever Buzz was around.

Buzz told me that he had been transferred to AKPS because of a clerical error. Someone at the orphanage had mixed up Buzz with another boy whose last name was similar to his. That young man had been transferred to an engineering apprenticeship intended for Buzz. Buzz had complained to the Ashur-Kesed registrar but was told that his paperwork was in order and that he'd be staying a full four years. His letters to the orphanage went unanswered (probably because the letters had been intercepted by the AKPS censors), and he became just another helpless victim of bureaucracy. That infuriated me. As I'd promised to help my brother, so I was determined to someday help Buzz.

At the moment, however, I wanted to go back to sleep. I covered my head with the thin, lumpy fabric that the school laughingly called a pillow and hoped he'd go away. "Go invent something, Buzz—like a new kind of muzzle for your big mouth," I moaned. I didn't feel like expending the effort to look at my watch, but I knew it was ridiculously early. The sun had not yet peeked through the windows of the barracks.

"Droll. I'm trying to help you, farm boy. The word came down that there's going to be a special inspection today. Bunks, boots…and foot-lockers." He paused dramatically before delivering that last tidbit, knowing it would galvanize me into action.

He was not disappointed. I ripped my covers off and jumped out of bed, banging my head for the hundredth time on the low metal edge of the top bunk. I stood there, holding my head and hopping on the cold floor while Buzz calmly continued.

"That was not a good move from either a medical or a strategic standpoint. Blunt trauma to the head does not facilitate hiding contraband." The pain was sharp, but not so sharp that I forgot the danger I was in. I was in possession of an illegal item. It wasn't the most common type of contraband—I didn't have any liquor, drugs, or cigarettes (for which I harbored a particular hatred). My possession was forbidden because it flew in the face of Ashur-Kesed's credo: *No rest, no weakness, no regrets.* Hidden in my footlocker, tucked inside the canvas lining of the lid, was a photograph of my home.

I don't know how Buzz got it, but I suspect he had high-level assistance. You didn't get something like that without serious connections.

The picture had cost me twenty-five dollars (which almost depleted my cash reserve), three liberty passes (which were the equivalent of platinum at AKPS), plus a pair of clean socks and a set of shoelaces. I had thrown in a dessert ration for extra incentive. It was a high price, but Buzz's contact on the outside had to go to a great deal of trouble to get it. First, he had to make a phone call to someone who lived in or near Lancaster, instruct the person to purchase a throwaway camera and wait for a sunny day (as per my instructions), snap and develop the picture, mail it to the contact who then had to smuggle the picture past the gatekeeper and the inspections, after which it would finally be delivered into my waiting hands.

As expensive as the photo had been, I had promised another bonus if the photographer was able to include even one member of my family in the shot. Sadly, that had not been possible.

The photo was my only link to my former life, and the only splash of color and joy in our dank, depressing barracks. *No rest, no weakness, no regrets.* No regrets? I had plenty.

Now I was in danger of losing my picture. The lining of my footlocker was an imperfect hiding place. Both the students and the barracks were inspected every morning and evening, but a BBF inspection, as we called it (bunks, boots, and footlockers), was relentlessly thorough and was intended to uncover just the sort of thing I was trying to conceal.

"Buzz, what am I going to do?" I whispered, assuming it was a rhetorical question. I began to search for hiding places. As I checked each place, Buzz offered commentary from his bunk. All I could see was his cropped blond head protruding over the side; the thin, standard-issue blanket covered the rest of him.

I checked under my mattress, hoping to find some...

"Nope," he said.

I examined the pillow.

"You must be joking!"

I considered the soles of my boots, one of which was loose and just might...

"Do you think you're dealing with amateurs here?"

I grew tired of his needling and snapped at him. "This isn't a spectator sport. You might consider helping me, you little..."

"Tut-tut-tut. Mind your terminology, young man. How do you know I haven't already figured it out?"

I ceased my frantic quest and looked up at him. "Are you kidding? You have a plan, and you let me go nuts here?"

"What are friends for? I help you out from time to time, and you provide me with unlimited entertainment. I think it's a fair deal." Buzz saw that I was about to attack him, so he decided to tell me his plan. He handed me a piece of pink, curved, rubbery material about four inches square. The edges were irregular and paper-thin; at its thickest point, it measured about an eighth of an inch.

"What's this?" I demanded.

"That, my friend, is your hiding place."

I fumed, waiting for an explanation. If this was a joke...

"Pay attention," Buzz said excitedly. "I cooked it up in a muffin pan last night. It's latex—looks a lot like skin, doesn't it?"

"So?"

"So, we fold the picture, slip it inside, then glue this to a part of you that the commandant will be most unwilling to examine, even if he suspects something is amiss."

I looked at the latex again, noting its curvature and drawing the only conclusion possible.

"My butt? You're gonna glue that thing to my *butt*? This is your grand plan?"

"I love your quaint, country naïveté, but I detect a note of ingratitude. It'll work. Even if they pat you down, all they'll notice is the proper feel and consistency of Grade A farmer boy's rump roast. What could be better? What could be more deliciously ironic?"

I stared at Buzz, admiring his creativity but frightened that his plan would fail. My alternatives were limited, though, and time had almost run out. After a quick moment of deliberation, I handed the picture to Buzz, and then leaned over.

Buzz performed the operation with every consideration for my dignity. He carefully tucked the picture into a fold in the latex, applied special glue to its thin edges, and then pressed it firmly against my upper right buttock.

"I learned how to work with latex from a Hollywood special effects magazine," he said.

I didn't care where he learned it as long as it worked. I tried not to think about what would happen if the barracks commandant walked in just then.

Buzz snickered as he finished up, and I joined in, relieved that the procedure had been completed in time. He gave the latex a final pat, then stood up.

"Take a look," he said proudly.

I turned away from the full-length mirror on the wall and looked over my shoulder. I marveled at my friend's craftsmanship.

"It won't stand up to a visual inspection, of course, but you should be okay in a pat-down," he said modestly.

By this time, the rest of the barracks was waking up. I quickly adjusted my clothing and carefully got back into bed; Buzz did the same. I looked up at the mattress above mine and whispered, "Thanks, Buzz. I owe you—again."

"We have to help each other out in here, kid. We're all we've got."

I did indeed pass the inspection, but Buzz's words were with me all day. *We're all we've got.*

Buzz was a good friend, and I hoped that I was the same for him. Yet, there was something empty in that phrase *We're all we've got.* It's not that I was ungrateful for Buzz and my other friends; it's just that I used to have a great deal more than friends. I used to have a mom, a dad, and a brother. I used to have a family.

* * *

"Not like that, Nick. You're the biggest city oaf I've ever known. Do you want some milk or not?"

Nick smiled and took the criticism in the spirit in which it had been offered. I smiled back and indicated that he should move aside and let me sit on the stool. I firmly grasped two of Billie's teats as she munched patiently on some fresh clover.

"You gotta pull like you mean it. You won't hurt her, believe me." I demonstrated again, and Nick's face was radiant with delight as twin, alternating streams of milk jetted into the pail with a watery, metallic sound. "See?" I continued. "It's a sort of squeeze, pull, squeeze, pull. Try again."

Nick sat down and reached under the cow's udder with a little more authority. He didn't say much; he never did. He simply looked, listened, and learned. We were both delighted when he finally succeeded in coaxing some milk out of Billie.

"That's the idea. Keep it up. When the bucket's full, dump it in the refrigeration tank like I showed you. Oh, and don't forget to jiggle that valve. I'll be in the next stall."

As I milked Elaine, I marveled once again at the way things had gone with Nick. His two-week visit was drawing to a close, and the time seemed to have flown by. I'd enjoyed the things Nick told me about the city, and he showed similar interest in my description of farm life.

In three days, Nick would be leaving, and I wanted to send him off properly. We revisited his favorite spots on the farm and tried to pack as much as we could into the time that remained. Of all the places we visited—the horse stalls, the hayloft, the pigsty—Nick loved my tree house best. We'd spent many evenings up there, playing cards and talking. Mom brought us fresh-baked cookies and Dad sometimes poked his head over the side to say hello. For the most part, it had been just the two of us. I knew my parents were watching, though, and that they observed our growing friendship with obvious pleasure.

I hadn't yet told Dad about Nick's feelings of guilt concerning his parents' death, but planned to do so when privacy permitted. I wanted to protect Nick from any further reminders of the tragedy until I could give him some good news.

In the meantime, I finally decided to introduce Nick to some of my friends. I planned to take him to one of our neighborhood baseball games. Nick and I had played catch a couple of times. He was pretty good with a glove, and I had no doubt he'd make a decent impression as long as he got a hit or two.

As I made these plans, I likened my actions to the simple agricultural principle of sowing and reaping. I was sharing my life and my friends with Nick, planting seeds of kindness in the dry soil of his broken heart. He loved baseball, and though he wasn't as good at fielding as I'd hoped, he tried his best. I loved the look on his face as he batted his first single even more than I enjoyed belting my own triple. When you plant generously, you also harvest generously. I planned to plant more seeds that night by inviting two of the guys up to the tree house for a farewell card game with Nick.

I forgot one thing. If you don't plant seeds deep enough, the rain sometimes washes them away and you get no crop at all. That's part of farming, too.

Chapter Eight

This is fun, I thought, as the punch connected with my left eye. The blow knocked me off balance, but instead of falling, which would at least have been dignified, I simply crumpled straight down onto my backside as if I'd had a sudden urge to sit down.

My antagonist laughed cruelly, along with the rest of the crowd that had formed. Some of the other students offered encouragement, such as "You should've shoveled more manure, farm boy," and "What's the matter? Did your sister forget to teach you how to fight?"

I wasn't bleeding, which was a plus, but my eye was already swelling shut. It would probably turn black and blue within the hour. I couldn't remember the specific penalty for fighting—there were far too many rules at AKPS to memorize them all—but I assumed it was severe. A disciplinary officer (D.O.) had been supervising the mess hall as usual, but D.O.s rarely interfered with brief scuffles like the one I'd been involved in. They preferred gambling on the outcome or merely enjoying the show.

Tonight, when I faced the barracks commandant, the D.O. would disavow all knowledge of the fight, or more likely, he would report that I had instigated the scuffle. I would be punished while my attacker went free. It was just another example of the many injustices that characterized the school.

I picked myself up and crossed over to an empty table to finish what was left of my dinner. As I poked at it, I thought about my new "home." I'd been tripped, pushed, mocked, and humiliated both in and out of class almost since the day I'd arrived, and most of the other new students were treated the same way. The environment in our barracks was better, but we spent comparatively little time there. Every day was a constant struggle to avoid harassment and even violence. Tonight I had been knocked down for moving too slowly out of an upperclass-man's way. I suppose I should have resisted, but I hated fighting. The last fight I'd been in had occurred in my tree house, and I still remem-bered the awful feeling of hitting another person.

I struggled against self-pity as I sat in that chilly mess hall that reeked of cabbage and chipped beef. Whenever something particularly unpleasant happened at school, I inevitably grieved over lost time and missed opportunities at home. I could no longer take refuge in the arms of my mother, nor could I seek my father's wisdom. I was growing up. Despite my recent desire to attain the status and privilege of adulthood, I found it overrated. What good was adulthood if the price tag included this wretched isolation from my family? I cried out in my mind as if my dad could hear me, and it grew into a habit as the months passed. *I'm sorry, Dad. I want to be your son again. I want to come home.*

So far, I had only heard from my family a few times. Dad's letters, brief and in his own handwriting, had contained messages like this one:

Dear Jake,

I hope this letter finds you in good spirits. We know that staying at Ashur-Kesed will be a difficult adjustment for you. It's not easy for us, either. I miss our chess games, and Mom misses your daily les-sons together. All the same, we know that you'll do well at school. Learn from everything that happens there. You're in our thoughts constantly...

There was more—news about the farm and such—but the true mes-sage of the letters had been clear: I would be staying at school until my education was complete, however long that took. I knew Dad well enough to know that he wasn't merely speaking of my classes, but of my character. My exile at Ashur-Kesed had been my own fault, precipitated by my own poor choices, but knowing that and knowing exactly how to change were two different things. I tried to be a willing part of the process.

I also began to make more friends. Buzz kept me on my toes, and I'd grown close to several other guys in my barracks. There was also the mysterious person who continued leaving me notes. Those short, secret correspondences served to break up the monotony of school life and provided me with a regular source of encouragement.

I had one of those notes in my pocket, and I pulled it out and read it again in an attempt to dilute my depressing thoughts. The note followed the same pattern as all the others: it was typewritten, optimistic, and ended with an unexplained word.

Jake,

Things can be tough here, but remember: you have friends. Stay strong. We'll meet soon. Trust my representative.

Best, E. (blue)

The notes were always unsigned, except for the initial "E." Obviously, my secret ally wished to remain anonymous, at least for now. What about the typewriter? Hardly anyone used them since the advent of the computer. Was that a clue?

I had carefully, secretly screened my schoolmates, but no one I'd met at school fit the profile. There was also something about the wording and tone of the notes that led me to suspect my friend might be female. That theory made little sense; this was an all-boy school and I hadn't even seen a girl for a long time. Still, the notes were somewhat fanciful, even affectionate, and they were always uplifting. I had not observed any of those traits in the hardened, cruel demeanor of the majority of my fellow students.

I'd wondered about the seemingly incongruous words at the end of the notes, but this note seemed to confirm my suspicion that they referred to the physical appearance of my benefactor. She (if it was a girl) had written the words "light brown," "five-seven," and "blue," among others. When combined, those words could describe someone's hair color, height, and eye color. However, that last line—"Trust my representative"—had me stumped.

I supposed I would find out soon enough. In the meantime, I looked forward to the mystery and excitement the notes brought to my otherwise drab existence. I also looked forward to meeting this unusual person, and I hoped this wasn't merely a trick played by the other students to embarrass or discourage me.

When dinner was over, we lined up and followed the disciplinary officer to our respective barracks. After we arrived, I endured the expected teasing as I examined my black eye in the mirror and tried to make myself presentable for evening inspection. The D.O. made his report to the commandant. Although I couldn't hear their conversation, I expected that my punishment was imminent.

The evening inspection occurred at 9:30 P.M. as usual, half an hour before lights-out. Its purpose was to maintain order and insure that the barracks were kept spotless twenty-four hours a day. The inspections were, like so many aspects of life at the school, a tiresome ritual.

The barracks commandant, a stocky man we knew only by the name of Sergeant Stenn, strolled down the line. He stopped when he spied my black eye.

"Student 3290, there appears to be something wrong with your eye."

"Yes, sir!"

"Did you trip over those clumsy feet of yours?"

"No, sir!"

"Did you poke yourself in the eye with a knitting needle?" That question elicited a snicker from the guards that trailed along behind the sergeant.

"No, sir!"

"Then what happened?

"I accidentally provoked an upperclassman, sir!"

"Oh, my. That was a mistake, wasn't it? Is there anything I can do? Get you some ice? Call your mommy?"

"Sir, no, sir!"

"Well, perhaps being neck-high in dirty underwear will give you some time to recover. Report to the quartermaster after classes tomorrow," he barked.

I sighed in relief as Stenn continued down the line. It could have been much worse. I crumpled onto my bunk the moment the door closed behind him.

"Laundry duty, eh? It's a good thing he liked your shiner, Jake," Buzz said brightly.

"Hmmm." I didn't feel like talking about it.

"So, are you gonna tell me what really happened?"

"What do you think happened? I didn't move fast enough out of Zack's way."

"Zack can't even move fast enough out of his *own* way. That big lummox...you want me to poison his soup tomorrow?"

I laughed. Buzz always knew how to cheer me up, even when I resisted. "Thanks, but no. Who would watch my back if you got arrested for murder?"

"Are you ladies gonna hug or what?" This came from Barker, so named for his laugh, which sounded like a seal with a bad cold. He wanted to be a lawyer but was terribly disorganized; I couldn't imagine what a judge would say the first time he caught sight of my boisterous, bedraggled friend.

"Aw, you're just jealous," Buzz replied.

"You're right, of course. If you two weren't such good friends, I wouldn't always have to scrounge for toiletries. *I* would be Buzz's very best pal, and privy to all the benefits accruing thereunto."

We all rolled our eyes at Barker's legalese.

"Elvin's a good bunkmate," the future attorney continued, "but he hogs the toothpaste—isn't that right, Southern Belle?"

Elvin, who was lying on the top bunk, grunted. He was studying with his usual ferocious concentration; I doubted that he'd heard one word of our exchange.

Barker addressed the rest of the barracks in a hilarious "closing statement" voice. "Fellow Ashur-Kesedians, I urge you to vote your conscience: doesn't our friend Buzz keep a beautiful boudoir?" We all laughed and agreed as Buzz modestly bowed.

"I'll say this for you, Jake," Barker added, referring to the way I had handled the commandant's questions, "you're learning how things work around here. Always make the upperclassmen look good."

We chatted, the three of us, and after a while, a few others joined the conversation. The pain of my eye was forgotten amidst the coarse but sincere bonding that was occurring more frequently in our barracks.

Later, after the lights had gone out, the throbbing in my face reminded me once again of another fight I'd been in, a fight that (unlike the one earlier this evening) I had started.

I'd handpicked Mal and Perry to come up to the tree house for a game of Kings on the Corners. It was a game best played with four people, and it was even more fun if two of them were terrible cardplayers like my friends were.

Nick and I were already up in the tree house when the other half of our foursome arrived. I had been demonstrating the finer points of the game when I heard a shout from below and the creak of the rope ladder. Soon, a dirty blond head made its appearance, followed by a brown-haired one. I made introductions all around, and I could see that Nick didn't quite meet with their approval. I'd expected that. Despite nearly two weeks on a farm, Nick's face and hands remained city-pale. He also retained the cautious air he'd had when I first met him. To top it off, Nick's errors on the baseball field had done nothing to endear him to my buddies. Mal and Perry hadn't played that day, but word had spread. I didn't care. I was optimistic about this evening and tried to move things along.

"Let's get down to business here, boys. The game is Kings on the Corners, and it isn't too hard to figure out," I said. Mal and Perry listened intently as I laid out the rules. *Not that it'll do you two any good,* I thought gleefully.

"Seven cards apiece, and four cards down around the draw deck, forming a sort of plus-sign. See? If a king had been thrown, you would have put it into a corner—"

"Which corner?" interrupted Perry.

"Any corner, lug wrench. May I continue?"

"Sure, dip stick." Dad disliked profanity, so I had established an alternative form of insult. This month, we used automobile parts; last month, it had been farm implements. It seemed a little childish—after all, most of us were teens by then—but it kept me out of trouble.

Nick observed our exchange with evident amusement. To my surprise, he spoke up. "Do you guys always talk to each other like that?"

"What do ya mean?"

"If I called someone in my old neighborhood a 'lug wrench,' I'd get beaten up."

"Yeah, that *was* a good one," I said.

"No, I mean I'd get beaten up for talking like a...a kid."

Mal chimed in at the insult. "Wouldja mind telling us how they talk down in the big city?"

"Sure. You'd call someone a..."

Three jaws simultaneously dropped. That was the first time I'd ever heard someone my age use that word, and from the delighted looks on my friends' faces, it was their first time, too. I'd only heard someone say it once before, when Mr. Modau's tractor broke down at the high point of the plowing season.

Nick had tossed off the word as if he used it every day. I saw admiration begin to gleam in Mal and Perry's eyes. Their faces seemed to say that this kid would do after all.

I experienced an odd mix of emotions. On the one hand, it was the perfect thing to bring to Dad's attention if I wanted to torpedo Nick's adoption. Dad would certainly not let someone who said words like *that* into our home. It wasn't that Dad was a tyrant or a man who made rules just for the sake of making rules. In his mind, there was right and there was wrong. He put it this way: "There are about a hundred thousand words in the English language. That's plenty to choose from without resorting to words which are coarse, crass, and common." That seemed to make good sense, so I had never gotten into the habit of swearing. At least, not the bad words.

On the other hand, as tempted as I was to blow the whistle on Nick, I also felt a strange desire to shelter him. I wanted to take my unlikely friend aside and tell him that on this farm, our family just didn't use cuss words. Not ever. Not if you banged your thumb with a hammer, not if you lost a game, not even if your team blew the play-offs for the hundredth time. As surprised as I was at Nick's loose vocabulary, I was even more surprised at the response it had evoked in me.

My initial astonishment wore off quickly, and I decided that the best thing to do was continue with the rules as if nothing had happened. My friends also tried to recover; they pretended that they heard (and used) such words every day. Nick seemed unaware that he had done anything wrong.

"Okay, well, once you put the king in the corner—*any* corner—you free up a space for one of your cards. You have to build by suits from the king down, and the ace closes out a run. The person to have no cards left wins. The more points you have in your hand when someone goes out, the worse you lose. Everyone got it?"

Everyone did, but I caught Perry smirking at me over his cards. What was on his sneaky little mind? He probably couldn't wait to try out that cuss word.

The game was fun, particularly since Mal and Perry lived up to their reputations and lost horribly. Nick didn't do half bad. We were nearing the end of the second game when he said in his quiet, wispy voice, "How about we up the stakes?"

"Steaks? You want some potatoes, too?" Mal was so corny sometimes, it hurt.

"Listen," Nick went on, ignoring the bad joke. "Do you guys have any baseball cards? Jake has quite a collection, but he's missing some from last season. Maybe you guys are missing a few yourself."

I realized where Nick was going with this. "Wait a minute," I said. "That's gambling, Nick."

"What if it is?"

"Well," I said, a little less sure of myself as I noticed the two other pairs of eyes that were now fixed on me, "Dad doesn't like gambling. He says it's a waste of money and makes a man greedy."

"Well, if it bothers you, look at it this way. You're missing some cards, and Mal and Perry here are probably missing some. Am I right, guys?" Nick's confidence appeared to grow before my very eyes; he finally seemed to be in his element.

My two hapless buddies nodded like puppy dogs, completely captivated by this stranger and his exciting, foreign ways.

"Remember, guys: you're not actually gambling, you're trading. Everybody wins."

I had to admit he was a smooth operator, but I'd never suspected that this side of Nick existed. Was he just trying to fit in, or was he attempting to dazzle us with this inappropriate demonstration of worldly wisdom?

I thought about what he'd said, and since it was sort of logical and no actual money was involved, I reluctantly agreed. Mal and Perry fished out their cards (which they carried around in their back pockets, of course) and threw them in the center of the rug where we were sitting. I did the same. Nick, I noticed, had nothing with which to ante. This fact did not escape the notice of my two friends, either.

"What do you got to put up, Nick old boy?"

"Hmm. I don't collect baseball cards, but I can ante up something just as valuable." With that, Nick pulled a somewhat crumpled pack of cigarettes out of his pocket and threw it into the pot.

This was an evening for surprises, or rather, for shocks. First swearing, then gambling, now smoking? I thought back over the last two weeks and felt a deep sense of loss. I didn't like this side of Nick, not one bit. Instead of an inquisitive, heartbroken young man I was suddenly sitting next to an enigma, and one laden with bad habits, at that. At the risk of being censured by Mal and Perry, I spoke up once more.

"Nick, where did you get those? Dad hates smoking even more than he hates gambling. He says it ruins your health and…"

"Rules, rules, rules; Dad, Dad, Dad," Nick exclaimed, his voice strident and unpleasant. He had never raised his voice before. "Don't you get to do *anything* around here? All you ever talk about is farming and your dad. What a pansy."

The next moment is frozen in my mind, the way bad memories often are. At Nick's scornful indictment of Dad, my arm instantly coiled and released, catching Nick on the upper cheek and cutting both his skin and my hand. All the accumulated tension and confusion of the past few months shot out in an angry torrent from the end of my clenched fist. With a surprised scream, he leaped at me and we rolled back and forth on the floor of the tree house, punching, thumping and scratching. Mal and Perry scrambled to keep out of our way. When they saw this was impossible, they waited for an opening, scooped up their baseball cards, flew down the rope ladder and disappeared into the night.

That left my fellow combatant and me. I naturally had the upper hand. Nick had never done a day's manual labor in his life and he was already panting from our brief exertion. *Who's the pansy now?* I thought, with great satisfaction. I was strong for my age. I flipped Nick onto his back, sat on his chest, and grabbed the pack of cigarettes. I leaned close to his face, which was red with humiliation, and hissed a warning.

"If you ever mention my dad's name with disrespect again, these will be the least of your health problems." I thought that sounded sufficiently threatening, and to amplify my words, I got off him, threw the cigarettes onto the floor and commanded him to leave my tree house. He slunk away, leaving me alone with my heart hammering and my shoulders heaving. Stripped of his bravado, he seemed more like the person I had grown to like, and I felt a pang of remorse. I slumped down on the beanbag chair.

My hand was bleeding, and I had a fat lip where Nick had landed a lucky punch. As upset as I was about this sudden revelation of Nick's character, my thoughts shifted to my father. How would I explain this? I was still oddly reluctant to reveal Nick's newly displayed shortcomings, but if I didn't, I would get punished, and good. There was no way I could avoid Dad before bed; we never skipped our nightly conversations. There was nothing to do except slowly descend from among the branches and tell Dad everything.

I climbed down and trudged across the lawn. As I approached the house, I thought about all the experiences Nick and I had shared, and how I had loved being the teacher for a change. With each step, I felt worse about hitting Nick. He had deserved a rebuke, not a beating. I also remembered Nick's face as I had delivered my warning. The look of the smooth operator had disappeared, replaced by the look of a frightened boy who'd gotten in over his head. I wanted to talk to Nick before I talked to Dad. If we could arrive at an understanding, if we could approach Dad having just reconciled, then perhaps we…

Nick was sitting next to my father on the family room couch.

I stopped short. It felt like I was standing on a train platform, watching my life pull slowly out of the station, never to return. I had come into view of the large family room windows and clearly saw my Dad tending to Nick's cheek, which was still bleeding. He appeared to be listening intently to something Nick was saying. What was that kid telling Dad?

I made myself walk up to the backdoor and open it. Every instinct told me to run, to go and hide somewhere until I awoke from this nightmare. The door opened directly into the family room, and I entered just as Dad finished putting a butterfly bandage on Nick's face. My dad glanced up at me, his brow crinkled with disappointment, then made sure that the bandage was neither too tight nor too loose.

"Looks like you boys have something to talk about," Dad said. He didn't seem too angry. *Maybe I won't get grounded after all.*

Dad stood up and amazed me with his next words. "Nick claims that the fight was his fault. Is that true, son?"

I tried to cover my surprise and appease Dad at the same time. "You've taught me that conflicts are usually two-sided, sir. It's my fault, too."

My father looked down at me, his hands on his hips, and I did my best to look penitent. I was eager to find out why Nick had claimed responsibility for what had just happened in the tree house. "You know I don't like fighting, son," Dad finally said. "You make this right. We'll talk afterwards."

He climbed the stairs and was gone. I was alone with Nick.

Perhaps it was the relief I felt at not incurring Dad's wrath, or maybe Dad's patience had rubbed off on me, but I was suddenly able to see Nick for what he was: a misguided, abandoned boy who had not had the benefits of a loving, supportive family. This momentary flash of maturity made it easier to do what I knew I had to do—sit down on the couch and make peace with him.

"Nice cut you got there," I said.

He looked down at the floor. I thought for a moment that he would ignore me, but then he mumbled, "You should see the other guy."

We laughed a little then, and it was better between us.

"Why did you do that?" I asked.

"Do what?"

"You know…take the blame."

Nick thought about my question for a moment. "Well, you know how you're always telling me, 'That's how we do things on the farm'?"

"Yeah."

"Well, that's how we do things in the city."

I didn't know what to say at first. As much as Dad had taught me about relationships, I had not yet been able to grasp the concept of sacrificing yourself for another. In my mind, when someone else was wrong, too bad for them. Yet tonight, even though I had thrown the first punch, Nick had put his own adoption at risk by accepting the blame. It would be years before I fully understood why.

Some tentative conversation followed, the obligatory apologies and handshakes were exchanged, and then we went upstairs. I knew Dad would be waiting in his study.

Sure enough, as we rounded the corner at the top of the stairs, I could see him at the end of the hall, poring over a booklet he'd received yesterday in the mail. I had been curious about it, but hadn't remembered to ask him what it was. He didn't look up as he said, "Is the war over?"

"Yes, sir," we mumbled. Dad closed the booklet and turned in his chair to face us. I marveled at the equanimity with which he seemed to be treating this whole affair.

"Nick, why don't you get some rest? Jake and I are going to talk."

Nick complied, and turned left into the guest room. Slowly, I entered Dad's study. He offered me a chair by his desk and looked at me for a moment. When he finally spoke, his voice was calm, even soothing.

"Jake, up to this point, you've always tried to solve conflicts peacefully. I've been very proud of you for that. Do you want to tell me what happened tonight?"

"There's not much to tell. Nick and I were having a good time, I guess, but we…had a difference of opinion."

"I've known you to disagree with your neighborhood friends from time to time. It's never come to blows before. Your difference of opinion must have been serious."

I shrugged. I planned to eventually tell Dad what I'd learned about Nick, but not yet. Not until I was sure the time was right.

"Well, I hope you two will learn to appreciate your differences rather than fight over them. You have a lot to offer each other. How's your hand?"

"Oh, it's fine," I said. "I should've tried to, I mean, I didn't want to hurt him." I was suddenly anxious to change the subject. I decided to satisfy my earlier curiosity. "What are you reading?"

"Ah, I'm glad you asked. It's a book about adoption. I realize that after what happened tonight this might be a sensitive topic, but Nick will be leaving the day after tomorrow. We—as a family—need to decide if he'll be coming back. To stay."

My mind whirled. I'd expected to discuss Nick's adoption with Dad, but I needed time to prepare my case. This was too soon. Nick hadn't even left yet.

I reviewed the events of the last few months. First, I had fretted about Nick's impending visit. Next, in an unexpected twist, we had become friends. After that, only days before his departure, I had discovered flaws that rendered him a totally unacceptable companion. Lastly, my Dad was actually thinking about *adopting* this swearing, gambling, smoking invader.

My family consisted of three people—no more, no less. I was determined to maintain that number at all costs. I had to tell Dad what I had discovered about Nick; I had to tell him everything. My conscience objected with a single question, causing me even more confusion: if I revealed Nick's faults and caused Dad to abandon the adoption, what would become of Nick?

I stared at Dad as I struggled to sort through these conflicting thoughts. Why did things have to change, anyway? Why did we have to adopt this kid, or any kid? Of all the families in the world, why did we have to be the saviors?

"Dad," I finally said, "I don't want a brother."

Dad thought about that for a moment.

"I see. Does this have something to do with your fight?"

"No. I, uh, we got on each other's nerves, that's all." It wasn't a lie, but I felt uncomfortable about the way I'd phrased it. "I just don't want him here. I like things the way they are."

"That's only natural. But shouldn't you think about it some more? It's important to your mom and me. I think it would be good for you, too, despite your misgivings. We don't have to decide anything tonight."

"Okay."

I hugged him good night and the embrace reaffirmed his ever-present strength and love. I knew more clearly than ever that anyone who came between my father and me was my mortal enemy.

In my world, enemies received no mercy. I hated to fight, but I had a feeling there was a war on the horizon. Reluctant participant or not, I would be ready when it arrived.

Chapter Nine

The airport. I stood just inside the automatic doors and stared at the controlled pandemonium of the terminal. The last time I'd been there was the day Dad sent me off to school. The place reawakened the same sense of unease and fearful anticipation I'd felt then. I hated flying, and my uncertainty about the reception that awaited me at home intensified my anxiety.

The shuttle had finally arrived and whisked me away from Ashur-Kesed. I'd watched the school recede with relief that was tinged, surprisingly enough, with sadness. I already missed my friends and had no idea when—or even *if*—I would see them again. As the shuttle picked up speed, the pine trees soon hid the fence, the buildings, and the gate. A part of my life officially drew to a close. I had arrived at the airport in plenty of time to make my flight, despite my fears to the contrary.

I obtained a boarding pass and checked my suitcase, but kept my attaché with me. People crammed the large, open concourse as I consulted one of the monitors suspended from the ceiling. My flight was on time. I had about twenty minutes. After buying a cup of coffee—a luxury I savored after drinking the bitter imitation they served at school—I sat down near gate A10 in an uncomfortable blue plastic chair.

As I tried to relax, I curiously examined my fellow travelers. Where were they going? Did they despise traveling by plane as much as I did?

Did they look forward to arriving at their destination, yet fear it at the same time?

I saw a couple sitting close together, closer than the blue chairs were designed to allow. They were young, dressed casually, and only interested in each other. They held hands and engaged in quiet conversation. Since they wore no rings, I assumed they were dating, and I envied their comfortable intimacy as I sat alone in the hurried, impersonal environment.

To my right was a middle-aged man in a business suit. He was reading a paper and wore the tired look of a frequent traveler. His eyes were red, and he gulped his bottled iced tea with an urgency that precluded enjoyment or refreshment. He was probably making a connection to another flight, continuing on in the pursuit of whatever business he was engaged in. I wondered if he spent much time at home and hoped that he did.

Across from me were two little boys and a young girl. The boys looked to be around four or five years old, the girl was about seven. They were accompanied by their mother, who studiously ignored the racket her children were making. The young girl was reading a paperback novel, her quiet activity punctuated by regular, angry shouts at the boys to *"Be quiet!"* Her brothers were failing at an attempt to share a handheld video game. One would play; the other decided he was bored and attempted to grab the game; his brother resisted with much screaming and hitting. In the process, the first boy would lose his grip on the game and complain to his preoccupied mother, who waved him off without even lifting her eyes from the magazine she was reading. The cycle repeated many times.

I wanted to tell them not to fight. I wanted to tell them that there are more important things than having your own way all the time. I wanted to admonish them for not being grateful for each other, for not appreciating the friendship and joy that a brother can bring. I didn't say anything. They wouldn't have listened, nor would they have been likely to understand.

Such lessons often have to be learned the hard way.

Nick left without fanfare two days after our fight. We never again discussed what had happened that night in the tree house, but things weren't the same between us. He was noticeably cautious around me, and my opinion of him had changed. Since Mal and Perry had spread the news of what had happened (the big blabbermouths), none of my other friends would come over until Nick was gone, lest they become embroiled in another scuffle. As a result, Nick and I bounced from activity to activity, trying to pass the time in a pantomime of our previous rapport. I was amazed at how fragile relationships are.

As Nick and I walked among the grapevines, milked the cows one last time, and took turns riding Swish, I reluctantly decided that I would have to tell Dad the whole story about what I'd discovered about Nick. I felt at peace with the decision; in fact, I felt noble about it. I didn't necessarily want to sabotage the adoption process, and I wasn't being spiteful. Nick simply wasn't a suitable addition to our family. Since I was the only one who knew that, it was my responsibility to speak up. I was still concerned about Nick's future, but I was forced to push that concern aside. After all, my family came first.

Nick and I said good-bye to each other at the front door with a handshake and a few awkward words. Mom, Dad, and I stood on the porch and waved good-bye as Paul drove him away. Paul had raised a bushy eyebrow when he'd caught sight of the still-healing cut on Nick's cheek, and I wondered what Dad had told him. The journalist would be disappointed that the visit hadn't worked out, but he traveled around a great deal. He would find someone else to help Nick.

When the dust from Paul's automobile had settled, I breathed a sigh of relief. Normalcy returned. That's all I wanted—for everything to be normal again. I looked forward to talking with Dad that night after dinner. It would hurt him to find out that Nick was not the innocent waif he appeared to be, but my duty was clear. I was about to head back into the house for an afternoon snack when Dad patted me comfortingly on the shoulder.

"Don't worry, son. You'll probably see him again soon."

"Huh?" Had Dad mistaken my sigh? What did he mean?

"Adoption takes a while, but Nick's a special case. Paul said that, if we all agree, Nick'll be back in about two months. Maybe less."

My mom and dad went inside without further comment, and I was left alone on the porch. "If we all agree"? It sounded like they had already decided. Dad had seemed so reasonable the other night. I'd been under the impression that I had some say in the matter. Two months. Maybe less.

How many times can a person's world be shaken before he loses his grip? It seemed to me that I really was losing my mind. It wasn't that my world was so horrible, or even so different than it had been. The problem was that I seemed to fit into it less and less. For reasons I couldn't understand or even pinpoint, my life was becoming a strange, confusing place where I was no longer welcome.

I wanted to be alone just then, but I also felt the need to do something that would help me to think clearly and come up with some kind of plan. I settled for an old standby: baseball.

I wandered down the road and discovered that a game was about to start. When my friends caught sight of me, they shouted a greeting and thrust me in line. The two captains, Philip and Jeb, began choosing teams. I was often picked early because I was a good catcher (I had a sneaky way of making the batter think a fastball was coming when it was really a curve, and vice versa). Today, however, Gib was there, and he was also good behind the plate (mostly because he was so dirty no one liked to stand near him in the batter's box). I stared off into the distance and waited while the teams were chosen. The sun felt good on my face, and it was one of those days when I should have been glad just to be alive. I wasn't glad; I wasn't anything. I just stood there like a sheep waiting for the slaughter, and wished that my life would return to the way it had been.

"I'll take that one—the ugly one." Cruel laughter ensued.

"They're *all* ugly, Upperclassman Rhodes! Could you be a bit more specific?"

"If you insist, Upperclassman Masterson. That one, the one with his scrawny knees knocking together."

"But Upperclassman, sir, *all* their knees are knocking together." More laughter.

It was a typically mean-spirited (and thoroughly unofficial) "spring cleaning" game the older boys played with the younger boys. To properly prepare first-yearmen for their incipient entry into mid-classman status, upperclassmen who excelled academically were permitted by custom to choose a "slave." For one week, this slave would have to do whatever the older boy commanded or face horrible reprisals. Beatings were the very least of the reprisals, and the tasks covered a wide range of humiliating and often disgusting cleaning and maintenance duties. The faculty looked the other way, as they often did when student activities such as this one provided them with some amusement.

Since I had started AKPS late—I would have been a junior if I were attending a regular high school—I wasn't a true first-yearman. I was thrown in with the rest of the first-yearmen because I was a new student and had never gone through the ritual. No one was exempt.

I was terrified. This was unlike anything I had ever experienced, and I'd recently faced the additional blow of discovering that I would not be returning home for the summer. Ashur-Kesed was a year-round boarding school, and apparently my parents did not feel I was ready to return home, even for a visit. I was disillusioned all over again, but my discouragement was lessened somewhat by the friends I'd made, particularly the one I still hadn't met. She (I was convinced by then that my anonymous friend *was* a girl) had written me an average of once every two weeks during my first year at school. I clung to each brief note like a man on a deserted island who finds a message in a floating bottle. It wasn't the same as being rescued, but it reminded me that I was still alive, and that someone out there was, too.

"Next!" the unofficial master of ceremonies bellowed. I tried to slink my way to the back of the line, but the number of potential slaves was quickly diminishing. A student named Abner Gale stepped forward.

"All right, Upperclassman Gale. Choose your loser!"

Abner didn't seem to fit in with the rest of this crew. He was tall, thin, and wore thick glasses. He was also brilliant. His "crime," I later discovered, was being born to parents who were too busy. He hadn't been a discipline problem; he had simply been in the way. His mother and father had shipped him to AKPS and promptly returned to their yacht. What a tragic waste of potential.

Gale scanned the crowd of boys more intently than his peers had done. He consulted a small sheet of paper in his hand.

"What's that? A wimp graph?" one of the other seniors asked.

Gale ignored them, and I saw him examine me, look down at the paper, then examine me again. He walked over and said, in a confident but quiet voice, "This one."

His choice was met with a cry of protest from a burly student with bushy black hair. He reminded me of the Incredible Hulk—strong, mean, and very dangerous when angry.

"Hey! You knew I wanted farm boy, Abner."

"When you earn a GPA of 4.4, you'll get to choose earlier."

I was shocked by Gale's boldness; he was no match for the Hulk. Then I discovered the reason for his boldness.

"Hey. Dufus." This remark came from Sam, who was heavily muscled and was by far the tallest student in the school. "Ab made his choice. End of discussion."

"Yeah, yeah, stop throwing your weight around."

I had just witnessed the inner workings of school politics. Here, as in other closed institutions, students split off into groups according to their abilities and preferences and then jockeyed for power, privilege, and position. The stronger students (like Sam) tended to become bullies, while the weaker students either survived by using their brains (like Abner), or else became little more than pawns who served the interests of the strong. It was a simple arrangement and you did well to quickly find your niche before someone else permanently chose it for you.

I was grateful that Abner, whoever he was, had taken a liking to me; the Hulk looked as though he'd had some particularly unpleasant tasks in store for me, though I had no idea what I had done to earn his wrath.

My new "owner" walked over to me as the slave trading continued. He slapped a sticker on me that said "PROPERTY OF U.C. GALE." He smiled a thin but not unfriendly smile and told me to follow him. I wondered what plans he had for me.

We walked outside into an uncharacteristically cold spring evening. The wind raced down from the nearby mountains, causing the pine trees outside the campus to confer in a rustling whisper. I wished that I had worn my school windbreaker, but the cold didn't seem to bother Abner. He led me without further comment past the neat, sterile row of barracks, and then turned left onto the gravel path that led all the way up the hill to the Hub. Along the right side of the path ran a tall, steel fence with razor wire along the top. Scenic. I wondered where we were going, but knew better than to ask. Ally or not, this was still AKPS and you didn't speak to upperclassmen without first being spoken to.

We turned a corner in the path and reached a spot where the fence was attached to a steel upright. I immediately noticed two things. One, the fence had been cut along the length of the pole; two, there was someone on the other side of it, obscured by a long hooded parka the same color as the pine trees. The person spoke—a female voice.

"Thanks, Abner. I owe you one—no, two. Keep this quiet, okay?"

Abner nodded, and as he turned to go, he smirked and said in a voice loud enough for only my ears, "You'll be warm soon enough, Jake." Suddenly, I understood the cryptic phrase at the end of the note I'd recently received: "Trust my representative." Abner *was* that representative, and that meant that the mysterious figure who was wriggling through the fence was my anonymous friend.

The young woman smiled, and now I understood Abner's remark, too. She was the first girl I'd seen for some time. I estimated that she was a little older than me, making her about seventeen or eighteen. The sight of her upturned lips cut through my loneliness and produced a warm sensation in my chest. I smiled back, hopelessly confused, but not about to complain.

"I'm Elise," the girl said. "It's great to finally see you up close." Her voice was of that rare type of contralto that sounds musical even when it's not engaged in song. She extended a small, gloved hand, which I gently and gratefully shook.

"So you *are* the person who's been writing those notes?"

"You'd prefer Abner?" she asked. Her laughter was so refreshing in light of the daily, rasping abuse of my instructors.

"Don't take this the wrong way, but I don't understand," I sputtered. "Why have you been helping me?" I was thoroughly knocked off balance by the unexpected turn this evening had taken. True, I had suspected that my secret friend was a girl, but I hadn't expected to meet her tonight. I also hadn't expected to be instantly attracted to her.

The wind picked up and I hugged my arms to my sides. Elise noticed, and chose to address my physical discomfort rather than answer my question.

"Do you want to go someplace warm? Ha! Silly question. Follow me."

I would soon discover that she was an expert at dodging questions. I admired her energy, though, and decided to temporarily forgo an explanation. She slipped back through the gate and held it for me. I froze, but not from the cold.

"Um, I can't leave the grounds."

"Sure you can. It's wide enough...see?"

She was teasing me. She knew I meant that it was against school regulations to leave the campus without proper written authorization. Any student found off the grounds was subject to "the Can," a narrow, virtually airless cell not much larger than a human body. It was one of the school's more inhumane punishments. I'd seen people come out of the Can, and it often took days for them to recover from the heat, lack of air, and subtle psychological agonies that one endured there. I'd even heard rumors that long ago, a timid first-yearman named Stewart had gone insane in the Can. He'd emerged gibbering and crying and was subsequently discharged. I experienced a sudden burst of anxiety. Was Elise playing a game? Worse, was one of the upperclassmen playing a game? I took a step back. I was grateful for this girl's friendship, but she was asking me to make a long leap of faith. She patiently slipped back through to my side of the fence.

"I know you're afraid of being caught, but you'll be perfectly safe. The guards don't patrol the place I have in mind, and no one will ever know you've been off-campus. You're either going to have to trust me or go back to your barracks. I don't know much about male bonding, but I'm pretty sure that hanging out with Buzz and the boys is not as interesting as what I have planned." She sized me up and concluded with a final question. "Are you saying that I'm not worth the risk?"

I struggled against my suspicions. Elise possessed detailed knowledge of the school, she knew Buzz, and she even knew the patrol patterns of the guards—but how? How could she claim such immunity, and more important, how could she offer it to me? I looked into her eyes and tried to detect insincerity. All I saw was playful affection mingled with a large measure of self-confidence.

I decided to follow her. I was not given to taking foolish chances, especially not in a hostile environment like Ashur-Kesed, but her contagious smile and the sense of adventure she offered were irresistible after so many months of drudgery.

We walked along a path that I had only seen from behind the fence. It wound along parallel to the fence for about thirty yards, and then dropped down a hill to the right. The path was muddy, so we were obliged to hold hands to maintain our footing. I didn't mind.

"Where are we going?" I whispered, feeling like a secret agent.

"Oh, you'll like it. It's not the most picturesque spot in the world, but it's warm," she replied in a somewhat louder than normal speaking voice. She was teasing me again by ignoring my attempts to keep quiet, but I wished she would be more careful. Even though most AKPS regulations contradicted my sense of right and wrong, it didn't pay to be cavalier about them.

I heard a low mechanical thrumming in the woods ahead of us, and caught sight of our destination through a thinning grove of pine trees.

Elise looked back at me and smiled, then led me through the unlocked rear door. We stepped inside and found ourselves in a long, high corridor.

"What is this place?"

"You know that huge house on the hill overlooking the school?"

"Yeah. We call it Dracula's Castle."

"This is what heats it."

"We're that far away from the school? Elise, I really need to get…"

She placed her finger on my lips to silence me. "If you try, I mean really try, you just might have a little fun. You do like to have fun, don't you?"

"AKPS isn't exactly a resort. I'm a little out of practice."

"Well, we'll have you fixed up in no time. Care for a tour?"

Without waiting for an answer, she grabbed my hand again and led me through the door. It opened onto a landing that overlooked a huge furnace room. Metal steps led down one flight to a concrete floor. Running down the center of the room was a massive boiler that belched steam at periodic intervals from a rusty relief valve. Hanging from the low ceiling was a twisted, greasy mass of piping and duct-work that wheezed, steamed and groaned. The overall impression was that we had entered the lair of a large, black, sleeping dragon whose many appendages spread all over the room, waiting to clutch an in-truder in its hot, oily grip.

Elise led me down the steps and past the boiler. As we ventured toward the far wall, we ducked under the dragon's slimy arms.

"You say that this place heats that mansion?"

"Yup."

"Why isn't it located *in* the mansion? This seems inefficient."

"Paranoia."

"I beg your pardon?"

"The owner of that house feels that having a large steam boiler sitting in your basement invites…sabotage."

"You're kidding."

"I wish I were."

"Who is he?"

"Let's just say that his family's eccentricities extend far beyond this little oddity. You know what? I'd rather talk about you. Come on; we're almost there."

We walked up another set of steps, through a door, and into another hallway where a table, two chairs, and a cooler had been set up. This adventure was getting better by the moment. I began to forget that I was in gross violation of school regulations and endangering my unsullied record.

I gallantly pulled out the chair for Elise. Now that the light was better, I took a good look at her. I was pleased that my guess about her notes had been correct—they *had* contained hints about her appearance. She was dressed in jeans and a sweater, and wore her light brown hair in a ponytail that accentuated her playful manner. She had fair skin and intense crystal blue eyes. "I've been wanting to thank you for a long time," I said as we sat down. "You're very…creative."

"How so?"

"The notes you sent me, all of this. I'm grateful. I'm a long way from home, and I never knew that a place like Ashur-Kesed existed, or that I would ever find a friend here." I paused. "Can I ask you a question?"

She smiled her impish smile. "I'm sure you have more than one."

"Why me?"

She thought about it for a moment before answering. "My life isn't very interesting," she finally said. "In a way, I go through the same dull routine you do. I happened to be…around…when you arrived. I've seen students come and go, but I've never seen anyone look the way you did that first day. Most of the guys that show up here have a certain hardness to them. Even though they know they messed up, they don't really care. You were different. You looked like you could use a friend. I liked you immediately."

She was direct, no doubt about that.

I mumbled something about the feeling being mutual, and Elise smiled as she opened the cooler and drew out two mugs, a thermos, and a sealed plastic container. She filled the mugs with a steaming, light brown beverage, and then opened the container to reveal strawberries, cantaloupe, grapes, and sections of Red Delicious apples. In the center of the container was a tub of caramel. My eyes widened at the sight. I had not tasted fresh fruit for almost a year. I missed it. And caramel? That luxury had never graced the mess hall of Ashur-Kesed and probably never would. I wanted to dig in but politely indicated that Elise go first. She picked up a plump strawberry and popped it into her mouth.

"See? No poison," she said. "Help yourself."

I did so, and the taste of the fruit instantly brought back memories of home. The mulled hot cider tasted even better. The drink reminded me of cool autumn nights by the fire, listening to Dad read aloud or watching Mom cross-stitch. I wondered where Elise had gotten it this early in the season; that was the farmer in me, I guess. Elise must have seen my face darken.

"Did I get it right?"

"Oh, it's perfect. I was just thinking about home."

"Share, please."

I did. There was something disarming about Elise, something that seemed to whisper that I could trust her with the sad tale of my past offenses. We began to talk—well, I did most of the talking—and Elise paid rapt attention. Her eyes never left me as she absorbed every detail, every word, and every description. I felt both exhausted and relieved when I finished the story, although I hadn't revealed every detail, especially not the part about why I had been sent here. Still, I had revealed more about myself than I had intended and now experienced a twinge of embarrassment.

"Wow, we farm boys sure can talk."

She was resting her chin on folded hands. Her eyes conveyed a knowing sort of sympathy, as if she could somehow relate to what I had told her. "I hope your story has a happy ending, Jake," she said quietly.

"I hope so, too." The old bitterness threatened to return and I suddenly didn't want to talk about myself anymore. I drained my mug, and Elise promptly refilled it. "Here I am babbling about myself," I said with forced congeniality, trying to fight off the oppressive memories of my last two years at home. "Your turn."

"Oh, my turn comes later."

"Now, wait a minute…" I objected.

"I insist." Her eyes grew mischievous again. "Where would the mystery be? A secret friend, a secluded boiler room, stolen moments in the forest—it wouldn't do to reveal all our secrets in one night, would it?"

"I guess not, but I didn't hear you objecting when I was spilling my guts a moment ago."

"Fair enough. You may ask one question, subject to approval."

There were so many things I wanted to ask her, but I decided to focus on the future, rather than the past or even the present. "When can I…when is our next 'stolen moment'?"

"Then, you would like to see me again?"

My blush gave her all the answer she needed, but her mood became serious as she answered my question. "We won't be able to see each other for quite a while. I don't think much of that school or its rules, but you're right to be cautious. We'll just have to be patient."

Patience again. My favorite character trait.

The minutes turned into hours as we continued to talk. I enjoyed the curve of her face, the sound of her laugh, and her razor-sharp intelligence. The unusual circumstances that had brought us together lent a strong sense of unreality to the evening, as though this was a pleasant dream that could end at any moment. Ashur-Kesed was the least conducive place I knew of to nurture a romantic relationship, but such a relationship seemed to be budding in that dingy hallway next to the boiler room.

In the midst of our conversation, I happened to glance at my watch. I stared down at the glowing blue numbers, shocked to discover that I'd missed the evening inspection. I looked up, stricken. Now I would catch it for sure. I opened my mouth, but she anticipated me once again.

"I told you—trust me. Inspection has been handled. You have nothing to worry about." She brushed a lock of hair away from my forehead, lightheartedly discounting my anxiety. "All the same," she continued, "we'd better get you back. No sense in being reckless."

She returned the mugs, thermos, and plastic bowl to the cooler and led me back under the pipes, past the boiler, down the other hallway, and out the back door.

Trust. Who was this girl who demanded my trust as if it were something I doled out for the asking? I supposed that was the nature of trust, though; you gave it when you weren't one hundred percent sure.

Elise led the way, and her hair smelled like wildflowers as it trailed behind her, gently tossed and lifted by the wind. Above, the stars were scattered across the sky in all their twinkling glory. Was it my imagination or were they somehow more beautiful tonight than they had ever been before?

We reached the fence, and Elise bid me good-bye with a firm handshake, looking into my eyes and saying, "I was right about you, Jake. I think we'll become very good friends. You watch your step in there, you hear?"

I nodded, and before she slipped through the fence, she reached up and kissed my cheek. She walked a few steps down the path, and then looked back over her shoulder. "By the way," she said with a wink, "you're fairly nice to look at." Then she was gone, leaving me in complete emotional turmoil. My heart hammered at the unexpected compliment and at the prospect of a much brighter future than I'd had any reason to hope for.

I watched her until she reached the bend in the path, and then raced to my barracks. Now that I was back on school grounds, I hoped she had been right about the inspection. If Elise could promise that I wouldn't get in trouble for missing it, she either had to know or be able to pay off the commandant. Meeting her had raised far more questions than it had answered, but I wouldn't have traded the experience for anything.

I half-crouched, half-ran across the campus, skirting the cameras and lights, and slipped quietly into my barracks. The fact that the doors were unlocked was in itself a miracle; the building was secured after nine o'clock, and it was almost eleven by the time I returned. There were no angry guards waiting for me, though, and everything seemed perfectly normal. I glanced up at the top bunk and saw that Buzz was asleep, his breathing slow and regular. I looked down at the inspection slip that was clipped to the front of my bunk, stamped with green inked letters: "PASSED." I shook my head as I undressed and slipped between the sheets. Who *was* she?

Chapter Ten

It was January, but the new year brought little hope.

Two months had passed since Nick's visit. During that time, Nick's imminent inclusion into our family hung over me like the sharp blade of a guillotine.

Dad and I continued to meet in the morning and evening, but it wasn't the same, at least for me. Dad still treated me with the same affection and generosity as always, but I couldn't understand why he was so determined to adopt Nick, and I refused to support his desire to do so. As a result, I became progressively less responsive to Dad's lessons.

I still hadn't revealed the flaws in Nick's character. I delayed partly because I didn't think it would make a difference, and partly because I had acquired the dangerous habit of sharing my feelings only with those who agreed with me. So far, I had confided in four friends (not counting Mal and Perry), and they all took my side. Dad had repeatedly tried to discuss the matter of Nick's adoption with me, but I always avoided the topic. I wanted to wait for the perfect time to drop my bombshell, and I wanted to hide my true feelings for as long as possible.

The opportunity to reveal Nick's "city ways" came sooner than I expected. Dad called a family meeting at the end of the month.

Family meetings were solemn occasions. Sometimes we met to

celebrate a successful harvest, other times to discuss a challenge or problem that could affect everyone on the farm. (We'd met just six months before to discuss ways we could save water during the coming dry season.) On this particular night, the topic of the meeting wasn't farming; it was Nick.

It had just been the three of us that night. We'd eaten a hearty meal of chicken croquettes, fresh broccoli, and twice-baked potatoes. I was stuffed but had just enough room for a piece of the cranberry-apple pie that was cooling on the stove. Dad got up from the table.

"Thank you, dear. That was delicious," Dad told my mom. He placed his hand on my shoulder and announced without preamble: "I'd like to have a family meeting. As soon as the dishes are done, let's all have a seat in front of the fire."

Mom didn't look surprised, so she must have known about it. They probably hadn't told me ahead of time so I wouldn't ruin dinner with my silent brooding, which had become an increasingly common habit of mine lately. Mom and I did the dishes while Dad went to stoke the fire that was popping and snapping in the family room.

A few subtle glances at my mother confirmed what I already knew: this would not be a good meeting. Ordinarily, Mom would chat with me about this or that, and we would laugh and sometimes even throw dish suds at each other (to the head-shaking amusement of my father, who stood at a safe distance during such battles). Tonight, she simply washed while I dried. Her face betrayed the tension she felt.

When we finished, I felt a familiar dread as I followed Mom into the family room. There were fewer and fewer places on the farm that were untainted by my growing anger and fear. Even my favorite places—the tree house, the barn loft, my own room—had now become like foxholes spread along a battlefront. These places provided nothing more than temporary, imperfect protection from a relentlessly advancing enemy. The problem was that the enemy was within me and I brought him wherever I went.

We all settled down in the family room. I perched stiffly on the divan by the fireplace, Mom sat in her rocker on Dad's right, and Dad lowered himself into his huge chair. He looked as regal as a monarch, and I felt a burst of admiration for him even as I loathed the topic I correctly assumed he was about to broach.

"Son," he began, "you know your mother and I have been talking about Nick's adoption for some time. We need to make a decision soon, but we haven't really heard from you on the matter."

"Yes, you have."

"Oh?"

"I told you already. I don't want him here."

"I thought we had agreed that you would think about it."

"I did think about it. I still don't want him here." I was defensive and angry. I stared down at the floor and tried to keep my tone respectful, but it wasn't easy.

My mother spoke. "Can't you explain why you feel that way, dear? Your father told me about the fight, but there's more to it, isn't there?"

It was now or never. I swallowed and finally said what had to be said.

"Nick doesn't belong here. I found out some stuff about him. You wouldn't like it."

My parents exchanged a glance. "Like what, son?" Dad asked. He sounded reasonable. I hope he stayed that way.

"He seemed decent enough when he got here," I began, "but when we were up in my tree house, I found out that he...that he talks really, uh, that he swears..." I was fumbling. My revelation of Nick's shortcoming didn't sound nearly as heinous as I wanted it to. I struggled on, hoping my next statement would seal his fate. "He also smokes and gambles, and he doesn't like all of Dad's rules and...he just wouldn't fit in," I finished lamely. I inwardly cursed myself for botching my one chance to keep Nick far away, where he belonged.

Mom and Dad were silent for what seemed an eternity. The fire crackled behind me, and Skipper sat at my feet, oblivious to the discomfort we all felt. Dad finally responded, "Son, we know Nick is far from perfect. In fact, we were already aware of the things you just told us. We want to adopt Nick *in spite* of the fact that he says and does those things. He needs a family who will teach him what it means to love and be loved. He's not going to replace you..."

"I never said he would!" I burst out. To my horror, I felt angry tears begin to run down my face. Dad's statement had touched a nerve that I hadn't even known was raw.

Mom got up to comfort me, but I couldn't have that. "Ma, don't.

I'm not a kid anymore. Look, I don't care what you do. You'll adopt him whether I want you to or not."

"Now, Jake, that's hardly fair," Dad said. "Don't you think that…"

The doorbell rang. We all froze, and then Dad stood up and headed down the hall to the front door. Mom and I remained seated, but I didn't look at her. I stroked Skipper's head, taking comfort in the fact that he would never betray me. Muted voices drifted back down the hall. I recognized our visitor's voice, and my relief at the interruption turned to disgust. It was Paul.

"Is this a bad time?" I heard him say.

"It's as good a time as any."

I asked Mom if I could go to my room. I didn't want Paul to see that I'd been crying. She nodded and I started up the stairs just as Dad and Paul entered the room. Dad didn't try to stop me.

Instead of going to my room, I crept to the edge of the stairs and tried to hear what they were saying. They skipped the small talk.

"Jake's not taking it well, I see," Paul said.

"That's putting it mildly," Dad responded. "Is this type of reaction common, Paul?"

"It depends. It's not unusual, I can tell you that."

"What do you recommend?" Mom asked.

"I recommend that you go ahead as planned. I think Jake is a re-markable young man. It'll be an adjustment for him, of course, but I think he and Nick will become fast friends in no time."

Why don't you go back to your newspaper and write about things you actually know something about, I thought.

I listened a little longer, hoping that my parents would reject Paul's advice. Unfortunately, Mom and Dad remained noncommittal.

I retreated to my room. As I lay on my bed, I realized that there was only one course of action open to me. If my parents decided to adopt Nick, I would do my very best to ensure that they regretted that decision. And, when Nick arrived, I resolved to make his life as miser-able as he had made mine.

A few days later, Mom and Dad told me that they'd decided to go ahead with the adoption. Dad tried to explain it to me, but I was past the point where explanations would suffice.

"Son," he'd concluded, "we don't expect you to fully understand or even agree with us, but we do ask you to trust us. Can you do that? Can you try?"

I nodded, which was a terrible lie. He walked out of the room and I simply sat there, wondering how this had happened. I was more determined than ever to make them all sorry that they'd done this to me. I began to think dangerous, violent thoughts.

Over the next three months my rage mutated into depression. I regularly feigned sickness because I couldn't bear meeting with Dad, watching the sunrise and chatting as though everything were normal. Despite my anger, I grieved over those lost moments. I imagined my father standing there in the fields, alone with his coffee and his thoughts, and I grew more resentful by the day. During my pretended illnesses, I stayed in bed and coughed every once in while so my mother could hear me. I often used the time to plan how best to harass my new "brother." It was easier to entertain these kinds of dark thoughts when Dad wasn't around. Without his steady, gentle wisdom, I was able to deceive myself into justifying my hateful schemes. In my mind, this was war. You didn't allow an invasion of your country's soil, and you didn't allow some foul-mouthed, tobacco-smoking, weasel-faced gambler to supplant you and ruin your perfect world. As I plotted and planned, Dad's lessons clamored for attention in the back of my mind. I tried to ignore them and mostly succeeded.

One morning in March, Dad came into my room before he went out for the day. He sat on the bed and felt my forehead. I looked up into his kind face, and a fresh wave of grief nearly overcame me. How badly I wanted things to return to normal, and how badly I wanted to go with him.

"Not feeling up to going out again?" he asked.

I shook my head mournfully.

"Too bad. I'm going to graft a branch onto the quince tree. I wanted you to give it a try."

That was too much to bear—Dad knew I'd always wanted to try my hand at grafting.

Dad stood up to leave, and the disappointment on his face was evident. He gave my hair a final tousle, then left the room. I heard his boots clop to the edge of the stairs, stop, and then return. He stuck his head through the doorway.

"You sure you're not feeling well enough?"

That did it; I swung my legs over the side of the bed.

"I'll give it a try, Dad. If I don't feel well, I can always come back to bed."

"Good enough," Dad said with a smile.

I dressed quickly while he got us coffee and headed out to the barn for the supplies. I felt my depression burn away like morning fog under the hot sun.

The quince is a small dessert pear, and Dad had planted a tree for Mom just outside the kitchen window. Mom enjoyed making pies with the firm, tart fruit; everyone else enjoyed eating the pies. It was a nice arrangement. I assumed that Dad wanted to graft another branch onto the tree to increase its yield. The technique, when done properly, caused faster fruit production than merely waiting for pollination to run its natural course. It was early in the season and we'd have to wait a few months for any rewards from our labor, but I was excited anyway.

I caught up to Dad at the foot of the tree, took the coffee mug he held out to me and sipped from it gratefully. One of the drawbacks of pretending to be sick is that you're not supposed to have an appetite; mine was screaming for food, and the coffee with fresh cream and sugar helped a little.

"Now, this is going to be exciting. I wonder if it'll work," Dad said.

"Why wouldn't it work?"

"Because we're not grafting a quince branch onto the tree, we're grafting a branch from a Bartlett pear tree."

"How come?"

"To see what'll happen. My theory is that we'll get Bartletts from this branch, and continue to get quinces from the rest of the tree."

"But even if it works, won't the Bartletts be smaller than normal?"

"I don't think so. We might get a hybrid if we used another kind of pear branch, like an Anjou, for instance. In this case, I think we'll end up with two distinct pears from a single tree."

"I don't know, Dad," I said doubtfully.

"Well, let's give it a try and see what happens. It'll be good practice for you, anyway."

We began to work. Dad brought out a square, homemade wooden box on which to cut the stem. He unwrapped the Bartlett branch (which had a water-filled tube on the end of it to keep the tissues moist) and showed me the proper way to notch it. He worked amidst the branches of the tree while I carefully followed his instructions. We finished our work at about the same time. I handed him the branch, but he gestured for me to do the honors.

I held my breath, hoping I'd done my job correctly. I had. The branch fit perfectly into its new home. Dad showed me how to wrap and tie the two carefully together, then let me slather on the gooey, black grafting paste. That was it—our job was finished. The quince tree looked the same as always, except that it had a new branch where one had not existed an hour before.

"Now," Dad said grandly, "we wait and hope."

That was a wonderful morning. There was something about joining those two separate fruit trees that made me feel good.

I didn't bother trying to maintain the fiction of my illness. I reported to Mom that I felt much better after getting some fresh air and asked for something to eat. She gladly complied as we talked about the tree. I told her in great detail about the technique of grafting. She smiled as she ladled pancake batter onto a well-greased skillet.

A few days later, after I'd finished my daily chores, I decided to check on the tree on my way back to the house. I didn't expect any significant growth, but I wanted to make sure that the paste and grafting tape were still in place.

As I approached, I noticed two white pieces of paper stuck in the branches of the tree, fluttering in the breeze. It was probably some trash that had blown in from the road. As I approached, however, I saw that the two pieces of paper weren't stuck there; they'd been purposely attached to two of the branches.

One piece of paper was tied to the quince branch and had the name "JAKE" printed on it in big letters. The other was tied to the Bartlett branch and had the name "NICK" printed on it in the same letters.

A tree that had been in our yard for sixteen years and a branch that had just become a part of the tree. They had been joined, for better or for worse. Time would tell whether they would form a bond, grow, and share the same nourishment from the roots. Time would tell if that unusual union would bear fruit, or if the host tree would reject the grafted branch, which would then dry up and die. The message was clear.

One part of me wanted to care, but another continued to loathe Nick. I looked toward the house. Were my parents in there now, watching my reaction? The caring part of my mind briefly scuffled with the hating part, and lost.

"Nice try, Dad, but people aren't pears."

"Do you two want to be alone?"

The words of my classmate shook me out of my reverie. I had been staring at the fruit on my plate, the bite I'd taken only partially chewed in my mouth. It seemed that everything reminded me of home.

"Those must be some pears, my man. I never liked the canned variety, myself. How're things?" Buzz sat across from me and slammed down his pile of books.

"Okay. I was just thinking about…"

"I know—home. Snore. Listen; let's talk about something I *am* interested in. How are things going with your girlfriend?"

I had shown Buzz some of the notes I'd received from Elise and asked for his opinion concerning her identity and apparent influence around campus. He hadn't ventured a guess, but seemed as curious as I was about her.

"Pretty well, but she's not my girlfriend."

"Yet."

"Cut it out."

"Come on, I see how your eyes flutter when you read one of her notes."

"Keep it up and I won't let you read them anymore."

"Killjoy. Hey, how'd you do on the physics test?" Buzz had a quick mind. Once he tired of a certain line of conversation, he immediately (and often unexpectedly) changed the subject.

"I passed, but just barely."

"Too busy dreaming about you-know-who, eh?"

"Zip it. Physics is easy for you. You'll probably win the Nobel prize when you get out of here."

"Hey, on that note, I invented a new kind of alarm system for the barracks. Wanna check it out?"

"Sure."

We trudged through late spring flurries that dusted the ground, but couldn't hide the mud and gravel of the campus. *Even the snow is gray here,* I thought ruefully. Buzz carried the same satisfied, confident air as always. Nothing, not even the weather, diminished his cheerfulness. He reminded me of Skipper—faithful, unassuming, always there when I needed encouragement.

Buzz strode with quiet purpose through the door of our barracks. We'd grown as close as brothers over the past year, and I still wondered what I had done to earn his encouragement and constant assistance. As soon as the door swung open, I heard a muffled beeping sound that lasted about three seconds.

"What was that?"

"That, my bovine-loving friend, was my newest invention."

He led me over to our bunks, lifted up his pillow and handed me a plastic box. It looked like a cross between a baby monitor and an army-issue field radio. A foot-long length of wire with an earpiece on the end extended out of the back of the device.

I asked the question that had become a tradition whenever Buzz introduced a new invention.

"That's great!" I paused. "What is it?"

"I'm glad you asked." (His response was also part of the tradition). "This is an E.W.I.A.—an Early Warning Inspection Alarm. Here's how it works."

Buzz leaped off the bunk and bounded over to the double doors that were the only way into or out of the barracks. He indicated one of the doorjambs, and I could see a tiny glass lens that glowed red when my friend passed his hand in front of it.

"I used a garage door sensor and wired it to this transmitter up here," he said, pointing to a tiny black box hidden behind the speakers that blared the daily announcements. "That, in turn, sends a signal to this receiver, which emits a short audio pulse. Bingo, no more surprise inspections."

"Buzz, if that sensor only goes off when the door opens, that means that we'll have about three seconds warning before the roll call. That's not much of an advantage."

"Good point; you're always thinking. Perhaps I need to position the infrared lens outside the doors, maybe at the entrance to the path. It will have to be done at night. You'll help, of course."

I groaned and flopped onto my bunk. "Can't you take an interest in literature or maybe basket weaving?"

"I'm already an expert in both those areas. Get some rest, because come midnight, we've got work to do."

Chapter Eleven

"Passengers seated in rows 24 through 18 may now board." I looked down at my ticket—seat 19A—and reluctantly approached the gate. An attendant told me to have a nice flight and a few moments later, I was boarding the DC-9. Another attendant greeted me with a broad smile and told me how glad she was that I had chosen to fly with them today. The other flight attendants were helping passengers stow their belongings; the crew was performing their preflight checks. It all seemed perfectly normal and perfectly safe—except for the air, which smelled canned and artificial. I couldn't wait to breathe the fresh, clean air of the country. I walked down the aisle, trying not to bump anyone with my luggage, and reached my seat in the middle of the aircraft. A window seat. Great.

With my carry-on safely stowed, I sat back, pulled down the plastic shade, and tried to get comfortable. Despite my uneasiness about air travel, I had one thing on my mind: home. As I pictured the farm in my mind, it seemed like a perfect, distant realm that existed only in my memories, a place characterized by undiluted happiness and peace. Home had been that way once, and I had been a part of it. I fought the nagging fear that I would never truly belong there again.

It was odd thinking these kinds of thoughts about the farm. I realized I had taken everything in my life for granted. When I was younger, I had devoted no more thought to the barn, the fields, or my home than

I had to breathing. Everything had simply been a backdrop against which the events of my life had unfolded. I promised myself that this time, I would be more grateful—for everything.

I made a valiant attempt to push back the regrets. The plane was awakening, preparing to lift me off the ground and take me back where I belonged. My mind continued to wander, carrying me from memory to memory as the huge jet turbines began to spin, then whine, then roar.

"Jake, get up!" Dad called. "You've got to see this!"

I fumbled for my alarm clock, thinking I'd overslept. Nope—it was only 4:45 A.M., fifteen minutes before my usual waking time.

I shook off my confusion, dressed quickly, and walked downstairs to the family room. I looked around for Dad, but he was nowhere in sight. It was too early for Mom. The kitchen was dark, the coffee pot was still in the cupboard, and the potbellied stove was unlit.

I looked out the window. It was late summer, but the farm still looked barren in the dark.

"Out here, Jake."

My father stood in the backyard. I opened the door and stepped out into the cool morning. Dew covered the ground, and my sneakers made small, wet imprints beside my dad's larger ones. He stood near the quince tree, and I hoped this wasn't another lesson.

A legal matter had delayed Nick's arrival. Apparently, there was a codicil in his parents' will that awarded custody to his nearest living relative. The relative—a second or third aunt—could not be found. The attorneys put the adoption on hold while they searched for her. I had taken it as a sign that my parents should reconsider the whole matter, but Mom and Dad had taken things into their own hands and were fighting for the adoption to be approved. I had lived in limbo for the past several months. I was in no frame of mind to endure any more lessons about brotherhood, especially not at a quarter to five in the morning.

As I approached the tree, I saw Dad waiting there, illuminated by an exterior floodlight. He looked pleased, and I soon understood why. The new branch had borne fruit, and the pears were unquestionably Bart-letts. In addition to the new, larger pears, there were many smaller quinces scattered amongst the branches of the tree. So, Dad's theory was correct. A Bartlett tree and a quince tree had been melded into one, both nourished by the same root system, both bearing their own individual fruits. Yeah. Whatever.

"You were right," I acknowledged quietly, cradling one of the large pears in my hand.

"Looks like we'll be having pie tonight. Would you care to pick the first one?"

I pulled on the pear and it came loose. It was firm and looked delicious. There was no lecture about what all this meant, no explanation of the underlying principles as they related to my life. Dad simply smiled and clapped me on the back.

"Good work, son! I'll have to let you graft some more. Make sure that the fruit makes it into the kitchen in time for Mom to do some baking, all right?"

I nodded and began picking. Dad strode off, whistling and leaving me to my thoughts. *Pears. Brothers. The future.*

Seven months passed. I celebrated my thirteenth birthday with the usual party, but the celebration was hollow and the gifts brought me no joy. Summer sped into the busy autumn season, and autumn slowly stripped the leaves from the trees and sent the farm into deep hibernation. Nick arrived just after the first snow of winter. What better time for my life to end than during the gloomiest time of the year?

The temperature plummeted and acres of farmland soon became unbroken vistas of snow. Vague lumps marked where the fence posts had been, and barren tree branches reached upward as though entreating the sun for more warmth. I felt trapped. The happiness of my childhood had fled, and my heart was as cold and hard as the ground. The significant difference between my situation and the seasons was that winter eventually ended and gave way to spring. My life offered no such hope.

As before, Paul personally delivered Nick to our farm and my parents hosted a party to welcome him. Our neighbors and many of my friends were invited.

I was not the life of the party. As Nick enjoyed all the attention, I could see that he was sizing me up, trying to assess whether or not he and I would get along. I couldn't wait to show him just how hostile his new home could be.

As the winter days dragged by, the rift between my father and me steadily grew. I must admit that Dad never moved. I'm the one who widened the gulf between us. He still tried to spend time with me, but I often rejected his efforts. I wondered what would happen when the gulf became too wide to cross.

The tree house was cold during the winter, and I didn't dare use a space heater up there. Only in the barn could I find the combination of warmth and solitude that I desired, so I spent most of my time there.

The chicken coop was also an effective hiding place. I was there one afternoon when Nick found me.

"I've been looking for you," he said.

"Get lost."

"Stop being a jerk. You're supposed to help me with the horses."

I turned to face him. "City boy can't even brush, feed, and water three horses? Why don't you ask Dad for help."

"Fine!" He stormed out of the coop and I checked my watch. If this confrontation ended in the usual way, I'd hear Dad's voice any minute.

"Jake!"

I didn't answer. When Dad entered the coop, we had another fight in a long, unpleasant series of fights. They were always the same.

"Jake, how many times do we have to go through this?"

"Sorry, sir."

"Don't you 'sorry, sir' me! I've told you time and time again: treat Nick with the kindness he deserves as a member of this family. I don't know how many different ways you want me to say it, son."

"He doesn't need me! He's already stolen some of my friends."

"That's not true, and it's not the point. He's your brother. Stop treating him like an enemy."

I usually tuned Dad out midway through these speeches. Sometimes he backed them up with punishment, sometimes not. Either way, the two years after Nick's arrival blended into one unending rhapsody of strife.

My one consolation was that, at the beginning, Nick got into trouble as often as he stayed out of it. He found it difficult to adapt to farm life, and his disrespect of anyone in authority often surfaced. Before long, however, he began to fit in. He made more friends in the neighborhood and wormed his way into the weekly ball games. He still wasn't much good at baseball, though, so he formed a basketball league instead. That thinned out our baseball teams, and the guys blamed me. The tension between Nick and me increased.

Spring finally arrived. The trees stretched their branches, glad to have awakened from their long, cold sleep. Despite my poor behavior, Dad continually tried to foster a relationship between Nick and me. One day, he suggested we all go fishing. That sounded good to me except for the "we" part. Dad and I were the fishermen; Nick still didn't know how to cast or even bait a hook properly.

We got up before the sun and rode in Dad's pickup down to the edge of the Saugatuck River. We'd be fishing for trout and using lures instead of live bait. That was a pity. I would have enjoyed watching Nick fidget at having to touch a worm. He was squeamish about things like that, and that characteristic had provided me with many opportunities to humiliate him.

The beautiful morning possessed enough power to penetrate even my cynicism. I stood on the bank of the river, admiring the way the rising sun played among the gentle ripples and eddies of flowing water. I looked forward to the next couple of hours. When I went fishing, I never cared if I caught a fish or not. I liked standing by the river, breathing the fresh, cool air and enjoying the peace of the nearby forest.

"Jake, show Nick how to cast, will you?"

With that statement, the beauty of the river dimmed as though a shade had been drawn over it. With my mouth twisted in distaste, I took the rod from Nick.

"Stand back, will you? You don't want to get one of these caught in the back of your head."

Nick complied. Being up this early excited him, especially since it involved learning something new. His black hair had defied earlier attempts to comb it and shot out in different directions. His eyes were wide, as if they wanted to gather as much information as possible. Nick had the look of an explorer on the brink of a new discovery. I envied him. I despised him.

"All right, watch me," I said. "You draw back, press in the button—see how it lets the line out? When you flick it forward, you release the button and out goes the lure. You have to release it just right, and don't reel it in too fast." Dad had given Nick my old training rod. Instead of a manual flip-over reel, Nick was using the simple push-button model that I had used for years. I thought he wouldn't be able to do it, and I'd have to baby-sit him all morning.

"Like this?" Nick snapped his wrist and the lure plinked into the water, just the right distance from shore.

That little show-off. Well, what would you expect? He was using a baby reel. I tried not to get too upset. After all, casting was one thing; catching a trout (which was a notoriously cautious fish) was another.

When I was sure Nick had the hang of it, I moved downriver to find my own spot. Dad was upriver, and I was sure he'd watched the entire casting lesson. I hoped he was happy. Another father-son tradition ruined.

I flipped, drew back, flicked forward, released. The golden spinner on the end of my line glinted in the sunlight, but not a single trout showed any interest in it. I cast for about half an hour and was about to move upriver when I heard a shout. I looked sharply in the direction of the noise and wondered what that dope was doing. Was he trying to scare all the fish away?

"Hey! Hey, I think I got one!" Nick cried out excitedly. I hadn't told him what to do in the unlikely event that he got a bite, but he was reeling it in pretty well. As I approached, I hoped against hope that Nick had snagged the lure on a rock, but then I saw the trout's golden-brown body break the surface of the river. I sympathized with the struggling fish and wished he would break free. Dad had trotted over to witness the momentous event, and we stood there while Nick landed his catch. It was small, but within the limit.

"Look! My first fish. Isn't it great, Dad?"

Hearing Dad's name come out of Nick's mouth caused me to turn to ice as I stood on the bank of that river. I don't know what devastated me more: the fact that Nick had addressed my father as "Dad," or hearing how casually—how naturally—he'd said it.

I dropped my rod and shouted, "He's not your dad, you idiot! He'll *never* be your dad!" Then, to seal my cruelty with the bitterest wax of all, I ended with: "Your dad is dead!"

Nick didn't argue with me. His smile vanished. He lowered the fish slowly and looked down at the riverbank. Tears ran down his cheeks and mingled with the flowing water. I angrily swiped away my own.

Dad dropped his rod and charged over to me.

"Jake, you have broken my heart!"

Dad's explosive rebuke shook me more than a physical blow.

"You'll learn something today, son, and you'll learn it well." Dad stood and drew Nick closer to us, encircling him with his arm. "This is your brother. He's no less a son to me than you are—*that's what adoption is*!" Dad's voice echoed off the hill across the river, causing the birds to scold us for the interruption of their morning song. "We have, as a family, extended our love to someone who *was* a stranger. Now it's you who have become the stranger."

Dad's scowl deepened as he concluded with a final, cryptic statement. "Strangers are welcome in our home, but not when they cause discord and pain. Change your mind, Jake. Change it soon."

Dad turned and left, leading Nick back to the pickup. My rage blotted out the import of Dad's words. All I'd gotten out of his speech was the fact that he had defended Nick. Later, when I'd had a chance to replay that scene in my mind, I really understood: Dad had called me a stranger.

That morning was a turning point. Over the course of that year, I began to take long walks by myself. I devoted hours to brooding and plotting. Perhaps worst of all, my behavior began to rub off on my friends. Years earlier, my father had warned me that bad company corrupts good character. Ironically, I was now the bad influence. Mal, Jeb, Perry, and the rest of the crew looked up to me. My poor example caused them to adopt my most pronounced characteristic: rebellion.

Some of my friends were able to drive by this time, and I couldn't wait for the freedom that driving promised. By the time I neared sixteen, I had my eye on one of the family cars. It was a large black sedan that showed its age in its worn upholstery and dulling paint, but it ran well and would get me far away from my family. A couple years earlier, I'd asked Dad if it might someday be mine. Dad never made a promise he didn't intend to keep. He'd merely said, "We'll see," and left it at that.

I'd once had a well-thought-out plan for my life. I intended to finish high school, get a bachelor's degree in agricultural science, and one day run the farm. My father had always been supportive, but he told me to keep my options open. He never pushed me to follow in his footsteps. Now, as much as I loved farming, I couldn't stand the thought of staying here one day past my eighteenth birthday. The problem was that I *hadn't* kept my options open. I'd neglected my pre-college work. I had no plan, no goals, and no real direction. Once again I felt trapped.

One day, after suffering through the drudgery of working the south hay fields, I noticed that the car was gone. I was only mildly concerned. Despite my increasingly hostile behavior, I firmly believed that I would soon be driving around in that car, far from my problems and my family. I was wrong. I discovered that Dad had given it away. Some deadbeat needed a vehicle so he could start some ill-conceived business venture, and Dad had fallen for it. He'd handed over the keys and my best chance to taste the freedom of the open road. I threw another one of my now-famous tantrums and was promptly disciplined.

When winter's grip had finally slipped away for good, the warm weather gave me a bad case of spring fever. Dad had indefinitely postponed my driving privileges because of my "poor attitude," but I didn't care about consequences, or my father's displeasure. I had to get away from the farm or I would burst.

I thought I had planned it well. Dad had left on his usual rounds; Mom was running some errand with the other family car. I was supposed to be taking Nick around, refreshing his memory about the spring routine so that he would be of more help during the growing season. Upon arriving at the horse stable, however, I pointed out how matted the horses' manes were (their manes weren't matted, of course). I suggested that Nick give the horses a good rubdown, and then spend fifteen minutes with each of them, brushing out those knots. He eagerly agreed, as I knew he would. He'd never seen a horse up close before arriving on the farm, and they still captivated him. At least he and I had something in common.

I left him with the horses and hurried to the truck. It was parked under a breezeway in between the garage and the maintenance shed. Despite being protected from the elements, its wheels had sunk into the soft earth. That gave me a moment's concern. I hoped I could back out without too much trouble and without leaving too much evidence.

Chapter Eleven

I got behind the wheel after checking to make sure no one was around. The smell of the vehicle brought back memories of fishing trips and rides up to the mountain; of pretending to steer when I was little and driving into town with Dad to get farm supplies. We'd always stop at the candy store on the way back. Dad would buy me a penny stick—green apple was my favorite—and I'd suck it with great enthusiasm all the way home. I was surprised to find myself on the verge of tears. Stupid memories, anyway. That was the past. Right now, I wanted a taste of freedom, not candy, and all I needed to do was turn the key, pop the clutch, and I'd be on my...

"Hey."

I jumped six inches. Nick stood at the passenger side of the truck with a scowl on his face.

"Brush the horses, huh? Do you think I'm that stupid?"

"Yeah. Actually, I do."

"Well, surprise. Where are you going?"

"None of your business."

Silence. I faced forward, wanting to bring the engine to life and escape, but I didn't know what to do with Nick standing there. I heard the door open, and my head snapped around.

"What do you think you're doing?"

"Coming with you."

"You don't even know where I'm going."

"I don't care."

"Get out," I said, not quite as forcefully as I'd intended.

"Okay. I think Dad's out by the orchards this time of day, isn't he?" The door opened and Nick swung his legs around as though he meant to get out.

What a little blackmailer. "Stop. Fine, come along. Just don't talk to me."

"Fine."

I halfheartedly turned the key. The whole point of "borrowing" the truck had been to get away from the boy sitting next to me. However, I didn't want to simply abandon my defiant little ride. That would make me look weak.

Finally, the engine cranked to life, and I briefly enjoyed the powerful roar of the eight-cylinder engine as I gunned it. I put my hand on the stick and tried to remember what Dad had done. I was familiar with a standard shift, but I'd never operated one in an automobile. I hoped they were similar to the tractor as I eased in the clutch and cranked the shift into reverse. No problems so far, so I let up the clutch a bit, turned around in the seat, slowly applied the gas…and promptly stalled.

I heard a giggle from beside me and shot a vicious glance Nick's way. "Not a word, grease ball. Don't push me today, I'm warning you."

Nick stifled himself and looked out his window. I tried again, and this time the truck crawled backward. I let the clutch up a little more while simultaneously giving it more gas, and we shot out and stalled again. Nick shook on the seat next to me, trying not to laugh. I vowed that if he made another peep, I would push him right out the door. I started the engine for the third time. After a few hard lurches, we were on our way down the driveway. My technique could have used some improvement, and I saw Nick fasten his seat belt. I decided to do what I usually did: ignore him.

By the time we got to the end of the driveway, I was starting to get the hang of it. I looked right, left, then right again, and eased out onto the road. I felt the need to demonstrate my superiority, so I stepped down hard on the gas pedal and we surged forward. The burst of speed intoxicated me. I almost forgot that Nick was sitting beside me, and I began to enjoy myself. Mailboxes sped by as I shifted into fourth gear and drove even faster.

A creek ran along the right side of the road. Although I had quickly mastered the technique of driving a stick shift, I hadn't counted on the shoulder being so soft. I rounded the next curve a little too quickly and felt the right front tire begin to skew toward the creek. I gritted my teeth and spun the wheel madly as I fought to keep the truck on the road, but I reacted too late. The front end of the pickup sank toward the swollen creek bed, and before I knew it, we'd plunged over the edge. Because I had neglected to put on my seat belt, I flew forward and rammed into the steering wheel. Pain erupted in my chest and right leg. The world suddenly turned black.

I regained consciousness to find Nick's stricken face only inches from mine. I was soaking wet, and I thought my right leg might be bro-ken. The pain grew worse by the moment. I moaned, and Nick said something about not moving, staying right there, that everything would be all right.

He kept asking if I was okay. He wanted to go for help but didn't want to leave me alone. I don't remember if I answered him or not. The pain drove me back towards unconsciousness, and the last thing I remember before blacking out again was that I was propped up in the passenger's seat.

I heard a beeping sound, and then a strange, antiseptic smell assaulted me. I opened my eyes and found myself lying on a bed with a curtain drawn around the left side, bisecting the small room.

A hospital. I lifted my head slightly and saw that my leg was suspended above the bed by an arrangement of white vinyl cords and metal pulleys. I heard voices in the adjoining section of the room. The owners of the voices weren't aware that the subject of their conversation was now awake.

"Your son suffered a compound fracture of the tibia. Although it punctured the skin, it was a clean break. It should heal without any lasting complications."

"What kind of complications?" Dad asked.

"Well, he might walk with a slight limp and the leg will ache whenever rain or snow is in the forecast. It shouldn't interfere with any of his usual activities. He's young; he'll bounce right back."

"Thank you, Doctor."

Silence. I drifted in and out. I couldn't see the label on the plastic IV bag that hung above my left shoulder, but I gratefully suspected that it contained some kind of painkiller. The voices resumed, but this time one was younger. Familiar. Despised.

"Will he be okay?"

"Thanks to your quick thinking. What happened?"

There was a pause. I thought I was imagining the next part of the conversation.

"I—I didn't mean to do it, Dad." I still cringed every time Nick called my father "Dad," but my irritation quickly turned to amazement as Nick continued. "I thought I knew how to drive the truck. I'd seen you do it a few times and it looked easy enough. I thought I'd take a short ride down the street. Jake caught me and tried to stop me, but I wouldn't listen. He jumped into the truck as I was backing out and kept telling me to go back, go back." I could hear emotion creeping into Nick's voice. I couldn't believe what he was doing.

"Go on." My father's voice betrayed nothing.

"When I got out onto the road, I took that first turn too fast. The ground all along the stream is muddy, and we just slid down into the water. Jake didn't have his seat belt on, and he was thrown out into the creek. I heard him screaming."

Another pause. I struggled against the drugs that were dulling my senses.

"I was wearing my seat belt and didn't get a scratch on me. That figures," he said woefully.

Wow, he's really laying it on thick, I thought. *Why is he trying to protect me?*

"I dragged him out of the creek and covered him with my shirt because I heard that when someone's in shock, you have to keep him warm. That's when I ran to get you."

I strained to hear Dad's response. My head ached—and not from the injury to my leg. Nick had pulled me from that truck, dragged me around to the passenger side, and lied to Dad in order to save me from getting into trouble. Why? This was the same Nick that I had relentlessly avoided, ignored, and despised since the day he arrived at the farm. This was the same Nick that I had insulted that very morning. Why would he sacrifice his good standing with his adopted father—for me? I remembered when Nick had tried to take the blame for our fight in the tree house. I hadn't understood his attempt to protect me then, either, but I understood this even less.

I heard the scuffling of feet and quickly shut my eyes. "We'll talk more about this tonight," Dad said. "Let's go see your brother."

Father and adopted son walked around the curtain and stood by my bed. I pretended to sleep, which wasn't difficult. Perhaps I was already sleeping and this was all a dream. When I woke up, maybe I would realize that my unwanted brother hadn't actually done this incredible, undeserved thing for me. I would awake and be able to hate him again without all this crushing guilt.

It wasn't a dream, of course. I felt Dad's warm hand on my head, and then heard him and Nick sit down on the green vinyl hospital couch. Sleep. All I wanted to do was sleep…and forget.

The drugs in my IV cooperated, and I drifted off.

Chapter Twelve

Time passed at AKPS, although not as quickly as we students would have preferred. Our professors droned on, the commandants and disciplinary officers continued to push us past our limits, and Vice-Chancellor Senna stalked about the campus with his dog, looking for the slightest excuse to condemn us.

I began to exhibit the outward signs of impending manhood. My shoulders broadened, my voice grew deeper, and my beard refused to be ignored any longer.

I welcomed the changes I saw in the mirror, but I wanted to grow in other ways, too. I wanted to be a man. The problem I faced was the sterile intellectual environment of Ashur-Kesed. While opportunities to grow had been plentiful on my family's farm, I had to search for them at school as if they were diamonds scattered amidst the barren sand of a desert.

As I grew, the hardships at school and the loss of everything that was familiar and precious to me continued to hone my mind and body. The jagged edges of my rebellious spirit began to wear away, revealing the values my father had implanted in my heart. Life polished those values to a brilliant shine, freeing them of the rough, ugly encumbrance of my selfishness.

My convalescence in the hospital lasted three days. I would have gone home sooner, but I had sustained a concussion in the accident and was under observation.

My friends visited, but it was a mixed blessing. They questioned what had happened. I didn't know what to tell them, and I didn't dare trust them with the truth. Although Nick had also come to visit me several times, someone was always within earshot, so I wasn't able to ask him why he'd lied to Dad. In the end, I decided to take a chance and repeat Nick's version of what had happened. To my shame, I even embellished the tale to make myself seem less like a wimp and more like a fallen hero—the big brother who had tried to keep his erring younger brother out of harm's way. In short, I lied.

Mom and Dad came every day, of course, but Dad was strangely reserved. He'd asked only general questions about the accident, which made me wonder if he suspected the truth.

On the third day, after Mom had stepped out to get us all some coffee from the hospital cafeteria, I decided to risk a few careful inquiries. "How's the truck, Dad?"

"That's not important, Jake. Trucks can be replaced; sons can't."

"Did Nick tell you what happened?"

"Yep." I could see he wasn't going to volunteer any information.

"What's gonna happen?" I tried to keep my questions vague, leaving my options open for a possible confession.

"Well, it's a serious matter. My rules are firm: no driving before sixteen unless I'm in the truck. Disobedience brings consequences." Dad avoided saying that Nick was guilty; neither did he indicate that he suspected me. His face betrayed nothing. Did Dad believe Nick's story? More important, should I allow him to believe it?

We didn't discuss the accident again until I returned home. The large hospital cast was replaced with a smaller one. I still found it cumbersome, and Mom restricted my activities for another couple of days. I hated my crutches and fretted about my recovery. What if I couldn't play baseball? What if I couldn't climb up to the tree house? I perfected self-recrimination into a fine art during the long hours of reduced activity.

Two days after my parents brought me home, Dad appeared at the door to my room.

"Good morning, son."

"G'morning, Dad."

"Do you feel like a little air? You've been cooped up for a while now."

"Sure." Grateful for any reprieve from boredom, I grabbed the crutches and followed Dad to the end of the hall. He took my arm and helped me down the spiral staircase, through the living room, down the hall, and out the front door. It was a beautiful day. Dad matched my slower pace and we chatted as we crossed the front lawn. As we passed the last few rows of corn, I was alarmed to discover that we were heading toward the truck.

Mr. Jackson from the gas station had pulled the pickup from the stream with his tow truck. It stood in its usual place, still splattered with mud, its front grille crumpled in. I wondered why Dad had chosen this particular spot for a morning walk. When we reached the truck, he lowered the tailgate so we could sit on it and then looked up at the sky, perfectly at ease despite the words he said next.

"Jake, perhaps having Nick around isn't the best thing for our family."

I wanted Nick gone but not this way, not while we were sitting on a vivid reminder of his attempt to spare me the punishment I deserved. My tongue felt like it was made of cotton as I spoke.

"Why, Dad?"

"He knew that driving the truck was forbidden for both of you, yet that rule was broken, and broken willfully. That's not something I can tolerate. That kind of behavior hurts the entire family."

"Oh." If Dad looked at me now, the decision about whether or not to confess would be taken out of my hands. I'm sure that my inner conflict was written in bold print in my eyes and on my flushed cheeks.

"Of course," Dad continued, "there are some things that don't add up. Maybe you can help me understand. Maybe Nick can stay after all."

Warily, I asked Dad what he meant.

"Well, you know that Nick tries very hard to fit in, but he's still not quite at home here. He's lived in apartments or townhouses all his life, and all of this"—Dad spread out his arms to encompass the whole farm— "it's just not second nature to him like it is for you or me. Did you know that Nick never takes off his shoes except to shower or sleep?" Dad chuckled. "He even walks through the pig sty with his sneakers on. He'd rather wash them off than get his feet dirty. He's not like you in that respect."

Dad was right. I didn't wear shoes from late April until August unless I had to plow or do lawn work. I loved the feel of the grass and soil beneath my feet, and in my opinion the heavy calluses I'd developed protected me as well as the sole of any sneaker would have done. Still, I wondered about the relevance of all this.

"The thing that confuses me, Jake, is that apparently Nick wasn't wearing shoes on the day of the accident."

"He wasn't?" I was confused. I distinctly remembered Nick wearing his trademark canvas tennis shoes that day.

"Here. Let me show you." Dad jumped off the tailgate, helped me to ease down onto the grass, then led me around the side of the truck to the driver's side door. He opened it, leaned down under the dash, and pointed.

"You remember that it was muddy that day. That's probably what caused the accident in the first place. I'm sure Nick could handle himself behind the wheel under ordinary conditions."

I nodded in agreement, still unsure where this was leading.

"Lean down here, son. Take a look at this."

I grabbed the driver's armrest while Dad helped to steady me. I followed my father's pointing finger and stared at the brake pedal with wide, frightened eyes. Now I understood.

Muddy footprints covered the mat and the pedals—bare, muddy footprints. I shot a glance over to the passenger side of the truck and saw the rest of the evidence that condemned me: there were footprints there, too, but they were clearly made by sneaker treads. The evidence was obvious. Dad knew that I had been driving, he knew that I had disobeyed, and he knew that I had lied.

I realized Dad had given me a final opportunity to confess. He had learned the truth, yet he had not accused me. I supposed he thought that I wouldn't grow that way, and even now, peering at the evidence of his son's disobedience and dishonesty, my father cared about my growth.

There was no point in delaying. Some remnants of inbred decency surfaced long enough for me to swallow and say what had to be said. "Dad?"

"Yes, son?"

"I was the one driving the truck, not Nick. I'm sorry."

Dad's deep green eyes didn't change as he gazed at me. The clear spring sky and wispy clouds framed his face. "I see," he finally said. "That would explain the footprints, wouldn't it?" He paused. The sparrows were singing, blissfully unaware of my suffering. Dad continued. "Would you tell me why?"

I wanted to explain, but couldn't find the words for what I felt. I knew I should say something else, something that would help Dad understand, but I merely fixed my eyes on the ground and remained silent.

Dad took my arm and helped me back to the tailgate. He didn't sit beside me but stood by the rear panel, gazing into the sky again.

"Jake, I foresee a future that neither of us wants. Our family is divided, and that's something I can't abide. I could stop it, I suppose, but it's not my way to force you or anyone else to do what I want. That wouldn't make me much of a father, and it wouldn't help you to become much of a man. I'd like to see you do the right thing, but that takes courage. To *do* right, you have to *be* right—here, inside. You've allowed bitterness to take root inside you, Jake, and I want to tell you now, while the sun is shining and there is still time, that you need to change that. I've been considering our options as a family. I've asked you to try to get along with Nick, and I've asked him to do the same. He's not always obedient, but he's doing a better job maintaining the peace than you. Perhaps it's because he feels he has more to lose. Nevertheless, there's a boarding school up north..."

"Are you threatening me, Dad?" I interrupted. My father ignored my biting tone and remained calm.

"Jake, you know me better than that. At this point, I haven't decided. Since you've expressed a desire to get away from home, it might be an opportunity for you to do that and even explore other options besides farming."

"Why? So Nick can steal the farm away from me, too?"

Dad was silent.

"Let's sum this up," I said. "Instead of getting rid of Nick, you want to send me away?"

"No. I want you and your brother to act like brothers. I want peace in our home. I want your mother to stop crying over you two before she goes to bed. Most of all, I want you to grow into the man I know you can be. If sending you to a boarding school will help achieve those things…"

"But I'm your *son*!"

"Yes, you are, but you still don't understand. Nick is my son, too. Would you have me extend to him lesser privileges because he wasn't born into the family? Or consider the reverse: pretend that Nick was the one who hated you. Would you have me treat him more harshly because he was adopted? No, Jake. You are my son, the product of your parents' love, but hatred must be treated as hatred, no matter who does the hating. It is precisely because you *are* my son that I expect great things from you. Besides, this isn't meant to be a punishment…"

"Oh, that's classic!" I interrupted. "Shipping me off to some school isn't a punishment? It's not my idea of a vacation."

"Jake…" Dad's voice conveyed his anger, but I wasn't finished yet.

"I've always tried to do what you say. Why am I being treated like a criminal just because I don't want a brother? And just so you know, little Mr. Perfect is anything *but* perfect."

"Son, I don't expect perfection from either you or Nick. You're right about one thing: you've been the joy of my life ever since you were born. But we're not talking about you forgetting to close the silo door or neglecting to do your chores. We're talking about you willfully, purposefully hating another human being." Dad's eyes once again searched my own. "Jake, I had hoped that you would understand why your mother and I felt so strongly about adopting Nick. I thought I'd given you ample opportunity to express your feelings. Most of all, I thought you would benefit from having a brother. I'm sorry for causing you pain. I'm also sorry that you feel you can't talk to me anymore."

Dad paused once more. "Hating Nick is wrong, Jake. I love you, and I've always made that plain. If you truly love your dad, please think about what I've said."

My father walked slowly towards the house, but I remained on that tailgate until my legs grew numb. I sat there and mourned the end of life as I knew it. When the pins and needles grew unbearable, I grabbed my crutches and hoisted myself off the truck.

"Time to move on, Jake," I told myself.

It was a warm night in June. A few of us were up in the tree house playing cards. We'd tried many other games, but our favorite continued to be 500 Rummy. Mo, Perry, Jeb, and I were silent as we hunched around a rickety card table. The game was close and the stakes were high. I didn't know where Nick was, nor did I care. He was probably off somewhere trying to impress Dad again.

My leg bothered me that night. True to the doctor's prediction, the recently healed bone ached whenever the humidity increased. Rain was in the forecast and the dull throb in my leg made me even more contrary than usual. The pain was actually twofold. Every time my leg hurt, I was reminded of the way Nick had tried to spare me the punishment I'd deserved, and I would inwardly grimace at the lack of gratitude I'd shown since then.

I had thanked Nick in a perfunctory manner after returning home from the hospital. I waited for him to explain why he'd lied for me, but I hadn't been able to swallow my pride enough to ask. He never volunteered the information.

I recalled his words from a couple years earlier. "That's the way we do things in the city," he had said. It galled me that an orphan who had been raised in a skyscraper knew more about forgiveness than I did. I was left to stew in my own unworthiness, and suffer from the nagging pain of owing a great debt to someone I wanted nothing to do with.

Nick had been disciplined for lying, of course; Dad approved of his intentions but not his methods. I had also been punished for lying, as well as for stealing and wrecking the truck. The punishment was in the past, but the memory of Nick's act of kindness remained, shaming me and highlighting my true nature. He had repaid my cruelty, jealousy, and indifference with the kind of love my father had always tried to instill in me. A startling realization caused me to recoil even farther from my family: Nick was more like Dad than I was. Tonight I had sought solace in the company of friends and in the repetitive but enjoyable diversion of card playing.

Rummy is a tense game when four people are playing. We were all good cardplayers that evening, except Perry. Despite my patient lessons, he continued to fail at cards. When he discarded the ace of hearts, I gobbled it up and added it to my queen and king. I had one card left.

"You stink," he muttered.

"You don't listen. Do you realize that's the third time you threw down the ace of hearts tonight? Every time you threw it down, someone picked it up and used it. Do you detect a pattern here? Listen, and I'll say it in English: don't throw down face cards unless it's absolutely your last resort."

"Shut your head."

"Fine."

We played for a while longer, joking around and enjoying the sense of solidarity we all shared. One of my friends—I think it was Jeb—came up with an idea.

"We should form a club. A card-playing club."

"Why?" I asked. I now questioned everything whether I agreed with it or not.

"So we could have tournaments and stuff. Maybe we could even make it interesting." By "make it interesting," Jeb meant we could gamble. The seeds Nick had planted long ago had only now begun to sprout in earnest. My friends loved to gamble, and I was starting to become more interested in it myself. We only gambled among ourselves, and hardly ever for money, but it was gambling just the same. I was sure my father wouldn't like a club based on gambling.

"Sure. That sounds good," I said.

"What do we call it?" Mo asked. "A good club has to have a good name."

"Yeah," Perry added. "Like that country club—what's it called? Oh, yeah—Cedar Crest. We need a name like that. What are you smirking at?"

"Nothing," I said, choking back laughter.

"Nothing," he said scornfully. "You look like a fox in a henhouse. Do you have an idea for the name?"

"I sure do."

"Well, what is it?"

"I don't think you'll like it."

By now, my other two friends were also curious and clamored for me to reveal the idea. "All right, all right. Are you ready?"

"We're ready."

"Gentlemen, I salute you as charter members of…the Ace of Hearts Club!" I pantomimed a trumpet blast and two of my friends laughed. The third sulked.

"Oh, come on, Perry. You know you stink at cards. It's an honor to have a club named after you," Jeb consoled.

"Are we in agreement?" I asked.

Jeb and Mo shouted, "Yeah," and Perry mumbled a "whatever," then smiled and gave in. He was always eager to please, sometimes *too* eager, as I would later learn.

We finished the hand and then discussed the guidelines and rules of the club. We would meet every Wednesday night. We'd draw up a schedule as to what games we'd play, what stakes we'd offer, and who we'd invite into the club.

"I suppose we should invite Nick to be a member," said Mo.

"Why?" I asked with a snip in my voice.

"I dunno. He's your brother, after all."

"How many times do I have to tell you guys? Nick is not my brother!"

They raised their hands in surrender and immediately dropped the subject. I was irritated that Mo had even brought it up. Everyone knew that Nick wasn't even welcome in the tree house, let alone in any club that might be formed there. I remembered my father's ominous warning about boarding school, and I'd intended to strike some kind of balance with Nick. In the end, though, I just couldn't do it. I couldn't even look at him without grimacing. In my heart, I guess I never believed that Dad would really send me away. I let my friends form the club, and assured myself that I'd get away with excluding Nick.

After about a half hour of planning, Jeb and Perry made a show of checking their watches.

"What's the matter?" I asked. "You guys got a date?"

They both laughed and exchanged a conspiratorial glance. "Nope. You do," they said together.

"What? What do you mean?"

"We asked Diane to drop by."

"Drop by? You mean, come up to the tree house? You guys need to grow up."

"We *are* growing up; that's why we invited her. You know she likes you. Why do you think she's always hanging around over here after school?"

"She likes everyone."

"Yeah, but she *especially* likes you." This sentence was delivered with clasped hands, fluttering eyelashes, and effeminate voices.

I shuffled the cards and pretended not to care. "I got better things to do, and better people to do them with." That didn't come out quite the way I'd intended, and it didn't fool my friends anyway. They could tell by the flush in my ears that I was secretly excited. Girls had become the topic of some interest among us boys. Sometimes they were even discussed at greater length than the most recent baseball game or fishing trip. I wondered just how interested Diane was in me, anyway. She had a reputation for being fickle, and I...

"Hi, guys."

How had she gotten up that rope ladder without my hearing her? That's what girls did to you, though. They dulled your important senses and unnaturally excited others. Diane certainly qualified as exciting. She was looking decidedly more like a girl than she had a couple of years ago. Her hair was a long, lustrous brown and was no longer hidden under a cap. Her eyes matched her hair and thick lashes and elegantly curved eyebrows adorned them. Instead of an ill-fitting baseball glove, she carried a black leather purse, that mysterious carryall which no man ever truly understands. Jeans and a blouse had replaced her dirty overalls, and she wore perfume—some kind of musk—as well as small diamond earrings. The overall effect was intoxicating.

"Hi, Diane," we all said, a united chorus of budding teenage masculinity.

"Come on in, make yourself at home," I said.

"No earwigs, right, Jake?" Her eyes twinkled. She looked pretty. This was bad.

"Uh, no, I haven't had any problem with those for quite a while."

"Maybe it's time for some curtains, then."

"Yeah, maybe."

My three friends decided it was time for them to leave and began to politely excuse themselves for the evening. I was facing the door of the tree house as Perry's head disappeared over the side. The last thing I saw was his hand, the thumb upraised in a salute. I grinned, and then I turned around and gave my full attention to Diane.

She was seated comfortably on the well-worn beanbag chair, and she looked a lot more at ease than I felt. I sat in one of the card chairs, and we talked about things like school, cars, and sports.

Diane and I had been seeing a lot of each other lately. She was a cheerleader and was quite popular at the local high school. Phil, a friend of mine who attended the same school, had introduced us. He promptly proclaimed (to my great embarrassment) that Diane and I were perfect for each other. She and I had never been on an actual date, but she usually wandered over to my house after school. We talked, sometimes leaning against Mr. Modau's rickety old fence, sometimes in our hayloft, sometimes on the short dock at Kent's Pond. I was fascinated by the way Diane tossed her hair, by the way she laughed, by the way she gestured with her long, slender fingers. She knew I was drawn to her, and the rumor was beginning to circulate that we were an "item."

That night in the tree house, after we'd covered all the usual topics of conversation, she finally gave up waiting for me to make the first move.

"Jake, what do you say we dim the lights?"

I swallowed audibly and hoped she hadn't noticed. I'd never kissed a girl, and I was fairly certain that was what she had in mind. I was desperate to make a good impression. I wasn't in love or even close to it, but I knew this was an important moment, and I didn't want to mess it up.

"Okay," I said. Simple words are best, or at least I hoped that was true. I flicked off the light switch and quickly glanced across the yard. I could just make out Dad's slippered feet through the family room window, so he was safely in his chair, relaxing by the fire. I assumed Mom was with Dad, and Nick knew better than to tell Dad what went on in the tree house. We'd have some privacy, at least for another half hour or so.

The moon was just short of full, so there was some natural light streaming through the windows. Diane waited silently on the beanbag and I made my way over to her and sat down. It was very cozy and warm, and before I knew it, she wrapped her arms around me, and I experienced my first kiss.

My first thought was less than romantic. *She tastes funny.*

I enjoyed the physical sensation of the kiss. She had thoroughly agreeable lips, and I had dreamed of a moment like this for a long time.

Still, I couldn't quite place that taste, probably because she was trying to mask it with spearmint gum.

After we had turned our heads several times and tried all the usual variations, we pulled away from each other slightly. She smiled.

"Not bad, Jake. You kiss even better than I thought."

"Thanks," I replied, then added as an afterthought, "You look nice tonight." *Oh, real smooth, Jake.*

She didn't seem to mind my verbal clumsiness. She leaned closer, and we kissed again with the awkward intensity that was typical of our age.

"I like you, Jake. Do you want to go with me?"

"Sure. Where?"

She giggled. "No, I mean, do you want to go steady?"

"Uh, sure." Steady? We hadn't even been on a date yet; now I had a girlfriend? Well, I guessed that was okay.

"What are you doing?" She was fumbling for something in her purse.

"I'm just getting a cigarette. Want one?"

That was it! I'd never tried cigarettes myself, but I couldn't stand them. I hated the smell, I didn't like the way people looked when they smoked, and (I had just discovered) I despised the way they made girls taste.

Diane had asked a question and I had only a few seconds to make an important decision: did her charms outweigh the smoking? I wasn't deciding whether or not to smoke; I had settled that issue long ago. The question was whether I wanted to date a girl who tasted like an ashtray. I looked at her face. Illuminated by the moonlight, she possessed a mysterious, almost hypnotic power. My decision was not totally free of conflict, but I made it quickly.

"No thanks. You go ahead, though."

"Sure you don't want to try one? They're menthol."

Menthol. Wasn't that something they put in cough syrup and chest rub?

I heard a click, saw a small flame, and noticed that in that flickering orange light, Diane didn't look quite as good as she had a moment ago. Then the flame was gone, and the moonlight reasserted itself.

My nose burned as the pungent smoke filled the tree house. If Dad saw or smelled it, he would be furious. I didn't want to lose my tree house privileges, especially not now after the formation of the Ace of Hearts Club. I found myself suddenly wishing that Diane would leave.

We continued to chat as she finished her cigarette, then kissed good night to seal our newly agreed upon relationship. Yuck. I lingered in the tree house for a little while, thinking about the busy evening I'd had. We'd established the Ace of Hearts Club, and that was good. I had experienced my first kiss, and that, too, was pretty good. I had a girl-friend who smoked. That was not good. I was both excited and weary, and I wondered what I had gotten myself into as I climbed down from the tree house and grabbed a cookie on the way up to my room.

Chapter Thirteen

"Soft drink, sir?"

I looked up at the flight attendant, then at her cart with its wide array of beverages. I managed a smile, but it must have looked forced. "Ginger ale, please."

The attendant popped the tab, poured the drink, and set it in front of me.

"First time on a plane, sir?"

"Second. Is it that obvious?"

"You're doing fine." She gave me a reassuring smile and asked my seatmate if she would like a beverage. The passenger next to me in 19B was an intelligent but quirky woman named Ruth. She was a grandmother in her early fifties who had two disconcerting habits: one, she ceaselessly chomped on a wad of gum, and two, she hardly ever stopped talking.

Most of Ruth's comments were inconsequential bits of small talk. At first I wished she would pipe down, but after a while I found myself actually wondering what she would say next. During the last hour I'd been updated on recent world events with short, raspy little bursts of information. "Didja hear that Joey Banks and his wife—what's her name, uh, Lisa something or other—are splitting up? They were on that sitcom together. Yeah, it's a shame. Everyone saw it coming, though." Or, "Do you play the stock market, Jake? No? A young man like you…" Or, more relevant to my situation, "What do you think about the educational system? This article talks about public education and how more and more people are home schooling now. You've been to school—do you think we learn more in a structured setting or in a loose setting?"

I enjoyed chatting with her. Ruth's easy way of jumping from topic to topic helped to distract me from the terrors of air travel. I'd told her an abbreviated version of my story and mentioned my distaste for airplanes. She reassured me that air travel was "safer than crossing the street," but I was still looking forward to the sound of the landing gear touching down on the runway.

Now my seatmate lifted her plastic cup of seltzer water and offered a toast. "Here's to getting home in one piece, Jake."

I laughed as we touched glasses. "I'll drink to that!"

At first, the Ace of Hearts Club was a huge success. After only two weeks, I was forced to increase the frequency of its meetings to accommodate the growing membership. Part of the attraction of the club was the poker games we played. We were still using baseball cards as currency, but they were worth a lot of money and offered the additional benefit of being easily scattered. If my dad made an unexpected appearance, they looked like a pile of innocent collectibles over which we had been comparing notes.

The card games passed the time after dinner, and that was vitally important to me now that I no longer spent the evening hours with my family. I knew that my absences pained my mother and father but they never nagged me about it. Every so often, they would ask if I'd like to join them for some coffee or a board game, but I always declined. I refused to share my place with Nick and retreated instead into the waiting branches of the oak tree.

Unfortunately, my tree house felt less like a refuge and more like a prison every day. For one thing, it had become crowded. There were sometimes as many as eight boys crammed into the tree house when club meetings were in session, and my friends and I had grown a few inches since the tree house had been built. For another thing, it was laden with memories of happier days. Its newly added curtains didn't help, either. They'd been Diane's idea to afford us more privacy, but because of her, they smelled like smoke.

Nick added an extra element of irritation to my evening activities. Whenever we convened a meeting of the Ace of Hearts Club, we would inevitably hear someone ascending the rope ladder. Next, Nick's head would appear over the side of the porch. He'd shout a greeting, which we generally ignored (one of the requirements for membership in the club was that you had to despise Nick as much as I did).

Despite the heartless creature I had become, I found it difficult to bear his looks of rejection. To further compound my guilt, Nick never told my father about the way I treated him. Whenever we dismissed and excluded him, he would simply leave. I grew to hate the creaking sound of the rope ladder as Nick descended. That sound seemed to represent both an opportunity and a condemnation. All I had to do was call out to Nick and invite him to come back up. I never did. Instead, I listened, transfixed by that sound, and let him leave, dejected and angry.

After Nick's attempted visits, I would usually lose the next two or three hands, laboring under a burden of frustration and guilt, until I remembered that it was he who had driven me to hide in the tree like a cockroach that scurries for cover when the light is turned on.

As time passed, my friends grew weary of Nick's intrusive attempts to join the club. It didn't matter that he was a good card player and would have contributed a fresh element to the somewhat monotonous ritual of shuffle, deal, play; what mattered was that I became irritable whenever he was around. In the interest of having enjoyable club meetings, someone suggested that we post a sign outside the clubhouse door. The suggestion gained support as the gang discussed it behind fists full of deuces, jacks, and kings, but I didn't care either way. I knew that sign or no sign, Nick would continue to appear in the vain hope of one day being welcomed into the club. I concentrated on my cards and let them blabber about it. Mal spoke up.

"What do you think, Jake?"

"About what?"

"About the *sign*. It should be simple, yet forceful."

"I think you should be quiet, yet silent. Can we play some cards here? I got a Carlton Fisk riding on this hand."

"Take a break for a second, will ya? This is important."

I slammed down my cards. "Make the sign, don't make the sign—I don't care! He's gonna come up anyway, you all know that."

There were mumbles of mild protest at my outburst, but we continued playing without further incident.

My friends wasted no time in implementing their plan. The next night, Mo proudly presented our club's official sign. They had created it on a computer and it proclaimed in big, black letters:

ACE OF HEARTS CLUB
Admittance to club meetings
is allowed to members or
BY INVITATION ONLY

I read the sign and had a terrible, uneasy feeling. There was something fundamentally wrong with it. To exclude someone for no good reason was bad enough; to put it in writing somehow made it worse.

"Hey, that's great," I said.

They tacked the sign to the tree house, directly under the window on the opposite side of the mailbox. They reasoned that Nick would see it when he came up, but it would not be visible from the house. We began the game—it was seven-card stud that night—and waited for the creak of the ladder. For some reason, it was a long time coming. We'd gone through five hands and still no Nick. I was restless. Poker was a risky game to play because there's only one use for poker chips. If Dad made a sudden appearance, the Ace of Hearts Club could very well be disbanded. In addition, I was anxious about how Nick would respond to this latest act of exclusion.

After the sixth hand, we all got up to stretch. I casually leaned out the window, pretending to grab a breath of fresh night air, and spotted two pairs of feet through the family room window. I couldn't see much more than that, but one glimpse was enough. Nick and Dad were talking. Maybe they were even sharing some cider or fresh lemonade. I didn't care. Let them drink their stupid drinks and have their stupid conversation. It would be a shame if Nick got a lemon seed caught in his throat. I remembered that Mom never left the seeds in her lemonade, and my mood grew even blacker.

We played later than usual because it was Friday night. Finally, after we'd switched games to thirty-one, I heard the rope ladder make its telltale sound. Nick's head appeared, and the greeting froze on his lips. He had seen the sign. I didn't look up, but I heard the pain in his voice.

"I don't care, you jerks! I hope your stupid tree house falls right out of the sky, with all of you in it." *Creak, creak, creak, creak, thump.* And Nick was gone. My friends laughed and I with them. Never have I uttered a more false, insincere sound. I hated who I had become and would have done just about anything to reverse my actions. Just about anything.

My father eventually found out about the club and the sign, of course, and he let me know about it in his usual fashion. I climbed up to the tree house after dinner one night. I wanted to take down the curtains and run them under the hose in the hopes of purging the horrible smell of smoke from the house. As I reached the top of the ladder, I noticed that there was something in my mailbox.

The miniature white box was a replica of our farmhouse's mailbox, which had always fascinated me as a boy. I'd loved the seemingly magical way an empty metal box seemed to generate a daily stream of letters, magazines, and packages. Dad used to let me pull the handle, retrieve the contents, and present the mail to my waiting mother.

Mailboxes, like everything else around our farm, were reminders of better days. I leaned over and looked.

There were two pears inside.

No note, no explanation, just two ripe pieces of pale green fruit.

On closer examination, I discovered I was wrong—one was a quince, the other was a pear. I knelt down on the porch as the shadows lengthened. The sun fled from my growing rage and disappeared below the western horizon, and the farm hid its face in the darkness. Two similar pieces of fruit, two very different boys. The quince belonged on the tree, but the pear was a cheap freeloader that should have grown from its own tree. I hefted the two pieces of fruit, one in my left hand, one in my right. My already strained self-control was insufficient against this insulting object lesson. I stood up and hurled the pear with all my strength onto the floor of the tree house porch. It splattered my legs as it smashed into small, wet chunks. I switched the quince to my other hand, brought it to my lips and took a bite. Bitter. How fitting.

Before entering the tree house that had now become a prison, I dropped the quince. It rolled through the remains of its fallen companion before plummeting over the side and hitting the ground with a dull, final *thump*.

It was one of my least favorite places on campus. From the outside it seemed inoffensive enough—the same clapboard gray as just about every other building, the same low roof and security-screened windows. Yet the stenciled sign on the door branded this building as an unwelcome reminder of my abandonment here: "Post Office."

I'd been assigned a mailbox when I arrived at school, but I didn't imagine that the letters would be pouring in from home. I was correct. During my first year I received only eight letters, and they seemed obligatory, meant merely to pass on information. They were all written by my dad and contained spending money for unanticipated expenses, news about the farm, and general affirmations.

At first, I was angry. It was bad enough that I had been banished; now I had to endure these vague, noncommittal letters that served only to increase my already unbearable sense of isolation. As time passed, however, I admitted that I was more lonely than angry. The envelopes from home could never deliver the thing I needed most: Dad's reassuring presence, his warm smile, his wry sense of humor.

I hated looking into my mailbox week after week and seeing nothing but empty space. Unfortunately, it was impossible to avoid the post office. Our weekly schedule was delivered to our mailbox, and I quickly learned that to deviate in any way from that document was to invite swift, harsh punishment. Actually, the innocuous-sounding term used by the faculty was "appropriate disciplinary action." I suspected that if people knew how Ashur-Kesed defined "appropriate" there would be a sharp decrease in enrollment and an avalanche of legal action.

So, here I was again at Box 1697. While the rest of the students occasionally got mail from the outside world—letters, approved magazines, and sometimes even care packages from home—I collected my single envelope without bothering to look for any other correspondence. I withdrew the schedule and quickly examined it. My classes never changed, but my biweekly work assignments did. I couldn't help but smile when I saw the first notation.

I had been assigned to lawn detail for three rotations in a row. The staff member responsible for scheduling had either forgotten or was unaware that I came from a farm. Under ordinary circumstances, the administration would never dispense a work assignment that a student would actually enjoy. I glanced over the remainder of my schedule, just to be sure there were no changes.

Nope. Everything was the same as always. I'd read as far as the lunch period when I heard a rustling sound in front of me. I glanced up. The mailroom worker was still sorting the morning mail and placing it into the slots. Strange; it sounded as though he had...

There was a letter in my mailbox.

I leaned down to take a better look—and there it was. It had to be a mistake. I grabbed it and read the box number, thinking he'd put it in my mailbox by mistake. I looked around and tried to remain casual as I examined the address. To my surprise, I found that there had been no mistake. The letter was for me.

There was no return address and my name and box number had been laser printed onto a label, defying identification. I supposed it could be from home, but Dad always hand-labeled his letters. I also noticed something else out of the ordinary—the envelope hadn't been opened. All correspondence that entered or left the academy was subject to the school censors. Their primary goal was to ensure that "no correspondence that violates the principles, tenets, restrictions, or guidelines of Ashur-Kesed" ever got through. How had this letter escaped examination?

I tucked the letter into my jacket pocket and waited in line until we were dismissed. I wanted to tear it open and read it on the spot, but I didn't want to draw attention to the fact that I rarely received word from home. It was Friday, and after dinner we were given two hours to study followed by one hour of in-barracks liberty. The only way to ensure my privacy was to wait until then to open and read the letter.

Dinner in the crowded mess hall seemed to drag on, and the two hours of study seemed to take forever. Finally, we were back in our barracks and I surreptitiously opened the envelope and placed the letter in one of my books. I pretended to read the book as my eyes raced over the letter. I was both disappointed and excited. The letter was not from Dad or from anyone else outside the school. The letter had come from Elise. I wondered why she had bothered to mail it when all of her previous communiqués had been slipped under my pillow or passed on through other students. The message was characteristically short:

Jake,

The weather's great this time of year. I enjoyed the unexpected warm front last spring. There are more in the forecast. By the way, one of the best ways to get a letter is to write a letter.

Soon, E.

I admired her style. She'd written in code, so she knew about the practice of censoring, yet the letter hadn't been censored or even opened. That was odd.

I assumed that the reference to warmth had to do with our first meeting the previous spring, and I smiled at that. Warm front, indeed.

I was also stumped by her last sentence. It had to be a coincidence. How could she possibly have known that I yearned for some word from home? I had shared much with her the night we met, but I hadn't said anything directly about the lack of any significant correspondence between my family and me. It seemed as though she were advising me to write home, as if she suspected that once I made the first move, my family would reciprocate.

I lay on my bunk, pondering the letter. With nothing else to do, I decided that I might as well take Elise's advice. I took a sheet of note-paper out of my binder and began to write. My letter home covered only one side of the page, but it was a start. I shared what little news I had, avoided any hint of negativity, and respectfully reiterated my desire to return home. I signed the letter and placed it in an envelope. Tomorrow I would drop it in the mail and see what happened.

Writing home inevitably caused me to think about my brother, and I wondered how Nick was doing. Did he remember that Princess tended to wander? Did he keep the henhouse clean? Was he taking good care of Skipper? I wondered if he thought about me. I hadn't even had the chance to apologize in person for the horrible thing I'd done to him, and for all my other offenses.

It also occurred to me that in all the chaos surrounding his adoption, I'd forgotten my promise to help ease his guilt over his parents' death. I had the considerable research facilities of the school at my disposal three nights a week; perhaps I could uncover some information here that would free him from his past. I could never make up for the way I'd mistreated Nick, but perhaps I had found a way to demonstrate my change of heart.

As the Ace of Hearts Club flourished and my hostility toward my family increased, I was continually confronted with my father's disapproval. Dad didn't like my attitude, my actions, or my friends. I told him that made us even—I didn't care for his choice of adopted sons, either. He was impossible to provoke, but that particular bit of disrespect cost me an inordinate amount of weekend freedom. There were many more such incidents. Our once-peaceful farm had become a domestic battlefield.

One day, without a word of warning, Dad appeared at the door of my tree house. I was startled by his ability to approach completely unheard and made a mental note to be more vigilant. Jeb, Cannon, and I had been playing blackjack. The game was innocent enough, but it wouldn't do to have Dad poking his head through the door when I was up there with Diane.

Dad stooped to enter and greeted my friends before addressing me.

"Jake, could you spare a minute? There's something I'd like to show you."

I sighed in disgust, risking his anger, but told the guys I would see them later. Dad and I descended, and he led me out to the massive woodpile where we stacked the logs for our stove and fireplace. Was my father going to have me carry wood into the house? Couldn't that have waited?

Imposing more chores upon me was not Dad's intention. He knelt in the dark soil behind the woodpile and pointed out a small mound of dirt. An anthill? He must be kidding.

"Dad, with all due respect…"

"Jake, I'm your father. If you understood the word *respect*, you'd look, listen, and learn."

Dad was patient, but when he sounded like that, it was best to submit. I closed my mouth and knelt beside the anthill. "Notice anything strange about this hill?" he asked.

I examined the nest. There was something unusual going on. Ants are usually the most industrious of creatures, but many of these ants appeared lazy. They were simply lying around the entrance to the anthill as others marched past on various errands. My natural curiosity briefly took over.

"What's going on? Did you spray them or something?"

Dad looked grim. "No, son. The anthill's been invaded. The trouble is, they don't even know it." My Dad sat back and looked out over the vast fields where we'd spent countless hours working, talking, and enjoying one another's company. "You see, there's a certain species of beetle that is able to release a pheromone that smells just like an ant's."

I found it fascinating that a beetle could duplicate ant pheromones so well, but I wasn't ignorant of my father's techniques. He had summoned me from the tree house for a reason. It wasn't ants he was concerned with; it was me.

"Once the beetle gains entrance into the hill by emitting the pheromone, it settles in. The ants don't attack it because it 'smells' just like them. The beetle begins to produce an intoxicating liquid that the ants can't resist. Soon they begin to neglect their young, which the beetle obligingly eats, and the ants either fight among themselves for the liquid or just lay around, inactive and unaware of the danger they're in. One beetle can destroy an entire nest, son, leaving behind disorder and death." My father paused, then did something he rarely did: he explained the lesson.

"Jake, some of your friends look and act as if they truly are friends, but they're affecting you in ways you're not even aware of. They're encouraging you to do things you never would have considered doing two years ago. Worse, you're not much of an example to them, either. You've changed, son, and not just in regards to your brother. You no longer care to spend time with your mother and me, you don't put the same effort into your work around the farm, and I know you're not happy about the person you've become. I'd like to help."

Dad was right about my unhappiness, but I found myself strangely unaffected by his lesson.

When crops are planted, most of the seeds fall on the fertile soil of the field, but some fall on the footpath beside the field. Those seeds bounce off the hard-packed dirt and never produce a crop because the birds come along and eat them.

That afternoon, as Dad and I knelt by the anthill, his words bounced off my heart the same way those seeds bounced off the path. Even worse, the birds were out. By the time Dad had finished speaking, it was as if he had never spoken at all. I found myself growing impatient, eager to return to my little anthill so I could play with the beetles. What a fool I had become.

"Am I dismissed?" I asked.

Dad's face was often unreadable, but that day I saw sorrow in his eyes. He remained seated in the soil and indicated that I was free to go.

I got up, brushed off my jeans, and walked away. His words followed me: "I'll be here, son." I wanted to turn around, but the beetles had done their work well. I kept walking and left my father alone by the woodpile.

A week or two passed, and that's when I found his letter. I had just climbed the rope ladder when I caught sight of an envelope protruding from my mailbox. The envelope it contained that day was addressed with a single name—Jake—and I was happily surprised as I tore it open. I thought it might be from Diane or from one of my other friends. I read the simple message, and felt my face go slack. It wasn't a pleasant greeting or a love letter; it was an intrusion. It was another poisoned arrow from my father's quiver, drawn back with full strength and released directly into my already wounded heart. The message was short and simple, and written in Dad's distinctive handwriting:

Jake,

I have a suggestion. Why don't you call it the "Far-Away Hearts Club" instead? That's a better name for a club that excludes some, hurts others, and alienates the rest. We miss you, son.

Dad

I stared at the letter in the fading light of the day before crumpling it up and tossing it into the corner of the tree house. Far-Away Hearts

Club. Very clever. Very funny.

I sat down, shuffled the cards, and awaited my friends' arrival. As an afterthought, I hung the Ace of Hearts Club sign on the door of the tree house. I pretended that Dad's letter hadn't bothered me, but in reality, I was haunted by it. I left it crumpled up on the floor and couldn't bring myself to discard it, even as I rebelled against its message.

Chapter Fourteen

"Hey, scum, how'd you pull that easy duty?"

I sighed as I shifted into neutral and turned to face Sam, one of the most dreaded students at Ashur-Kesed.

I had been in the midst of my assigned lawn work. Although there was hardly any grass on the campus proper, there were two large athletic fields where we did our morning exercises and sometimes played rugby or soccer, if we cared to use our liberty passes for that purpose. I had been driving the school tractor back and forth along the length of the north field, enjoying the sun and fresh air. The tractor, similar to the one I had driven twice a week at home, vibrated heartily beneath me. Of all the days for Sam to harass me...

"Hello? Anyone home?" Sam growled impatiently.

I responded with the proper etiquette. Sam did not look happy, and it was wise to be extra cautious around him—even when he *was* happy. "Uh, Upperclassman, I assume I was chosen because of my farming background, sir." Right etiquette, wrong answer.

"You assume, huh? What about the school motto?

"No rest, no weakness, no regrets!" I shouted, desperately wishing he would go away.

"Right. Did I catch you reminiscing about the olden days, John Boy? Get off that machine! We can't have your skinny butt relaxing while other more worthy students get stuck with menial labor. I'll mow, while you run behind me and pick up the clippings—by hand."

I set the brakes and climbed down with an air of resignation. Sam was a perpetual agent of misery and possessed a dangerous combination of height, muscle, and a complete disregard for consequences. In addition to bowling over anyone who got in his way, he plagued everyone with ridiculous riddles. If Sam posed a riddle and you couldn't answer it, you would "owe" him a liberty pass or some other precious commodity. If you somehow managed to answer the riddle, he would fabricate a different answer and you would still owe him. He had no trouble enforcing his directives, and since the staff of Ashur-Kesed never interfered with anything that promoted an increased level of fear, Sam was free to engage in his activities more or less unhindered by the administration. (In fact, on one occasion when Sam was tossing me around the Hub courtyard like a rag doll, I saw Vice-Chancellor Senna part the curtains of his office, smile, and calmly return to whatever he had been doing.)

Still, I wasn't afraid that day, not really. With the regular encouragement of my friends, I was shaken less and less by the various torments and harassments I was forced to endure. They had given me hope—hope that I was valuable after all, hope that failure doesn't have to be permanent.

I was able to face Sam with a calm, steady assurance. I remained respectfully silent.

"What's the matter?" Sam asked as he boarded the tractor. "Has all the fresh air made your tongue stick to the roof of your mouth?" He laughed broadly, then eyed the controls.

I knew in an instant that he'd never driven a tractor. His overconfidence visibly melted into fierce concentration as he realized he had only a few seconds to convince me that he knew what he was doing. I foresaw the error he was about to make and opened my mouth to shout a warning. As was often the case at AKPS, my warning came too late.

Sam correctly surmised that the tractor had a manual transmission. What he didn't realize was that the controls for each front tire were separate; therefore, he only released one of the parking brakes. When he engaged the clutch, cranked the motor and leaned forward on the throttle, the tractor sprang to life and immediately began to spin in a furious circle. Sam was thrown to his right as I scrambled to get out of the way. He made a valiant effort, but inertia took over and hurled him off the side. Fortunately for him (depending on one's point of view), his belt caught on the fender and he was dragged along the ground in a recumbent position, his legs pumping furiously in the air as he tried to free himself. Sam strained to keep his head and back away from the ground, but, even with his considerable strength, the power of the tractor was winning out.

If I'd had to think about what to do, it would have been too late. I ran around the tractor, getting a feel for its speed, then jumped into the seat and grabbed the steering bars. Leaning to the left to counter the centrifugal force, I slowly pushed on the left control bar while releasing the right emergency brake. I eased down on the brakes as soon as I was able. The tractor came to a stop, and I turned off the engine and pocketed the key. I jumped down to help free Sam.

Sam was okay and he proved it by calling me a number of colorful names. He was lying on his back with his legs up in the air, still attached to the fender. In that position, I thought he looked a little like an Apollo astronaut reclining in the command capsule—except for the mud and grass stains. I couldn't help but chuckle at that thought, which sent Sam into a fresh tirade. I knelt down and tried to assist him.

"Will you stay still for a minute? Your belt's caught," I said.

"When I get loose, I'm gonna run your face over with this tractor!" Sam said.

"Really? That doesn't give me much incentive to help you, does it?"

"You'll help me, farmer freaky. You'll help me or I'll…" Sam's lower body fell to the ground as I finally succeeded in freeing his belt. As he fell, his tailbone struck the edge of the fender, and I winced on his behalf. He screamed in anger, leveled another volley of crude names at me, and leaped to his feet. He fell just as quickly to his knees, grabbing at the small of his back.

"What did you do to me? Why does it…" His questions dissolved into howls of pain.

"What did *I* do to you?" I shook my head. "You hop onto a tractor you've never driven before, nearly get yourself killed, and then ask the person who saved your life what he did to you." I suddenly remembered my own accident with my father's truck and had an inspiration: why not follow Nick's example? It was a long shot, but worth the attempt. I addressed my would-be tormentor, who was still clutching his back. "I'll show you what I *will* do for you."

With that, I threw myself to the ground and rolled around until I had stained my own uniform with grass and soil. Sam seemed to forget his discomfort and watched my gyrations with an amazed, comical expression. When I had finished, I stood and helped him up. His back was fine, despite all the noise he'd made. He waited for me to explain, and I plunged ahead quickly.

"Your barracks commander will ask about those stains," I said. "You were teaching me the fine points of wrestling. I lost." I hoped he would understand.

Sam opened his mouth to speak, closed it, opened it, and then closed it again. He understood perfectly, but was having a hard time accepting the fact that someone whom he had so often victimized would now offer him a chance to save face. He wore the look of someone who never offered mercy to others, and who therefore could not recognize it when it was extended to him. Dad's oft-repeated words from my childhood were simple, yet powerful: *An act of kindness can turn the worst enemy into a best friend.* It was a lesson that Nick had learned before I had; a lesson he'd practiced one day as I lay unconscious by the side of a creek.

Sam ended up not saying anything at all. He simply turned and walked away, limping slightly. I shook my head, not really surprised but trying not to be judgmental. After all, I hadn't responded to my brother's gesture either, at least not at first. It had been worth a try. Sam would have made a powerful ally.

I climbed back up onto the tractor and prepared to resume my lawn work. *You're welcome,* I said to myself as the tractor roared back to life.

Sam turned out to be grateful after all.

One of the benefits of being an upperclassman of his stature and physical strength was that he could choose his friends with little fear of reprisal. Sam chose to announce his friendship for me one day after morning calisthenics.

In its typically sadistic fashion, the faculty of Ashur-Kesed scheduled physical education first thing in the morning. The bell roused us as always. We changed quickly into our singlets and athletic shoes, and rushed through a breakfast of thick, buttered bread, strong coffee, and two hard-boiled eggs. From breakfast, we marched out to the south athletic field, where Mr. Paroh waited.

Mr. Paroh fancied himself a drill sergeant but employed methods that would shock his military counterparts. He was unrivalled in the areas of verbal abuse and the relentless infliction of pain. He pushed us so hard that we regularly feared our hearts would burst in our chests. We did standard training camp exercises: jumping jacks, sprints, sit-ups, push-ups, and the hated leg lifts, plus torturous little modifications that often drove us to the brink of unconsciousness. All the while Mr. Paroh would bombard us with an unending stream of insults, and I was often repulsed by his perverse creativity. His square jaw constantly gnawed at an unlit cigar, even when his lips parted to blow maniacally on his whistle. He would only light his cigar when he had tortured us to his heart's content, grouped us into sweating, gasping lines, and shouted out the words we'd waited all morning to hear: "Sissies, dismissed!"

One morning about a week or two after I rescued Sam from his own ineptitude, Sam shocked me by standing next to me in line. That was unprecedented. The various cliques at AKPS never fraternized with each other, and Sam and I belonged to two completely different groups. What was he doing next to me? I assumed he was planning to cheat me out of a liberty pass with one of his absurd riddles, but I didn't dare ask him. If either of us spoke, Paroh would order us to do push-ups until our elbows gave out. At any rate, my leg ached that morning, and I was in no mood for Sam's little games.

Mr. Paroh stalked up and down the long line of students, assessing our level of preparedness and making sure we were all attired according to the dress code. We stood there, side by side, our hands behind our backs in the "parade rest" position, while the pleasant strains of one of our instructor's favorite songs drifted over to us. Mr. Paroh sang while the rest of us responded:

"You're a bunch of slimy worms!"
"We're a bunch of slimy worms!"
"You're past the point of no return!"

"We're past the point of no return!"
"You are losers, there's no doubt!"
"We are losers, there's no doubt!"
"You're gonna run till you pass out!"
"We're gonna run till we pass out!"

Oh, great. Running. Just the thing to transform the throb in my leg to full-blown agony. We jogged off in the direction of the quarter-mile cinder track, and Sam stuck to me like glue. We all ran until we were snorting like racehorses. Afterward, we struggled through our standing exercises until finally we were dismissed.

I understood why Sam had shadowed me all morning when we returned to the locker rooms. The showers were communal, adding humiliation to the morning's regime of suffering. Since the officers didn't enter the bathrooms with us, the showers were often the site of acts of malice or revenge. One of my classmates had widely publicized that today "the farm boy would get what was coming to him." I'd known about the threat, but I was tired of running from trouble. I intended to stand up to the bully and hope for the best.

We filed into the large bathroom and took our turns in the shower. The hot water felt great after the raw morning air. As I was drying myself, I suddenly felt the sharp snap of a towel on my backside. I let out an involuntary yelp, to the great delight of my tormenter and his cronies.

The towel-snapper's name was Spencer. He was a well-built second-degree upperclassman (the equivalent of a junior in regular high schools), and he was just getting started. "So, farm boy, you think you're better than us 'losers' in 794? You think it's funny to pass a literature exam when the rest of us fail it? Well, strap on the plow, boy. It's time to go to school…"

It was a typically petty reason to harass me. I prepared to defend myself, but a strong hand on my shoulder pushed me aside. It was Sam, and his response to Spencer's threat was swift and ferocious. He attacked Spencer, dragged him into the shower, and thrust Spencer under the nozzle. Sam twisted the knob to the left and steam began to billow out into the locker room. Spencer struggled as the water reached dangerously hot temperatures, but Sam's tree-trunk biceps barely twitched as he maintained his hold. Sam shouted with all his strength, and his reverberated words sent an unmistakable message: "No one messes with Jake. *IS THAT CLEAR?*" Spencer nodded vigorously. When Sam released him, he scurried out of harm's way. Everyone in the locker room laughed uproariously at the unexpected entertainment. At Ashur-Kesed, this was the average student's idea of a great way to begin the day.

I understood what Sam had done, and I marveled once again at the complexity of school politics. He couldn't simply announce that he and I were friends—that would have made him look weak. Instead, Sam had proclaimed his friendship for me in a language that was spoken fluently at school: physical force. I glanced at him and thanked him with my eyes.

"This is it," Ruth said with an exaggerated tremor in her voice. "They say that the most dangerous parts of air travel are the takeoffs and landings. Hold on tight, kid." She grasped the arms of her seat and pretended to be frightened, contorting her face into an expression more akin to indigestion than to the terror I felt. As an afterthought she assumed the voice of a flight attendant and added, "Keep in mind that in the event of a water landing, your seat cushions will have absolutely no value except to give the sharks a nasty case of foam poisoning. Not that I'd care about that, mind you. If a shark has the bad manners to eat a defenseless crash victim, he deserves whatever he gets, right? Anyway, we're not even over water so it's a moot point. I love the beach, Jake, don't you? You make sure and take your lady over to Virginia Beach, buy her a nice dinner and tell her that Ruthie got you through one of the worst air disasters in history. But don't take her swimming." Ruth leaned in close and whispered through clenched teeth, "Sharrrks!"

I laughed in spite of my efforts to concentrate on my fear. How did I get seated next to this lovable maniac? I both pitied and admired her husband, who was, coincidentally, a farmer.

When I recovered and looked up, the plane was on the ground.

I looked at Ruth with a mixture of admiration and gratitude. She was innocently freshening up her lipstick and blush.

"Sharks, huh?" I said to her.

"You can't be too careful, kid."

"I'll remember."

She smiled and put her lipstick back into her purse as the plane taxied toward the gate, toward home.

Chapter Fifteen

"Is this safe?" Barker asked.

"Yeah, it's one of the top ten resorts on the East Coast," I replied.

"Sarcasm does not become you."

"Just keep shoveling. You know what'll happen if we look like we're having a good time."

"No worries there, Jake," Elvin gasped.

My friends and I had been sent to the place we called "the dungeon." The black dust and brutal heat made this one of the most unpleasant (and unhealthy) work assignments on campus. Our job was to feed and stoke the huge coal boilers that heated the Hub.

Barker, Elvin, and I tried to make the best of it as we shoveled the fist-sized chunks of rock at a strong, steady pace. The sweat poured off our bodies and coal dust covered us from head to toe. Older students supervised us, so neither teachers nor officers would be subjected to this misery. Even the student supervisor sat in an observation booth. He wore full respiration gear while my two friends and I wore only white allergy masks and plastic safety glasses.

The six cylindrical boilers were crammed into a low, underground room located about fifty yards east of the Hub. The loud, ancient machines needed repair. We expected one or all of them to blow up someday and kept a sharp eye on the pressure gauges as we worked down there. Everyone who had ever tended the boilers hoped that the school would convert to oil or natural gas, but I'd heard that the shareholders continually voted down such proposals. They felt that tuition money was better spent "educating young men." What a laugh.

As I shoveled, it occurred to me that the boiler room bore an unusual similarity to the furnace building where Elise and I had spent our first evening together. Both heating structures were offset from the buildings they serviced, and I was once again struck by the inefficiency of such an arrangement. Elise had attributed this design quirk to paranoia, and I wondered now if the person who lived in that spooky mansion had something to do with Ashur-Kesed. That would be an interesting twist on the rumors I'd heard.

A cloud of coal dust blinded me and interrupted my thoughts. I dropped my shovel and squeezed my eyes shut, waiting for the tears to wash the dust away. Thankfully, the sound of a whistle pierced the thick air of the confined room. It was time for our break. As my vision cleared, my friends threw their shovels into the coal bin and helped me over to the hatch that led up to ground level. We couldn't leave, but we could remove our meager equipment and try to gulp some fresh air before returning to work.

The upperclassman supervising us sat arrogantly at the far end of the room, reading a scientific journal. We sat on the floor at the base of the access ladder.

"Promise me if I ever get that jerky that you guys will beat the tar out of me," Barker requested, referring to the upperclassman.

"No problem there, B. In fact, I'll throw you a little beating now, just to show my good faith," Elvin said in his cheerful Southern drawl.

My eyes felt better, but I was too winded to join the conversation. I was in good shape but hadn't been sleeping well lately. I spent far too many nights staring up at the bottom of Buzz's bunk, thinking about home, thinking about Dad, and thinking about Elise.

The guys continued joking as they took turns standing under the narrow opening where the ladder ascended to the ground floor. When it was my turn, I gratefully lifted my face, closed my eyes, and enjoyed the cool air that rushed down the passageway. I was startled when a small, balled-up piece of paper fell from the opening, bounced off my forehead, and rolled to a stop at our feet. I jumped back and heard someone scurry up the ladder and run lightly across the floor above.

None of us moved for a split second, then Barker began to talk loudly, indicating with widened eyes that someone should cautiously attempt to pick up the paper. I joined in the conversation, laughing along with my two friends, and glanced down. We were all curious but had to make sure our supervisor didn't see what we were doing. If that paper projectile did contain a message, it was vital that it didn't fall into the older student's hands. Elvin laughed especially hard, slapping his knee and kicking the balled paper to his left, where it came to rest behind a boiler just out of the supervisor's line of sight. Barker made a show of stretching and then sat down on the floor to flex his quadriceps. As he got up, he pocketed the paper. Elvin and I slowly maneuvered our way around Barker so that we subtly blocked his hands from view. Our position wouldn't be likely to arouse the upperclassman's suspicions, since we were all still in plain sight. Slowly, carefully, Barker pulled the paper from his pocket as we continued to laugh and talk. We weren't even sure the paper contained a message, but it broke the monotony.

Barker unwrapped the paper and shot his eyes down in careful little glimpses. A wide smirk spread across his face as he looked in my direction. It *was* a message, and it was apparently addressed to me. Excited, I inclined my head slightly, indicating that Barker should turn the paper over and let me read it. Instead, Barker glanced at Elvin, pursed his lips, and raised his eyebrows.

I felt a familiar rush of adrenaline—was the note from Elise? I should have known—only she could have found a way into a locked, guarded access corridor.

I moved one step closer to Barker. He saw that I was about to grab the note, so he quickly flipped it over so I could read it. It said,

Dear Jake,

I miss you! Meet me this Friday night after lights-out. You know where.

E.

Oh, terrific. What would these two gossips make of that? I was thrilled to hear from Elise, but Barker and Elvin were well known for their relentless pursuit of news, or more accurately, any information that someone else wanted to keep a secret. No amount of begging, pleading, or threatening would keep them from spreading the contents of Elise's note around the barracks. I groaned inwardly at the prospect of all the questions that would result.

The whistle blew again, and as we returned to our stations Barker and Elvin continued to make subtle faces and gestures. I tried to ignore their ribbing but my silent grin only encouraged them. As we resumed our dusty, backbreaking work, I focused on Friday and began to mentally plan every word, every facial expression, and every movement.

When we were dismissed from the boiler room, we headed back to the barracks and the nice, hot showers that awaited us. We weren't allowed to speak during the brief walk, but as soon as we entered our quarters and heard the door secured from the outside, my two coal-encrusted friends made a slashing motion to Buzz. My bunkmate quickly engaged his newly retooled alarm system, and the two scoops burst out laughing as they addressed the entire barracks: "Jake has a girlfriend!"

The news elicited shouts of amazement and everyone bombarded me with questions. Since I still didn't know exactly who Elise was or how she had attained such influence around the campus, I stalled them by promising to tell them more after I saw her. They gaped at me—I was actually going to *see* this girl? They demanded to know how I was going to manage that, but I told them to be patient. Secretly, it amused me. They would have hoisted me onto their shoulders and paraded me around the barracks if I'd told them that I had already seen her, and off campus, no less.

I showered and climbed into my bunk. I was coughing from my stint in the dungeon and my eyes still stung from the dust, but at least I was clean. As I tried to rest my battered body, I couldn't help but smile. Things seemed to be looking up.

"Are you gonna discard, or are we trying to grow beards?"

Perry and I were playing rummy in the tree house and he was losing as usual. "Shut your face! I give *you* plenty of time," he bit back sharply. His irritability told me that he had to choose between two high cards. Perry chewed his upper lip as he often did when he was about to do something foolish.

"You give me plenty of time because I don't *take* any time." I spoke with a light, relaxed tone that made Perry even more nervous. After scanning his two cards with a final burst of intensity, he plucked one out and threw it down. The ace of hearts—what else? Poor Perry was so intent on trying to read my face that he wasn't even mindful of the irony of his discard. He was aware, however, that his fate would be decided right now. If I picked up that card, I would win the hand and maybe even the game.

I pretended to examine my remaining cards and squinted with contrived indecision for added effect. When I was sure that Perry had a sliver of hope, I scooped up the ace, added it to the two others in my hand, slammed the winning trio down, and flipped out my discard in one fluid, triumphant motion.

Perry screamed.

"I can't help someone who doesn't want to be helped," I said. "I've told you a million times: never, ever throw out high cards. You hold them until they rot in your hand, or until you can shove them down your opponent's throat." I spoke with the confident air of a master card shark.

"That's the dumbest thing I've ever heard," Perry mumbled. "You gotta throw 'em sometimes."

"You're hopeless," I concluded as I added up the score. "You wanna keep going?"

"Naw. I'll never catch up now, and you already have all my best baseball cards. You wanna spit?"

"Okay."

When we were younger, we'd often demonstrated our masculinity by trying to hit certain leaves on the tree. Whoever achieved the best combination of accuracy and distance was, naturally, the better man. Neither of us wanted to admit it, but we no longer enjoyed the game. It used to be a good kicker after a game of cards, but it had become little more than a stale throwback to our younger days. We couldn't abandon it, though, without crossing some invisible line in the aging process, so we spat and pretended it still meant something. I handed Perry two squares of gum. The sugary burst of saliva made for greater distance.

"So, how are things going with your brother?" Perry asked. *Spit*; partial hit.

I nailed a broad leaf with a nice, fat one before turning on Perry. "He's not my brother," I said, for what seemed like the thousandth time.

"I know, I know. I mean, he's fitting in pretty well, isn't he?" *Spit.*

"Yeah." *Spit*; miss.

"Well, what are you gonna do about it?" *Spit*; solid hit.

"You may not be able to play cards, but you sure take the prize for dumb questions. What can I do?" *Spit.* Way short.

"Well, you could always hope for a bad crop of, say, wheat."

I turned to face Perry, appalled by his suggestion. "Are you nuts? Hope for a bad crop...if that doesn't beat all! We're farmers, remember? That's our livelihood. Besides, what does wheat have to do with Nick?" *Spit*; too scattered. How could anyone hope to spit properly during a conversation like this?

"Well, it would be a shame if he made some kind of costly mistake," Perry continued with an air of wily confidence that made him look like a demented fox.

I stared at Perry, impatiently waiting for him to continue his incomprehensible train of thought.

"How could your parents keep this kid around if, say, the wheat harvest was short? Your dad just planted it, and wheat can be funny sometimes."

"I don't know if you've noticed, Perry, but my dad's a pretty good farmer. I've seen different size harvests, but I've never seen a bad one. If you're trying to cheer me up, you'll have to do better than that."

Perry studied me as he landed a final shot onto a distant leaf. "Let's just wait and see what the harvest brings, shall we?"

"Yeah, okay," I said, dismissing him. Where did I get friends like him, anyway?

A short while later, we climbed down and bid each other good night with the traditional punch on the arm (that, too, was a throwback to our younger days). I walked across the lawn to our farmhouse, slipped inside, and went to bed. I didn't devote another thought to Perry's foolish words.

About two months later, Remmy came running in from the fields. "Boss, you'd better take a look," he said. "It's the wheat."

My dad and I had been cleaning the cow stall. Dad put down the shovel and followed Remmy with strong, purposeful steps. I went too, of course.

The fields rolled out in front of us, the strip crops forming beautiful, alternating patterns of green and gold. When we got to the edge of the field, Remmy walked in among the young heads of grain and seemed to be searching for something. He plucked first one, then two heads and held them in his hands for my father to examine. Dad's jaw tightened. He took the stems from Remmy and showed them to me.

"Do you see it, son?"

I examined the grain carefully but saw nothing. Both of the heads looked healthy to me. The fruit wasn't fully ripe, but that was normal for this stage of its growth.

Dad glanced at Remmy. "Bearded darnel," he concluded. Remmy nodded grimly.

I had no idea what they were talking about. As much as I knew about farming, this was a new one on me.

"Bearded *what*?" I asked. My father bent down and held up the two stems.

"Bearded darnel. The grain in my right hand is wheat, Jake. The grain in my left hand is a poisonous weed. They look almost identical, and there's no way to tell the difference until they start growing. You see the darnel head? It's smaller than the wheat."

This was awful. Dad had planted Red Spring wheat in the field. It was a hard grain used for making high-quality bread flour. The loss of any portion of this crop would be expensive.

"How did it happen, Dad? Did Mr. Amos sell us bad seed?"

Dad got up and shared another look with Remmy. "No, son. Someone did this on purpose. Someone came in here after we sowed the wheat and scattered darnel seed."

Dad looked down at the tainted crop. He was very angry.

Perry's words, "Wheat can be funny sometimes…" came flooding back. I felt my ears and face grow hot. I knew I was probably as red as the ace of hearts. I was glad my father wasn't looking at me.

He held a piece of dirty cloth in his hand. He kept turning it over and over. I barely trusted my voice, but I had to know.

"What's that, Dad?"

"Remmy found it among the wheat plants. It's Nick's t-shirt. Funny thing is, he was looking for it the other day. He asked your mom if she'd seen it. Why would he look for a t-shirt that he lost doing this?"

I felt like I was going to faint. Had Perry actually poisoned our crop and planted that t-shirt in the vain hope of implicating Nick?

I had to say something before Dad became suspicious, but I wasn't ready to tell him about Perry. I cleared my throat and asked, "What can we do?"

Dad, still looking at his crop, said quietly, "Wait until the harvest and separate the grain by hand. Then we'll bundle the wheat and burn the darnel. It'll take extra men, extra time, and extra money. What a shame." With that, Dad walked slowly back to the barn.

I swallowed the bowling-ball-sized lump in my throat, nodded to Remmy, and followed Dad.

As soon as feasible, I ran off down the road. There was an ex-friend who deserved a good pounding.

I found Perry in his barn, sitting lazily on the edge of a horse stall. As usual, he was wasting time. He saw me coming up the road and called out.

"Hiya, J! How're things on the farm?" His smile faded as he noticed the set of my jaw and my clenched fists.

I ran at him, screaming with rage, and pushed him backward with all my might. He flew off the back of the gate and landed on a pile of hay. His arm came down on a heap of fresh manure, adding a nice touch to my vengeful act. He was too shocked to scream, too scared to run, and had too little breath to cry. He simply stared up at me as I leapt over the gate and thrust my face into his.

"Are you out of your mind?" I bellowed. "Do you have any idea what you've done? You ruined our Red Spring and there's no way Dad is going to believe it was Nick, so that means that I'll be the one to catch it for all of this!"

He still couldn't speak. He had never seen me like this.

Fortunately for him, my rage suddenly fizzled out. As furious as I was with Perry, I was even angrier with myself. I realized that I had opened the door to this act with my incessant complaining. What profit would there be in hurting this cowering dolt? Still, what Perry had done was unthinkable and unforgivable. I spat on the ground near his feet and severed our friendship.

"Don't ever come near my house or my farm or my family again."

With that, I left. I thought I heard Perry crying as he sat dumbstruck on the floor of the barn. I didn't care; I had my own problems. How was I going to tell my father?

"Jake, we spoke about this, didn't we?"

I nodded unhappily. I'd just finished telling Dad what Perry had done and wondered what kind of punishment I'd receive for my part in it. Despite my rebellious spirit and my ever-present anger about Nick, I felt bad about the wheat.

"Son, you tried to tell me before Nick arrived that he would cause trouble. It seems the opposite has turned out to be true. I know you weren't directly involved with damaging the wheat, but you do bear part of the responsibility. If you had welcomed Nick into your circle of friends, this probably wouldn't have happened. You'll be the one to organize the harvest, separate the grain from the darnel, and make sure we don't ever face such a loss again. I'm disappointed, son. Now, I think it's time I called Perry's father…"

I was dismissed, and I walked slowly out to the edge of the wheat field. I wondered why you still got into trouble even when you told the truth. Shouldn't confession count for something? *Yeah, it counted for something. It got you put in charge of the worst job on the farm.*

I walked a few steps into the grain field and picked two heads. There were two types of plants in this strip of land; one was good, one was bad. As I held the heads of grain and examined them closely, I still couldn't tell the difference between the good and the bad. I wondered if people had anything in common with grain. I wondered if you could only tell the good from the bad when it's too late, when the only thing you can do is separate them and then light the fire…

I stood there as the sun went down and found myself rooting for the bad grain. There had to be some hope for it. There had to be.

Hailing a cab outside the airport terminal was more difficult than I'd expected. Ruth had wished me well a moment before and then disappeared into the crowd. I needed to get to the bus station for the final leg of my trip, but all I saw were shuttles and private cars. As I tried to decide what to do next, a limo pulled up to the curb. It was long, black, and polished to a high shine.

The limo slid smoothly to a stop, and the motor purred as the driver's door opened. The chauffeur stepped out. He noticed me immediately and walked over to where I was standing. I thought maybe he was going to ask me for directions. The man, dressed in a black tuxedo, bowed and spoke to me with a crisp British accent.

"Excuse me, sir. Are you Jake?"

I nodded. The man's next statement would have brought a smile to my face had it not totally bewildered me.

"Could I take your bags, sir? I'm here to conduct you home."

Chapter Sixteen

History was the only subject I enjoyed at AKPS. The class reminded me of Dad, or rather, the teacher did. This one instructor, a glaring exception at AKPS, cared deeply about his subject. His name was Mr. Collard-Hill. He had often substituted for our regular professor, a booming, blustering man named Mr. Rabab. One day at the beginning of my second year, we were overjoyed to hear that Mr. Rabab had taken a position at a school up north and that our substitute teacher had been offered tenure.

Mr. Collard-Hill's opening statements on his first day as our full-time instructor had proven he didn't fit in at Ashur-Kesed. "My goal is to make history come alive for you," he announced, his enthusiasm clearly apparent in his eyes and voice. He was young but suffered from some kind of blood disorder that made him physically weak and caused him to walk with a pronounced limp. As a result, he couldn't move around the classroom as he taught, but he made up for his immobility with the passion of his delivery and the incredible visual images he painted.

Mr. Collard-Hill avoided the history text unless it was time to review for an exam. He preferred to begin every class with a dramatic introduction, followed by a fascinating exposition of some pivotal event from the past. Today, his opening statement had particularly riveted my attention.

"If you dive down to the wreck of the *Empress of Ireland*," he began, "the first problem you'll encounter is the icy water. You'll also have to contend with strong currents. If you actually make it to the bottom, you'll find yourself immersed in a black, silent graveyard. Take a deep breath as you get closer to the river bed, because you're about to come face to face with a ghost—a rusting, metal reminder of an error in judgment that occurred in spring, 1914. Ah…but whose error was it?"

Dive on a wreck? Graveyard? Underwater mysteries? I was hooked.

Mr. Collard-Hill went on to explain how the *Empress* had sunk in the St. Lawrence River on May 29, 1914. He described the sudden terror of the passengers and crew as the *Empress* collided with the *Storstad*, a coal ship out of Norway. I listened intently, trying to imagine what it must have been like to be sleeping one minute and struggling in freezing cold water the next. We relived the heroic efforts of the captain and crew to save the hundreds of passengers who survived, and evaluated several eyewitness accounts of the tragedy. The ship had foundered in only fourteen minutes and the exact cause of the collision was still a mystery. There had been a thick fog, but the ships had sighted each other earlier in the evening and had taken steps to avoid disaster. Why, then, had disaster occurred?

Mr. Collard-Hill paused at that point in his lecture to give us our assignment. We were to research the event, examine the testimony of both crews, and draw any conclusions we felt were warranted. We were also required to devote a section of our paper to the lessons one could learn from the *Empress* tragedy. Mr. Collard-Hill was like that. He refused to merely spew dates, facts, and figures. Like my father, he believed that the study of history was useless unless we actively learned from it.

After a brief question and answer period, he dismissed us. As I collected my books and left the classroom, I looked forward to exploring today's lesson in greater detail. We were allowed to visit the school library three nights a week, and I knew exactly how I would spend my two-hour allotment that night.

I ate a hasty dinner and marched across campus to the library, which was a recent addition to Ashur-Kesed.

The outside of the building commanded immediate attention because it was made of brick rather than the gray-painted wood that characterized most of the other school buildings. It was an unusually shaped building, with a central cylindrical section surrounded by three single-floored wings. Both the central structure and the wings had skylights, and the overall effect made the library look like a large, brick space-craft.

The floor of the lobby was covered with white, polished marble that had been cut in diamond-shaped slabs; a rich, burgundy carpet covered the study areas and corridors. The cubicles and tables were made of hand-carved walnut complete with individual banker's lights, and the huge central skylight—a stained glass mosaic of various literary fig-ures—illuminated the lobby with myriad colors. The checkout desk dominated the lobby, but was eclipsed by the library's most impressive feature: its carved walnut shelves. Through a brilliant stroke of archi-tectural genius, they stretched in one curved piece all the way up from the ground level to the fourth floor. There were no stairs leading to the upper levels, only a long, gently sloping ramp that followed the curve of the shelves. You could stop and browse for books at any point on the ramp. The shelves were open in the back, so from the ground floor it looked as though the entire building was being embraced by thousands upon thousands of volumes, and that the books themselves welcomed those who sought knowledge.

The building also housed advanced research equipment, such as computer card catalogs, cable internet access (monitored by faculty censors, of course), and digital microfiche machines.

In a way, the library was incongruous, since the founders and fac-ulty of the school had little interest in true knowledge. Like the Hub, this building was the gift of a rich donor, and I, for one, was grateful.

I sat in my usual cubicle and began to sketch an outline for my as-signment. I decided to collect all the relevant data I could, collate it, and then analyze it in my barracks over the weekend.

I sat at the computerized card catalog and searched through a long list of books. The computer screen bathed my face in green light as I jotted down the five most likely candidates. I ascended to the second level, where the ramp opened up into a large, square room with a bal-cony that overlooked the lobby. Teachers used the balconies as watch-towers. They monitored the study areas and strictly enforced the "no talking" and "no socializing" rules.

Consulting the notes I'd made, I selected a thick book filled with underwater photos. I flipped it open.

"I enjoy that one myself. It brings back memories."

I looked up, startled. Across the aisle, I saw two eyes and a pair of white, bushy eyebrows that contrasted sharply with the dark, leathery skin of the owner's face. The voice was deep and rich.

"How do you know which book I have? You can't see the binding from that side," I said.

"Oh, when you've been up and down these aisles for so many years, you get to know what's here. You're reading about the *Empress*, aren't you?"

"Yes."

The man came around the side of the shelf. He looked about sixty, his balding head balanced by a neatly trimmed salt and pepper beard. He stood a bit taller than my own five feet eleven inches, and wore casual faculty attire: a vest embroidered with the gold AKPS seal, a white shirt, and black trousers. The man smiled and extended his hand, which I politely shook.

"That's a good grip," he said. "My pop always said you could tell a lot about a man from his grip. Eli's the name. I'm not as full of information as some of these books, but I'm certainly at your service, Jake."

My eyebrows shot up, silently asking the obvious question.

"How'd I know your name? Well, it's my business to know who's handling my books. You're a careful one. You don't like getting your greasy"—he pronounced it *greezy*—"fingers all over the photos, you don't dog-ear, and you always put the books back. I figure you for a person who loves to read. My kind of person."

I smiled, completely disarmed by the man's openness. He'd obviously been watching me, but he had me at a disadvantage. I'd never seen Eli during my weekly trips to the library. Not once. As far as I'd ever known, there was only one librarian. His name was Mr. Miktab, and he seemed as much a part of the furnishings as the paintings that hung in the lobby or the wall fixtures that lit the ramp.

I'd often been amused by Mr. Miktab's resemblance to a writing instrument: he was tall and thin, with hair slicked back almost to a point, just like a quill pen. He never strayed from his post behind the huge central checkout desk. From that vantage point, he supervised the students and staff who helped re-shelf books, never touching the volumes himself, but fastidiously obsessing over their proper care and organization. His stiffness precluded sitting down, and the only parts of him that seemed to move were his arms and eyes. When you slid a book across the checkout desk, his bony fingers snatched it from you, deftly flipped it open, plucked the red card out, stamped it vigorously, replaced it with a yellow reminder card, and slid it back before you could exhale. All the while, his shifty eyes examined you, silently proclaimed you unfit to borrow one of his books, and dared you to return it past the due date. His voice sounded like the high notes of a clarinet, thin and reedy, and the only words he ever spoke pertained to his precious paper possessions.

"Due 4 April, 19:37 hours!"

To which you simply replied, "Sir, yes, sir, and not a minute later!"

Who was this stranger in front of me who claimed to be the librarian, usurping the quirky Mr. Miktab? I certainly preferred Eli's warmth to Miktab's icy glare.

"It's nice to meet you, sir, but why haven't I ever seen you before?"

"Oh, I mostly just float around until someone needs me. Writin' a paper, are you?"

He hadn't really answered my question, but I answered his.

"Yes. A research paper."

"Collard-Hill?" he inquired.

"Right."

Eli leaned in conspiratorially. "There may be some hope for him, eh?" He chuckled quietly, and I joined in.

"I was there, you know," he said casually.

"Where?"

"The *Empress of Ireland*. I dove that wreck about thirty five years ago."

"You did?" I couldn't restrain my excitement, and the question burst out far louder than was allowed. The library monitors shushed me. Eli and I ducked back down the aisle, out of sight. Any residual questions I had about Eli's sudden appearance in the library were forgotten.

"You did?" I repeated. "How? Why? I thought you were a librarian. Will you tell me about it?"

Eli led me to a study room. "I'll be here," he said. "Go get your notebook and come on back. We'll have ourselves a story time."

I tried to appear nonchalant as I descended the ramp to retrieve my belongings from the cubicle where I'd left them. I feigned another book search before proceeding back up to the second level and into the study room. I wasn't breaking any rules, but you couldn't be too careful at AKPS. Sometimes a teacher would forbid something simply for the sake of exerting his authority, and I didn't want to chance that. This was too important and too much fun. I settled across from Eli. He folded his hands and was about to begin when a thought struck me. I didn't really like the thought, but I knew I shouldn't push it away. I remembered that there was something I needed to do, something more important than listening to interesting stories. Eli was the perfect person to assist me with some research that had nothing to do with history class.

"Excuse me, Eli." He obligingly stopped. "I know we just met, but I could also use your help on a different research project."

"Well, surely. How can I help you?"

"Actually, it's for someone else. I need to…set a friend's mind at ease."

"That's right noble of you, Jake."

"I don't deserve any credit, believe me. Here's what I need to find out…" I spelled out the particulars of the tragedy that had taken the lives of Nick's parents. I told Eli that Nick blamed himself, and that he thought the fire had been caused by his carelessness in the basement.

Eli listened, stroking his short beard and nodding. "This will take some doing, but we can manage it, Jake. You said that Nick lived in Chicago? I tell you what: I'll check with the Chicago fire department. They might give me the information. If that turns out to be a dead end, I'll check the on-line newspaper morgues. We need to find out where that fire started. If the authorities say it started somewhere on the upper floors, we're home free. If they say the basement, we'll do a little more digging and try to find the exact cause. I'll send word as soon as I can. Jot down your mailbox number for me."

I did so, and Eli sat back in his chair as he slipped the piece of paper into his shirt pocket. He was appraising me in the same way Dad used to do.

"This person you're trying to help, Jake. Are you two close?"

"Not exactly, but we should be."

"Should be? You'll have to clear that one up for me, my man."

"He's my adopted brother. I…did some things I regret."

"Ah, a guilty conscience, eh?"

"Yes, but that's not why I want to do this," I said quickly. "He deserves to know, that's all. I don't like to think of anyone living with that kind of guilt. I was taught that if you can help someone, you should help someone."

"Sounds like me and your pop would get along fine." Eli leaned across the table. "We've still got time to talk about sunken ships before you go back to the barracks, but I hope you'll take a bit of advice from an old sailor. I did a couple submarine tours back when I was just a little older than you. On a sub, there's a captain and there's a crew, but you're all in that fish together. Each man depends upon the next to do his part, whatever it may be. We all came from different backgrounds. Some liked their food this way, some squeezed their toothpaste tube that way, and some were as ornery as polecats. If we had a problem with each other, though, we solved it because our lives depended on us acting and thinking as one.

"I figure a family's got a few things in common with a sub. You have the mom and dad, and they're responsible for leading and teaching, but everyone in the house has to pull together. My point is that on a sub, there's no such thing as an 'adopted' chief of the boat or an 'adopted' mate; in a family, there's no such thing as an 'adopted' brother. Either he's your brother, Jake, or he isn't. Does that make any sense?"

While Eli was speaking, I couldn't help but marvel at the similarities between his advice and my father's, down to the same metaphorical style Dad often used. In fact, Dad had tried to teach me this very lesson. I decided that this time I would pay closer attention.

"Yes, sir, it makes a lot of sense."

"Good. Now let's start with my very first dive, and then I'll tell you about the *Empress*. I was in Aruba, snorkeling on the wreck of a German freighter named *Antilla*. She was sunk just off the coast, and her old rusty belly stuck right out of the water…"

Eli spoke for the better part of my two-hour study allotment. He effortlessly wove the different elements of his stories into chronicles that were as entertaining as they were informative. When Eli described the cold waters of the St. Lawrence River, I could almost feel the chill. When he spoke about the dangers of scuba diving, I could almost hear the hiss of the regulator and feel the pressure of the ocean bearing down upon me. When he described the sunken wrecks he'd explored, I could almost see the looming shapes of dead ships as they lay there in the darkness of the sea, corroded by rust, surrounded by silt, filled with memories and history.

"Yes sir, Jake—the sea is a dark mistress. She'll let you wine and dine her, but if you scorn her power, down you go—forever."

We heard the bosun's whistle that announced our library time was over. The faculty had added that naval accessory to their grab bag of patched-together military conventions, and I was amazed to hear its shrill call so soon—had two hours passed already? I stood and thanked Eli for his help.

"Don't mention it, m'boy, and don't forget to check your mailbox. I'll send word as soon as I can."

"That sounds great. Thanks again for everything. It was good to meet you."

"And you. This is gonna be some paper, eh?" He laughed a deep, wonderful laugh, disregarding the rules and earning another volley of disapproving *shhhhhh*s from the three faculty monitors. "Gotta keep 'em on their toes, right, my friend?" With a wink, he was gone, disappearing into the stacks as if he were some strange type of book—one that walked and talked and knew your name. And called you his friend.

I joined my classmates as they lined up by the main door. I was in for a shock when I returned to the barracks, and I later thought that for a place so full of monotony, AKPS certainly had more than its share of mysteries.

Library research was not mandatory, so Buzz had spent the evening on his bunk, tweaking one of his inventions. Several guys were gathered in the common area, studying for an exam. Excitedly, I told them about my experience in the library and shared some of the things I'd learned. As I spoke, one of my classmates—a solidly built Scot named Fergus—looked puzzled.

"What's up, Fergie?" I asked.

"Beggin' yer pardon, Jake. I didna catch this mon's name."

"Eli."

At the mention of that name, a hush fell over the little knot of friends that had congregated near my bunk.

"Eli, eh? What did he look like?"

I described him, and Fergie's look turned cynical.

"I get it. You know, you really had us going, laddie. Who told you about Eli? Was it that joker?" He cocked his thumb at Buzz, who remained strangely quiet.

"Fergie, what are you talking about? No one *told* me about him. I met him tonight. I thought it was funny that I hadn't seen him before, but it's a big library and I'd never spent much time on the upper levels…"

"Look, it was a nice try, and I admit you had me creeped out for a second. However, you canna pull one over on Ferguson Liddel." The rest of my friends broke into uneasy laughter. Once again, Buzz abstained and simply listened.

I was frustrated now, and thoroughly confused. "Guys, what am I missing here?"

The laughter trickled into silence. Fergie examined me for a few seconds more before speaking quietly.

"Okay, farm boy. If you're actin', ye deserve an award. I'll play along."

He leaned closer.

"Eli *was* the librarian. He's been dead for five years."

"So you still got in trouble?"

I had just told Gib the story of what Perry had done to the wheat field, my confession, and the resulting punishment. My friend was incredulous.

"It's just what I've been saying all along: you may as well lie. If you get away with it, great; if you get caught, it's no worse."

Despite the fact that I had told the story in order to receive sympathy, I was in no mood for Gib's faulty philosophical ramblings. We were sitting in the loft above the dairy stalls, wasting time. I was in a foul mood. My harsh treatment of Perry had circulated around the neighborhood. Although most of my friends supported my decision, some sided with Perry. I'd lost more than one friend over that stupid wheat. It was just wheat. So what if there were a few weeds in it? That was part of farming, wasn't it?

I hadn't learned my lesson, though. I was still complaining to biased friends who couldn't possibly offer mature perspective or guidance, and Gib wasn't through rambling. He wore the same devious look that Perry had that night in the tree house. I paid attention this time. Next thing you knew, one of my fool friends would be burning down our house.

"Look, I'm no mastermind or anything, but it seems to me you have an opportunity here."

"Opportunity?" I didn't bother trying to hide my boredom.

"Yeah. You had to suffer for a botched job of sabotage. Why not do the job yourself, the right way?"

That was interesting. "What do you mean?"

"Well, Perry's got no common sense. Everyone knows you never mess with a farmer's crops. Plus, the way he tried to frame Nick was just plain dumb. That's not the way you would have done it. If you were to frame that little punk, you'd do it proper. Am I right?"

"I suppose." I didn't know why, but the conversation was beginning to appeal to me. It offered the combination of an intellectual challenge and a way to discredit Nick. I was so sick of seeing his pasty face everywhere I went, I was tired of hearing his inane chatter at every meal, and most of all I couldn't bear hearing him call my father—*my* father—Dad. Gib was still talking.

"…you just have to figure out what to sabotage."

What to sabotage, indeed. There were countless ways to trip up Nick on a farm this large. The answer came, ironically, from a low, deep "moooo" from below us. I crawled to the edge of the loft and stuck my head over the side. Inspiration struck; I rolled over and jumped to my feet.

"I know how to do it, but we have to hurry."

"What do you mean, 'we'?"

"Don't make me throw you over the side of this loft. This was your idea, and I need your help. All you have to do is keep watch for me."

Gib reluctantly agreed, and I scurried down the ladder like a barn rat and trotted into the adjoining room, where we kept the refrigeration tanks for the milk. Gib stood nervously by the door, looking painfully conspicuous. I gestured for him to step back so no one would see him, then quickly did my work.

When you do the same thing every day for years, you get to know the idiosyncrasies of every piece of equipment, every tool, every vehicle. Tank #2 had developed a twitchy valve. Dad had fixed it once, but the mechanism was defective and we needed to replace the entire valve assembly. If you didn't jiggle it before you poured your bucket in, the valve would lock open and you'd lose the precious milk you'd just worked so hard to obtain, as well as the rest of the milk in the tank. If I jammed it open, Nick could jiggle it all he wanted to; the milk would still pour out all over the floor. It was a good, entry-level act of treachery. At worst, we'd lose a little milk. At best, Nick would be drenched, humiliated, and possibly chastised.

My conscience was remarkably silent as I jammed open the valve. The tank was about three-quarters full, and the trick was to jam the valve in such a way that the slightest pressure from within would cause all the milk to pour out. It was more difficult than I thought it would be. Finally, I succeeded and motioned to Gib that it was safe to come in.

"Okay, it's almost time for the afternoon milking. Hide up there and watch the show."

Gib was excited as well as relieved. He hadn't played an overly large part in this wasteful act, and so could easily disavow any knowledge if caught.

I checked my watch and sure enough, Nick showed up right on time. I waited until he had bent down to inspect and prepare the pumps, then I quietly climbed down the ladder, exited the barn, then entered loudly through the same door. I greeted Nick in a friendly manner but received a look of suspicion in return.

"Hi, Jake. What are you so cheerful about? Did you find out I have a terminal illness or something?"

That stung, but I easily shook it off. Apparently, my conscience was sleeping. "Come on, I don't treat you that badly."

"Yes, you do."

"Well, whatever. Need a hand?"

"Nope. You showed me, and I can handle it. How much did they produce this morning?"

"Normal. You should have a good load."

"All right. Well, I'll see you at dinner. You going out for the sheep?"

"In a few. Bye."

"Bye."

I left the barn and pretended to head for the pasture. What a creep, talking to me about milking as if he'd done it every day of his life. I crept back and shot a glance up at Gib. He indicated that it was safe to sneak back up to the loft. I sidled around the corner of the barn and quickly, silently ascended. We leaned over as far as was safe and watched my brother.

Nick proceeded with the milking, and the proficient way he handled the pumps filled me with even more ire. *Well, don't forget—he had an excellent teacher.* That thought brought me little comfort, and I couldn't wait for him to fill the bucket. Gib and I held our breaths as Nick shut off the first pump and hauled the container of fresh milk to the back room. The only variable was whether he would pour the milk into Tank #2 first. We heard the sloshy sound of him pouring the milk, but no screams ensued, so we knew he had poured it into #1 or #3. So much the better; now our chances were fifty-fifty. Nick was about to get a well-deserved surprise.

As Nick worked on the second bucket, my conscience suddenly awoke. It was very angry with me. I watched Nick down there, so industrious, wanting so badly to please. He wasn't trying to replace me; he was trying to imitate me. Was that a crime? I wrestled with it as Gib lay beside me on the hay, leering like a greedy child in front of a toy shop window. As Nick finished the second bucket, I couldn't stand it any longer. I got up and moved toward the ladder. That's when I heard my father's voice drift into the barn. He was probably on his way in from the fields.

"Son?"

Nick stopped in his tracks and called out over his shoulder, "Yes, Dad?"

I froze, lay back down on my stomach, and told my conscience to shut its meddling mouth. Instead of correcting Nick and telling him that, no, he had been calling his real son, my father had responded.

"Has Jake gone out for the sheep yet?"

"I think so."

"Very good. I'll see you in the house."

"Okay, Dad!"

Stop calling him Dad! I screamed in my mind. *Pour the milk, come on, pour the milk...*

Gib and I waited in feverish anticipation as Nick rounded the corner and began to pour the milk. We were rewarded by the sound of milk jetting out of the tank and onto the ground, the metallic crash as Nick dropped the bucket, and as an extra bonus, Nick's startled cry of frustration. It was all Gib and I could do not to laugh. Mission accomplished!

Nick tried in vain to stop the flow of milk, but it was no use. He ran out of the barn and into the house. We had to hurry now. I quickly climbed down the ladder with Gib in tow, reversed my work on the valve, then grabbed my staff and headed out to get the sheep. Gib ran off to tell our friends what we'd done, and I strolled cheerfully into the pastures. That hadn't been so hard. I wondered what my next act of sabotage would be.

A little later, as I checked the doors on the sheep pens, I thought about dinner and the wonderful misery that Nick was no doubt suffering at this very moment. How pleasant it would be to eat a meal without hearing about how much he was learning and how much he enjoyed farming and blah, blah, blah. Since Dad usually rebuked people in private, I doubted I would be privy to Nick's chastisement, but I could hope, couldn't I? I called out a light-hearted "good night" to the sheep and strolled toward the house, whistling as I went.

I went in through the backdoor, took off my muddy shoes, and strolled into the kitchen for a sample of whatever we were having for dinner. Mom was there, stirring a pot of thick beef stew. It smelled wonderful, and without me having to ask, she scooped out a chunk of meat and placed it in the small, decorative dish on the stovetop for me. I plucked it up with two fingers, popped it in my mouth, and kissed her on the cheek. She smiled and examined my expression.

"Good beef?"

"Gweat," I said, the hot meat muffling my voice.

"Good day?"

"Yeah, pretty good." *Liar.* The word had jumped unbidden into my mind. My grumpy conscience again. "Where's Dad?" I asked, "and Nick?" I quickly added.

"In the dairy barn. There was a problem with #2, I guess."

"It sticks. I told Nick that. Bad?"

"He lost the entire tank. That's a lot of milk."

"Sure is. How's Dad?"

"Oh, you know. He's angrier with the refrigerator repairman than he is with Nick. Your father just had that valve replaced last week."

My face must have registered my shock, and it was fortunate that my mother was tending to the vegetables. I hadn't known that the valve had been replaced. The accident would look suspicious now. That stupid Gib! Why did I listen to him? To make matters worse, Dad's anger would mostly be directed at the repairman rather than at Nick, where I wanted it. Mission status: failed. I sat down at the table and tried to distract myself by asking Mom if she wanted any help.

"Sure. You can grab the napkins and glasses. Dad and Nick should be in any minute."

I complied, but I was too quiet. Mom noticed and waved a carrot under my nose.

"Carrot for your thoughts?"

"You know I don't like carrots, Mom."

"Potato?"

"Nope."

"Another piece of beef?"

I finally laughed, but I obviously couldn't tell her what was on my mind. I made up something lame about being tired and my leg giving me trouble again. I instantly regretted that as her maternal instincts switched into medical doctor mode.

"Are you using your cream?"

"Yeah."

"And you're taking it easy, right?"

"Mom!"

I was spared a physical examination by the sound of the backdoor opening and...laughter.

Dad and Nick were chuckling about something. That figured. I realized as they walked into the kitchen that it didn't matter anymore if Nick stayed or left. Things would never be the same. I also had to reluctantly admit that I didn't know my father as well as I thought I did.

Dinner was yet another exercise in theatrics. I chewed my food mechanically, not tasting it, not enjoying it, as Dad and Nick joked about that "clunky old valve." Remmy was eating dinner with us that night and he laughed along with them. I noticed that Mom had her eye on me. I had to be more careful about my facial expressions. Had she caught me grimacing at the interaction between my father and brother?

Dad asked me how my day was, trying in his usual caring way to draw me into the conversation. I offered nondescript answers. Nick must have sensed that something was wrong, and he was careful not to provoke me. Twerp.

After dinner, we went into the den for the evening's activities. I grabbed a book and sat on one of the couches. Although that comfortable room held painful memories, I wanted to see if there might be some residual fallout from the milk accident. Sometimes when I broke a rule or failed to follow the right procedure for doing an assigned task, Dad would delay his rebuke to give me time to think about my offense. Maybe the same would be true with Nick. As the night wore on, it became apparent that no such rebuke was forthcoming. Mom was reading, Dad was using a glue gun to repair something or other, and Nick was watching Dad. Of course. I wondered if some of the hot glue from that gun had dripped onto Nick and attached him to my father's hip. Bitter, sarcastic thoughts. I felt an overwhelming desire to flee from this sickly little family montage.

I excused myself, and as always Dad cordially invited me to stay a little longer. I declined. I thought about my foolish regrets in the barn, when I had almost called off the sabotage. There had been a moment when I believed Nick wasn't trying to replace me. That was partly true. Nick wasn't trying to replace me.

Nick *had* replaced me.

In the hallway upstairs, the grandfather clock took up where my conscience had left off, accusing me and reminding me of an inescapable and unbearable fact: *Your fault your fault your fault your fault your fault your fault...*

I wasn't going to listen to that until I finally fell asleep. I decided to risk something I'd been considering for a long time. I went into the sewing room, gathered my nerve, and opened the window. The night was warm as I crept out onto the eave of the roof. I had to be careful because I was right over the den where my family was still engaged in their activities. I crept to the far end of the roof. It was closer to the ground, but not low enough for a safe jump. I looked out across the lawn at my tree house. That was where I wanted to be. Although it was small and saturated with memories and nostalgia, it was a place where Mom, Dad, and Nick were not. But how to get there? I needed another rope ladder. Tomorrow I'd buy one with my allowance, keep it hidden in my room, and use it whenever I needed to escape. I would climb down to the lawn, run quickly across the grass, and hide amidst the comforting embrace of those huge oak branches. I didn't need a family. I didn't need anyone.

Chapter Seventeen

I had never experienced anything like it. The inside of the limousine was covered with leather and smelled brand-new. I had my own climate, radio, and window controls, and even access to a mini-refrigerator filled with cans of various soft drinks. I was thirsty but thought I should ask permission before taking one. Since the smoked glass window between the passenger compartment and the front seat was open, I moved to the seat nearest the partition and addressed the driver.

"Is it okay if I have a soda?"

"Of course, sir. You'll also find snacks in the compartment on the opposite side of the cabin."

I switched seats again, grabbed a cola and a bag of chips, and decided to ask the question I really wanted to ask. This man seemed friendly enough.

"Excuse me—what's your name?"

"Arnold, sir."

"Who hired you, Arnold?"

"I'm terribly sorry, sir. I'm not at liberty to say."

"Come on. It had to be my father; who else could it have been?" While this was certainly true, I still wanted confirmation. If Dad had hired a limo to come and get me, if he had gone to all that trouble and expense to bring me home, maybe he really had forgiven me.

"Nevertheless, sir, I'm sure you understand."

Polite but immovable. I made one last attempt.

"I'll give you a soda if you tell me."

The chauffeur chuckled at that, toasted me with the bottled seltzer he'd been sipping, and examined me closely through the mirror. "Let's leave it at this," he said in that formal accent of his. "You have many friends, Jake."

"So I've been told," I said with a sigh. "I just wish my friends were a little more talkative."

Arnold smiled and turned his attention back to the highway. There was nothing else to do except sit back, sip my drink, and enjoy the trip home.

It was around 9:45 at night, and we were planning my impending "date," as everyone insisted on calling it. Actually, my bunkmates were doing the planning; I was merely swept along by their vicarious enjoyment of my good fortune. Simon, a rough kid but great to have on your side in a conflict, cut right to the heart of the matter.

"Hey, Jake...didja kiss her yet?"

"Aye, laddie, ye canna tell us the opportunity's nae arisen!" Fergus added gleefully.

I wasn't going to satisfy their curiosity that easily; besides, there wasn't much to tell. "A gentleman doesn't discuss such details."

That remark was met with a loud chorus of disdainful skepticism. Dan summed up everyone's opinion: "He didn't kiss her, guys." Laughter. They were such a bunch of...

"Hey." This was from Joe. "Has she told you who she is?"

Buzz perked up on his bunk. Until now, he had remained relatively silent, but Joe's question seemed to irritate him for some reason. "Hey, Joe. Clam up."

"Well, he's gonna find out sooner or..."

"I said be quiet!"

That caught my attention, and everyone else's. I studied my friend's face and noted his unusually serious frown.

"What's up, Buzz?" I asked. "What am I going to find out?"

"Jake, if I were you, I'd ignore this bozo." Buzz threw a dirty sock at Joe to further illustrate his displeasure. Joe caught it in midair and pretended to cram it into his face while inhaling deeply. Everyone laughed, but I refused to be deflected. I opened my mouth again to ask what Joe had meant when Buzz caught my eye and gave me a wink, as if to say "we'll talk about it later." I closed my mouth and frowned. There was such a thing as too much mystery.

The guys continued to grill me about Elise, demanding that I fill them in on as many details as my "gentlemanly upbringing" would permit. They also offered many pointers on what to do and say on my date. Some of the suggestions were helpful, some were impractical, others were ludicrous—but all were appreciated. We talked and laughed until the lights-out warning bell sounded, and then everyone headed for his own bunk. The main doors were locked, and another day at Ashur-Kesed ended. I lay back, put my hands behind my head, and closed my eyes.

I needed rest, but first I wanted to discover the reasons for Joe's comment and Buzz's inexplicable behavior. After the final bell sounded and the room was plunged into darkness, I felt Buzz shift on the mattress above me.

"I assume you'll need a wake-up call?" he inquired innocently.

"Don't you dare try to get out of explaining," I whispered. "You winked at me. That means 'drop it for now, I'll tell you later.'"

"Actually, it means 'I'm very fond of you.'"

"Look…"

"Come on, Jake. I'm trying to save you some trouble. Do you trust me?"

I sighed. Whenever someone asked me that question at AKPS, it meant that I wasn't going to get the information I wanted. Since I'd had ample experience with Buzz's stubbornness and had little chance of forcing the information out of him, I merely grunted in reply.

"That's a good boy. Be patient and don't try to be such a detective all the time. Most of all, enjoy yourself tonight. Now, as I was saying," he concluded cheerfully, "do you need a wake-up call or not?"

"I guess so, but how are you going to manage that?"

"Don't be insulting. I can wire an infrared warning system that will go off if a guard so much as belches, and you wonder if I can wake up my friend for his secret tête à tête." He clucked his tongue disapprovingly.

"No offense, bud. What's a 'tet ah tet'?"

"Your accent is atrocious. It's French. It literally means 'head to head,' but in your case it means a date, farm boy, a good old-fashioned date."

"I've been telling you guys all night: it's not a date. She's a friend, that's all."

"More insults. Why don't you just say 'I think you're stupid, Buzz.' It'd be more honest."

I loved the way Buzz could turn a phrase. He had lain back down on his bunk, and I heard his voice through the mattress as I began to get drowsy.

"You know, you'd better start sharing some juicy tidbits. I can be of more help than you know, but I must be paid with information. Keep that in mind, O wiry tiller of the soil."

"I'll do that. Don't forget to…"

"Wake up! Wake up, you dope! You're gonna miss your date."

I sat up in bed; I didn't even remember falling asleep. I felt Buzz's hand shaking me from above.

"I'm up, I'm up. What time is it?"

"It's time to go. Make sure you chew this before you talk to her or it'll be a short evening." I felt him press a stick of gum into my hand. Buzz thought of everything. "Now get out of here—and take notes. I want to hear all about it tomorrow."

"Thanks, Buzz."

I dressed quickly and climbed out the bathroom window. It was locked and alarmed of course, but Roy had rigged the lock and disabled the magnetic contacts in case we ever needed to get out (or in case someone bearing contraband needed to get in). In the event of an inspection, Roy could restore the window to its original condition in about thirty seconds, assuming he had ample warning. It was a dangerous game we played, but everyone in the barracks had agreed it was worth it.

My feet landed solidly on the crushed gravel under the window. I looked around carefully, stayed low and in the shadows, and ran for the fence along the outer path where I knew Elise would be waiting. I arrived a few minutes later, breathless and excited.

She wasn't there. I unwrapped the stick of gum and popped it into my mouth as I searched for some sign of Elise on the path beyond the fence. I fought bravely against disappointment. She had said to meet her an hour after lights-out, and it was five minutes after that now. Maybe something had happened; maybe she…

"Hi."

Relief flooded my body as I turned around. "Hi. I expected you to be on the other side of the fence."

"Sorry. A guard came by. It wouldn't do for me to be caught on campus, and I didn't want to give away my 'door.' I hid behind the mess hall." Elise looked beautiful, her cheeks flushed by her short jog back to the fence. "Well," she said cheerfully, "let's get going."

"Sounds great. Where to?"

"Follow me." Elise promptly led me back the way she had come—onto school grounds.

"I thought you didn't want to get caught on campus."

"I'm not going to get caught. The guards never patrol the north end of the campus past ten or eleven at night."

She was right, of course, but how did she know that? We skirted the path, using the buildings for cover. It was obvious why no trees had been planted in the main area of the campus: if any student tried to slip off the grounds or even engage in unauthorized travel between buildings, he would find little to hide behind. The darkness helped. We kept to the shadows and soon arrived at the library, which stood due north of the Hub and was the last structure before the athletic fields. As we'd anticipated, there was no guard activity here. We crept behind the library building undetected.

Elise led me down some crumbling concrete stairs to an old door. She motioned for me to wait there while she climbed back up the stairs. I watched as she knelt by a small cellar window, operated a hidden latch, and crawled through the narrow opening headfirst. She held her legs straight out like a gymnast's before drawing them through the opening in one fluid motion. In just a few moments, the door—which didn't squeak despite its age—slowly opened. Elise stood there with outspread arms and an expectant look on her face.

"What do you think?"

"I'm speechless."

"Try, or you can't come in."

"Let's see…you are the most resourceful, amazing girl I've ever known. How's that?"

"I don't know. How many girls have you known?"

Elise flashed her radiant smile, which quickly dissolved into laughter. She grabbed my arm and pulled me inside, shutting the door behind us. We walked down a dark cinder block passageway that was lit only by the flashlight that Elise held. A moist, musty odor pervaded the place and reminded me of our root cellar back on the farm.

"Why the library?" I asked. "Are we going to do some research?"

"Well, we can," she said with a smile, "but you might like what I have planned a little better. Duck low, Jake."

I ducked and just missed hitting my head on a four-inch metal pipe that ran across the top of the passage. It would have floored me. How many times had Elise been down here? And where were we, anyway? I knew we were beneath the library, and I assumed this was some sort of maintenance tunnel, but I couldn't imagine where we were headed.

We turned the corner, passed through a steel fire door, and emerged from the dingy, sewer-like tunnel into a well-lit corridor lined with doors on both sides. Rows of buzzing, fluorescent lights revealed peeling paint and faded linoleum tiles. The doors were labeled with blue plastic nameplates: JANITOR, ELECTRICAL, STORAGE.

Elise led me to the only door in the hallway that did not have a label, opened it, and flipped on a light switch.

We stepped into a combination office/living space that bore little resemblance to the industrial passageways that led to it. The room was warm, cozy, and unoccupied. A throw carpet covered the concrete floor, and a couple of mismatched but comfortable-looking couches lined the room. A battered television on a rickety wooden stand was plopped in front of one of the couches, and there was even a fireplace against the outside wall in which a small fire was crackling. Pictures and mementos on the walls told the story of someone's life, and a roll-top desk in the corner was strewn with even more photos and clippings.

I had so many questions, but I didn't want to spend the evening interrogating Elise. Instead, I wanted very much to follow Buzz's advice: simply enjoy the evening and leave any explanations to her.

Elise sat on one of the couches opposite the fireplace and patted the cushion beside her. I obediently sat down and tried to look at ease. The firelight caressed her face and made her look even more mysterious than her words and actions had already rendered her. She anticipated my curiosity with her next statement.

"You have many questions."

If ever I was going to satisfy my curiosity, now was the time. However, my instincts told me to settle for whatever information Elise offered. "I suppose they can wait," I responded casually.

"I can help with the most obvious question: no, this isn't where I live. This is the apartment of a dear friend of mine, a friend I believe you've already met."

I thought about that for a moment. We were in the library, and the only person I'd met recently was…"Eli?"

She nodded, and when I looked around more closely, I noticed that many of the pictures lining the walls had the blue-green tint of underwater photography—some of the sunken wrecks that Eli had explored? I suddenly saw an opportunity to uncover the truth of Fergie's unnerving announcement the other night. I momentarily set aside the fact that this was a romantic setting and that there was a beautiful girl sitting just inches away from me. Despite my earlier resolve, I had to ask about Eli. The only problem, I quickly realized, was how to phrase the question. Fergie had told me that Eli had been dead for five years, yet here we sat in what Elise claimed was his apartment. It made sense that the librarian would find it more convenient to live on campus, and the apartment was obviously lived-in and furnished in a manner that was consistent with what I knew of him. I didn't want to sound accusatory, but someone wasn't telling the truth. I decided to approach the topic through the backdoor, so to speak.

"You know, one of my friends tried to freak me out the other night."

"How so?"

"I told the guys about Eli, and Fergie got all weird on me and said…well, it's silly, really…"

"No, go on."

"He said that Eli has been dead for five years."

"Ah." Elise wore a strangely neutral expression. "Did he look dead to you when you met him the other day?"

Hmm. That wasn't exactly a denial. Was she being evasive? *Be careful, Jake.*

"Well, no," I responded, "but it was odd that I'd been in that library every week since I've been here, and I'd never seen him once. The only librarian I knew anything about was Mr. Miktab." This conversation didn't have the light, casual tone I'd hoped for. Elise still wore that neutral expression, and I was concerned that I had ruined the evening. She quickly dispelled that fear.

"Jake, I'll give you some advice, and I hope you'll take it in the right spirit. Sometimes you don't have to explain a good thing, you just have to enjoy it."

That sounded just like the advice Buzz had given me only hours before. Elise had mentioned Buzz's name a few other times. Was it possible they knew each other and, for reasons unknown, were keeping their relationship a secret from me?

Elise interrupted my thoughts. "You like Eli, don't you?"

I nodded.

"So do I. Don't let ghost stories keep you from benefiting from the friendship of a man who's seen and experienced what he has. Eli can help you, Jake, if you let him. Okay?"

She seemed so wise. I wanted to let it go but couldn't shake the feeling that something was off-kilter here. Still, I supposed that on this topic, my premonitions didn't matter. After all, I had spoken to Eli myself. He hadn't disappeared, walked through a wall, or done anything else that ghosts are supposed to do. If I was still curious, I could ask him for an explanation myself. For the moment, I allowed my beautiful but confusing friend's blue eyes to distract me from any further contemplation of ghosts and/or librarians.

"This library was literally built around his house," Elise continued, looking around the room and effectively closing the subject. "That's why there's a fireplace down here. The kindhearted moguls who founded this school graciously paid him a modest sum and allowed him to keep his home. They never told him they planned to build a library three feet from his front door. He got a court order at the last minute, but Ashur and Kesed had the contractors pour the foundation around Eli's house out of spite. This room is all that's left." Elise frowned as she looked down at her hands, which she had unconsciously clenched. "But I don't have to tell you sad stories, do I? You've got your own problems."

"Not at the moment," I responded, as sympathetically as I could. "He's a good man. I'm sorry about what happened. Someday, every injustice that has ever happened at this school will be made right." I didn't know how I was going to keep that vow, but I was nevertheless determined to carry it out.

She looked into my eyes but did not reply to my promise.

"It's nice, isn't it?" she said, referring to the apartment. "He's comfortable here, and I guess that's what matters most."

"It's perfect. Where's Eli now?"

"He's out haunting that old mansion on the hill." She laughed at my expression, and I joined in when I realized she was teasing me. "Sorry," she said. "I couldn't resist. Eli is being very considerate. When I told him we wanted to spend some time together, he offered to go upstairs and catch up on his reading so we could meet in a more comfortable setting than, say, a boiler room."

She examined me again with a look that made my heart hammer in my chest. Despite everything—the rigors of school, the dangers of sneaking around, and the mysteries that surrounded Elise—I felt my affection for her growing at an alarming rate. Nothing I'd experienced with Diane had prepared me for this. I felt certain that it was time to kiss her.

Elise's mention of the boiler room reminded me of the way I had received her "invitation" to this evening's excursion. I tried to steer the conversation toward our blossoming relationship.

"By the way, nice shot in the boiler room. You should have seen Barker and Elvin when they read your note."

She laughed. "I felt silly sending you a note that way, but one does have to be careful around here. Still, it was fun. You should've seen the look on your cute little face when that paper hit you." *Do you need a better opening than that, Jake? Kiss her. Now.*

"You see, that's the trouble," I said, good-naturedly. "Whatever we talk about raises an average of ten questions. How did you get into the Hub that night? How did you get past the guards?"

"Am I going to have to do something drastic to quiet you down?"

This is it!

"Absolutely."

She got up, but instead of moving closer to me, she walked over to the rolltop. A record player sat atop the desk, and though it looked old, it seemed to be in good working order. Elise inspected the fifty or so records that were neatly organized on a shelf nearby. She selected one, pulled it carefully out of its sleeve, and placed it on the turntable.

"It's not a CD player, but it'll do just fine," she said.

I waited on the couch as she set the speed and flicked a switch. The stylus arm rose automatically and traveled to the first cut. Elise walked over and held out her hand. "Dance with me?"

Mellow jazz filled the room and suited the mood of the evening perfectly. The pops and scratches of the old vinyl actually enhanced the muted trumpet and quiet rhythm section. We danced slowly, her head on my shoulder. Any tenuous control I thought I possessed drifted away on the gentle wind of her breath.

"Say something poetic," she whispered.

She was so direct, yet so disarming. Her combination of business-like efficiency and playfulness were a double blow that I found impossible to dodge. I tried to recall some of the sonnets I'd read or some poetry my mother had taught me in literature class, but I couldn't remember a single line. I was about to apologize for my poor memory when I suddenly remembered a few verses I'd learned long ago during a family visit to Boston. The words were part of an old sailor's song that I'd seen engraved on a ship's dedication plaque. The tour guide had taught us the tune, and the song had stuck in my mind. I cleared my throat nervously and said, "I, uh, I'm not much of a poet, but here goes:

"I walked to the sea by the light of the moon
The sand and the waves whispered softly as one
I searched by the sea on an evening in June
And waited for morning to come.
I sat on the shore as the sun showed its face
The surf flowed around without worry or sigh
Whenever I miss you I come to this place
To see the deep blue of your eyes."

I tried to remember more, but it was enough. Elise looked up at me. Her eyes really were like the sea—a deep, liquid blue that only hinted at the greater beauty found below the surface.

"That was perfect, Jake. I hope we can see the ocean together someday. You make it sound wonderful."

For once, I knew better than to say anything. Elise put her head back on my shoulder, and we danced for a long time. At the end of the third song, Elise suddenly embraced me, hard. I could feel her breath on my neck. It came faster than normal. The voice inside my head became frantic. *Would you please, for the love of your sanity and everything you hold dear, just KISS HER!* I hugged her back, hesitated, and then the moment ended. The opportunity evaporated.

"Thank you for the dance," she said as she performed a formal curtsy.

I bowed, mentally kicking myself but thrilled that whatever I felt for her was reciprocated.

"So," Elise said as we settled back onto the couch, "tell me more about your brother."

I would rather have discussed our growing relationship, but I saw an opportunity. "On one condition," I replied.

"Yes?"

"Tell me something—anything—about yourself."

"I suppose I should," she said, laughing. "You first, though."

"Yeah, I figured that. All right, you want to know about my brother…" I paused, thinking back to the day I met Nick. "I have to admit that I liked him at first. He was quiet, but he had a good sense of humor. He was a fast learner, too."

"You say that almost as though it's a bad thing."

"No, I just remember how eager he was to fit in. There was so much more I could have done to make him feel welcome. He made friends and he even did a pretty good job around the farm, but he succeeded in spite of me, not because of me."

"You'll get the chance to make it up to him."

"How? I doubt that 'sorry' would cut it in this case."

"You still haven't told me what you did to Nick, I mean, the 'straw that broke the camel's back,' as you put it."

"Isn't what I've told you enough?"

"You're terribly hard on yourself. I have a feeling that your family is far more willing to forgive you than you are to forgive yourself."

"If that were true, I wouldn't be here."

The remark came out more sharply than I had intended. I instantly regretted it.

"Well, I happen to be glad you're here," Elise replied.

There was no anger in her eyes, only a look that instantly returned my thoughts to the present.

"I'm sorry, I didn't mean you. I just meant that…"

"I know. It's all right. My turn."

"Finally!"

"Let's see, where should I start? Hmm…can't tell you that, *definitely* can't tell you that…"

"Hey!"

"Just kidding. I'll start with my job. I work in town at the *Messenger*. I'm an administrative assistant to the editor."

"The *Messenger*. That's a national newspaper. How'd you land that job?"

"I had some family issues that made home life unpleasant. I decided to work hard, graduate high school early, and try to find work in my field. I did an internship at the *Messenger*, then worked my way up. I also take courses at the community college when I have the time."

I was interested in Elise's occupation, but something she'd said had seized my attention. "What do you mean by family issues?"

"You, sir, are exceeding your boundaries," she said with a smile.

I sighed, not surprised by her answer. "Sorry. You want to become a journalist, then?"

"Actually, I want to write books. I do freelance articles for the paper now, but that's just to gain experience."

"You know, I happen to know one of the most famous journalists of our day."

"Who?"

"Paul Tarsean."

"How do you know Paul Tarsean?"

"Actually, he's the one who introduced Nick to me and my family. Maybe I could introduce you to him someday. He loves to help people out. I'm sure he could help you find a publisher."

"That sounds great."

We talked for another couple of hours. The conversation drifted comfortably here and there, mingled with our laughter and growing affection. As the evening drew to a close, I remembered Elise's most recent note. "By the way, you give good advice," I said.

"You mean about writing home?"

"Yes."

"Did you?"

"It was easier than I thought it would be." I looked into the fire, which we'd kept well fed with logs throughout the evening. "How did you know I felt that way? Are you that perceptive, or am I that transparent?"

"Both." A giggle. "I love to listen to you talk. When you describe your home or your tree house or your Dad, it's as though I can see them in my mind. It wasn't hard to come to the conclusion that you miss everyone and that you're reluctant to write…"

I missed the last part of her sentence. She'd just given me a great idea for the next time we met. *I can see them in my mind,* she'd said. The only challenge was where to get the things I'd need. I made a mental note to consult Buzz tomorrow. I felt a finger in my stomach and realized I'd zoned out.

"Sorry—you asked me what I wrote in my letter home, right?"

"Right, and you have nice abs."

My face felt red hot.

She attempted to stifle her laughter. "Well, you do."

I thanked her, and stuttered through a brief description of my letter. She nodded approvingly.

After a warm, comfortable, near-perfect evening, we left Eli's apartment and exited the library. I walked Elise back to the fence, where we embraced again. On a sudden impulse, I leaned forward. She stopped me cold with one of her well-timed statements: "Isn't it great to be friends without the added burden and confusion of all that physical stuff?"

"Absolutely. Feel the same way," I responded woodenly.

She touched two fingers to her lips, and then placed them gently upon mine. My heart felt as though it would explode.

"Good night, Jake. I had the best time."

"Me, too."

"Soon?"

"Soon." And then we parted.

I watched her slip through the fence and disappear down the path. She still hadn't told me exactly where she lived, but it had to be nearby. At the moment, however, my curiosity had faded, thoroughly overrun by more powerful feelings.

I sneaked back into the barracks, my head spinning from a combination of weariness and excitement. First bell would ring in about three hours, and I would have a hard time getting through the day. I'd make it, though. As great as my despair had been when I'd arrived at school, the joy I felt that night far surpassed it.

I grabbed a couple hours of sleep. The bell rang and I listened to my classmates stir for a moment before joining them as they jumped out of their bunks for pre-inspection and head count. I stood in line with my classmates, exhausted but happy.

Chapter Eighteen

"Whatsa the matter, Jake? Didda you other one breaka?" There was genuine concern in Mr. Agorazzo's voice, but I considered his question an invasion of my privacy. I had walked into the hardware store with cash and I wanted to buy a rope ladder. Was that a crime? Did that warrant a federal investigation?

Mr. Aggy, as the townspeople called him, had sold Dad a rope ladder for the barn a few months ago. I guessed the shopkeeper was worried that his reputation might be tarnished if he had sold my father an inferior product. I didn't have time for this. I simply wanted to buy my ladder and go.

"This is for me, Mr. Aggy. I wanted an extra one for the tree house. You know, in case the one Mom made breaks or something. I don't want to be stuck up there." It was amazing how natural lying became once you started doing it. It was also amazing that you stopped feeling bad about it, especially when it got you out of trouble or, as in this case, when it sped you out the door of a hardware shop.

"Ah, very wise, Jake. You're justa lika you father. Still, I don't thinka that something you mama make issa gonna break anytime soon."

His accent, which had always been a source of delight when I was younger, irritated me. Or maybe it was the words themselves, rather than the way they were said. *You're just like your father.*

"Are you sure you don'ta wanna save you money?" he asked.

I assured him with thinly veiled impatience that I did indeed want to buy the ladder—immediately. With a shrug, Mr. Aggy rang me up, took the exact change I passed across the counter and handed me a receipt. He smiled and called out behind me as I took my package and headed quickly for the door.

"You tella you father I say hello, eh?"

I waved in response and walked through the door. The small bell that hung there tinkled a cheerful good-bye as I left.

This was not good. The next time Dad saw Mr. Agorazzo, he would surely tell him about my purchase. Dad would find it unusual that I was buying another rope ladder when there was a perfectly good one hanging from my tree house porch. Well, it couldn't be helped. If my father asked about the ladder, I would tell him the same story I had told Mr. Aggy. It wasn't really a lie. I really did buy the ladder for my tree house, right? I was just leaving out a few things, like wanting to escape from my home and family, hating the sight of my brother, and wishing I could live alone. I cheerfully walked home. Tonight after dinner, things would be different.

"May I be excused?"

Mom's eyebrows rose. "You hardly touched your dinner, Jake. Are you feeling all right?"

Dad looked up from his plate of pot roast and mashed potatoes. "Let him go, dear. He's not a little boy anymore."

"He is to me—and so are you, for that matter," Mom replied, affectionately patting my father's hand. "I saw you in the yard today, chasing after Skipper as though you were ten years old. Honestly. It's a wonder you don't pull your back out or…"

"May I be excused?" I repeated. My parents' spontaneous ramblings, once endearing, were now sickening to me.

"Of course, Jake. Backgammon later? There's pie."

"No, thanks."

I pushed back from the table, acknowledged Nick and headed up to my room, leaving my family to coddle each other.

I'd hidden the rope ladder and some other supplies in a canvas knapsack under my bed. The ladder was made of strong yellow nylon. It was marketed towards households as a means of escape in the event of a fire. I didn't care what it was supposed to be used for; it was perfect for my plan.

I waited until I heard my family leave the kitchen before making my move. I tiptoed into the sewing room, quietly opened the window, climbed out onto the eave, and crossed to the end of the roof. I didn't want to risk attaching the ladder to the gutter, so I'd brought two heavy eye hooks. After making some careful measurements, I positioned the first hook about three inches above the edge of the roof, bore down, and screwed it through the shingles and into the wood beneath. I repeated the process with the second hook. I pulled the ladder out of my knapsack and attached it to the hooks.

I'd done my work well. There was nothing left to do except climb down, but I hesitated for a moment. I wasn't afraid of heights, but I had a perfectly normal fear of falling. As I sat on the roof trying to work up enough nerve to step onto the ladder, I heard laughter from the room below. That was all the motivation I needed. I got on my hands and knees, inched out over the edge of the roof, and placed my foot on the first rung. Gingerly, I placed my other foot on the rung and began to climb down. I was thrilled when I safely reached the ground. While my family was inside talking, laughing, and thinking that I was up in bed, here I was on the back lawn. I felt wonderfully sneaky.

I ran across the yard to the tree house, which in the fading light was nothing more than a dark, hulking blot among the leaves. Suddenly, it didn't seem so inviting. With diminished enthusiasm, I ascended. Only when I reached the top did I remember that I couldn't turn on the lights. Dad would see them from the house and my secret escape would be revealed.

I sat there in the dark and listened to the crickets while Nick ate the pie I should have been eating, played the games I should have been playing, and enjoyed the companionship that was rightfully mine. Worse, I didn't really need to sneak out to the tree house. Mom and Dad allowed me to come and go as I pleased, as long as my evening activities did not interfere with my 5 A.M. waking time. I felt deeply sorry for myself, but I was far too proud to rejoin the family or to let them know I sought the solace of the tree house.

I'd sure shown them, hadn't I?

Loneliness and bitterness are a volatile combination. With nothing better to do, I devised my next act of sabotage. Self-pity gave way to crafty determination. I came up with several workable possibilities. Perhaps I could call a special meeting of the Ace of Hearts Club tomorrow and ask for suggestions—in secret, of course, and in direct defiance of my curfew.

After about an hour of such thoughts I felt a little better. I climbed down from the tree house, crossed the yard, carefully climbed my new ladder, and reentered the house. This was going to be a busy week.

His name was Jeffrey. He was the son of one of the adjunct professors, and we saw him from time to time when his father substituted for another instructor. He had Down syndrome, but to me that wasn't his defining characteristic. What I loved most about Jeffrey was the fact that he never had an unkind word to say about anyone. Most students (including me) went out of their way to befriend him. His outlook was so simple it was profound: enjoy life, avoid worry, and be thankful for everything. If the sun was shining, Jeffrey considered it a good day to be alive. If a bird sang a cheerful song, he counted himself blessed. If Jeffrey's father bought him a coffee cake on the way to school, he was full of praise both for his father and for the baker. Jeffrey steadfastly refused to focus on anything negative, and I learned much from him during the short time we spent together.

Since he possessed the enormous physical strength that sometimes characterizes his condition, his father placed him under the care of Mr. Tubal, the metal shop instructor. Jeffrey's father probably assumed that his son would spend the day lifting heavy objects and helping to keep the shop clean. Mr. Tubal was skeptical at first, but soon observed that Jeffrey could do more than lift and clean. He taught his young apprentice how to use the blowtorch, which caused quite a stir and earned Jeffrey the nickname "Torch." Before long, Jeffrey became an unqualified expert in metal craft. He loved his new hobby and lost no time in creating a large variety of useful and beautiful objects.

I passed the metal shop on my way to class one day and saw his familiar, helmeted face laboring behind the fierce blue flame of the blowtorch. I marveled at the dexterity with which he wielded the clumsy instrument. Jeffrey was working on a very small piece of metal, and I let the other guys cut me in line just so I could watch him for a few more seconds.

Jeffrey finished what he was doing, extinguished the torch, and carefully set it down. He lifted the blast plate on his helmet and beamed when he saw me.

"Jake is my friend!" he shouted.

I smiled. "Hi, Jeffrey. What are you making?"

"Fly away, Chippy! Fly away!" he said, picking up the little piece of still-glowing metal with a pair of tongs and waving it around the room.

It was a perfect metal cardinal. Since the steel was still red-hot, it was even the correct color. Its crest was tall and proud and its beak was just the right shape. As the bird cooled, I could see that the seams were as tight as if they had been machine-molded.

"Jeffrey, that's your best yet. Did you know that cardinals are my favorite birds?"

"They are? Mine, too! I'll make you one, Jake. Fly away, Chippy!"

"Student 3290, have I made an error?"

I snapped to attention. Our line officer had noticed that one student was missing and had come to investigate. It had been careless of me to let that happen. "No, sir," I responded.

"Then tell me why you are not in line, upperclassman."

"I...I was just admiring the work of apprentice craftsman Holland, sir." I inwardly groaned. My answer was perfectly valid—anywhere but here. At Ashur-Kesed, admiration was reserved only for abstract principles of proper behavior. It was never to be wasted on people.

"You were *admiring*," the officer repeated disdainfully. "The school credo, please?"

I shouted the familiar phrase, hoping to somehow wiggle out of this. Out of the corner of my eye, I saw Jeffrey approach. He was still holding the tongs and cradling his bird in a thick steel worker's gauntlet.

"3290, I don't believe I heard enough school spirit in your voice. Again!"

I began to comply, but Jeffrey interrupted.

"Jake is my friend. Like my bird? Fly, Chippy!"

The officer looked at Jeffrey with thinly disguised irritation. No one on the faculty wanted to offend their colleague, but behind his back they wished that he would make some other arrangement for Jeffrey. "Sir, why don't you go back to your little project and let me do my job."

"Okay. Do you like my bird?"

The officer was unsure what to do. He glared at me, then at Jeffrey, and realized that the wind had been taken out of his sails. "Get back in line, upperclassman," he barked at me. "You'll run an extra two miles tomorrow morning. Maybe that will bleed off some of your excess energy." With that, he strode off, frustrated. I rejoined the line, but not before winking gratefully at Jeffrey.

Jeffrey had come to mind because I needed his optimism just then. I had been beaten up again and I had a pounding headache as a result. I also needed to prepare for a calculus exam but was finding it difficult to study as my mind kept replaying the events of that morning.

The fight had been characteristically brief and one-sided. I had unwittingly broken another upperclassman's record for the hundred-yard dash during morning calisthenics. Instead of praising me for the accomplishment, Mr. Paroh (in typical AKPS style) had ridiculed the other student, accusing him of unthinkable weakness for letting a "skinny, weak-kneed, farm boy" beat his record. During lunch, my classmate had expressed his displeasure with a volley of body blows and one knockdown belt against my jaw. The mess hall guards didn't interfere; in fact, they even gambled on the outcome. As I picked myself up off the floor, I saw money being passed from one group of guards to another. *Well, at least someone bet on me. That's something.*

Now, as waves of pain radiated through my forehead, I needed any inspiration I could get. Sam, who still fiercely protected me, hadn't witnessed the fight. When he found out what had happened, he would certainly visit my adversary with swift retribution, but that didn't help me now. Thoughts of Torch and his unconquerable spirit always brought a smile to my face, so I tried to draw strength from the example of my cheerful, hardworking friend. If Jeffrey had been in my barracks, he would have told me to cheer up, and I would have done so. I hadn't seen him on campus for a while. I hoped that his father hadn't finally bowed to pressure from the rest of the staff and made other arrangements.

Chapter Eighteen

My improved outlook gave way to anxiety as I thought about everything I needed to accomplish that week. In addition to my many exams and academic projects, I had to finish preparations for a special date with Elise. She'd contacted me via Abner, and she and I had made tentative plans for the weekend. This time, I'd asked to be in charge of the location. Buzz and the group pitched in enthusiastically. I was expecting a delivery anytime now. Through Buzz's many connections, I had been able to obtain most of the materials I needed for the date. As I took a break from the endless parade of slope equations that I'd scrawled, worked, and re-worked, I heard Buzz's homemade alarm system go off. He listened carefully, and then made the announcement I'd been waiting for.

"It's a number two, guys. Jake, it's your delivery."

There were three kinds of alarm signals. A number one was a scheduled appearance of a guard or the barracks commandant. They showed up at the exact same time every day, but Buzz announced them anyway to keep us on our toes and to ensure that the system was working properly. A number two was a "friendly." When there was a contraband delivery, the courier would wave his hand in front of the sensor in a pre-determined pattern, thus alerting Buzz that there was no cause for concern. A number three was the alarm we all dreaded. It signified an unannounced inspection. These inspections were actually excuses to punish us. Someone was always caught doing, saying, wearing, or having something that was against school regulations.

I looked up as a thin, red-haired mid-classman came in through the bathroom window. He was carrying a small package wrapped in brown paper. He sauntered over to me and placed the package carefully on the desk.

"Here you go, courtesy of Mr. Keran's chemistry lab. What do you need this stuff for, anyway? You makin' a bomb to blow the place up?"

"Now, now, friend," Buzz admonished. "You know the rule: couriers ask no questions."

"What's eatin' you, Buzzard? Never broke a rule before?"

"Yes, but only after breakfast or before dinner." This non sequitur seemed to greatly amuse the redheaded courier, judging by his guffaw. The sound of it threatened to split my head wide open.

"So long, guys. It was real." The courier left, and I sat on my bunk and opened the package. In it was a coded note telling me what the items would cost and when payment was due. Everything seemed in order, but I needed somewhere to hide the supplies. A hand appeared from the bunk above mine.

"Hand it over, farm boy. I'll keep it safe."

I gratefully passed it to my friend.

"Now, why don't you get some rest? You don't look so good."

Stalking, I soon discovered, was even more fun than sabotage.

I was in the midst of pursuing my prey. He was humming to himself and preparing to work among the cornstalks, weeding and clearing away any fallen or damaged cobs. I had a full bag of ammunition—grapes—and was maneuvering around the vineyard, keeping out of sight and waiting for the right moment. This was so much more entertaining than the game I had played in my youth. That game had been in my imagination; this one had a real, live enemy.

Nick turned away from me, blissfully unaware of the impending attack. I pulled out my first shell and crept to the edge of the cornfield. I estimated the distance to my target, cocked my arm, and fired. The shot missed by an eighth of an inch, buzzing past my quarry's uppity little nose.

His head snapped around, but I was already gone. I knew the field so well I could probably have navigated it blindfolded. Even better, there was a stiff wind that day and the rustling corn stalks masked the sound of my footsteps. I had changed position so that as he faced the spot I had occupied just a moment ago, I now had a straight line to his right profile.

I stayed extra low. He was on guard now, although he wasn't sure exactly what was going on. I selected a plump, juicy shell from among my munitions, reared back again, and launched. *Splat!* It struck his right temple. From the way he recoiled, you'd have thought he really had been hit by live ammunition.

"Hey!" he yelled, wiping the sticky residue from the side of his head. I was choking with laughter and barely changed positions in time to avoid his charge through the corn.

Now I was behind him and I could see his head turning this way and that as he searched for some sign of movement. Aim, rear back, fire—a direct hit! This time it caught him at the base of the skull and he spun around, more irritated by the fact that he couldn't predict the direction of the next attack than by any pain caused by the grapes. I could hear a touch of hysterical frustration in his voice as he demanded to know who was there. *Frustrated? Join the club, Nicky my boy, join the club. That's how I feel every single...DAY!*

I doubled back, because I could see he had enough brains to expect that the next attack would come from the direction of the stone wall. He screamed loud and long when the grape took him on the neck from the exact opposite direction. I decided to pelt him with one final barrage before creeping off. I enjoyed the mental image of him searching in vain for his invisible enemy, nerves and muscles taught as he expected at any time to be struck again. How long would he stand there? A minute? Two? Ah, this was the way to spend a sunny afternoon.

I decided on a multiple mortar attack—I would throw as many grapes as I could cram into my fist. I watched him turn this way and that, trying to anticipate my next move. I waited him out. He surprised me by suddenly speaking in a calm, casual voice.

"I know it's you, you lazy, jealous child." The smile faded from my lips. What had he just called me?

"Yeah, I guess I'd feel bad, too, if I had everything you have. A Mom, a Dad, a home, a future. Poor Jake has it so tough. How does he even make it through the day, burdened by such hardships?"

My right fist clenched involuntarily, crushing a handful of grapes into wet, mushy pulp. *He'd better close his mouth. He had better just close his dirty mouth.* But Nick was just getting started.

"Yes, Jake's had a rough time, but he makes up for it, folks! He's clever. He knows how to sneak around in a cornfield and throw grapes at his brother. Well, listen up, Jake. All the grapes in the vineyard won't change one fact." Nick's voice dropped down low and mean. He spaced each word with clipped, brutal intensity: "Dad...loves...me...*more!*"

I leaped out from among the corn stalks like a ravenous lion, landing on Nick and wrapping my hands around his throat. It was my turn to scream now, something incoherent, something about him not being my brother, something about hating him. Angry tears blurred my vision, but I saw that he didn't seem afraid, nor did he try to resist. I was unable to squeeze as hard as I wanted to, restrained by meddlesome images of Dad. I gave Nick a final, vicious shake and let him go. He looked up at me and said, quietly and triumphantly, "I guess you're not as smart as you thought you were."

I released him and fled, abandoning my chores. I spent the rest of the day and much of the evening on top of the silo. More than once I considered throwing myself over the side. I finally returned to the house long after the sun had set.

Dad was waiting for me, of course. He sat alone in front of the fire. The TV was off, the newspaper and almanac had been laid aside, and the rest of the house was dark and quiet. When I opened the door and stepped into the family room, he stood up. I felt the anger radiating from him in waves. As always, however, I clearly sensed that the anger was directed not at me, but at my actions. How was he able to make that distinction? How did he continue to love me despite the horrible things I did, despite the horrible person I had become? It's nearly impossible to despise someone who loves you like that, no matter how unfair you think they are.

And so it was on this occasion. Despite my rage, I suddenly regretted the cruel trick I had played on Nick, and I even felt bad about nearly choking him. I felt like a Ping-Pong ball, hit back and forth by two fiercely determined opponents—one good, one evil.

My father took a step toward me and uttered a single sentence.

"Son, let's talk about grapes."

Chapter Nineteen

It was difficult to focus on my work. The book on the study table in front of me seemed to blur in and out, as if I were viewing it through a microscope that someone kept adjusting. I looked up and rubbed my eyes. My headache, which had not abated since my fight three days before, throbbed behind my right eye. My throat was raw, my nose ran continually, and I was certain I had a fever. I reluctantly concluded that I had a bad cold, or maybe the flu.

What lousy timing! I had only been sick once or twice in the last few years. Now, when I was planning my first official date with Elise, I had caught some kind of bug. I wrestled with the idea of going to the infirmary. If the medic determined that I had a communicable disease (no matter how common it might be), I would be quarantined for at least forty-eight hours. That was unthinkable; I had too much to do. At the same time, I didn't want to be selfish. By not reporting to the infirmary I could easily infect my classmates. I was pondering my limited options when I heard a now-familiar voice.

"Jake, my man, you don't look so hot."

I looked up at Eli's concerned face.

"Oh, you know. It's probably just a virus or something," I whispered.

Eli sat down across from me. "Not the best time to get sick, is it? I understand you have a special night coming up."

I smiled, even though I could barely hold my head up. "She told you?"

"Sure did. Buzz and Sam added their two cents. Say you're running 'em ragged chasing after supplies." He paused for a moment, examining me closely. "You know, I'm just a librarian, but if you'd pay an old man some mind, I'd say that you and your girl make a mighty fine pair. You give any thought to the future?"

"That's what keeps me going."

"Ain't it the truth? How's the plan coming along? Do you have everything you need?"

"I'm still short on a couple of supplies, and I haven't figured out where to take her yet."

"It'll come to you. Just wait for inspiration, my man. Listen, do you have a list of what you need? Eli used to be a man who could obtain certain items, for a price."

"A price, huh?"

"Sure. Got to keep you accountable, don't I? Tell me what else you need, and I'll see to as much as I can. In the meantime, you'd better get yourself to the doc."

I gratefully scrawled the last half-dozen items I needed and passed the list across the table. The librarian's eyebrows shot up as he read the list, but his smile told me that I was in good hands.

"Eli's on the case, Jakey-boy. Get better soon."

With that he was gone, vanishing into the stacks of books in that unusual way he had. I stared at the stack for a moment. My pain-wracked head wrestled with something. What had Eli just called me? Jakey-boy. That was an amazing coincidence—that was the same name that Yasha had coined for me one summer on the farm. Then again, I supposed it was a somewhat natural nickname for Jake. It was so hard to concentrate. Maybe I should get to the doctor after all. What was I just thinking about? Oh, yes: nicknames. It didn't seem important. I collected my books and slowly climbed the steps to the second level to request permission to report to the infirmary.

I'd more or less solved the mystery concerning Eli's alleged "death." It had been easy enough. When I told him about the rumors I'd heard concerning his demise, he'd gladly explained everything.

Five years ago, he had taken a leave of absence to do some consulting for the U.S. Navy. They wanted to salvage some battleships that had been sunk during World War II and had assembled a panel of experts to assist in the operation. Mr. Miktab had been hired as an interim librarian in Eli's absence, but no explanation had ever been given to the student body as to where Eli had gone. Rumors began to circulate that Mr. Miktab had murdered Eli and hidden his body in one of the walls of the library. Some particularly imaginative students reported that his ghost could sometimes be heard in the night, groaning in righteous indignation and lurking amidst the books he'd loved so dearly. The truth was that when Eli returned after his year's sabbatical, Mr. Miktab was firmly entrenched as librarian. Rather than fight for his position, Eli had simply stayed on as an assistant, helping wherever he was needed. He didn't mind. His downgraded responsibilities gave him more time for research.

I had laughed along with Eli at the silly rumor about Mr. Miktab, but I secretly evaluated the truth of Eli's claims. I wanted to believe his story, but the explanation seemed too perfect, as if it had been carefully scripted and rehearsed. There was also a huge gap in his explanation: since I had arrived at AKPS, no one had mentioned or even seen Eli until the day I met him. From that day on, however, he quickly became well known among certain members of the student body, all of whom were friends or acquaintances of mine. When I questioned my friends about their account of Eli's death, they said they'd been joking. I suppose Eli *could* have been in the library all along, quietly doing his job, staying out of everyone's way, but that seemed implausible.

In the end, I had to bow to practicality: Eli was obviously flesh and blood, and whether or not he was who he claimed to be, he was a great friend.

Eli had also worked hard to retrieve the information I'd requested concerning Nick's parents. I was overjoyed to discover that Nick was not to blame: an overloaded socket in the penthouse apartment had caused the fire that claimed his family and neighbors. I quickly sent a copy of the article to Nick along with a brief note: "Nick, I thought you might want to read this. Sleep well. Jake." I hadn't heard back from him, but that was okay. The important thing was that he didn't have to go through life blaming himself for a mistake he never made. I wished I could experience the same freedom, but I certainly couldn't claim innocence. I had learned that mistakes are expensive and that the price can only be deferred, never avoided.

I reached the top of the stairs and approached Mr. Printiss. He was among the more inoffensive instructors. We'd nicknamed him "Mono" because he generally spoke in short, dull bursts, rather like a semiautomatic weapon that fires rubber bullets. I waited for him to notice and address me before speaking.

"Upperclassman?"

"Yes, sir. Requesting permission to report to the infirmary."

"Reason?"

"Possible communicable disease, sir. Influenza."

"Dismissed. Guard?"

I breathed a sigh of relief as a guard stepped forward to escort me across campus to the medical facility.

Although I had only visited the MedFac a couple times, I was grateful for it now. Ashur-Kesed did not want its students to appear unhealthy or mistreated. The many bruises, black eyes, contusions, and sometimes even broken bones that occurred at the school demanded a twenty-four hour medical staff. The nurse at the front desk looked over his shoulder as we came in. He had been watching some sporting event and looked irritated at being interrupted, especially since I wasn't bleeding and had walked in under my own power.

"What's this?"

"Sir, upperclassman with possible communicable disease," the guard said.

The nurse grumpily clicked the mute button on the television and shuffled papers, looking for a form.

"Symptoms?" he barked.

"Headache, runny nose, sore throat, chills," I replied.

"What am I, your mommy? Is that all?"

"Yes, sir."

The nurse thrust a digital thermometer into my ear. A single glance convinced him that he couldn't send me back to the barracks.

"Guard, I'll admit him. You can return to post." My escort nodded and left as the nurse—his nametag identified him as DAWBER, R.N.—pushed some papers toward me. He reactivated the sound on his small TV (he'd been watching basketball, I now noticed) and put his feet up on the reception desk.

"Fill these out," he instructed. "There's a chair over...oh, come on! You don't try for a three-pointer when you're down by that many...aw, what losers!" He shook his head in disgust. "I don't know why I watch the finals. Some of these guys just can't take the pressure, you know?"

I didn't know. All I knew was that if I didn't sit down I would fall down, so I grabbed the clipboard and hurried to the nearest chair in the waiting area. The forms were blessedly simple, since the fees for any medical treatment would be added to my tuition. I scrawled my name, barracks number, and nature of my illness, then signed the release form that permitted the infirmary staff to treat me. Lastly, I wrote the name and phone number of my nearest relative.

"Done?" Nurse Dawber stood over me, increasingly irate at the poor performance of his team.

I nodded and handed back the clipboard. The nurse seemed to notice for the first time how horrible I looked. He forgot about his game for a moment and led me to an examination room. After checking my blood pressure, reflexes, and pupil dilation, he drew a vial of blood and stepped out into the hall. When he returned, he took a long, cotton swab and unceremoniously stuck it down my throat. I gagged, but he had gotten what he came for and left the room again.

The next time the door opened, it was the doctor. After consulting the contents of a manila folder he'd brought with him, he smiled thinly and pronounced his diagnosis.

"Upperclassman, you have a nasty little infestation known as *streptococcus bacillus*, more commonly known as..."

"Strep throat," I groaned.

"Yes, indeed. The good news is you'll be feeling better in about two days. The bad news is you'll be staying here with us. Can't have you spreading that little bug around. The nurse will set you up in a room. Don't look so glum. I'll run the antibiotics from an IV to get you back on your feet faster, and I'll give you something for that headache. Best of all," he concluded conspiratorially, "you'll miss a few days of class."

Great. That ended the possibility of being prepared for my date with Elise. I didn't even have a way to postpone it, since I still had no idea how to contact her. As the nurse led me to my room, which was thankfully a private room, I remembered that Eli knew that I had reported to the infirmary. He would tell Buzz, who would hopefully find a way to relay the message to Elise.

I didn't have the strength for any further thoughts about Buzz, Eli, or even Elise. I undressed and lay down between the crisp white sheets of the infirmary bed. The doctor came in a few moments later to start the IV, and I slowly, gratefully fell into a deep sleep.

I awoke to see a massive, warped eye peering down at me. When the cyclops saw that I was awake, it withdrew and became more familiar.

"Rise and shine, farm boy!" Buzz exclaimed. "You gave us quite a scare."

My tongue felt swollen and my mouth was bone dry. I gazed up at my friend, groggy from the medication and the residual effects of my illness. He was wearing his Scotland Yard glasses, as he called them. Buzz had designed the odd-looking eyewear, of course. It consisted of two magnifying glasses (minus the handles) attached to a pair of old tortoiseshell frames and secured around his head with a thick leather strap. With the flip of a spring-loaded switch, he could lower one or both lenses, although lowering both at the same time gave him a headache. As with most of Buzz's inventions, it was a work in progress.

I smiled and wondered what time it was, and how Buzz had gotten here so fast. I had just fallen asleep, hadn't I?

"What time..." My voice cracked. My throat was still raw.

Buzz affected a melodramatic look and his best detective movie voice, and grasped both my shoulders. "Look, kid, I see how it is. Your number is up, your ticket's been punched, it's all over for you. It's a tough break, and I know we've had our differences, but that's in the past, see? Tell me where you hid the map. Tell me where you hid the map!"

I laughed but no sound came out. Buzz lifted a plastic cup to my lips and I took a cautious sip. The moisture felt good, and I repeated my question with more success.

"What time is it?"

Buzz smirked. "Don't you mean what *day* is it?" He shook his head at my confusion. "You know, Jakester, the fact that you're allergic to penicillin might have been information worth sharing before they pumped you full of the stuff. It's been two days since you last graced us with coherence." He grew a bit more serious. "You almost didn't make it—no kidding. It's good to see you awake." His creased brow was pushed aside by a wide grin. "And someone—a very pretty someone—told me to tell you to stop stalling and sweep her off her feet."

"Elise?"

"No, my grandmother—of course, Elise!"

I sat up, feeling more alert and sipping more water. "Did she tell you when? I think I'll be here a while longer."

"She told me you should play it as it comes, and she'll contact you in the usual way. Don't worry, bud. When you get out of here, we'll have everything ready. The guys are all excited—they're taking bets on the outcome."

"Reassuring. How'd you bet?"

"Are you kidding? I'm the bookie."

We laughed and talked a bit more, and then I felt myself drifting off again.

I was roused by a hand on my shoulder, shaking me gently. It was a doctor, although not the same one who had treated me a couple days earlier. This one was younger. He had jet-black hair except for vivid strips of gray that extended back from both temples. He reminded me of a skunk.

Why did I feel so odd?

The doctor examined my chart. I watched him as long as I could, but my eyes started to cross. I wondered what kind of painkiller they'd put in my IV. Dimly, I wondered why they were giving me painkillers at all. Hadn't I been feeling better yesterday?

The doctor put down the chart. "Jake, it looks like your vacation is over," he said. "Your last blood test was clear enough for you to return to your barracks and to your studies—not that that's good news, right? By the way, did you fill out a medical form when you enrolled here?"

I tried to think about it, but I was having trouble remembering much of anything. I shrugged.

"Well, that was a bad thing, your being allergic to penicillin. You pulled through okay, though, so all's well that ends well, right? Right. The doctor suddenly leaned forward, staring at the IV bag that hung just above my bed. "Hey, who put you on this stuff? You're not due for surgery. Someone's going to hear about this, I promise you. Let me just…"

"Don't touch that, doctor."

Dr. Skunk swung around, startled by both the words and who had said them. I moved my eyes, which felt like balls of lead, and tried to focus on the tall, thin figure standing in the doorway. It was a man whose presence was guaranteed to inspire terror—a man who, under the guise of being an educator, ruthlessly intimidated and oppressed the students and staff under his control. He didn't scare me, not then. I greeted him cheerfully.

"Hi, Vice-Chancellor Senna! Thanks for visiting me!" I noticed that Sabrina, his faithful Doberman, was not with him, and added, "Where's your doggy?"

The vice-chancellor's pale lips wrestled with one another, each trying to outdo its counterpart in a display of utter contempt. In fact, the vice-chancellor's entire face seemed to have no other purpose than to express his displeasure. His head resembled an angular piece of carved granite, mounted on his shoulders without the benefit of a neck. Tiny wisps of white hair clung desperately to the sides of his head. His nose jutted out like the blade of an axe, ready to hack away at any transgressors he encountered. Wrinkles, permanently etched into a scowl, marred his forehead.

He strode across the room with the sports-loving nurse in tow. Senna towered by the side of my bed and glared down at me.

"I assure you, Upperclassman 3290, this is not a social call." His lips enjoyed a brief respite as they twisted upward in a smile.

"I see the medication has taken effect. Thank you, Nurse Dawber. That will be all for now." The nurse nodded and left the room, glancing once over his shoulder with a look that almost crossed over into concern.

I hoped whatever was troubling him wasn't too serious. Maybe his basketball team had lost again. "Three-pointer!" I exclaimed, then repeated the phrase several times because I liked the way it sounded. I felt very good.

The doctor looked alarmed and reached over to take my pulse. "Say, what's going on here, vice-chancellor? The boy's nearly unconscious. Did you order this medication?"

"I did indeed, doctor, and you are dismissed. It seems we have a rat problem here at AKPS. I have a few questions for our sick upperclassman."

"But you can't…"

"I *CAN*!" Senna bellowed. "Leave!"

"I don't know who you think you are…," the doctor said as he left, not intimidated, but also unwilling to scuffle with his superior.

The vice-chancellor returned his attention to me. "Now," he said in his best approximation of a pleasant tone of voice, "I understand that someone in your barracks has been taking midnight strolls. A few of my most trusted men have done some rather tidy detective work. Do you know what they discovered?"

"The cure for the common cold?" I said, imitating his accent.

"No, twit." He leaned in close. His breath reeked of stale meat, an odor I assumed a lion's breath would have the instant before he sank his fangs into your neck. "They discovered that it was you. Would you care to tell me where you were going?"

"Sure."

Senna seemed to be waiting for something. He sure looked mad, and that made his face even more ugly than usual. "You look uglier than usual," I said with a giggle.

"On the contrary, 3290, ugly is what I will become if you don't tell me what I want to know."

"Well, why didn't you ask?"

"I did ask," he said between clenched teeth. "Nurse!" he called.

The nurse rushed into the room as if he'd been just outside the door. "Yes, sir?"

"This dosage is making him incoherent. He's suggestible but unable to focus. That's useless to me. Fix it."

"Yes, sir."

The nurse adjusted the controls. My head began to clear, but I still did not understand the danger I was in.

"Now, I'll ask you again. Where did you go and what did you do?"

"I went on a date," I replied cheerfully. "In fact, I went on a couple of dates."

Senna looked sharply at the nurse and snapped, "What drug are you using?"

"Thiopental sodium."

"What's your assessment? Is he telling the truth?"

"Probably, but remember: he'll only tell you what he wants to tell you. If he's hiding something, thiopental won't force it out of him."

"Then why did you use it?" Senna demanded.

"Well, it's a common anesthetic. I thought it would be a bit safer than…"

"At what point did I ask you to think, Nurse Dawber?"

Dawber scowled but held his tongue.

Senna looked back at me. I wasn't sure what he'd expected, but my admission had clearly surprised him. "You went on a date, eh?" he said. "With a young woman?"

"Of course, you big banana."

"Describe her."

"Oh, she's beautiful. She has brown hair and blue eyes and great lips and I think I'll ask her to marry me someday. We have another date coming up, but I don't know when because I don't know what's today, uh, what today is."

Dr. Senna's expression suddenly changed. He smiled craftily—an even more disturbing sight than his usual scowl—and patted my shoulder.

"Thank you, 3290. I came here for one thing, and you supplied me with something even more valuable."

"Glad to help," I said. "You know, while I have your attention, the mess hall could stand a little variety in the menu department, like some real meat for a change and maybe some…"

"This medication will no longer be required," Senna cut me off. "Nurse, he is well, yes?"

"Uh, yes. The infection is just about licked."

"Good. Get him lucid, dressed, and in my office in one hour. Use another drug, if necessary, to clear his mind."

The nurse nodded. I got my first inkling that maybe he wasn't upset about basketball. He seemed to be worried about me. That was nice of him.

I was happy.

Then the thiopental started to wear off and the first precursors of terror made their appearance at the edge of my consciousness.

"So. Not quite as chipper as the last time we met, eh, 3290?"

I stood in that most dreaded of places, the suite of offices occupied by Dr. Charles Senna. I stood at attention in full dress uniform. The vice-chancellor sat behind his polished ebony desk, tapping a gold fountain pen on his blotter and thoroughly enjoying the moment. Sabrina sat beside the desk, looking deceptively docile.

"I'll be brief," Senna continued smugly. "We've known of your rebellious little excursions for some time. I came to that infirmary room hoping for confirmation, and I did that for one reason: I require information."

He let that statement hang in the air and gazed out huge windows that had the distinctively thick, curved look of bulletproof glass. *He's more paranoid than we suspected*, I thought. The drug they gave me lingered. I felt not quite there, but I was grateful that I could face Dr. Senna with a measure of courage. Silently, secretly, I thought of my dad and wished he were there. He would know how to handle this arrogant, evil man. Senna calmly lit a pipe, which looked completely out of place in his mouth. A pipe was something that scholarly professors smoked as they discussed deep things in well-lit studies. Clenched between the vice-chancellor's teeth, it was a vain and hypocritical accessory. The fragrant smoke drifted upward as he took a few puffs.

"Where was I?" he asked, knowing full well where he had left off. "Oh, yes…information. You see, I believe that order is one of the foundations of an excellent education. When order breaks down, it is virtually impossible to maintain the proper environment in which to prepare young men for the future that awaits them. This I cannot, in good conscience, allow."

Good conscience? What an obscene joke. A good conscience would run screaming from Senna's mind if it ever had the misfortune of arriving there. I couldn't help but smile, and the vice-chancellor noticed.

"You'll soon have little reason for mirth, I assure you," he snapped. "Order has broken down at this school. It has happened slowly but has now reached epidemic proportions. It occurs in the form of smuggling, unauthorized communications, nighttime wanderings as in your case, and many other violations of the strict—but just—regulations of Ashur-Kesed Preparatory School for Young Men. What I need from you, 3290, are names, times, and places. Simple, yes?"

"Student 3290 does not understand, vice-chancellor, sir!"

Senna unceremoniously thrust the pipe into a thick glass ashtray. His large leather chair flew backwards as he stood up. "You squirming, disrespectful little worm," he ranted. "You understand perfectly! If you lie to me again, I'll cleave your head with this walking stick. Do you understand *that*?"

"Perfectly, vice-chancellor, sir!"

"Good." The storm blew over as quickly as it had begun, and my adversary reseated himself. "Now, you will tell me who leads the contraband ring, how and when they communicate with their customers, and…"

"No, sir, I will not."

Senna's eyes protruded so far out of his head that I expected them to pop out and dangle onto his cheekbones. "What did you say?" he breathed dangerously.

"I will not divulge any of the information you requested, sir. Not now, not ever."

He was around the desk in a moment. He drew back his right arm and backhanded me. My head rocked back, but I remained rooted to the spot, eyes forward and unwavering. He drew his arm back for another blow, but checked himself and called for a guard. One appeared almost instantly.

"Take this lying pig to the disciplinary facility." He placed his mouth close to my ear and breathed into it with his foul, carnivore breath: "I believe you students call it the *Can*."

So, I would finally experience the worst known punishment that AKPS could administer. I had managed to avoid it longer than most, but in the end, I had underestimated Senna and his ever-watchful guards. Idly, I wondered what had given me away. Had I forgotten to cover up my footprints one night? Had I left some other telltale sign of my activities? I supposed it didn't really matter how I'd gotten caught. I thought of Elise, and knew I would do it all again. The guard herded me out of the office, and Senna called after us. "We'll talk again, upperclassman, after you've had some time to think."

Chapter Twenty

My evening excursions to the tree house had proven to be a good idea. Sneaking out onto the roof while everyone thought I was in my room made me feel powerful and in control. I was neither, of course, but I settled for the illusion.

I climbed out through the sewing room window and carefully stood on the roof. In the family room below, Mom, Dad, and the Intruder were enjoying a wonderful evening as usual. My mouth twisted in a grimace and my heart grew a little bit darker.

I walked carefully to the edge of the roof, sat down, and positioned the rubberized hooks of the ladder onto the hardware I'd installed earlier. Climbing down was still my least favorite part of these nightly escapes and I paused for a moment, looking up at the extraordinary majesty of the evening sky.

I noticed with an aching sense of loss that I no longer enjoyed the stars as I once did. Instead of appreciating their light and beauty, I focused on the distance between each one. I was repelled by their unchanging isolation. We had much in common that night, the stars and I.

The evening breeze carried with it the scent of impending summer, and the leaves rustled their excitement. I closed my eyes and searched inside for something I had lost. The memories were there, the knowledge was there, but the joy was gone. I heaved a great, shuddering sigh and looked up one more time. I'd learned about the constellations during my daily lessons and had made a game of inventing stories about those ancient patterns of twinkling light. Orion was hunting again and had little time for foolish young men. His belt gleamed and his upraised club would be victorious that night, as always. To the west, the Herdsman kept watch over his flock just as I had done with mine. I ignored the Twins since they reminded me of the reason I was sitting on this roof in the first place, but I sympathized with Andromeda, chained to the rock, awaiting the hero who would save her. I wondered who would save me...

"Nice night for stargazing, isn't it?"

I jumped. Dad was sitting on the roof just ten feet away. He was dressed in his black fisherman's turtleneck and work pants, and cradled a steaming mug of coffee in his hands. Beside him on the roof were a thermos and another mug.

Well, it had to happen sometime. I knew my father would find out about this, and I wondered if he had spoken to Mr. Agorazzo or had just figured it out on his own.

Although I didn't find Dad's presence on the roof the least bit amusing, I had to smile. The average father would have confronted his son directly, sternly informing him that this sort of behavior wouldn't be tolerated. Dad sat on the roof and waited for me—with coffee, no less!

"I suppose it is a nice night," I cautiously replied.

"You know, the door would probably be safer than that ladder. You're free to come and go as long as you stay within the boundaries your Mom and I have set."

He knew that wasn't the point. I wondered why he had come up here.

"Coffee?" he asked.

"Okay."

He sidled over and handed me the extra mug, which he then filled. I took a sip as the silence stretched between us, imitating the black expanse above. I wanted to speak, but words failed me once again. I felt cold and dead.

As we sipped the coffee and gazed at the sky, I remembered that sometimes even stars died. For reasons not fully understood, the reactions within a star occasionally intensify, causing it to explode with unspeakable violence. After the explosion, the dying star slowly collapses in upon itself, growing ever smaller, cooler, and darker. Its brilliance disappears, and it vacates its place in the heavens. The rest of the stars bear distant witness to this event, unable to prevent it, unable to offer the slightest assistance.

What could I say to Dad? How could things ever be made right between us? I had changed. I, too, had lashed out with great fury and was now slowly shrinking in upon myself. All my family could do was watch it happen.

"What are they saying tonight, Jake?" Dad asked, as I continued to gaze upward.

"Same as always, I guess." A voice inside urged me to say more. I couldn't.

Dad waited an appropriate amount of time, then got up in one fluid motion. "Well, I guess I'll turn in. Don't stay out too late, son. I'll be in my study for a while."

And he was gone. His arms were always open; he always extended the invitation. I mourned the lost opportunity even as I raged about what Dad had done to me by adopting Nick. I stayed out there a while longer and finished my coffee. I didn't bother going to the tree house. There was nothing there for me now, and no point in denying that fact any longer.

"The Can" was actually an industrial locker, a storage compartment that had been converted to a purpose never intended by its creators. There was a row of twelve such lockers in the maintenance garage. Each was made of steel and measured about two feet wide by five and a half feet tall. They had faded from their original factory green to a dull, sick color reminiscent of a stagnant swamp. They stank of silicone and petroleum. I'm sure there are places of confinement more unpleasant, but the Can was thoroughly dreaded as the low point of the AKPS experience. The administration pretended the torture was for our own good. Wayward students were expected to ponder their crimes against Ashur-Kesed and emerge humbled and remorseful.

We knew better. To us, the Can was nothing more than a sadistic form of intimidation and manipulation. Its purpose was to control us, not rehabilitate us.

The Can offered equal doses of physical and emotional punishment. The converted locker deprived its victims of both oxygen and proper blood circulation. Ventilation through the slits in the door was barely adequate and the air soon grew stale in such a cramped space. Fumes from the cleaning rags stored nearby further polluted the air and caused light-headedness and reflexive coughing.

Most students couldn't stand up straight in the Can. The body was forced into a position where the neck was bent forward, causing severe headaches and cramped neck muscles. The victim had to keep his arms crossed over his chest, reinforcing the illusion of being buried alive. The knees, slightly bent and forced into the front of the locker door, often tightened up. I had never ventured near the maintenance shed when someone had been in the Can, but I'd heard that after about six hours, the screaming began.

The second area of suffering was psychological. If you were claustrophobic to begin with, the Can could drive you insane in minutes; if not, you were only slightly better off. The pain, the shortage of oxygen, and the tight quarters soon began to conspire against rational thought. Growing panic threatened to cause a "freak-out," as it was called. Over the years, some students had tried to punch and kick their way out of the locker. They achieved only unconsciousness or broken bones.

The isolation also inflicted harm. In this smelly, steel coffin where I had been incarcerated now for three hours, there could be no notes from Elise, no inventions from Buzz, no stories from Eli.

To make matters worse, I was the recipient of a little extra touch the guards referred to as "the broiler." After being pushed into the locker, I'd heard the solid snap of the padlock followed by laughter as the guards dragged something across the floor. There were other sounds I could not identify—muted scuffling, then a single click followed by a low buzzing noise. A minute later, I felt warmer and realized what they had done. They'd positioned a space heater directly in front of the locker.

As my physical discomfort grew, my mental anguish kept pace. I began to worry about the drugged portion of my "interview" with Dr. Senna the day before. I couldn't remember it. Had I said something that could further compromise both my own safety and that of my classmates? I had a vague recollection that I'd mentioned Elise, but I hoped

I was wrong about that.

As my breathing grew more labored and the sweat poured off me, I thought about the date I still hoped to enjoy with Elise. Our first kiss would be perfect, everything would be perfect...I was looking forward to...*Breathe in, breathe out.* Hard to think. So thirsty. Could you die of dehydration? *Ding, dong, ding, dong*—the school bell. Who rings that thing, anyway? *Bong, bong, bong.* I wonder what time it is. Three "bongs," three o'clock. Where was I, what was I thinking? Oh, yes— the date. The bell. The bell tower! Our first date—the perfect place! Bell tower—great view, no interruptions, romantic with the right touches. Have to be careful, though, Jake old boy. Senna will be watching you like a hawk, like a vicious old hawk...careful...

My disjointed reveries were suddenly interrupted by a voice.

"Hurry up! He's outside talking to the other guard. We don't have much time."

"Jake!" The whispered voice came from the air slits.

"Buzz? Is that you?"

"No, it's Santa Claus. I checked my list, and you've been a good boy this year, so I brought your present early."

Buzz, amazing Buzz, moved back from the door and spoke to someone else. "Okay, let her rip. Jake, you might want to keep your hands and knees away from the door—and whatever you do, don't scream."

"Scream? Why would I scream? How did you get in here?"

I was startled by a loud *whoosh* and saw sparks leaping up past the air slits. I took Buzz's advice and pulled in my arms and knees as best I could. Even so, it soon became furiously hot in the locker. "Buzz," I whispered frantically. "What are you doing? It's getting hot in here..."

The whooshing sound and the sparks suddenly ceased. Someone began pulling the door outward, and I heard a screech as the newly cut hinges grated against each other. In another moment, the door was wrenched from its frame, still locked but with its hinges severed. Cool air flooded the locker as two gauntlet-clad hands placed the door against an adjacent locker and flipped up the blast shield of a welder's mask. I could just make out the identity of my other rescuer through a cloud of dissipating smoke.

"Jake is my friend!" he said.

It was Jeffrey, smiling as always, wielding his heavy torch and looking as though he had just finished a simple project in metal shop. My smile rivaled his as I tumbled out of the locker, mindful to avoid the still glowing edges where the hinges had been. My legs gave out but strong arms caught me. The surprises kept coming: Sam was there, and so was the object of my most recent thoughts.

"Elise!"

I saw tears in her eyes just before I hugged her. "I can't believe he would do this to you!" she said.

"I'm okay." I gazed around the small circle of rescuers. I would carry this moment with me for the rest of my life. "This is incredible, guys. I don't know what to say."

"We're not out of the woods yet, farm boy," Buzz whispered. "I had Jeffrey cut you out of there to give you some fresh air, but we've got to get you back before the evening watch or we'll all be joining you."

"How'd you get in here?"

"The sewer, of course," Buzz said.

"What?"

"Just kidding. There's a grease pit under the main garage where they used to do oil changes and stuff. An access corridor connects it to a door behind the building. We broke in, climbed the ladder, waited until the guard wasn't looking, and voilà!"

"Brilliant, as always."

"Hi, Jake!" Jeffrey interjected.

"Hi, Jeffrey! You did a great job on that locker."

"It was easy. I brought you a bird. I told you I would make you one, and Jeffrey Holland keeps his promises because that's the right thing to do. You keep your promises, that's all." With evident pleasure, Jeffrey withdrew a metal cardinal like the one I'd admired a week or so earlier. This one was fully painted and was an absolute treasure of painstaking craftsmanship. I turned it over in my hands and thanked Jeffrey with an embrace. I handed the bird to Elise for safekeeping, and she carefully tucked it into the flap pocket of her jacket. Next, I turned to Sam.

"You old softy. Are you sure you want to risk this?"

"Aw, I'm on the six-year plan anyway. What more can they do to me?"

We laughed and joked for about fifteen minutes. Buzz and Sam kept careful watch as I stretched and enjoyed the relatively fresh air. A guard was still on duty, but he stood at the far end of the garage, bored and inattentive now that his companion had left to patrol the campus. The main door was the only visible way in or out, so he obviously didn't think security would be much of a problem. As my friends made sure that the guard didn't suddenly decide to stroll this way, Elise and I finally had a moment to ourselves. She'd brought me a sandwich, an apple, and a thermos filled with cold water. I gratefully gulped down the water before attacking the food.

"Don't forget, mister, you owe me a date."

Nothing would have pleased me more, but I expressed my doubts around a mouthful of ham and cheese. "They'll be watching me. It'll be more difficult than before."

"Haven't you learned not to underestimate your friends?" she asked, disconcertingly close and moving even closer. Jeffrey watched with interest, but I didn't have the heart to ask him to excuse us.

"Jake," Elise began, her arms suddenly around my neck, "I've wanted to tell you...well, lots of things, and I was waiting for the right moment, but we may have to wait longer than I expected for that, so..."

"Break it up, you two. We have a serious problem." Buzz said.

"What's wrong?" I asked.

"Another guard just walked in. He's probably coming to check on that space heater, making sure you don't fry in there. Quick, get back in. Jeffrey, you've got to seal him up fast."

"That's not good enough," Elise said. "The hinges won't cool by the time they get here."

Sam took charge. "I've got an idea. Elise, stay with Jeffrey and get him out as soon as he's done. Buzz, you're with me. Jake, stay fresh," he said, heading in the direction of the guards.

Buzz followed him without argument, and they both crouched down behind a group of rusty fifty-five gallon drums. As I folded myself back into the locker, I heard bits and pieces of their plan and felt another burst of gratitude for their friendship.

"So we circle around from that direction? Then what?"

I didn't hear the response, but Buzz apparently understood.

"That's all well and good, but take it easy. I'm a brilliant inventor, not a pugilist."

"You and your twenty-dollar words. Just roll with 'em, Buzzard. Let's save the day."

"I'm ready when you are."

Jeffrey was about to return the door to its proper place when Elise leaned in and kissed my cheek. "I'll be waiting. You hang in there, okay? I love you."

Before I had a chance to respond, the door was back in place and the sparks from Jeffrey's blowtorch were flying. I was stunned. The beauty of those three words stood out against the repulsive backdrop of the Can, like roses that managed to bloom amidst the rubble of an earthquake. I couldn't respond to Elise's words, not now with the noise of the blowtorch, but I vowed that when I emerged from this...*ouch*! I had neglected to keep my hands away from the locker door, and the pain refocused my attention on the present. I pushed myself back into the locker as far as I could go and waited for Jeffrey to finish his work.

I soon discovered what Sam and Buzz had in mind. I heard a crash, then lots of shouting, then the unmistakable sound of flesh striking flesh. The heavy patter of running footsteps echoed throughout the cavernous building as the guards began to shout, too. Sam and Buzz evaded them, making a great deal of noise as they continued hollering and calling each other names. I heard a few heavy thuds, and then a rough voice—a guard—addressing the trespassing students.

"What do you think you're doing here?"

"Begging your pardon, sir, my classmate and I had a little wager going. He lost, and I was having difficulty collecting. I bet that 3290 would be whimpering like a baby by now, while Buzz here figured he'd still be hanging strong."

I couldn't see anything that was going on, but Jeffrey had finished his work and I could hear better now. One of the guards snorted and agreed with Sam, who had known just what to say, but had he and Buzz bought enough time?

Jeffrey brought out a can of freon-propelled compressed air. My friends had thought of everything. If the guards discovered red-hot hinges they would certainly become suspicious, although I doubted they would guess what had actually happened. Jeffrey looked at Elise for confirmation. She in turn looked at me, touched her fingers to her lips, then pressed them against the air slits. She whispered, "Scream on three," and then she was gone. I counted to three and then screamed with all my strength, covering the sound that Jeffrey made when he released two bursts of chilled air at the hinges to cool them. There was a chance that cooling the hinges so rapidly could cause them to fracture, but it was a necessary risk. When I heard the hissing stop, Jeffrey crept away, whispering a final "Jake is my friend," before circling with Elise and exiting through the main doors while my other two friends maintained their diversion.

"Keep an eye on them," one of the guards said to the other. "It was a close bet, you two. He's sure screaming now." The footsteps got closer, and I saw the guard's chest, then his eyes as he bent down. I quickly started screaming again, then slumped forward, pretending to swoon.

"Hey, are you completely stupid?" the guard demanded of his comrade. "This locker door is blazing hot. You wanna kill this kid?"

Despite my discomfort, I had to stifle a laugh. It had worked. The guard thought the space heater was to blame for the heat that radiated off the welded hinges.

"Senna said to give him the full treatment," a distant voice replied.

"I'm turning this off. Leave it off, per my orders. He's had enough. Is he scheduled to be released tonight?"

"Yeah, after the second dinner shift."

"All right, I'm going to bring these two out for some fun. They look like they'd enjoy a little exercise, isn't that right boys?"

"Sir, yes, sir!"

"In the future, remember to control your curiosity. And student 5818, if you can't pay your debts, you shouldn't gamble."

They were gone and I was safe, but at what price? The brief period of fresh air and exercise had done me good. I felt that I could endure the next few hours until my release, but my thoughts revolved around two topics: the three life-transforming words that Elise had spoken, and concern over what would become of my friends.

I was released from the Can as scheduled, and I sensed that the guard expected me to be in worse shape than I was. He made no comment, though and simply handed me a liter of water before marching me back to the barracks. It was obvious that I would be denied food until the following morning and my stomach made loud noises as it rebelled. I paced, waiting for the guys to return from dinner.

I wondered what the vice-chancellor had in store for me. He'd probably permitted the relative luxury of a shower and a good night's sleep in order to lull me into a false feeling of security. Tomorrow, I would no doubt face him again. He would pose the same questions, and I would once again refuse to answer. I was afraid of returning to the Can but only in a distant, detached way. The loyalty of my friends had given me incredible strength. I felt invincible.

My barracks mates started to trickle in, and they quickly gathered around to ask about my experience in the Can. They were awed by my apparent good spirits, but I kept quiet about the brief respite I'd enjoyed. It was possible that Senna had the barracks bugged, especially since he knew I possessed valuable information. I had no intention of betraying Buzz, Sam, Jeffrey, and Elise by carelessly boasting about the way they'd come to my aid earlier that day.

"Here, Jake. I brought ye some grub," Fergie said, passing me a napkin-wrapped bundle. The guard had stepped outside to secure the perimeter of the barracks, and I gratefully wolfed down the food.

"So why'd you get canned?" Joe asked.

"Senna wanted…information," I said, in a good approximation of the vice-chancellor's creepy voice. Everyone laughed, but quickly grew serious as I continued. "He knows about the contraband ring and he's trying to get me to give up the names. He seems to think he has something to hold over my head."

"He does," drawled Elvin. "Your life!"

"Aye, lad. It doesna pay to be careless. Ye dinna tell him anythin', did ye?"

"Not a word!"

They were relieved at that, and we talked for a while longer, devising ways to thwart Senna's investigation. After everyone dispersed, I sat down on my bunk and heard a distinctive crinkle. I got up quickly and saw that an envelope had been placed right on top of the gray bedspread. Was it from Elise? I snatched it up, concerned about the guard who had just returned from his patrol. I threw a quick glance over my shoulder, but he was watching our television monitor, which alternated between a cable news program and an in-house video bulletin board.

He was engrossed in a special report about the NCAA finals, so I had a few moments of privacy.

I turned my attention back to the letter and was instantly disappointed. It wasn't from Elise. The envelope bore the embossed gold stamp of Ashur-Kesed. I slid my finger under the flap and withdrew the crisp linen stationery. I pulled out a form letter from Dr. Senna and read,

Student 3290,

As of this date, you are hereby informed that you will be formally discharged from Ashur-Kesed with full graduation credits two weeks from today. This request was authorized by your parents/guardians and approved by the faculty. Your textbooks will be collected the day before your departure. Be sure to hand in any outstanding work or your transcript will not be released to any university you may be planning to attend. Do not remove any items from your barracks, such as blankets, extra toiletries, or...

I didn't read the rest. I had dreamed about going home since the day I'd arrived. To my surprise, I realized that I wasn't ready yet. This was too soon. I had things to resolve, preparations to make. I wasn't ready to say good-bye to Elise or to my other friends. Why had Mom and Dad suddenly decided to bring me home now?

I needed advice from Buzz. He would know what to do. I paced the barracks, drawing curious stares from the students who sat conversing or studying, and I waited for him to return from dinner.

Fifteen minutes passed. The last of the boys who ate second shift dinner returned, but Buzz was not among them. Barker swung up onto the top bunk, greeting me as usual.

"Hey, Jake. Glad you're okay. Tough break about Buzz, huh?"

"What do you mean?"

"He's pulling mud duty tonight with Sam. They got caught near the Can." Barker seemed to consider that for the first time. "That was pretty careless, come to think of it. Maybe they were trying to pay you a little visit."

"Yeah, maybe," I said. In my anxiety over the letter, I had forgotten that my friends had sacrificed themselves so that I could escape the Can—and what a sacrifice. Mud duty was an exhausting, frustrating disciplinary assignment. It was meted out to students who committed a mid-level offense and was particularly suited to a pair of offenders.

An officer would conduct the students to the east athletic field. Just beyond the field was a plot of useless, barren land that served as the perfect setting for the punishment. They'd give the two offenders shovels. The officer in charge would begin to spray the students and the dirt with water from an irrigation hose, soaking them to the skin and turning the dirt into mud. The students were made to dig. While one was digging a trench, the other filled it. It was messy, backbreaking, futile work, and it lasted as long as the offense warranted. The severity also depended on the mood of the officer in charge. At his discretion, he could forgo the water altogether or reduce the length of the trench or both. He could also intensify the punishment if he wished.

There was nothing I could do for them except hope that the officer in charge was in a merciful mood. I waited in the barracks, agonized over their suffering and worried about my premature departure from AKPS. I hoped that the morning would bring fresh perspective.

Chapter Twenty-One

I committed my final offense on a hot, dry night in August.

It was about 9:30 and the meeting of the Ace of Hearts Club had just ended. It had been another boring exercise in beating a good thing to death. Games can be entertaining, and friends are a necessity, but the club had squeezed the fun out of both. When you *had* to play cards and hang out with friends, the activity suddenly became less like recreation and more like a chore. I partially blamed Dad, too, him and his "Far-Away Hearts Club" note. That note (or more specifically, his name for our club) overshadowed every moment I spent in the tree house.

I was constantly burdened by the dual life I lived. Nagging guilt mingled with ferocious resentment. I desired reconciliation, but I also blamed Mom, Dad, and Nick for what I considered my ruined life.

On that particular evening, Diane and I had planned to spend some time together after my club meeting. She'd climbed up into the tree house as the guys were leaving and asked the question that had become a running joke: could she join the club? Everyone laughed and promised that they'd think about it.

We all thought it was just a typical summer night. My friends didn't know that they would never visit the tree house again. I didn't know that my days at home were numbered. Diane didn't know that her relationship with me was about to end.

As the sound of my companion's voices faded, I reluctantly admit-

ted to myself that having a girlfriend was not as "awesome" as everyone claimed. Diane and I had settled into a routine that was every bit as
burdensome as the Ace of Hearts Club meetings. She would come over,
we would talk for a little while, she would remove her gum (which sig-
naled her desire to begin kissing), and then we would engage in that
peculiar teenage ritual.

I don't mean to say that I found it unpleasant. I enjoyed the rush of
knowing that someone of the opposite sex liked me enough to kiss me.
The problem was that I was so starved for affection that I settled for
any intimacy at all, even the superficial companionship that Diane provided. I knew perfectly well that she and I would never last for more
than a year or two. Even then, our relationship was showing signs of
strain, due largely to my poor attitude.

That night the small talk soon ended, and Diane's hand moved to
her mouth to remove the wad of pink bubble gum she was chewing.
Oh, well. At least I liked the taste of bubble gum. I moved over to the
beanbag where she waited. We began to kiss, and I really wanted it to
mean something. I wanted to *feel* something, anything besides this
emptiness; but no, there was only the usual tickle in the pit of my stomach. I almost sighed as I leaned in for another round. That's when I
heard the snicker.

At first, I thought it was Diane. I pulled back and asked her what
was funny. She merely raised her eyebrows in unspoken confusion.
Then I heard it again, and knew it was behind me. It had to be Nick. I
wondered what he had seen. If Mom and Dad found out I was up in my
tree house making out with a girl, Dad would probably ground me for a
month. Although a part of me didn't mind spending time away from the
tree house, it was completely unacceptable for it to happen because of
this little snitch.

My parents were neither unrealistic nor unromantic, but they had
warned me about putting myself in situations where my physical desires might overpower good sense. They still trusted me to some extent,
but of all the family rules, remaining pure until marriage was among the
most sacred. Whatever Nick had seen, it wouldn't look good to Mom and
Dad, even though it was relatively harmless.

I tried direct confrontation. I spun around, making a scrunchy beanbag sound that made me feel ridiculous.

"Hey! Do I spy on you, weasel?"

"No," he replied calmly, "but then again, I don't really do anything worth spying on. At least, not lately."

He really knew how to get under my skin. I crawled to the door of the tree house. "Get lost, and keep your mouth shut," I said.

Nick's head disappeared from view. I turned back to Diane and saw that cursed little orange flame that indicated she had lit a cigarette.

"I thought you were trying to quit."

"I am." *Puff.*

"You couldn't wait two seconds while I got rid of him?"

"I knew you'd be in no mood." *Drag*, exhale while talking. How unbelievably irritating. "Why don't you let him come up? He's a good kid."

"Why don't you mind your own business?" I was shocked that those words came out of my mouth. I had never spoken to her like that, but then again, she had never before meddled in my affairs. I could see that I'd hurt her feelings, and I supposed I should be sorry. I was just about to apologize when she looked over my shoulder and smiled.

"Hi, Nick," she said.

I looked back and saw his head, barely visible over the edge of the narrow porch. That did it. I turned and rushed toward the porch, unable to restrain my rage any longer.

Nick's eyes went wide and he scrambled down the ladder. I lost sight of him, and then suddenly, I heard him scream. A massive shock rumbled through the floorboards of the tree house. Horror supplanted rage. I rushed to the edge of the porch.

Nick had somehow lost his grip on the rope ladder. As he fell, his foot had become entangled in the rungs and he hung there, his arms hanging down, his face growing redder by the moment as the blood rushed to his head. He was too afraid to scream again, or do anything else that might cause him to fall.

For a moment, I couldn't move. No one had ever fallen out of the tree house. In fact, I had never even thought of the possibility until now. The house was rock-solid and barely even swayed in a stiff wind. Of all the people to fall out, why did it have to be Nick, and why did it have to be my fault?

Diane leaned over the edge. She gasped when she saw Nick hanging by one foot. The sound shook me out of my paralysis. I leaned over the edge and spoke to Nick quietly, trying not to panic him.

"Okay, Nick, it's gonna be fine, it's gonna be fine, just hang on. I'm coming down, just don't move, okay? Don't move…"

He didn't reply, and I started down the ladder, slowly, carefully. If he had fallen any other way, he could have grabbed the ladder himself and climbed to safety, but his foot had caught the rope in such a way that any movement on his part might cause him to plunge headlong into the hard ground below. I hoped to help him grab the end of the ladder so he could safely reach the ground. I told myself it would be simple. Afterwards, we'd have a good laugh about it. It never occurred to me to call for Dad. I had to save Nick, because I had made him fall.

I balanced precariously in midair, only a few feet from him but seemingly miles apart. I vowed that I would close the distance between Nick and me, not only right there on the ladder, but every day from then on. I slowly inched my way closer to him, gingerly placing each foot on the rung below. I realized something in those few seconds of remorse. I realized that I loved my brother.

"Okay, Nick, almost there, hang on…"

He was only inches away now. No need to be nervous. I reached for his leg, knowing even as I did so that it would be better if I descended just one more rung. My balance was just a hair off. I was afraid, I was trembling, and I was impatient.

I missed.

The ladder swayed dangerously, and I watched in stunned disbelief as Nick's foot slid off the rung. I knew I wouldn't be able to catch him and I knew it was my fault, all of it, and then I heard Nick screaming and…

Silence.

The screaming suddenly resumed and I realized it was coming from me. It was an automatic, uncontrollable scream that ripped from my throat, mingled with Diane's, and brought Mom and Dad running. I don't remember how or when I got off the ladder. The next half hour was a blur. Red and blue lights flashed, and local volunteer paramedics were soon joined by police and hospital ambulance attendants. The ambulance cut deep, muddy grooves into our backyard, and the attendants brought out a special stretcher that they only used for people with serious back injuries.

Nick didn't move. Nick made no sound. I wanted to rush over to him, to tell him to stop fooling around and get up, just get up. Wave after wave of guilt battered me as I thought about all the terrible things I'd said and done to Nick. He was my brother, and brothers are supposed to look after one another. Hadn't he always tried to look after me? I wanted so badly to invite him into the tree house for a game of cards. I would rip up that stupid sign, and it would be *our* tree house. I wanted to erase the past two years and start over. I would do it differently, I would do everything differently, I would *be* different.

I felt a hand on my shoulder and looked up, startled out of my growing hysteria. Dad's expression was the same as always, but his eyes registered grief. I wanted to ask about Nick, about why he was so still and quiet, but I was afraid of the answer. Mom stood with us, but she, like Dad, seemed distant. I felt outside of my family, as though I were looking at them through a gate I had slammed shut.

I hadn't yet considered the ramifications of what had happened. It didn't occur to me that this accident looked suspicious in light of my much-publicized feelings for Nick. For once, I was focused on others. I wanted to take away some of the pain in Dad's eyes, to say I was sorry—for everything. I didn't get the chance. As I looked up at my father and began to speak, I noticed that his face was suddenly illuminated by a strange, flickering light. He noticed it, too, and looked up towards the source of the orange glow. His eyes changed, and I followed his gaze skyward.

My tree house was on fire.

It took a moment to register. Diane was talking with one of the paramedics; I think they had dated once. She saw the blaze, cried out a warning and pointed up at the tree house. I understood what had happened. *Where did you put your cigarette, Diane?* I thought fiercely. I wanted to run for the barn to get the hose, but I couldn't move. Something was holding me back.

I turned and saw my father, looking upward at the growing fury of the flames. He had clamped his hand around my upper arm. I struggled uselessly against his grip.

"Dad, let me go! Maybe we can save it, maybe there's something we can…"

"No." He looked down at me. His eyes had changed again. There was still love there, there was always love there, but there was also a terrible finality. "Let it burn, Jake. It's too late." I felt a chill zip its way down my spine. There was something about the way Dad said those words that made me certain they bore a double meaning.

I suddenly realized that the tree house had drawn my attention away from an important fact: my brother was being loaded into the back of the ambulance, and I was to blame for it. For the first time, I understood what Dad had meant by the name "Far-Away Hearts Club." My heart—my thoughts, my decisions, and my emotions—had steadily drifted away from my father and everything he'd taught me. I had chosen to reject things of substance in favor of things that didn't last—things that burned.

As the paramedics made final preparations to take Nick to the hospital, my parents and I watched the fire slowly consume the tree house.

The rope ladder burst into flame and fell to the ground, forever cutting off access to my childhood haven. The well-worn pile of hemp lay there, announcing the end of an era.

The night was hot, and the fire made it hotter still, but I shuddered.

Dad called for Yasha and Remmy. He had already cut power to the tree house. Now he instructed them to wet down the smoldering debris while the three of us went to the emergency room. Mom, Dad, and I climbed into the car and followed the ambulance to the hospital.

We arrived there just as they were rushing Nick inside. Mom and I sat in the waiting room while Dad attended to the paperwork. We spoke very little. All we could do was wait as the minutes turned to hours. Yasha and Remmy showed up after they'd finished extinguishing the remains of the tree house. Mr. Modau walked in with Mr. Aggy, and several other people from town stopped by. They did their best to encourage us, but my only thought was *What if Nick dies?*

"Jake, Nick issa gonna be all right," Mr. Aggy said as he took a seat next to me. "This is a good hospital. You don'ta worry, eh?"

I tried to smile, but I couldn't speak. Mom came over.

"How are you holding up?"

"Okay. Why is it taking so long? What are they doing in there?"

"Their best, I hope. It'll be all right."

Why did everyone insist on saying that? How could everything be all right? They didn't see Nick slip through their fingers, they didn't hear that awful sound when he hit.

Finally, a young doctor emerged through the swinging doors. She looked tired. *Please have good news,* I silently urged.

"Nick's a tough young man," she said. "I transferred him up to critical care. You can't see him tonight, but he's out of danger for the moment."

We all wept with joy. Even so, I'm sorry to say that the instant I was sure that Nick was out of danger, my focus shifted back to myself.

I thought about the accident. I wondered what I'd been planning to do when I'd rushed toward Nick. Had I really been about to push him? If he hadn't fallen by accident, would he have become the victim of his brother's rage?

It was time for all this to end. I still wasn't sure how I felt about having a brother, but I knew one thing: I was ready to try. I decided to wait until the shock of the accident wore off a little, then I would have a talk with Mom and Dad.

We went home soon after the doctor's report. Mom and Dad (who still hadn't asked for details about the accident) stayed up for a while after I collapsed into bed. My fear began to subside and my hopes for the future began to grow stronger.

I awoke to the sounds of conversation in the kitchen. The sun had been up for some time and I was surprised that Dad had allowed me to sleep through my chores. I swung my legs out of bed and stretched. I felt a little better after a good night's sleep.

I smelled breakfast downstairs and cautiously entered the kitchen. Mom had laid out a simple meal of muffins, juice, fresh bread, and coffee. She and Dad had already eaten. They looked grim.

"Sit down, son," my father said.

"Is anything wrong? Is Nick still okay?"

"Yes, he's fine."

Mom and Dad told me that Nick had fractured one of his vertebrae, but the break had not injured his spinal cord. He would suffer no paralysis, although his recovery would be long and painful.

"Jake," my mother said, "what happened last night in that tree house?"

I stuttered through a description of the accident. It was impossible to gloss over the role I'd played in it, so I didn't try. My face grew red as I described my reaction to Nick's intrusion.

"Son, you know we treasure honesty in this house," Dad said. "Did you mean to push Nick out of the tree house?"

The question shocked me, because Dad hadn't asked if I *had* pushed him; he asked if I'd *meant* to push him. And I wasn't sure of the answer.

"I…I don't think…no, no I didn't mean to push him. I didn't want to kill him, I just didn't want him spying on me."

"Son, this is certainly not the time for a lecture, but I'm sure you understand how serious this is. Nick is going to be okay, and that's the most important thing, but we need to talk later in the week about…" Dad stopped and looked down at the table in a fashion that made me turn ice cold. "We need to talk about the future."

The next couple of days were difficult. Mom and Dad seemed different somehow. The business of the farm went on as usual, except that my parents went back and forth to the hospital whenever they had a free moment. Nick was still sedated most of the time, so visiting him consisted of sitting there, watching him breathe through a tube.

Three days after the accident, Mom and Dad asked me if I wanted to visit Nick. I said yes, and we went after lunch.

It was awful. The antiseptic smell, the drawn faces of the patients, the sound of monitors that announced life and death with impersonal electronic beeps—all of it paled in comparison to the sight of my brother.

Nick had four holes drilled into his skull. Metal posts were screwed into the holes and a thick plastic device called a "halo" encircled his head, keeping his fractured vertebra immobile. He was unconscious and would remain so for at least another day. I didn't see him again for two years, and every time he came to mind in those intervening years, that image of him in the hospital assaulted me, blamed me, and humbled me.

When we got home from the hospital, Mom and Dad asked me to have a seat in the living room. They spoke in quiet, measured tones that assured me they were leading up to something awful. They pointed out the way my attitude had deteriorated over the past few years. They reminded me of the many warnings they had given. They mentioned Nick's growth and the way he had yearned for (and never received) my friendship. Lastly, they told me that they thought it would be best if I spent some time away from home. They had selected a school in Vermont called Ashur-Kesed. They reaffirmed that this was not a punishment. The purpose was to teach me things I apparently could not—or would not—learn at home. They told me they loved me and that this was difficult for them, and they said a great many other things, but as they spoke one sentence overlapped their words in my mind, contradicting them like a drum that thumps along just off the beat: *You're being thrown out of your own family.*

When my parents were through, they asked me if I wanted to say anything. I had many things to say. There had been apologies to make, words to regret, actions to recant. However, like an attorney who knows the case is lost, I couldn't see the point in making a closing statement that would only serve to lengthen my defeat. I said nothing. By the time my parents gave me permission to leave the room, my bitterness had returned. All my anger and resentment, unhappy at having been shut out of my mind for even a brief moment, barreled back into my consciousness with great fury.

I went upstairs, packed, and lay down on my bed. Mom and Dad took me to the airport later that week. My emotions vacillated between anger and fear. As my parents stood at the gate and watched me board the plane, the tears streamed down both their faces. I'd never seen Dad cry like that before.

I gripped the arms of my seat as the plane took me away from my home, my family, and my life.

Chapter Twenty-Two

It was three o'clock in the morning. I'd had a hard time sleeping and was just rolling over for the hundredth time when Buzz finally stumbled into the barracks. A thick layer of mud covered him from head to foot, and exhaustion pinched his face. Thankfully, the disciplinary officer extended unusual clemency and allowed Buzz to shower for as long as he wanted.

After a full fifteen minutes under the hot water, Buzz limped over to our bunk where I impatiently waited for him. I noticed that his lower lip and right eye were swollen. He and Sam must have been throwing real punches during their diversion in the maintenance garage.

As Buzz approached, I reminded myself to wait an appropriate amount of time before asking for his advice. *You should be more concerned about him than you are about yourself.* I sighed. The same old selfishness.

"Buzz, I don't know what to say," I whispered. "Thanks for everything."

"I told you, farm boy. We have to look after each other." He crouched by the side of my bunk, keeping an eye on the main doors. (The barracks commandant sometimes showed up in the middle of the night to do a bed check). "How are you feeling?" he asked. "Any permanent damage from the Can?"

"I don't think so. How's Sam?"

"Oh, he's fine. Pain just makes him tougher and meaner." Buzz yawned and stretched painfully. "I'm looking forward to the hour of sleep they've graciously allowed me."

I realized that if I didn't ask for Buzz's advice now, I might not get another chance until the next night after dinner. I wanted to be considerate, but my worries suddenly tumbled out, seemingly of their own accord.

I held up the letter. "I found this on my bunk when I got back from the Can," I whispered urgently. "I'm going home in two weeks."

"I sense that for some insane reason you're not happy about that."

"Well, I have some unfinished business," I said, a little defensively. I'd expected him to be more sympathetic.

"*She* would be happy that you're going home, especially after you were canned."

"It's not just Elise. I…"

Buzz was no longer listening. I could tell because he suddenly slumped face first toward the floor. The many hours of exhaustive labor had apparently caught up with him, and I barely caught him in time. I helped him up to his bunk where his swoon immediately turned into a deep sleep.

I watched him long enough to assure myself that he was all right, then lay down on my own bunk and finally fell asleep.

The next day, I'd hoped to speak with Buzz before we headed off to class. Instead, I was awakened by two of Senna's personal guards. They made me dress quickly, and then they dragged me into the vestibule of the vice-chancellor's office. I was tired, but the burst of adrenaline from being awakened so suddenly gave me an extra measure of vigilance. Perhaps Senna anticipated that. He made me wait for a half hour before opening the double doors to his office. By that time, my exhaustion had reasserted itself.

"Good morning, student 3290. I trust you had a pleasant night's sleep?" The vice-chancellor's cultured accent was like a coat of paint on a rusty dumpster. It did nothing to hide the stench of his malicious intentions. "Tell me," he continued as he waved me into his inner chambers, "is the Can as uncomfortable as everyone says it is?"

I ignored his taunt, walked stiffly into the room…and froze in the doorway.

Elise stood next to the vice-chancellor's desk.

My eyes went wide, but she shook her head subtly, once.

"Thank you, my friends," Senna said graciously as he seated himself in his high-backed chair. "Your clumsy attempt at subterfuge only confirmed what I already knew. You two are acquainted."

One of the guards placed a strong hand on my back and propelled me into the room. Sabrina, who was in her usual position by the desk, growled low in her brown-black throat. I straightened up and waited for Senna to get on with it, my mind full of questions. How had he found out about Elise? Was it something I'd said while under the influence of those drugs the other day?

"Let's get right to the point," the vice-chancellor said. "3290, yesterday I asked you for some information, which you were strangely reluctant to provide. I summoned you here to tell you a story, and I think you'll find it both amusing and relevant. Afterwards, you might be more inclined to cooperate. Shall we begin? Once upon a time there was a wicked little girl who thought she could write…"

Elise stared straight ahead, but I could see the rage in her eyes. Why had she even agreed to be here? She wasn't a student at Ashur-Kesed; Senna had no hold over her.

"You see, Jake—may I call you Jake?—this wicked little girl wrote a slanderous article about an excellent educational institution—this educational institution. She filled her article with lies, but since perception is often reality, I was reluctant to allow that piece of yellow journalism to be printed. This next part is scandalous, but why dress up the truth? The girl blackmailed me. She told me that every week she made a 'special' phone call. If I refused to agree to her terms, she would fail to make that call and her article would appear in every major newspaper from here to the West Coast. Her terms were simple: she was to be allowed access to the campus without harassment and without penalty at whatever hour she chose. She refused to divulge her reasons for this strange request, so I assigned some of my men to uncover it for me. Do you know what happened?"

I remained silent.

"I discovered that my own guards couldn't find out what this little tramp was doing during her evening visits." Senna selected a pipe from his desk rack, filled it and lit it. "More important," he said with the pipe clenched between his teeth, "they couldn't find out who she was doing it with." He exhaled and the smoke curled around his head, intensifying his sinister appearance.

I stood at attention, trying not to react to his speech. So many things made sense now. I'd known that Elise was a writer and that she worked for a newspaper, but I never dreamed that she'd put her talents to use in such an extraordinary (and dangerous) way. It amazed me that all this time she'd had the vice-chancellor under her thumb…for my sake.

Dr. Senna continued, assuming the mournful expression of one who had been unjustly wounded. "Apparently, she convinced some of my own employees to turn against me. I must admit that I am not the easiest man to work for. My standards are high, and I brook no impertinence or disobedience. I gradually discovered that she had taken advantage of a small group of dissatisfied, weak-minded fools who were just looking for an opportunity to betray me."

Ha! I thought. *That probably wasn't too difficult.*

I admired Elise's cleverness; Senna did not. "This state of affairs is intolerable," he concluded as he took another drag on his pipe. Despite these words, he wore a thin smile that implied he'd found a way to turn the events to his advantage.

I jumped slightly when the intercom buzzer on his desk sounded.

"Ms. Jessep, did I lapse into a foreign tongue when I instructed you not to disturb me this morning or were you calling to tender your resignation?" Senna snapped.

"Vice-chancellor, the Code One you warned me about is on line seven," a tinny, female voice replied from the speaker.

"Put him on hold, stall him, *do your job*." Senna thrust the pipe back into its holder and redirected his attention toward me.

"It seems we need to hasten this along. Fortunately for me and Ashur-Kesed, there was a flaw in this young woman's plan. Two days ago, while making a routine visit to a sick student in the infirmary, I discovered who this young woman was so desperate to see." Senna leaned forward. "It's you, Jake. Isn't that charming?"

Suddenly, as if he'd thrown a switch, Senna dropped his grandfatherly tone and reverted to his usual biting cadence. "Student 3290, the balance of power has changed. I will not be blackmailed by no-talent hacks, I will not have students smuggling contraband and sneaking around, and I will not have my own guards taking this woman's side and betraying me. I will have *order*."

Sabrina snarled as if to punctuate her master's diatribe. "If this snipe fails to make her phone call, I will hurt you. Badly. If you fail to give me the information I desire, I will hurt you. Badly. Since you're going home in two weeks, we're short on time, but please believe me when I say that these will be the worst two weeks of your life if you fail to cooperate. The moral of this little tale? I always win in the end." He paused, withdrew a small tape recorder from the breast pocket of his suit and clicked it on with a flourish.

"Now," he said with renewed cordiality, "shall we start with the contraband smugglers?"

"No, sir."

Senna's expression darkened, his eyes narrowed, and his lips squeezed together. "Sabrina, darling, did he just say no? What should we do about that, precious, hmm? Up!"

At that command, the Doberman stood and advanced one step in my direction. She crouched in a pre-attack position and awaited further instructions. This wasn't good. I remembered a few experiences I'd had on the farm and knew that I had to take a chance.

"Do you love your dog, vice-chancellor?"

That caught him off guard. "What?"

"I asked if you love your dog."

"Don't play games with me, 3290. Abandon this ill-advised ploy for more time and simply answer my question. If you refuse, I fear that Sabrina will become unhappy."

"Vice-chancellor, I was raised on a farm. I've killed wolves with nothing more than a three-foot hickory staff. If you love your dog, tell her to sit down. If she comes one step closer, I'll blind her. If need be, I'll kill her."

My voice was steady, and I knew that my experience would serve me well if the situation called for self-defense. Nevertheless, I hoped Senna would relent. I watched him closely as he slowly walked around his desk and stroked his growling pet behind the ears. His face underwent terrible contortions as he attempted to evaluate my bold threat.

"Do you think you can take him, my darling?" he said, almost too softly for me to hear. "Is he bluffing, precious? Can this puny weakling really subdue a magnificent animal such as you? Hmm?" Senna's sunken eyes bore into me with disturbing intensity. He looked quite insane, and his lips curled upward as he announced his decision. *"HIT!"* he thundered.

The dog leapt forward, even as I crouched into a ready position. My reflexes and experience took over. As the Doberman jumped, I thrust two fingers into her left eye, rolled to the right, and prepared for another attack. I'd pulled the blow at the last second because I didn't want to permanently injure her, but my maneuver had been sufficient. Sabrina recoiled, whining in pain, her legs slipping and scratching on the polished floor. She was, however, a well-trained attack dog. She quickly regained her footing and leaped for my throat again.

"Sabrina, *down*! Rest!" The dog abruptly stopped and retreated behind the desk, even as my head jerked around in amazement. That command had come from Elise, not Senna. The vice-chancellor was temporarily speechless. He seemed stunned that Elise had presumed to command his dog, and worse, that Sabrina had obeyed. In the midst of the commotion, the intercom sounded again. Senna bashed the intercom button with his fist.

"What do I have to do to make this clear?" he screamed. "I do not want—"

"Vice-chancellor," the disembodied voice interrupted, "the Code One says that if you don't speak with him right now, he'll get on a plane and be in your office before the school day is out." There was a brief pause. "He says—these are his words—he doesn't recommend that you force him to take that measure. Sir."

"He doesn't recommend…?" Senna, his near victory spoiled by his dog's failed attack and by this troublesome and apparently influential caller, snarled orders to the two guards stationed at the door. "Get *her* off campus, and confine him to barracks for the remainder of the day. Move, move! Ms. Jessup, call the veterinarian—this savage has injured my dog. Give me line seven…"

The guards led Elise out first. We didn't even have the opportunity to exchange a glance. She disappeared down a side hallway while they hustled me down the steps, through the main lobby, and out into the

Hub quadrangle. From there, one of the guards escorted me to my barracks and then remained outside to stand watch. I carefully pondered everything I'd learned about Elise and whispered a silent "thank you" to her and to that caller, whomever he or she was.

I expected Senna to call me into his office for the conclusion of my interrogation, but no one came to get me. I knew I'd go crazy if I just paced back and forth all day, so I passed the time by studying.

At lunchtime, I heard excellent news from one of my barracks mates. Dr. Senna had been called off campus to an emergency meeting of the AKPS board of directors, over which the aged Chancellor himself, Rodney N. Kesed III, presided. I couldn't wait to tell Buzz, but I was even more eager to hear from Elise. This was a perfect opportunity for us to meet one last time before I left school. The trouble was I still didn't know how to contact her. I hoped she'd get a message to me, but I was concerned about Senna. I had no idea how far off-campus his influence reached. Did he have people watching her? What if they intercepted her message and destroyed it, or worse, what if they allowed us to meet and ambushed us? What if...

"You're the biggest worrier I've ever known."

The voice came from the door of the barracks and I looked up, interrupted from my anxious reveries by Buzz's observation. He and a group of friends had just returned from lunch.

"What makes you think I was worrying?"

"I could smell the smoke coming out of your ears from a hundred yards away."

"Doesn't that usually mean that a person is thinking?"

"Well, if you were thinking you wouldn't be worrying."

I had to concede his point. I leaned against our bunk, adopted a casual air and tried to appear calm.

"Better?" I asked.

"Much. You look like you're waiting for Senna to perform an appendectomy on you—without anesthesia." Buzz's lip and eye looked better today, but he was still cradling his side. After helping him up to his bunk, I convened a private meeting with my battered bunkmate and five other friends. I told them what had happened that morning, including the letter informing me of my early release, Elise's unusual presence in the vice-chancellor's office, and Senna's impending absence from the campus. Boys being boys, they were especially impressed by the way I'd handled Sabrina.

"Ye really knew how to set that mutt on her backside, lad!" Fergus exclaimed.

"I suppose. It's nothing when you grow up on a farm. What really surprised me was the way that dog listened to Elise."

Buzz jumped in. "Oh, that's easy. Anyone who knows the commands can do that. Dogs respond to specific phrases."

"Sure, but what good is it to have an attack dog if, say, a robber or a mugger can just call the dog off?"

"Maybe Sabrina was confused from that poke in the eye you gave her," Barker suggested.

"Maybe," I said doubtfully. "Anyway, I still have the problem of going home early with no way to contact Elise."

"What would she say if she were here?" Buzz asked.

"She'd say to trust her," I sulked.

"Right. You need to get your mind off your problem—which, by the way, doesn't seem terribly pressing to anyone in this room besides you. Hey, boys," he said, addressing the rest of the barracks. "Jake just found out he's going home. Anyone feel sorry for him?"

The room was suddenly filled with shouts of outrage. I was pelted with dirty clothing, notebooks, pillows, and anything that came to hand. I was laughing hard by the time they relented. Buzz, who had overseen my assassination, poked his head over the side of the top bunk.

"Now that you've been given a lesson in perspective, let's go over your preparations. Obviously, the big date is on again. You've figured out the place; do you know how you're going to get into the bell tower?"

"Uh, no. I guess it would be locked, wouldn't it?"

"No problem. I have a friend in 694 who knows how to pick locks. I'll have him see to it. What if there're bats up there?"

"Bats?"

"You'd better check it out first. Winged, blood-sucking mammals would probably put a damper on the evening. You'll have to sneak out tonight, but those are the chances we take." Buzz pushed up his nose with his index finger and made bat noises.

Among his other talents, Buzz was good at distracting me. We discussed my date with Elise and before long the rest of the barracks drifted over. All of them had helped in one way or another, so they all had a stake in this. I welcomed their input.

I looked from one happily scheming face to the next. Two years ago, these faces had all been unwelcome reminders that I was hundreds of miles away from home. Now, I actually took comfort from the group. They'd all been rejected by friends, family, and society, but had latched onto each other (and to me) with unshakeable loyalty. Senna had once compared our friendship to the desperate camaraderie of "rats clinging to debris," but I was glad to be a part of this crew and proud to call them my friends. I thought of Nick, and how well he would fit in. I hoped that I could build this kind of friendship with him. He certainly deserved that.

We "visioned" (that was Elvin's word for our imaginative planning session) until lights-out. By then, we were ready for action. Dan, who loved spy movies, coined the name for this grand event and everyone loved it. The name was more militaristic than romantic, but I let them have their fun.

As soon as I received word from Elise, we'd implement Operation: Bell Tower.

Later that week, I felt something under my blanket as I awoke to the familiar sound of the school bell. I fumbled for whatever it was and discovered an envelope. I quickly tore it open. It was a note from Elise, and it said,

Dear Jake,

Surprise! You're cute when you're sleeping. I'm glad you're safe. I hear that someone is going to be gone for a while. Sounds like a good opportunity. Third quarter, 10 P.M. The usual place.

Love, Elise

I consulted the small calendar on the wall and found that the moon would enter the third quarter tomorrow night. Perfect, since I'd completed my preparations the day before.

So far, there had been no repercussions from the incident in Senna's office. I wondered what his big emergency was, and hoped it was severe enough to keep him away for a long, long time.

I had been commanded to attend classes as usual, and I was happy to comply. Despite my concerns about safety, despite my anxieties about returning home so far ahead of schedule, my thoughts kept returning to Elise. "I love you," she had said. Since hearing those words, I'd walked a little taller. My instructors would have perceived the change in me if it had been their practice to notice things like that; but since happiness hardly ever made an appearance on campus, none of the faculty recognized it when they saw it. They simply droned on in their usual way, oblivious to my barely suppressed joy.

I found it difficult to believe that my days at AKPS were now numbered in the teens. I felt no sentimentality for the place itself, but I would miss my friends. It was time for another major adjustment in my life. As before, I felt ill-prepared for it. As before, I did the best I could.

After dinner, I once again conferred with my friends and told them that the date would take place in about twenty-four hours. None of us slept very much that night.

The next day crawled by. After dinner, my friends and I had one last meeting before lights out. When 10 P.M. finally came, I crept out the barracks window amidst whispered encouragement and parting advice.

This is either going to be a success or a catastrophe, I thought as I made my way across campus. One part of me was confident that everything was in place, but another part cautioned that Elise might think the whole thing was foolish.

I arrived at the fence and glanced at my watch. I feared that Dr. Senna would suddenly appear with Sabrina and some well-armed guards, but then I heard footsteps on the path and all thoughts of Senna disappeared.

"There he is—the man who isn't even afraid of Dobermans," Elise called out playfully.

"Look who's talking: the world-class journalist-slash-blackmailer." We laughed as she slipped through the fence, and then embraced, thrilled to see each other again.

"Where are you sweeping me off to tonight?" she asked. She looked radiant in the moonlight.

"Do you trust me?"

"What a question. You know I do."

"Follow me." *Too terse, you idiot. She's not a farmhand; she's a girl—a woman. Say something intelligent, will you?* I wanted everything to be perfect, and I was a little hard on myself that night.

"Nice moon tonight." *Oh, brilliant. What are you, a werewolf?*

"It is. I wish it weren't so bright, though. I'd never forgive myself if you were caught 'fraternizing' with me. Especially after we've been discovered by Senna."

"Well, you're worth it." *Good one, Jake—for a hair-coloring commercial. Cliché Man strikes again.*

"Jake?" Elise had stopped and I turned to face her, desperately afraid that I'd already spoiled the evening. I never had been a smooth talker.

"Yeah?"

Before I knew what was happening, she reached up and kissed me—a warm, surprising kiss that stopped the breath in my throat and made time melt. It was over before I could fully appreciate it.

"What was that for?" I said.

"That was for the wonderful evening I know we're going to have," she replied, perfectly calm. "I figured that if we got that out of the way and stopped worrying about it—should we kiss, shouldn't we kiss?— we'd be able to relax and enjoy ourselves. Good idea?"

I tried to recover from the pleasant shock she'd given me. "Practical, yet romantic. A superb idea."

She took my hand and indicated that I should lead the way. My hopes for the evening soared.

We traversed the path on the east side of the campus. The sounds of a basketball game floated on the night air, which further explained why we didn't see a single guard. The Final Four was in progress, and since Senna was gone, I'd been told that every officer on duty would be watching the game on the TV in the main security room of the Hub. I was glad the guards were distracted since the Hub was precisely where we were heading. We approached the building and crept toward the locked door that provided access to the bell tower.

When Elise saw our destination, her eyes widened in surprise and admiration. She put her mouth near my ear (causing a jolt to race through every nerve ending of my body) and told me that I was really coming along.

Fortunately, the door was located on the opposite side of the building from the security center. We reached it without incident. As I turned the knob, I held my breath and hoped that Buzz's lock-picking friend had done his work. The knob turned; so far so good. I opened the door and we began the long ascent to the tower. I used Elvin's flashlight as we climbed the winding stone steps.

In the course of my visit to the tower the day before, I'd discovered a disappointing (but not surprising) secret: the AKPS bell with its deep, mighty toll was actually non-functional. The clapper had been removed for some reason, perhaps for a repair that had never been performed. The bell hung there, silent and impotent, putting on a charade of auditory bluster. It seemed to unwittingly imitate the faculty and founders of the school: sound, but no substance; volume, but no power. What everyone thought was the sound of the bell was actually a digital recording amplified by four large speakers. It was their lying voice I heard every day, jolting me out of bed, announcing lunch and dinner and classes. Thankfully, I had also discovered that there were no bats in the tower. I'd smiled at that. Perhaps they refused to make their home in the presence of such a large, silent hypocrite as that bell.

Elise and I spoke little on the way up the stairs, each of us lost in thought. Her hand grasped mine tightly. When we reached the top, everything was just as I'd hoped it would be. The moon filled the tower with pure light that illuminated the small table and chairs I'd set up. The bell hung in the center, ashamed that its secret had been discovered, but trying to redeem itself by enhancing the atmosphere of our impromptu café. We might have been on an outdoor terrace in France except for the razor wire fence and unbroken rows of plain buildings that were visible beyond the lip of the tower.

The table was adorned with two roses and covered with a white linen tablecloth (courtesy of Johnny, who had laundry duty this week); silverware (courtesy of Elvin, who had sticky fingers and loved to deprive AKPS of anything that wasn't nailed down); and plates (courtesy of Eli, who had more than he could use). There was no candle, but I soon remedied that. With a flourish, I cracked open a chemical light stick that we used during nighttime obstacle drills and inserted it into an extra glass.

"Jake, it's…I don't know what to say."

"Try, or you can't come in." Ah, what fun it was to turn her mischievous ways back on her.

"Well, how about this: I am of the opinion that people waste time and words, and I don't want to be guilty of either. I know that I haven't been generous with the personal details of my life, and I know that we've gotten to know each other in a pretty unusual way, but I think we have a future together, Jake."

Just when I thought I had one up on her, she proved how far out of my league I actually was. She not only stole my thunder, she unleashed it back at me with double strength. I told her I felt the same way and earned myself a smile. Dinner consisted of filet mignon, baked potatoes, and broccoli "acquired" from the faculty dining area. I hadn't asked any questions, but Buzz had promised it would be waiting for us in the tower, hot and freshly-prepared. As usual, he had come through.

The first topic of conversation was, naturally, the face-off between Senna and us. Elise told me that she'd been outraged by the school and its cruel practices for years. Finally—the same week I arrived—she did something about it. She spoke with her editor, who expressed an interest in proposal to write an in-depth article about AKPS. The person she called every week was a powerful, influential man whose identity she wouldn't divulge. When I asked how Senna discovered where she lived, Elise gave yet another evasive response. I expressed my frustration.

"Jake, you're still in danger at this school, and so are my 'assistants' on campus," Elise reasoned. "Senna used drugs on you once; what's to keep him from doing it again? Remember: he found out about me from your own lips. If I tell you everything you want to know, think about what could happen the next time."

She was right, of course. I dropped the subject, and then Elise asked me a question of her own.

"Jake, what did Senna mean when he said you'd be leaving in two weeks?"

I looked down and poked at the remnants of my dinner. "I'm going home. I guess my parents called and arranged an early release. I don't know why."

"That's good. I'll sleep a lot easier knowing you're safe at home. Are you nervous?"

"Oh, I suppose, depending on how much I think about it," I replied. "Right now, I'm not thinking about what's going to happen there. I'm thinking about who I'm leaving behind here."

"Oh, you can't get rid of me just by going home. I know where to find you. It's better this way, especially after everything that's happened." She looked out over the quiet campus, and her face belied the cheerful, encouraging words she'd spoken. "Still," she said, "I'll miss you."

I didn't know why things had taken such a gloomy turn, but I was determined not to let anything spoil the evening. "I have a surprise for you," I said, inviting her out of her thoughts and back into the bell tower.

"I like surprises. What is it?"

Elise looked vulnerable for the first time since I'd known her. I felt an overwhelming desire to sweep her away from AKPS, but I had to settle for the miniature "journey" I'd hidden in my backpack. "Are you sure you trust me?" I asked again.

"Of course."

"Then sit back while I blindfold you."

Her eyebrows shot up in curious amusement. "That's not something you usually hear on a first date. What are you up to?"

"Questions later. Trust me."

She closed her eyes and leaned back. I secured the blindfold around her head, and then reached for a fishing tackle box that contained a number of small bottles. I'd left it in the tower the night before.

"Okay. This isn't the best place for a date, so I thought I'd take you somewhere else, somewhere you'd love."

She smiled and waited.

"Now, this is what we would have done on our first date," I began. "First, we'd get in my car and…"

"What kind of car?" Elise broke in.

"Work with me, here. I don't have a car yet."

Chapter Twenty-Two

"Sorry," she said. "Please go on."

"That's better. Okay, first we would drive to Philadelphia. There's a great seafood restaurant there. It's right on the beach and they serve the best scallops." I uncapped a bottle and waved it under her nose. I couldn't see her eyes, but I'm sure they widened.

"Hey! That smells like…well, like the sea!"

I hurriedly put the first vial away and grabbed the next. "After dinner, I'd take you over to the pier. They sell hot peanuts, cotton candy, caramel apples…"

It hadn't been easy to manufacture the scents. I'd told Buzz about my mother's lesson in aromatics, then told him what I had in mind. For a moment, I was afraid I'd requested something that exceeded even his considerable resources. However, after scouring his memory, he remembered a local health food storekeeper who did aromatherapy on the side. She couldn't help us personally but had introduced Buzz to a friend of hers who worked at a candle factory. Buzz had connected that woman with our friend, Abner, who was an expert chemist. The two experts had combined forces and broken into the school chemistry lab to produce the specific aromas I'd requested. The result of their collaboration was the simulated date that I'd brought in my tackle box. Thus far, it seemed to be having the desired effect.

With each scene I described I waved a new scent under Elise's nose. She was so delighted that she stopped commenting on the various aromas and merely sat back and enjoyed the experience. In the realm of our imaginations, I took Elise to the shops where they sold knickknacks and potpourri, past the bakery where they made huge cinnamon rolls served with hot, dark-roasted coffee, and finally to the deck of the *Robert Morgan*, an eighteenth century sailing vessel that bobbed gently in its berth by the dock. We listened to the seagulls and the bustle of the port behind us as we looked at the stars together and spoke of the future.

When our imaginary date was almost over I waved the last vial under Elise's nose. Since a forest of conifers surrounded the school grounds, the vial contained the perfect aroma with which to transition back to reality: the smell of pine trees. I removed the blindfold and looked down into Elise's moist eyes.

"Where did you learn to do that?" she asked. "Don't tell me—your dad."

"Actually, it was my mom."

"I will thank that woman someday. In the meantime, come here."

We kissed again, and on this occasion, I had plenty of time to enjoy it.

Later, we sat quietly with our arms around each other. Clouds had obscured the moon, and that would make traveling back to the fence safer. Elise broke the comfortable silence with an unusual question.

"What does the word *love* mean to you, Jake?"

"You mean, the kind of love we have for each other?"

"We can start there."

"Um, it means that I think about you all the time. When I'm not with you, I want to be with you. When I am with you, I don't ever want it to end." I fell silent, searching my heart for a deeper explanation.

Elise was happy to direct my thoughts. "What about bad times or…flaws?"

"Flaws?"

"If you don't know by now that I'm not perfect, you'll find out pretty quickly once we spend more time together. Then what?"

"You want to talk about flaws? You already know I'm not perfect, and you've still been the best friend anyone could ask for. I want to be the same for you."

"Hmm. So in your opinion, love endures problems, imperfections, et cetera?"

I began to get the idea that these were not idle questions. I shifted my gaze away from the night sky. "Elise, are you trying to tell me something?" As I looked down at her, I was dismayed to discover that she was on the verge of tears. "What is it?" I asked.

"As a matter of fact, Jake, I am trying to tell you something." She paused to gather her resolve. "I need to tell you who I am."

"I know who you are. You're the person who helped me through the worst years of my life. You're my best friend. You're the woman I want to spend…a lot more time with."

I was hoping to quell her anxiety but she ignored the compliments. "Jake, I know this is totally ridiculous, but would you come someplace with me? Someplace where I can show you what I mean?"

I didn't know what to think, but I also had no intention of letting the evening end on a negative note.

"Lead the way."

Chapter Twenty-Three

We crossed the Pennsylvania state line and it suddenly became real to me: I was actually going home. Arnold and I had fallen silent. We'd talked for quite a while, and though our conversation had passed the time and helped to alleviate some of my anxiety, he now left me to my thoughts. He understood that this was a momentous occasion for me.

I liked Arnold; he was a decent man. He told me how he'd suffered a string of misfortunes some years ago—something concerning the stock market—but that a few people along the way had reached out and helped him start over. I told him I could relate to that.

As the increasingly familiar landmarks sped by at sixty-five miles per hour, I thought about the friends who had helped me find *my* way. Throughout my journey, there had been many amazing people who, like spectators at a marathon, had urged me on to the finish line. It was both wonderful and strange: each friend had, in his or her own way, reinforced the lessons my parents had tried so diligently to teach me. Buzz exemplified loyalty and taught me to never give up. Eli showed me that kindness crosses every boundary. Elise taught me that I was of value simply because of who I was.

The final fifteen minutes of the ride were the worst. I squirmed and fidgeted on those gray leather seats, much to Arnold's amusement. I turned the air conditioning up, then turned it down. I tried to listen to music but gave up after only a few moments. I wanted to prepare myself, to chart every possible eventuality and reaction, and to envision what I would say when I finally saw my family again. I wanted everything to be...

"We're here."

My eyes shot up. Sure enough, we were turning down my road. The same trees, the same houses, the same place where I'd grown up. And there was our house.

I wasn't surprised by its appearance. I'd known exactly how it would look because it never changed. Every flower, every paving stone, and every blade of grass was in place. The house was flawlessly white, the barn was the same rich red, and the well-tended crops still stretched out in all directions.

One thing was different, however, and it instantly caught my attention: there was a new driveway about fifty yards north of our own. It was still on our property, though I saw no accompanying mailbox. Had Dad sold off part of the farm? Since I'd expected everything to be the same, this long strip of new asphalt bothered me.

I was also surprised to see that our driveway was filled with cars. I hadn't expected a welcome home party, but it would be good to see my neighborhood friends again.

I looked up and saw a pair of eyes examining me from the rearview mirror.

"It's been a privilege driving you home, Master Jake."

"Thanks for the ride, Arnold. I'll have to recommend your services to all my friends...assuming you tell me who hired you."

"Sorry, sir. Not just yet."

"You know, you'd fit well into our family."

"Oh? Why's that?"

"You're as stubborn as I am."

"All in good time, my friend. I'm reminded of a mystery novel—you could flip to the back and read the ending, but where's the fun in that?"

"Oh, brother!"

Arnold winked as he stepped out of the limousine to open my door. He carried my bags as I walked up the cobblestone path that led to the house.

Elise guided me through the fence, off school property, and over the steadily sloping path. She hadn't spoken since we'd left the bell tower, and I attempted in vain to guess where we were going. We soon passed the mechanical shed where she and I had first spoken face to face. The structure would have brought back pleasant memories if not for the unusual circumstances. I felt a twinge of uneasiness.

We reached a clearing a few minutes later, and my apprehension quadrupled. Looming in front of us, surrounded by a high, iron fence and gate that was more appropriate for a graveyard than for a residence, was the mansion we students had nicknamed "Dracula's Castle."

"Elise, what are we doing here? We're not going in there, are we?"

She looked up at me. This time there was no adventure in her eyes, no mystery. She was carrying a heavy burden and the only path to freedom appeared to lead inside that house—but why? What did this have to do with her?

"It's safe, Jake. No one's home," she said quietly.

"How do you know that? Because the lights aren't on? Elise, I don't understand. I thought we were having a good time. I…"

"It's important."

I closed my mouth but I wasn't happy. The last thing I wanted to do was explore that creepy house. There were countless rumors about who lived there, but no one had ever uncovered the truth. Any student who attempted a firsthand investigation of the mansion quickly learned that straying off campus simply wasn't worth the punishment. Legends had sprung up in the absence of facts, and those legends often involved grisly creatures, both living and dead. I wasn't afraid of monsters, nor did I believe in ghosts, but trespassing on someone's property didn't fit with the romantic plans I'd had for the evening.

"We talked about love tonight," Elise continued. "I'm asking you to show me how far it goes. I know the people who live here and you have my word that they're not home. You'll understand in a moment, Jake. Now, *please…*"

Elise grabbed my hand and pulled me through the front gate as though she feared she might lose her nerve if we didn't hurry. We climbed the crumbling stone steps and walked through the front door. It wasn't locked, and that fact did nothing to lessen my apprehension.

The inside of the house fulfilled every one of my friends' conjectures. It was like something out of an Edgar Allan Poe story. A high chandelier hung above the marble floor of the foyer and dimly illuminated the broad, winding staircase that disappeared into the gloom above. Grim portraits stared at us; odd statuary crouched in recessed niches in the walls. To my amusement there was even a suit of armor to complete the "haunted mansion" look of the house. The only things missing were the cobwebs and the deceptively gracious host who turned out to be a madman. I was fascinated despite myself. Elise knew the people who lived *here*?

She led me up the staircase into an upper hallway lined with doors. Elise opened the first door on the right and flipped a switch. I stopped short as we entered the room. It was as though we had passed through a magical portal that transported us from one mysterious realm to another. This room differed in every way from the rest of the house. It was a huge suite, decorated with ornately framed watercolors, alder wood furniture, and a light-colored carpet. Bookshelves lined the walls, and in one corner stood a canopied bed hung with cream-colored lace. A massive fireplace, much like the one in my own home, dominated the far wall. The room was like an enclave, an embassy of light in a foreign, shadowy land.

"This is my room, Jake," Elise said with no warning and no inflection.

"*Your* room?" I waited for the punch line or an explanation, something that would make sense of Elise's statement. She remained silent. I reexamined the suite in light of this new information: this was Elise's bedroom? It certainly fit my idea of what her room would be like, but something wasn't right, and it wasn't merely the incongruity between the room and the rest of the house. Elise's bearing had changed upon entering the room. She seemed strangely out of place here—more like a prisoner in a comfortable cell than a willing resident. I wondered about her parents. Why had they let the house and grounds fall into such disrepair?

I noticed a typewriter sitting atop a spacious desk. I walked over to it and rested my hand on it, as if to confirm the reality of the place.

"I had to use a typewriter whenever I wrote to you," Elise explained, anxious to elicit some other response from me. "My father has a computer, but I didn't want to risk him finding out about us."

"This is your room," I repeated." Elise nodded as I continued putting the pieces together. "That's how you knew no one was home."

"My father is on a business trip. Tonight seemed like the right time to show you where I live."

"This is what you wanted to tell me? That you live in Dracula's, uh, that you live here? Elise, that's certainly a surprise, but it's nothing to get…"

She shook her head. "I wanted to tell you who I am, and bringing you to the place where I live seemed like a logical first step. Let's take a look at the rest of the house," she said, although she looked unhappy at the prospect. I followed her into the hallway and we turned left to go back downstairs.

After crossing through the foyer, we walked down a long corridor that led into the west wing of the mansion. The floor plan was curiously similar to that of the Hub, but I missed the significance of that fact as I tried to guess what her secret could be. I glimpsed various details of the rooms we passed. There was a large library, a sitting room, an office, and what looked and smelled like a cigar room. The hallway terminated in a circular atrium that opened into an impressive trophy room. Elise paused by the double doors.

In the dark, the mounted heads of the various game animals looked hideous, a gallery of dead prey silently accusing their killer. Elise flipped on the light, and the room assumed a somewhat less frightening ambiance. I stepped through the door and looked around. A large, framed photograph at the far end of the room immediately caught my eye. The photo showed a hunter holding an elephant gun as he stood next to his prize.

If Elise's dad was the hunter, he was an accomplished one. The room resembled the safari clubs of the late 1800s and boasted trophies of every kind. Mounted gazelle, moose, and caribou heads encircled the room, along with a massive elephant head—the same elephant as in the picture? There were other smaller photos on the walls, various weapons and pieces of survival equipment, many souvenirs from distant continents, and a large mirror above the mantle. A full-sized bear rug was spread out on the floor, and a male lion crouched menacingly in the center of the room, safely encased in a glass display box. In one corner, several overstuffed chairs and couches formed a semi-circle around one central armchair. I imagined that this was where the host and his fellow hunters swapped stories of adventure and danger.

I had almost reached the far end of the room when I noticed that Elise hadn't followed me. She indicated that I should take a closer look at the large photograph. There was something familiar about that hunter, although a pith helmet obscured part of his face. I took a few more steps and realized why he looked familiar. The man in the picture was Vice-Chancellor Charles Senna.

"Hey!" I began. "You don't mean to tell me that your father is friends with…"

That's when I understood. I understood why Elise had been in a unique position to help me, and that it wasn't just because of the article she had written. I knew how Senna had known where to find her, why she had been present in his office the other day, and why Sabrina had obeyed her command to stop attacking me. I knew who Elise was.

"Dr. Senna is your *father*?"

I could see Elise tense up from across the room. We stood there, separated by about eighteen feet and that ridiculous lion as my memories caught up with this new knowledge. Hadn't she told me long ago that the owner of this house was paranoid? Hadn't she always avoided any discussion of her parents? She'd mentioned just a few minutes ago that her father was on a business trip. Dr. Senna was on a trip, all right—attending the emergency board meeting that so conveniently allowed his daughter and me to get together that evening.

I searched my feelings carefully and came to a wonderful conclusion: nothing had changed. Elise was still Elise. In fact, I found this turn of events to be wonderfully ironic: student 3290 had fallen in love with the vice-chancellor's daughter. More important, I determined that student 3290 would soon rescue the vice-chancellor's daughter.

"So what's the big news?" I asked as I walked over to her. "Is this the 'flaw' you mentioned? Did you really think this would change how I feel about you?"

"It doesn't?" Her relief caused fresh tears to well up, and I wiped them away and kissed her in view of that photograph of her father.

We went back up to her room, and I made a fire while Elise revealed the secrets she'd been compelled to keep for so long. I discovered some of the reasons for Dr. Senna's spiteful demeanor. He had always been a stern, pragmatic man and had married according to his family's prearranged plan. His wife had been the daughter of a rich family friend and the marriage had been lifeless in every way but one: Elise had been born two years after the wedding. Elise's mother quickly grew bored with Charles's stiff academic life and sought other "opportunities" overseas. She never returned, causing Senna to retreat from public circles, utterly humiliated.

Elise, who was viewed as little more than an inconvenience, was left to the care of an aunt who came to live with Senna and his infant daughter. The aunt was the only positive influence in Elise's early life. She imparted to Elise that gentle yet mischievous spirit that so characterized her personality. The aunt and her little charge made it a point to enjoy life despite the overbearing presence of the master of the house. The two did everything together. They cooked, cleaned, sewed, and— most importantly—laughed. When Elise's aunt became ill, Elise cared for her throughout the long years of her infirmity. She'd died a couple years before my arrival at Ashur-Kesed. Upon her death, the servants she'd paid for with her own money were dismissed and the house began to show signs of neglect. Senna refused to hire any more housekeepers, and Elise couldn't manage all the work herself. It hadn't taken long for the once-beautiful mansion to assume its current appearance.

Senna hardly ever spoke to his daughter except to demand food or the performance of some household duty. He seemed to feel she was in some way responsible for the sudden departure of her mother. Elise refused to be discouraged. In the terrible void left by her aunt, she turned to the students and staff of the school for companionship. She soon became a favorite on campus but was constrained to enjoy her newfound friendships secretly. Senna disapproved of friendship as much as he disapproved of every other good thing.

Elise had been chatting with the gatekeeper the day I arrived at school. If I had glanced to my left as I walked through the gate, I would have seen her, but I had been too self-absorbed and miserable to notice much of anything that day. She, however, had noticed me. The rest was history.

I didn't learn the most fantastic part of her—our—story until later that night, when it was almost time for us to say good-bye. It was after midnight, and we sat silently in front of the fire. The evening had turned out well after all, but I wondered when I would see Elise again. I had an idea.

"Elise, why don't you come home with me when I leave school? I want you to meet my parents. They helped Nick, and I'm sure they would help you. My dad could introduce you to Paul and maybe find you another newspaper job..." I stopped speaking. Elise was smiling ear to ear. "What's that for?"

"I might as well tell you. This certainly is a night for revelations, isn't it?"

"Tell me what?"

"I've already met your parents."

"What?"

"I can't tell you all the details—your father bound me to secrecy— but he and your mom came to the school unannounced at the beginning of this year. Buzz gave them the scoop on everything that was going on here, including me..."

"Buzz met them, too?"

She laughed at my incredulity. "Yes, but you can't say anything to him, not one word. Promise?"

"Yeah, yeah, get back to the part about you meeting my parents. *I* haven't even seen them since the day I got here."

"They're every bit as wonderful as you described them. When your parents enrolled you here, Senna gave them the usual propaganda, complete with false testimonials from former students. As far as your parents knew, this was nothing more than a strict boarding school. When they found out what was really going on, they knew they had to get you out of here. But they had an idea."

"What kind of idea?"

"They knew that with a little help, they could shut this place down. Your parents never abandoned you, and they never stopped loving you. They wanted to make sure that there was someone here who would keep an eye on you and let them know if things got too dangerous. They asked Buzz, a few others, and me to watch out for you, which of course, we were already doing. You know that Code One phone call my dad got?"

I nodded.

"That was your dad. He's the man I call every week. I told him about my father's little stunt with the drugs in the infirmary. Was your father *mad*! Anyway, I imagine that the emergency meeting of the board of directors had something to do with the fact that your dad and Paul have released my story to the national press. This school's days are numbered."

"I suppose you're good friends with Paul, too?"

"Of course. My boss introduced us at a convention."

"If I hear one more shocking, surprising, totally unexpected thing tonight, I'm going to explode," I said, shaking my head.

"In that case, no more talking, mister." She turned my face towards hers and did an effective job of kissing away my amazement.

Although we delayed it as long as possible, we finally admitted that it was time to say good-bye. Elise presented me with a going-away present: a black canvas attaché that contained two of her journals. She'd kept a record of our relationship but made me promise not to read them until after I arrived home. She suggested I write a book someday about my experiences on the farm and at Ashur-Kesed, and thought the journals would be a good starting place. In the meantime, they would remind me of her until we could find a way to be together again.

As we left Elise's room and passed through the dreary, neglected house, I marveled again that such a beautiful person had flourished in such a barren environment.

After we passed through the forest and arrived at the fence, I felt a lump in my throat and tried to get a grip on my emotions. Dad had taught me that a true man cries when there's something to cry about, and stands firm when courage is required of him. I supposed this was an occasion for both courage and tears. I saw that Elise agreed. We laughed a little as we wiped each other's eyes and then embraced tightly.

"I love you," we said at nearly the same time, then laughed again.

"Will I see you before I leave?" I asked, knowing the answer.

"Probably not. I'm sure you've noticed that my father has taken a rather intense disliking to you. He'll make it difficult for us to see each other again."

"How will I get in touch with you once I'm home?"

"My address and phone number are in my journals. Call during the day, if you can." She looked down, then brightened a little. "Things are going to go great with your family. I have a feeling."

"I wish I had the same feeling."

"Don't worry. Promise?"

"I'll try."

We held onto each other for a long time. After a final kiss, Elise slipped through the fence and disappeared. Her absence left a deep, cold void in my heart as I walked slowly back to the barracks.

The next week and a half passed quickly. Dr. Senna returned shortly after my final date with Elise. He looked ill and studiously avoided any contact with me, for which I was thankful. His standoffishness gave me the freedom to achieve a certain closure during my final days at Ashur-Kesed. I was able to say my good-byes, pay off my outstanding debts (of which there were many), sneak back into the bell tower to clean up the remnants of our date, and submit my final tests and papers—all without harassment or further punishment. A few days before my departure, I received a package from Dad. The large envelope contained my plane ticket and instructions for the journey home. I was encouraged by this tangible evidence of my release, but I was still unsure about what awaited me back home.

The night before I took the shuttle to the airport, the guys in my barracks gave me an unauthorized going-away party. Buzz's alarm system served us well, but it wasn't needed that night. Not a single guard showed up to spoil our fun. We exchanged gifts and stories, and I was hailed as a conquering hero. When it was all over and the barracks were silent and dark, Buzz and I had a moment to reminisce. I was desperate for details about his interaction with Mom and Dad, but I kept my word and refrained from asking. Instead, I let Buzz do most of the talking and tried to preserve the moment in my mind.

"Well, farm boy, you made it," he said with great pride. "You turned out pretty well, too, just as I predicted. Didn't I predict it?"

"Yup. You sure did."

"Now, don't get all mushy on me. We might have to embrace, and then what would happen to my reputation?"

We laughed quietly and continued to relive some of our favorite experiences. It was our way of acknowledging that we'd miss these days, even though discouragement and suffering had surrounded them. More than that, we'd miss each other.

Buzz's going-away present was safely hidden among my other gifts. My brilliant friend had tinkered with an electric shaver, combining it with—of all things—a handheld tape recorder. If a guard found it and flipped the switch, all it would do was buzz (I liked the irony of that). However, if I pressed the hidden switch on the back, I would hear the recorded advice and farewells of all my AKPS friends. It was a great gift from a great friend.

When we'd said all that there was to say, we shook hands and climbed into our respective bunks for the last time as bunkmates. I had hoped for a sunny day for the trip home, but Buzz informed me as we were drifting off to sleep that I should expect rain. His homemade barometer indicated that the air pressure was falling fast.

There would be no good-byes the next day, and no send-off. The faculty would never suspend the normal routine of the school merely to discharge a student. When I awoke in the morning, the barracks would be empty and I would leave as I had arrived—alone. Yet, I would leave a far richer person than I had been, and I would always be grateful for the years I spent at Ashur-Kesed Preparatory School for Young Men.

Chapter Twenty-Four

I felt good, all things considered. My crisp uniform helped me walk up to the front door with a certain dignity, and the clacking of my polished black boots on the cobblestone walk sounded sufficiently impressive. I remembered my barefoot jaunts around the farm and wondered if I would feel comfortable in cutoff shorts and a t-shirt after having worn the uniform for so long. Time would tell. I looked forward to finding out.

In joyous contrast to the gray environment of Ashur-Kesed, the color and beauty of my home delighted my senses. The sky had attained that pure shade of light blue that often follows a good rain, as though it had been washed clean in preparation for spring. Wispy clouds promised good weather, and the birds agreed with that prediction as they flitted amidst the branches of the slowly awakening trees. Well-tended flower beds added more color to the front yard, as though an artist had splashed her paints in a random arc along the walk.

Off in the distance I heard a tractor and the muted sounds of cows and chickens. I inhaled the pure air, and found that I'd even missed the smell of the farm—that distinctive mixture of aromas produced by hay, soil, and animals. I was truly home.

I reached the door and raised my hand to knock, but it suddenly flew open. Mom and Nick stood in the foyer. All my prearranged greetings dissolved into a blur. I'm not sure who was happier, who started crying first, or who hugged whom the hardest. We stood there on the porch, our words and laughter jumbling together as we enjoyed this long-awaited reunion.

Mom looked wonderful as always and Nick had grown at least four inches. Surprisingly, my father was nowhere to be seen. Mom bustled me inside and addressed the chauffeur, who was standing back at a respectful distance.

"Thank you for bringing Jake home safely, Arnold. How was the traffic?"

"Not as heavy as one would expect for this time of day, ma'am. We both enjoyed the ride."

Mom invited Arnold in, and they chatted as we all entered the house. Nick and I had a few moments to ourselves as we followed them. My brother seemed in perfect health. I could see toned muscles beneath his polo shirt, and he walked with a confident stride. His well-tanned face no longer held the expression of a timid, fearful boy. Nick, like me, had grown up. The only reminders of his accident were the two scars on his forehead marking the place where the halo had been attached. I caught him eyeing my uniform.

"Like it?"

"It's pretty slick. Did they give you a gun with that outfit?"

I laughed. "They didn't dare!"

"Skipper missed you, but I remembered to feed him," Nick said with a slight smile.

"Thanks. Where is he?"

"With the sheep."

I opened my mouth to protest. Skipper had always been too rambunctious to be of any real use in the pastures. Nick anticipated my objection.

"I taught him a few things. The sheep love him now, and he and Issy are great partners out there."

Nick also mentioned his new hobby: volunteer firefighting.

"You got my letter, then?"

"Yeah. Thanks." I could tell he wanted to say more, but that it was not the right time. Instead, we joked about the changes each of us had undergone. It was comfortable banter, and I liked the direction in which the day was heading. The only part of my homecoming that was not to my liking was Dad's conspicuous absence.

We reached the rear of the house and entered the family room, but there were no guests and no Dad. There was, however, lots of food. Mom had prepared a huge buffet like the one she'd laid out when Nick had first come to visit. I searched my heart carefully for any remnant of jealousy or bitterness and couldn't find any. That was a relief. I was about to ask about the cars in the driveway when I was startled by a sudden shout from the kitchen.

"WELCOME HOME, JAKE!"

I looked in the direction of the voices and dropped my bags when I saw who our guests were. Of all the mysteries I'd endured at school, of all the surprises I had experienced, none was so utterly unexpected as the huge mass of people that streamed out into the family room that day. They wore party hats, blew into those silly paper noisemakers, and seemed to thoroughly enjoy the look on my face.

Mixed in among my neighbors and childhood buddies were friends I'd made more recently: Buzz, Eli, Mr. Collard-Hill, Fergie, Barker, Elvin, Sam—and still they kept coming. Barracks-mates, classmates, even Jeffrey and his father—they all came pouring out of the kitchen. And finally, there was Elise. Shock, astonishment, joy, confusion…a jumble of emotions assaulted me, overcame me, and delighted me. I threw myself at the crowd of friends, desperately curious, desperately happy.

Paul was also among the guests, and he thumped me on the back and shook my hand. Fergie's Scottish brogue was even more unintelligible than usual; Barker was, well, barking; and Elvin treated us to a horrible operatic version of "For He's a Jolly Good Fellow."

The room was filled with people I'd thought I'd never see again, all helping me celebrate the best day of my life. Elise topped it off and kissed me right in front of everyone, provoking a long, delighted "oooohhhh" from the entire group.

I continued to search the crowd in vain for Dad, even as I greeted my friends. The welcome had exceeded my wildest dreams, but it didn't seem official, not yet.

In the course of being bounced from person to person and exchanging handshakes and hugs, I suddenly stood face to face with someone else I had never expected to see again.

"Ruth?"

"Hiya, Jake! I see you made it home in one piece."

"I don't understand."

"No one told you?" She laughed a wheezy, raspy laugh. "We're neighbors. I moved in down the road while you were at school. Your folks and I got to be real tight. They told me when you'd be coming home and that you hated to fly, so I volunteered to help see you through. I knew I'd be on my way back from a wedding, so I rearranged my plans a bit. It was worth it just to see your face as that plane swooped in for a landing."

Everyone laughed, and then Paul took me by the arm and led me to the center of the room. He told the assembled group to grab a glass of punch and raise it high.

"To Jake: returning son, brother, and friend!"

"To Jake!"

Glasses clinked, punch was consumed, and the applause continued loud and long. I looked around from face to cheering face and happily shouted the question that begged to be asked: "What are you all doing here?"

Buzz answered for everyone, of course. "Jake the private investigator strikes again. Don't you know a welcome home party when you see one? We wouldn't miss this for the world—especially since we helped you get here. Nice place, by the way. I don't suppose you need another hired hand—one with a knack for inventing useful items at a reasonable price?" There was more laughter; but it didn't hide the fact that, as usual, Buzz had managed to answer my question and evade it at the same time. I would have to get my answers elsewhere.

Elise disappeared into the kitchen to help Mom, and Buzz and my other friends from school lost no time attacking the food. As they did so, they delighted Nick, Mal, Jeb, and the other guests with stories of their many adventures with me at AKPS. I saw my opportunity and drew Paul aside.

"Mr. Tarsean, please tell me you know what's going on," I said.

"It's Paul, and I think I can help you. I even have an idea how it's all going to end," he said with a conspiratorial wink and a glance in Elise's direction. He grew serious. "Jake, I know you want to see your father, so I'll be brief. I'd like to let you in on a little secret."

"Well, it's about time!"

He laughed a gigantic laugh, throwing his head back and nearly spilling his punch. "I'm glad to see that you haven't lost your sense of humor, my boy. Our friend Buzz is right: all these people helped your father and me perform a very important task. Now, listen carefully..."

The sounds of silverware clinking and people talking overlaid Paul's incredible story. He provided the final pieces of the puzzle, summarizing the amazing things that had gone on behind the scenes at Ashur-Kesed. I listened carefully as the journalist knit together the last two years, and I marveled at the great lengths to which my family and friends had gone to ensure both my safety and my eventual return home.

Paul had many contacts in the world of mass media. About a year ago, the editor of a small town newspaper had introduced Paul to a young woman named Elise who showed great journalistic promise. He'd asked Paul to read several articles she had written. Paul recognized her ability and noticed that she happened to live on the very doorstep of Ashur-Kesed. He contacted Elise and asked her about the school. He didn't like what he heard.

"I told your father what I learned about AKPS," Paul said. "His first reaction was to pull you out. He and your mom flew up and met with Buzz and Elise. When they returned, he'd changed his mind. She'd convinced him that they'd keep you safe. So, we sat down and planned how we were going to go about shutting down AKPS for good."

"How come I didn't know about my parents' visit?" I asked.

"From what Elise told your parents, it sounded as if you were growing despite the school. They didn't want to disrupt that. To ensure your safety and to keep Senna in check, Elise proposed the article exposing AKPS's illegal practices. After she researched and wrote the piece, she sent a copy to me, and then presented it to Senna."

I shook my head. "They did all that for me?"

"You have it right, Jake. Is it so difficult to believe that you inspire such friendship?"

"Well, yeah."

"You sell yourself short. No one who helped you at school ever regretted it. Now, let me finish. I haven't gotten to the end yet.

"Your friend Buzz is quite an enterprising young man," Paul chuckled. "He gave the rest of the students a vested interest in helping you out. He passed the word that a plot was afoot to close down Ashur-Kesed. He announced that anyone who wanted to participate needed to rally around the student whose father was responsible for this significant event: you, Jake. As you can imagine, Buzz soon had an army of support, all unified by a common purpose: to gain their freedom by bringing about the downfall of Ashur-Kesed."

I listened to the rest of the story, amazed that my friends had kept the secret the entire time I was at school. There had been close calls, of course, but I never suspected that I was the focal point of such a concerted effort. I thought of all the occasions when Buzz had protected Elise's identity, and vice versa. I remembered all the times they'd steered me away from negativity and kept me moving in the right direction, and how neither one was ever far away when trouble came. I smiled at the way the whole barracks had rallied around me when I was preparing for my final date with Elise. They had gone far above the call of duty, all of them.

I learned that my father called Dr. Senna on a monthly basis, delivering subtle warnings concerning the treatment of AKPS students. Senna naturally hated those anonymous phone calls, especially since they were coupled with the threat of Elise's letter. Throughout my schooling, Senna never discovered that the troublesome student with the meddling father and the mysterious subject of his daughter's attention were the same person. If it hadn't been for my recent illness, he may never have realized the connection. Paul drew his remarkable tale to a close and resolved one of the most nagging mysteries of all.

"Towards the end, your father enlisted the aid of an old navy buddy by the name of Ian."

"Ian? I never met anyone by that name."

"You know him as Eli."

"So that's why everyone thought he was dead."

"The real Eli did pass away five years ago, although not in such an unpleasant fashion as the rumor mill would have you believe. He died quietly in a rest home, surrounded by his family. It is true that Ashur-Kesed lied to him and stole his property, but they'll get everything they have coming to them. We strategically placed Ian in the library because we knew that things were about to get more difficult for you. The name change was his idea. He thought a little touch of mystery would be better than making up an elaborate cover story."

"A *little* touch of mystery?" I exclaimed.

Paul laughed, clapped me on the shoulder and continued. "We needed someone who could get into position quickly and have the ability to interact with you privately. By that time, Senna was tired of our 'suggestions' and little adjustments of the rules. He suspected what we were up to and he didn't intend to go down without making himself look like a hero, or at least a martyr. Buzz and Elise felt that he was preparing to do something rash.

"When Elise contacted your father and told him that Senna had used drugs on you, your Dad immediately signed your release papers. He knew it was no longer safe for you, and he knew something even more important." Paul leaned closer. "He knew by that time that you'd learned all that you needed to learn. When a man's education is complete, hand him a diploma and set him loose—don't you agree, Jake?"

I did indeed. I now realized that I'd never been alone at school, and that my education had never been left to chance. After that first year, my father had handpicked a few people who had served, whether knowingly or not, as substitute teachers, taking over where he and Mom had purposely left off. My friends had done their job well. I wished for a moment that I had known all of this earlier, but realized that this was the way it had to be. Some lessons can be learned when the sun is shining and all is well; other lessons can only be learned in the dead of night, when hope and help seem far away. I understood the wisdom of my father's plan, and was more desperate than ever to see him.

"Thanks, Paul. This would make a great story in your newspaper—maybe a miniseries."

"That's a good idea. Get to work on that, will you?"

"I'm not a writer, but I am acquainted with one."

He raised his punch glass again as my mother and Elise emerged from the kitchen, obviously sharing a secret. I could only imagine what havoc those two could wreak once they joined forces. I smiled at the prospect. Elise stood at my side and squeezed my hand as Mom said the words I'd been longing to hear.

"Jake, your father is out back. He's waiting for you."

I slipped out the backdoor, once again reveling in how wonderful it felt to be home. My mother had pointed in the direction of my old tree house. I wondered if there was some vestige of that grand old fort left among the branches of the chestnut oak. I also wondered why Dad wanted me to meet him out there, alone.

My boots imprinted the tender spring grass as I walked up the hill. Odd that I didn't see the branches of the oak; they were usually visible from there. I wondered if the tree had caught some disease or been struck by lightning. I was disappointed at the prospect. The oak was a powerful reminder, and I'd hoped it would always stand there to speak to me about the past.

I reached the top of the hill and discovered why the tree was gone.

Standing in its place was a modest colonial similar to our farm-house. I walked up to the new home and understood the purpose of the new driveway I had seen earlier: it led right up to the house and fed into the cul-de-sac in front. But whose house was it, and why was it standing in the middle of our backyard?

As I approached, I saw a gleaming brass nameplate. It was affixed to the right of the door, just like the nameplate on my tree house had been. After taking a few more steps, I could see the word "JAKE" engraved upon its surface. It *was* my old nameplate, polished to a high shine and adding to my confusion.

The door suddenly opened. My father's face, illuminated once again by his broad smile, peeked around the corner. He looked the same as always, and the sight of him caused a tidal wave of happiness to break over me. Dad said only two words. They were words he'd said years before on a similar occasion, and words I'd dreamed of hearing again:

"Welcome home!"

I can't imagine a day containing more joy than that one. My father and I embraced at the front door and wept for a long time. Neither of us said much at first.

After he'd taken a good look at me, Dad took great delight in showing me around the house—my house. It had that wonderful smell of fresh paint, clean carpeting, and new lumber.

Dad conducted me around the ground floor, with its large fireplace and spacious, furnished rooms. I could sense the love and care that Dad had put into the house. The walls, like the walls of our farmhouse, were covered with personal memorabilia: photos, blue ribbons from country fairs, and shelves containing an assortment of my childhood possessions. There were two bedrooms and a library upstairs.

When the tour was over, Dad and I sat down in the library. "Well, Jake, here it is, and it's yours if you want it. You'll be eighteen soon, and I wanted to celebrate your birthday and your homecoming in a dramatic way." Dad grew serious. "But I want to make something clear, son. This house is not meant to manipulate you into taking one path or another. It may be that you want to go out on your own for a while. It may be that you've decided on another career besides farming. You're free to do those things, no strings attached."

"Dad, I've considered a lot of things over the past two years. Leaving home again isn't one of them. It's just that…"

"What is it?"

"It's strange to come home and be treated like a hero when I did all those things. I made everyone miserable. I just don't feel like I deserve this, that's all."

Dad smiled and beckoned me to the window. He gestured out over the farm.

"Jake, *all* of this—the farm, the equipment, the barns and stables, even the other house—will someday belong to you and your brother. You'll inherit it because you're my sons, not because of the things you've done or haven't done." Dad paused to collect his thoughts. "Don't think of this house as something to be deserved. It's a gift, and it's meant to convey just a tiny portion of our love for you. Enjoy it."

"I never even got the chance to say I'm sorry."

"Son, you told us you were sorry by the life you lived and by the choices you made. Your mother and I hoped for growth, not perfection. You've shown us that, and more. We've had many occasions to be proud of you since you left for Ashur-Kesed." He examined me for a moment then seemed to abruptly change the subject.

"By the way—did you enjoy the limousine ride?"

"*You* hired Arnold. I knew it."

Dad smiled and withdrew an envelope from his pocket. "Actually, I didn't. Arnold wanted me to give you this when the time was right. I suppose now is as right a time as ever."

I opened the envelope and removed two pieces of paper. One was a new, expensive-looking sheet of stationery; the other was an old scrap torn from a paper bag. As I read the words that were laser-printed on the newer stationery, I experienced a strange combination of joy and remorse.

It said,

Dear Jake,

I hope you enjoyed my gift. I offered to drive you home. It was the very least I could do for the person who changed my life. Permit me to retell a story you already know.

A long time ago, I put my life's savings into the stock market. I had just come over from England and received some poor advice about a "sure thing." The only sure thing was the loss of every penny I had. I couldn't find work in my particular field, so I was reduced to begging. Things became so bad that I was forced to steal corn right out of a local farmer's front yard. You remember the rest of the story. A kind young man left some food for me—along with a note.

I was blessed by your generosity. I put aside my pride, asked your father to forgive my theft, and sought his help. I'd never met anyone so gracious. He found me a job in town, and when I wanted to reestablish my family business—chauffeuring—he gave me his own car so I could get a better job in the city and begin to save some money.

I own the limousine that you rode home in and many more like it. I owe everything to you and to your family and I've been waiting for years to say this in some fitting way: thank you, Jake. You truly understand "the value of one," as your father has always boasted of you.

Your dear friend, Arnold

It was amazing that such a seemingly small act of kindness could mean so much to someone. I still remembered how wonderful it felt to help a person in need and at the same time please my parents. I glanced down at the other piece of paper and was transported back in time to that day by the stone wall. I remembered every item in that brown paper bag, and I remembered the note. I couldn't believe he'd saved it.

Dear Poor Person,

I'm sorry you're so hungry. I got you something better to eat. You must be sick of all that corn. I hope things get better for you soon.

~~*Bone appateet*~~
Sincerely, Jake

We were silent then as we looked out over the farm, father and son together again. I thought about the school, and the many students still trapped under its oppressive yoke.

"Dad, Paul tells me that you're going to close down the school. Is that true?"

"Yes, it is. We waited until everything was in place. With all the evidence we've amassed, no judge in the world will allow it to remain open. Your mother is going to help place those boys in environments more suited to their abilities."

"That's a relief."

"Coffee before we join the others?"

"Sure."

We descended the stairs, which Dad had constructed from the trunk of the chestnut oak. (He told me the tree had sustained damage from the fire and had to be cut down. He hadn't wanted it to go to waste).

As we sipped our coffee and watched the sun fade over the fields—another custom I had sorely missed—I thought about the extraordinary measures my father had taken: secret friends, newspaper articles, a trip to school, and a new house. "Dad, wasn't there some easier way to teach me these things? Why did you go to all this trouble?" I asked, suspecting the answer but wanting to hear it anyway.

Dad smiled as he lifted the mug to his lips. "What trouble?"

The party lasted late into the evening. I had the opportunity to speak with everyone at some point. I discovered that Ian was an engineer at a submarine base two hours east of our farm. He promised to give me a tour of his facility and maybe even a ride on a submarine. I looked forward to that. I thanked Mr. Collard-Hill for his contribution, spent some time with Jeffrey and his father (who was not the gruff man he had pretended to be), and floated from conversation to conversation, more at peace than I'd ever been in my life. I also reconciled with Perry, which added yet another happy reunion to a day that was already full of them.

Nick had turned out to be a remarkable young man. I clearly saw the stamp of my father's influence upon him. He was doing all the tasks around the farm that I had done, and from all reports was doing them well. He told me that he'd collected every one of the baseball cards I'd lost in the tree house fire. He said he knew it wasn't the same as having the originals back, but his gesture brought a lump to my throat. I looked forward to spending a great deal of time with him. I was sure he could get me back up to speed on some of the new farm equipment I'd seen out back.

Elise and I half-jokingly mentioned the possibility of marriage, and my former schoolmates immediately began planning it. Nick was named the best man, and Buzz insisted on instituting a new tradition: the *second*-best man, who would be in charge of all the special effects at the wedding. I groaned at the idea and was instantly accused of being hopelessly old-fashioned. They forced me to give in, but I made the stipulation that there be no fireworks of any kind during the ceremony.

When the evening ended, my parents told everyone that there were plenty of guest rooms upstairs. Buzz, Sam, Elvin, and Elise stayed the night.

Elise and I had a few moments to ourselves after everyone had either gone home or gone to bed. We sat on the couch in front of the dying embers of the fire. Skipper, who'd left his puppy days far behind, rested contentedly at our feet.

"I can't believe that two weeks ago, we sat in front of another fire and wondered when we would see each other again," I said.

"Well, *you* wondered," Elise said. "I knew exactly when I'd see you again."

"And you let me think…there will be repercussions."

Chapter Twenty-Four

"Yeah, sure. You forget how well I know you. You'll forgive me and move on."

I laughed quietly, reminding myself not to underestimate her. We talked long into the night. We discussed some of our dreams for the future; we wondered where Elise might find work, where I would fit in on the farm, and we discussed the possibility of attending college. Sometime in the midst of our conversation, we fell asleep, bringing that day to a gentle close.

The sun rose the next morning, unhindered by clouds. It spread its warmth and light upon a sleeping farm, a restored family, and a new beginning.

Epilogue

I can hear my grandchildren downstairs, begging for a sample of their grandmother's leftover cookie batter. I'd like to join them—she makes the most wonderful cookies—but first I wanted to add these final words to our manuscript.

Ashur-Kesed was closed a few months after I left. Vice-Chancellor Senna disappeared just before the resulting media firestorm, and neither Elise nor I have seen him since. I heard that many former students went back to the school under cover of darkness. They burned it down after collecting mementos from the abandoned classrooms and barracks. Although I mourned the loss of the library, I never returned to the campus. I had taken with me everything of value the day I left.

Nick and his wife live across the yard in the house we grew up in. My brother and his wife Maria had four children, all of whom I promptly spoiled. He was a great farmer but pursued his first love and became the fire chief of our little town. He's done a great job and refuses to retire. We're best friends.

Elise and I didn't get married right away. First, we planned our careers and attended a local college. Paul's newspaper provided a full journalism scholarship for Elise. I studied agriculture and business. During that time, Elise and I dated in a more conventional manner than was possible at AKPS: no sneaking around, no boiler rooms, and no Dobermans. Our long courtship enabled us to sort through our pasts and build a strong foundation for marriage. After graduation, I proposed to Elise during a trip to our favorite seafood restaurant in Philadelphia.

After college, Elise once again worked her way up through the ranks of a local newspaper and eventually became editor-in-chief. Along the way, she pursued her dream of writing novels. I followed in my father's footsteps and became a farmer. I had many other career options, but I could never imagine a more fulfilling occupation. My study overlooks the family farm, which my sons have taken over. They've done a great job. They're good boys. Their sister keeps the books, and she's expecting my twelfth grandchild.

I kept in touch with many of my friends from school and we even shared a few more adventures over the years. Buzz became a great success, of course. He settled into the architectural field but continued to invent "gizmos and gadgets," as we called them in our phone calls and letters to each other. We organize an AKPS reunion every year. The stories seem to get better each time we tell them. I also keep in touch with my childhood friends, many of whom also became farmers.

Elise…well, she's downstairs right now, taking those cookies out of the oven. To me, she hasn't changed much since those days; her smile is just as beautiful, her eyes are just as blue. In between writing novels (she's on her tenth now) and raising our children, she enjoys teasing me as much as ever. I couldn't have asked for a better companion with whom to spend my life.

She and I wrote this account many years ago, using both her journals and Dad's journals to supplement our own memories. We enjoyed editing the story after dinner and whenever else we had time, polishing the narrative and trying to be as accurate as possible. When our first child came, we continued to work on the manuscript now and then. When our second child came, we put the book in a trunk in the attic and forgot about it. It was our story and it was important to us, but somehow we never got around to finishing it. Every now and then, one of us would remind the other, but there always seemed to be something else that needed our attention: the cry of a baby, the neighing of horses, the fields that needed tending. To us, the story continued on in the business of everyday living.

As I look out my window and listen to those precious children in the kitchen, I am reminded that one person's story is many people's story. A few weeks ago, we decided to pull this old book out of the attic, complete it, and tack on a brief last word.

Tree houses burn and hearts are easily broken, but love endures. I've tried to live out that truth every day of my life since I returned home, and like my father, I've tried to instill it in my own children and grandchildren. We've passed on our story because if just one other person realizes the power that love wields, then our story will continue long after our names are forgotten.

Love confers immortality; love itself lives forever.

Mom and Dad? They'll live forever, too, remembered and cherished because of the way they raised, taught, and loved a boy named Jake.

Acknowledgments

One of the unexpected pleasures of writing a book is the opportunity to thank some of the people who helped along the way. I'd like to express my gratitude to these friends and family members:

To those who provided valuable feedback on the first draft: my wife Natalie; Lara Santamaria; Matt and Sheri-ann Armentano; Laida Kearney; June Adams; Steven Mann; Stephanie Santamaria; my fifth through eighth grade students at Fellowship Christian School (2001-2002); and Amy Barton. Roy and Beth Cooper also provided unswerving support and legal advice.

To my parents and grandparents, who encouraged me to read, and placed the best books ever written into my hands.

To my many teachers (whom I never properly thanked for the tremendous investment they made in my life), particularly: Joan Kasper, Walter Hawkes, Linda Gregory, Frank Gawle, Elissa Getto, Marcella Jackson, Robert Moore, Gerald Wilson, Hans Collischonn, Kermit Finstad, and Dr. Russell P. Getz.

To Carolyn Arends, whose song "Seize the Day" was like a lighthouse to me during many dark days. Her music and commitment to our Savior continue to inspire me.

To Philip Keller, whose book *A Shepherd's Look at Psalm 23* gave me important insights into both sheep and shepherds.

To my editor, Lou Belcher, whose keen eye and commitment to excellence helped make this novel what it is. She did far more than check for continuity, pacing, and grammar; she also helped me to become a better writer. I'm also grateful to Mynderd Vosloo, my art designer, who beautifully translated the spirit of the story into the cover, and to Cheri Carroll and Jana Rade, who guided me through the design process. To Bonnie Schenk Darrington, my copyeditor, who offered valuable insight and did a great job of cleaning up the manuscript; and Diane Black, who painstakingly converted my manuscript into its preproduction format.

Finally, to everyone else at American Book Publishing who had a hand in bringing *The Far-Away Hearts Club* to life: your professionalism and love of your craft were constant sources of joy.

About the Author

Patrick Spadaccino has expressed his passion for writing since early childhood. Born in New Haven, Connecticut in 1965, he began his writing career by submitting an article to the editor of his high school newspaper. During his years at Gettysburg College, he continued to study writing and expanded his interests to music and theatre. He sang and played piano in local coffeehouses and performed in several theatrical productions, including *Ah, Wilderness!* and Shakespeare's *The Tempest*.

After college, he worked as morning show producer and on-air personality for KC101 FM radio. He performed stand-up comedy and often appeared in the southern Connecticut area with his band, Reel to Real. In addition to writing books, Patrick recently wrote and starred in a musical stage adaptation of Charles Dickens's *A Christmas Carol,* which includes seven original songs. Yearly, the proceeds from the production are donated to local and national charities.

Patrick lives in Connecticut with his wife, Natalie, and is currently working on his second novel.